In a
Sweet
Magnolia Time

In a
Sweet
Magnolia Time

Robert Wintner

Twice-Baked Books

This book was originally published in 2005, The Permanent Press,
Sag Harbor, NY.
Wintner, Robert

In a Sweet Magnolia Time / Robert Wintner

ISBN: 978-1-7366222-6-1
1. Waring, Julius Waties, 1880-1968—Fiction. 2. Charleston
(S.C.)—Fiction. 3. Race relations—Fiction. 4. Civil rights—
Fiction. 5. Judges—Fiction.

Layout & design by Keith Christie

Twice-Baked Books

$11.00
ISBN 978-1-7366222-6-1
51100>

9 781736 622261

Also by Robert Wintner

Fiction:
 Whirlaway
 Lizard Blue
 Reefdog
 A California Closing
 Homunculus
 The Prophet Pasqual
 Hagan's Trial & Other Stories

Memoir:
 Brainstorm
 1969 and Then Some

Reef Politic in narrative and photo/video:
 Dragon Walk
 Neptune Speaks
 Reef Libre, An In-Depth Look at Cuban Exceptionalism &
 the Last, Best Reefs in the World
 Every Fish Tells a Story
 Some Fishes I Have Known

Author's Note:

Septima Clark (1898-1987) lived in Charleston, South Carolina when I began this novel. She was old at that time and had carried her gentility and soft touch into those years. As a Civil Rights activist in the NAACP, she focused on education as a tool of change and granted me two interviews in 1977 to that end, setting the story straight on a firsthand account. Most generous with her time, she recalled plantation days with composure, seemingly inured to bitterness, as long as the facts got rendered. Her father had been a slave. Septima Clark was born and died in Charleston and is remembered as the mother of the Civil Rights Movement. Rosa Parks also benefitted from Ms. Clark's timeless generosity, attending one of Ms. Clark's workshops three months prior to keeping her seat on a Montgomery, Alabama bus.

Special gratitude is also due to Tom Waring (1907-1993), a newspaper editor in Charleston in '76 and nephew to Judge Waties Waring. A man as genteel as Septima Clark, Tom Waring was also above old-family superiority common to any town with a history. He too became a generous source of facts and events and insight from the troubling past. As a journalist of the old school, where accuracy reined, his keen eye and mind helped fill in the blanks, providing what no record showed.

This story is true. As a city magazine editor in Charleston, in 1976, I needed a cover story to rattle some old bones in that socially complacent town. Nothing stood out but more of the same: beauty, flowers, quaint charm, antebellum architecture and on and on, until my art director, Jack C. Thames, gifted water-colorist, born and raised as a very best bubba, said, "Take a look at the Waring story." Jack was fifty-two then; he'd been a young man in town twenty-four years prior, when a few pleasantries got ruffled. Most of the principles were still around as well in '76 and talking freely, albeit in low tones.

Many people regret the reframing of history for one cause or another, but reframing is convenient, even if misleading.

This narrative is based on actual events, with the course of history accurately represented. The characters are also true. Some names have been changed, though most were not.

—Robert Wintner

Memoriam:
Marty Shepherd, in faith.

_2_

In a Sweet Magnolia Time

Magnolia Cemetery lies on the southern edge of the no-man's land called North Charleston, a gray-brown collection of dirty brick and smoke stacks under a sickly yellow sky, where God and state senators make jobs for the people. You'll count six new car lots and eight used on the way up to North Charleston. Two tenement projects sit across the road from the graveyard and seem just as peaceful. A paper mill and a chemical plant a half sniff yonder round out the neighborhood. Salvation is what North Charleston means to the nitty gritty folk who work there. Elsewhere it only means ugly.

North Charleston grew and spread, painless as a brain tumor, while the body proper carried on as usual with delusions of antebellum, though now the antebellum remnants are mostly cordoned off for the edification of Yankee tourists, much as a mental patient might be subdued for her own good and confined to a padded cell with a one-way window, so the doctors and concerned passersby can take a closer look. What's left of antebellum on the street is tired talk of what was and the same tired sigh at the old houses it lived in.

Magnolia Cemetery sits on the southern verge, appropriately at the top of old Charleston, bearing down from the North. Magnolia marks the passing epochs with forty thousand headstones showing the names of forty thousand white people. Forty thousand graves makes for history to the horizon, the family names carved into granite as testament to the greatness that was.

To that day all was white, and white was the lasting intention. But the day Waties Waring went under was different. He was white too, with a discordant note echoing down the years. It was 1968, and only Waties Waring in a century and a half and forty thousand graves had a colored funeral.

I finished early in town and rode on up. Everyone knew about the funeral but wouldn't discuss it, and I'd frankly had enough of pretending it didn't exist. Talking a thing to death went along with our chronic circumspection, so the absence of banter was refreshing. We weren't short on intelligence, genetically speaking, though I'm certain that massive cerebral segments collectively atrophy by middle age, what with such caution in keeping things polite. Take the industrial ugliness of the unspeakable North, with the paper mill stench and lunchbox mentality; better yet, take the aforementioned senators responsible for such "growth." A senatorial appearance for cocktails off the cuff could send a murmur through our crowd in town, but anyone stepping back to see what any senator had actually done in accordance to what we truly hold dear would concur: we are represented at the capitol by bumpkin politicians with no regard whatever but for jobs for the people indirectly as they translate to job security for themselves. Oh, you might ask what's wrong with that. Nothing, if you eat lunch from a metal box, have more children than you can afford, yearn for another car, and care not a shred for the countryside making this region unique. And the conversation of these politicos could drive a sane man twitchy.

Waties Waring never ran for office. He was appointed but was as much a politician as all the professional men in Charleston needed to be, maneuvering, strategizing, polling, lobbying, cajoling and ruling as necessary, always politely, and never more so than when conversing. The topic went to power, always power, whether tomorrow is Election Day or this afternoon bodes ominous for lunkers in the surf because of a spring flood near dusk. You had to consider the power in the fish or the man catching the fish, or the man who had no time to fish, because he was too busy working for the betterment of all, don't you know. New ideas were not trusted or tested or talked about too much, lest the talker be deemed impolite. Polite is the root derivative of politic in our town.

I don't think I ever grew out of our local scheme of things but rather grew away from it or maybe stepped aside of it so I could breathe. I loved our society and still recall certain times fondly, but something changed. I needed air long before that day in '68, and I wouldn't call that day cathartic, though it does mark the beginning of my removal from civilization, physically speaking, that is.

I needed to get away from town and its strained consensus that served as a collective assurance, sort of a safety net. You could sense and feel a topic being avoided by the mere traffic jam of glances here and there seeking insight to what was understood as terribly coarse and possibly abrasive and certainly not grist for our pleasant mill.

Waties Waring was the federal judge to first rule: *Separate but equal is not equal.* He gave life to an appeal process leading to the historic ruling by the Supreme Court of the United States in *Brown v. The Board of Education*, changing life as we knew it. That is, he was the first judge in the history of the United States of

America to rule in favor of the Negro struggle for civil rights, yet his ruling is not considered historic, and that of the Supreme Court is. But he set the wheels in motion and garnered a niche in Charleston history, or rather in local notoriety. The notion of civil rights was safely constrained before his ruling. His jurist's logic was simple, with deadly results. He cost us millions in funding, knowing we could never, nor would we want to, comply with the integration standards resulting from what he started.

He cost me more in many ways. I was him; he was me. In a manner of speaking we were bound at the hip by self-destruction. You outlive the age of realization and realize it's all turned bad on you, and destruction has a warm fuzzy feel to it, maybe revealing what the afterlife has in store, which may not be so bad after all; I don't know. God knows this vale of tears had yet to stack up to what it promised. As I live, my search continues, though I wonder now if continuation is better than the alternative.

Waties Waring and I were born in Charleston, where The War began. His family was eighth generation landed, three hundred years in the same town. He suffered cross burnings in front of his house and brickbats through his windows before he was driven out of Charleston and South Carolina, ostracized in every way and shamed into exile in New York for his last fifteen years. New York; it can make a man tremble. After three hundred years of Lowcountry, a man approaching the age of reckoning could damn near swoon.

I had to get out of town the day of the funeral because town seethed with silence on the subject, people milling outside their offices on the street, quite a few bankers and real estate agents and most of all the other lawyers, all convened informally to participate in not talking about it, to shore up the bond, whatever it was. The judge died five or six days prior to the funeral, so the newspaper had enough time to stoke the old coals, see if a little spark hiding in there could ignite the old fires. Everyone downtown knew the self-evident truth of the story, because we grew up and grew old with the fact that Waties Waring practiced separation of the races with the best of us. His radical decision from the bench was motivated by revenge—on us—urged not by sudden epiphany but by the woman who cost him his life. I say his life in the figurative sense; he didn't die for another fifteen years, which is like doing time in the federal slammer if you spent the first sixty-five years all warm and cozy in the garden out back, scotched up past smelling the flowers and making chitchat easy as you please. Sure, it gets stifling, but try New York on for size and you'll feel a hair shirt of a different itch.

The Broad Street regulars and those who yearned to be viewed as Broad Street regulars were predictable as sunrise the day the judge got put under; they'd mosey up and down the sidewalk, never straying farther from their office façades than they ventured otherwise in life, as if the phone might ring. It wouldn't. They'd look up slow as wise men receptive to cosmic truth, and they'd stay calm, coming on back down to street level for some meteorological prognostication and potential variants on the diagnosis, which local insight factored years of experience equal to great wisdom, don't you know. Each would predict or agree, staying so painfully superficial that what they weren't discussing felt tangible as a force 5 hurricane blowing in from the Battery. Might rain. Might get right torrential, but not before noon, maybe twelve thirty, or one, but not likely before noon. Therein, practicing that perfected habit of old Charleston—that happy, deliberate ignorance of the blissfully better off—they gave the bond meaning and strengthened it with consensus on what was being lived and protected here. Or so they thought, and many still do, though the hard core is down to octo and nonagenarian. There were more of them back then, talking of the tides, the seasons, prospects and past catches.

Modern population density dilutes what was so clear and concise just a few decades ago. Simply put: we had a death in the family, a sudden, tragic and grotesque fatality, but he was either insane or criminal and best forgotten and certainly not worth soiling a perfectly normal morning on morbid recollection of a most unfortunate turn of events.

Most of the in-town crowd weren't born stupid but learned by example: stick your head in the mud and see if it doesn't feel all right. Moreover, just you take a good look and see if the safe view from down in the dark won't make the unpleasantries plain damn go away. You can't do anything about North Charleston but ignore it, even when it smolders and festers, its gray and yellow flatulence drifting south at sunrise after a night of chemical burn— night, so nobody complains, unless they wake up and ponder gratitude for a fortified tax base. Maybe that wasteland serves as paradigm for our cares and woe; no matter how awful things seem, we wake up sunny and cheerful to a brand new day, and the stink blows away by lunch, for us, taken at a table with a cloth and dishes and silver service.

We lost one of the keenest minds our little town ever produced, and if the loss was unavoidable, just as the old society crumbled along with the houses it lived in, and the rot and ruin of the industrial hinterland to the north filled our noses, we could have paused at least to ask each other why. We could have examined this man's faults in the light of our own, if we could have seen that light. I don't know how much longer this part of the world, this Lowcountry, can go on; so many people want jobs with more factories or more resorts with more promotion for that shrinking part of it called quaint and historical; come on down, y'all. Park your car and take a look. The outlanders want to see Blacks on City Council now, but they want to see them out weaving baskets by the highway too. They want it old; they want it new; they want it all. Maybe that's what people do, but whatever quaint charm was there seems so poorly defended anymore from within.

I went one night about twenty years prior to the judge's funeral with another lawyer, a shrimper and a real estate man to the small park between the post office and the judge's house. I hadn't thought about it much since then, because I repressed it—put a lid on it, shut it down. We stood a wooden cross in an iron pot filled with dirt, since the judge's steps led right down from the house to the sidewalk with no dirt anywhere to stick a cross. Now what must they have been thinking, building a house with no dirt in front for a cross? We carried our cross over as close as we could and doused it with gasoline, then lit it and threw four or five brickbats through the windows, yelling all kinds of sonsabitches. Then we ran.

I have pondered motivation since. Was I so ambitious? Well, yes, I was; but, moreover, frustration drove me to tantrum, with the bricks and burning cross. So, am I to be excused, like a modern defendant pleading temporary crisis of the emotions? It doesn't matter, not to anyone or me; what matters is the wheel of life, as the Buddhists call it. Oh, you challenge the notion of a dyed-in-the-wool redneck reading The Book of the Dead? Go ahead and challenge, then come on down, park your car and take a look. The wheel doesn't stop, but if we pause to view it, we may gain a greater meaning for the ashes and broken glass littering its periphery.

I attended the funeral because I was practically part of the family. His daughter and I were close once; that seems lifetimes ago, though I recall wondering if she thought it was my forearm that her little hand grasped in our shared bed of youth, like it was only moments ago. That sort of thing was not the basis of our love, and it was love, but I'm a man on the far side of a failed, meager marriage to a woman now clearly perceived as a total stranger. I no longer wonder what might have been with Anne. And I digress;

Anne's mischief notwithstanding, I saw no reason to bear a grudge against the old man. Forgive and forget, after a fashion, had become my practice, in keeping with the smug summation we excelled at; forgiveness was for those who got caught, with smugness reserved for the unexposed.

The last time I saw him was in New York a year or so before he died, though what kept him alive then was a mystery of nature. Flat pitiful, shrunk down, bent, shriveled and plain worn out, he looked dead and done for, but he surprised me, perking up when I apologized for any ill will between us, meaning the social resentment he suffered when nobody invited him and his new wife anywhere, including me, which was no surprise to me, after all, but may have surprised him; we were such colleagues. Professional resentment was an equally gravid potential, because every lawyer in town declined his company and/or counsel, including me, which must have hurt as much as intended and then some. He said he'd dealt with that ill will foolishness long ago. Any bad feelings left were for my town and me to resolve.

He was just that good, casually waving off the rancor that went blood deep with a foolishness disclaimer.

I arrived at the cemetery early and drove on down toward Belvedere Section, the headstones reading like road signs on the past, back through a nether world that actually existed prior to the myth of itself, where spoken names flowed like currency, their value emanating directly from the mellifluous accent, correct intonation and languidly precise enunciation of the speaker. Because the state of being and being able to talk about it in the genealogical *patois* capturing the soul of the region seemed damn well heaven on earth for a singular-minded group of white people. The dialect is a singsong rhythm of bloodlines with denomination in the names: Pringle, Prioleau, Drayton, Lowden, Bowden, Snowden, Drydon, Reardon, Jervey, Gasque, Gaillard, Grimble, Greeley, Pinckney/Taveau, Montague, Manigault, Rasque, Rhett,

Rutledge, Sumner, Smythe, Stillwell, Cromwell, Hopewell and Gervaise.

Burma Shave. The road reads with a French flair at the outset, because the Huguenots were first. But the Tory influence mixes in before too long, and the resulting lilt is uniquely Charlestonian. Most Warings are in Belvedere Section, as are the Covingdales. Covingdale begins with Arthur, who landed in '41. (The Seventeenth Century is presumed here; that's 1641 for those of you who went to public school.) The Covingdale line continues roadside to Henry, Richard, Charles, Edward, James, George, and here I be, Arthur again, just like the first, and like the judge, eighth generation landed. The Warings came a few years earlier than the Covingdales but only buried six generations in Magnolia, the others having died sometime before the cemetery opened and settling somewhere between the Ashley and the Edisto Rivers. No one knows where, but they call it the Old Waring Burial Ground. Less cavalier than that, the Covingdales knew exactly where their roots were sunk. We transplanted our earliest antecedents to achieve a more concisely visible continuity of our history, family, longevity and grandeur, whatever those lofty principles were worth, which was plenty, or at least plentiful was the perception.

Magnolia proper is only Nineteenth Century, but with notable foresight and apparent good taste, the Covingdales moved their old bones to the best place to be, once development could accommodate the more civilized traditions. Anything 1800's doesn't count for much around here, it's so recent (besides being the Century of our Misfortune) but some of us saw the value of disinterring the forbears so whole families could stay together like a matched set in a different sort of hutch, rendering the soil at Magnolia more venerable from the outset. Because a century or two does make a difference in esteem, socially, in this part of the world, and I suppose the cemetery's grand opening was a good chance to free up some prime garden space behind the house too, since the antecedents got planted out back before Magnolia. We lived up next to the ancestral shrine, the house only a step and a stumble from our proper inevitability, our rightful place in the limestone lineup. All that changed with the advent of Magnolia Cemetery, kind of.

A man leaned on a spade over the open grave, his head bent in an attitude of chronic neck curvature, or maybe he watched the gasoline-driven pump chug and sputter water from the grave out a long siphon tube. He spoke as I approached but not to me, most likely encouraging himself onward through his thankless task, his voice audible before it was comprehensible, him nodding at me briefly but then speaking down at the empty grave, saying he never was one of those people to holler about progress, try to stop it or anything. "But you get them things cranked up all at once..." He gazed up to the northeast and scanned the smokestacks to the northwest. "It'll like to choke you."

A simple fellow, he was nonetheless engaging for a cemetarian, even in this part of the world, where the departed are still recalled and often addressed personally, where death is regarded as little different from life, so long as you have a good view. The dead ones don't actually partake in the tea and scotch and talk, but then they have much less fuss to deal with too. He said it wasn't easy, adjusting to cemetery life, which phrase in itself reflected massive adaptation, but he did adjust, even to the browning. That is, everything in and around Magnolia turned brown, which he accepted as reminiscent of the old sepia tone movies he saw as a child. He called it old Tarzan brown, and said take a look; it covers everything in time, from the tombs and trees, even out to their leaves, to the little wrought iron fences the families put up between themselves, all brown. He'd grown accustomed to the brown and didn't mind the smell, since it too recalled old photographs from his youth just back from the druggist. "But the smoke and yellow stuff'll like to choke you."

He said he read the newspaper from his former home, one home or another, because he'd had quite a few homes, any one of which was better for newspapers than this home, where you couldn't count on the local newspaper but for bad news. That or old news. He'd read that the process was called inversion, whereby pollutants are discharged into the air, where they remain trapped by the cloud cover, so the yellow grit rolls from one end of the county to the other—"Like a big old turd won't flush."

"Well put," I said.

He said, "Howdy. Walter Snole's my name. U.S. Navy, retired."

"Arthur Covingdale. My pleasure."

He looked at his dirty hands as compensation to the gentlemanly thing to do and shrugged instead of shaking. "I'll tell you the truth," he said. "These people don't care. They're dead. But you wait till their cousins come out in a while; by God you'll see some grunting and snorting. You a Waring?"

"No. Covingdale."

"That's right. You're in here. This is a strange one, though." He nodded at the headstone over the hole and called it a rare marker. "First off, no epitaph. Most all of them have epitaphs, even if they're little short ones like, *Loving Father* or something. Secondly, wife put her name on the other side already. You won't see that too often when he dies first. They usually wait to put their names on till they die too. I figure they don't want to get out of the running before they have to, you know what I mean? Guess this gal must be old. I'd bet you she's old."

"You'd win," I said. "She's old, and she's been out of the running a long time. She can run her mouth though. I'm certain you'll get a whiff of that too, if you stay for the funeral."

"Oh, I'll be here," he said. "This fellow was a judge, pretty high up."

"Yes, I know."

"We got twenty governors of South Carolina here and a good many senators too. Robert E. Lee's grandson is here. I like to sit in on the famous ones. I don't know much of what this fellow did, except he was famous for helping the Negroes one way or another. I guess that's rare too, around here. Maybe you know."

"I know," I said. "He's not fondly remembered here. He made a few decisions as a judge that were controversial to the point of violence, and he lived the last fifteen years in New York because of it. The thing was, he never was a liberal, you know, he was only getting revenge on Charleston and South Carolina for the condemnation that came his way after his divorce and remarriage."

"Well," Walter Snole said. "I don't know nothing about all that."

"No. It's a long story. Most people don't."

"I never had a bone to pick with those people. The Negroes, I mean. Colored preacher come out here this morning to tell me his people would be here for the funeral. He told me and just stood there gawking at me like a child knew he was in for a beating, like I was supposed to slap him with my shovel or something. I told him I didn't care if he brought a whole damn fleet of Negroes and stayed all night. He says to me, 'No. Call us Black. Not Negro, Black.' Used to be they didn't like that. 'Course they like it better than nigger, but there wasn't much difference between Black and darky. I don't suppose you could call them darkies now without they'd get real excited. I don't believe they like colored anymore either, but Black is all right. He asked for Black." He leaned on the spade, pondering the grave. "Next thing you know they'll be wanting us to call them shines or rugheads. I don't care. I'll call them anything they damn well want. I got no bone to pick with those people. I just don't want trouble. That's all."

"There won't be any trouble."

He looked at me, as if to ask how I could be so sure, unless I had ties to trouble. As I composed my safe response, his gaze went over my shoulder. "Well, here they come. You didn't go to the service in town?"

"No. This is plenty for me."

"Me too," he said, shutting down the pump and pulling the siphon from under the catafalque as the generator backfired, slurped a last swallow, belched and stopped before giving up its last two gallons of drivel back to the water still in the hole.

They arrived in single file, parked and moved in a strained, hesitant manner toward the grave, five white people, maybe twenty-five Blacks. I knew them all and exchanged pleasantries briefly till the colored preacher grew restless and loud-voiced over the tardiness of a designated pallbearer, Jim Cohen. The next few minutes were given over to speculation on where he be and whether a man might make better time in crossing the River Jordan by getting an early start, even if it meant crossing with only five pallbearers.

The tardy party finally arrived, sputtering and smoking like North Charleston, in a Fleetwood Brougham with no trunk lid and no back seat, and looking, as we were wont to say on many a sad and sorry Sunday morning, shot at and missed and shit at and hit. He carried a huge and handsome load of produce looking ready to sell on the road if it didn't fall out before he got to his place of commerce, which I hoped he planned to do rather than announce specials there at the funeral. He parked next to my car, which I'd parked forty paces down to avoid the traffic. Then he opened his door into mine, carefully, so the ding wouldn't be too big. He emerged slowly, taking time as required for what had to be two hundred fifty pounds of him, or maybe three hundred. Once out and more or less stable on his own two feet, he straightened what was supposed to be a black sport coat over his bib overalls with a tie apparently knotted by a child. He brushed the crumbs from the front of it and smoothed his gray-flecked temples before looking up like a seasoned thespian to grin for all the folks waiting and watching. But this was no act; I knew Jim Cohen from way back when and from regular stops out on Savannah Highway too, where I bought his corn and root relish, and maybe bought into his repartee as well, calling him Mr. Jim as he called me Mist Aht. Just so, we paid homage to our common source, odd peers meeting as if randomly.

Glancing here and there like a creature of instinct taking stock, his alert eyes eased down to the natural fatigue of a man his age facing yet another task. The grin shrank to a smile of hope, and he said, "Ey! Ey you be?"

"Awright. Awright," the Blacks refrained.

Jim Cohen re-adjusted his tie as a matter of onerous process, ending with a headshake indicating certainty that this uptown clothing would never adjust as it should. So he waddled to the hearse, where he grasped the remaining unmanned handle and looked around, more sanguine now, to pronounce, "Awright."

The six pallbearers hefted the soul-departed burden never before borne by those of African descent in Magnolia, and so the book of history creaked slowly open as the procession proceeded, post haste.

22

The River Jordan

The Reverend Mr. Whitehead read his funeral passage verbatim and with dispatch from the page marked Funeral Reading in a leather-bound, gilt-rimmed, flawlessly maintained edition of the King James, extemporizing only at the end to tell us the judge was a loving father. I saw Walter Snole nod behind the crowd where he rested both hands on top of his spade handle and his chin on top of that, pumping his head as if his itch was scratched, and now he could shovel the dirt. The Reverend Mr. Whitehead paused like a preacher at a wedding, waiting for anyone to speak now or forever hold his peace. Then he was finished, so he stooped for a few clods and tossed them on the casket, and it was over.

Except that the Reverend Mr. Washington, the colored preacher, stepped up to announce that Jedus be telling him to preach some too, to which the vast majority of attendees agreed as one,

Yeah!

Pray, Jedus!

He'p me now!

Riding the crest of affirmation and allowing no time for dissent, Reverend Washington then imprinted the book of history indelibly, his falsetto preaching voice rising over the thousands upon thousands of white graves having yet in their hundreds of years of repose to hear a Black man preaching Magnolia, and for all we knew still waiting to hear. Never mind, on that day the shrill voice assured all those living and dead in hearing range that we are on our way to Jordan on the same path trodden ever since when. Reverend Washington exhorted that the souls know where they want to go, and there come a time when the going is suddenly free of earthly burden for heavenly taking, and this be such a time for our dearly departed judge.

He'p me Jedus!

His dog-eared paperback Bible looked soaked down and dried out, and in a minute he shook it in the air, picking up the pace and finding his stride. The man had heart, ranting down the road to Jordan, surmounting obstacles on the way with further pleas. *He'p me, Jedus!* Or *Walk! wid me*, the other Blacks and one or two of the whites repeating those lines and otherwise affirming, *Yeah!*

A light rain started not halfway to Jordan, but most of the Blacks didn't open their eyes. When the drizzle picked up, the Reverend Mr. Whitehead touched the Reverend Mr. Washington on the arm and looked up, to God and the dirty rain. Reverend Washington grinned and fast-forwarded his exhortation directly to the riverbank just across from Jordan.

He'p me, Jedus!

He prepared to cross quickly and actually began the crossing when the torrent gushed from the sky. Reverend Washington was already knee deep in the river and deigned to turn back but had to wade on alone since everybody else took to their cars, until finally he did too. It poured ten minutes or so, and when it stopped no clods remained for Reverend Washington to toss on the box. Just mud.

I waited through the rain and came out again into the mud since I wanted to hear firsthand and not the second- or third- or fourth-hand accounts, soon to circulate in town, of the judge's wife's eulogy. I knew she'd start up sooner or later; the New York Times called her a lively, talkative woman, but we didn't see that as emulation of our euphemistic custom, because we knew her to be loud and hateful and mad as a hatter. I wanted a moment with Anne too, the judge's daughter. I reasoned my motivation here clearly; we literally shared childhood, spending every day together for years, but hadn't seen each other since she moved north to live with her father and his new wife. It seemed an odd move and an odd arrangement and most odd that she left her mother alone here, especially since that was just before her mother died, but then the whole topsy-turvy world around here was past reckoning and just wanted to get back to its old self, and maybe she did too. I can only speculate. With the principals removed from the arena, the tension died down directly and the cruel memories faded, till they were disinterred for the old man's funeral. I thought we'd go for coffee or something.

She saw me when she arrived but didn't acknowledge. It'd been fifteen years, so maybe she didn't recognize me, though I doubted that. She looked good, plain but healthy, like her mother had looked. Her short dark hair and black tweed suit and plain white blouse highlighted her cheeks, rosy with life, not rouge, or maybe she'd only chilled on a permanent basis up there in New York. She looked fit and strong and kept a proud posture, and I concede that a flicker of hope rose in me. My moorings had loosened long ago, so maybe a coffee date seemed easy, one more step on an old, familiar path.

She hovered protectively over her stepmother, who didn't utter a sound that day and hardly looked like the femme fatale who stood this town on its ear. I remembered the mongered accounts swirling around town like dust devils then. You had one story of the bed sheets found at the beach on Sullivan's Island not too far from Henry and Heloise Middleton's beach house. Whether imagined or real didn't matter since those bloodstained sheets spawned the most recorded history of any single skirmish since The War. One Mrs. Gervais Grimble (née Pringle {née Grumble}) said a spot of blood was found near the end of one sheet. She was certain it was the bottom sheet, which sleuthing was deemed significant then, in those historic times prior to fitted bottom sheets. She was certain too that the stain was at the foot of the bed. Pressed on her certainty, she said, "I swear it was!" She knew because Mary Green told her so. Mary Green was the Warings' housemaid then and heard about the sheets from Flo Manigo, the Middletons' housemaid, whose beach house was a trysting place for the judge and the Yankee spitfire. Mrs. Gervais Grimble had that disarming ability to raise one eyebrow. It implied something devious, like sodomy or pedophilia or worse, the devil's curse. Devious potential lurked everywhere, counterbalancing what she strove so diligently to make nice, like tea and cookies and a little visit. She was remembered for her debutante years, when she once asserted with characteristic vigor that she did so know about the fallopian tubes; they were a small island chain off the coast of Maine, and indeed they *could* get cold, which anybody could plainly know without having to visit Maine, because all you had to do was look at those pictures in those books, and you could practically *feel* the cold. "I don't know why *any*body would want to live *there!*"

Some years later, at the crux of the scandal, she asked, "Don't you see? At the foot of the bed!" She'd pieced it together, and though nobody needed to get ugly about it, and this was obviously not in need of further analysis, it most certainly did not appear to be nice. So whoever tolerated that rant was left to picture the blood, the bottom sheet, the foot of the bed and the obvious scene transpiring. Trouble was, the scene wasn't obvious but obscure, leaving nothing to be seen or conjured or by any sane or stable means fantasized.

I gave it my best nonetheless, venturing that the blood could have been from a razor cut; the judge was such a stickler for personal appearance, and it reopened under duress as he knelt at the foot of the bed in passionate abandon to suck the Yankee spitfire's toes, which is just the sort of thing that kind of woman wants, and if that bottom sheet with the blood at the foot wasn't proof, then what?

The theory was laughable, but nobody laughed, nor was humor intended. Oh, yes, I was dead serious in my effort to sleuth any component of this scandalous crime against morality; I made myself blush. Mrs. Grimble raised the other eyebrow on the case made by the prosecution, also more amazed, frankly, than she cared to be. Toe sucking was simply not discussed, though astonishment was general and pervasive in town those days, all sourcing back to this new wife, this font of sadism and perversion, this Svengali, this siren, this Eve come to spoil our garden with easy cootch, which, if you think about it at all, would be the logical next stop after the feet.

Hunched, short-winded, sexless and old beyond her years, the new wife only mourned in silence.

I approached Anne and her stepmother as the crowd dispersed. Half the cars started and rolled out while the other half tried to start and failed, the drivers finally raising their hoods and asking each other who had a decent set of cables.

"Anne."

"Hello, Arthur. How've you been?" She responded well enough but wouldn't look at me, rendering the air between us colder than the fallopian tubes.

"Good." I touched her arm, warming things up, I thought. She looked up, so I smiled and opened our new discourse warmly, "I've been good. Very busy...."

"Like a set of jumper cables at a nigger funeral?"

What? What cause did she have to talk to me like that or to use that language here? "Anne. I want you to know how...good it is to see you. I'm sorry about your father. I want you to know that too. You know I...."

"Do you?"

"Yes. I do. You know I visited him last year. I was sorry I missed you. Your...stepmother can tell you. We had quite a chat. He...."

"Arthur."

"Yes."

"I know." She turned away from me and guided her stepmother slowly toward the parking area. I walked along, thinking her bitterness nurtured and aggressive, but I hardly suspected the arrow waiting in her quiver.

"In town long?" I asked.

"Too long, I'm afraid. We arrived last night, and we're not leaving till this afternoon."

"I see."

Finally she stopped to look at me directly in the eyes. "I do too," she said.

"Anne...."

"Arthur." She parked her stepmother on a sound footing, then turned to me. "Arthur. I know what you did. I saw you. I'll never forgive you. I can't. If my father chose to, that's his business. He was always fond of you. He...loved you. Thank God he was crazy by the time you started throwing brickbats through the window. We're leaving now. Goodbye, Arthur."

She knew. But how could she? Never mind. I'd have time to sort that out. In the meantime, she was getting away, leaving me nothing for it but to tighten my drag. What was I thinking, as I lashed back? That she would commiserate at last and come for coffee? "Do you think he ever got as crazy as your mother?" They both turned back to face me. The old lady's eyes opened wide. Anne said, "Leave my mother out of this, Arthur. She's no more of your business than any of this ever was."

"She was everybody's business, as I recall."

As startled as her stepmother and as hateful as I'd seen her stepmother in the past, as though the hatred was learned, Anne nearly snarled. "Goodbye, Arthur. You take my mother and make her your business and keep her your business. Just don't bother me with it. Do you understand?"

"Yes. I think I do."

"She's right over there." She pointed. "This cemetery has a special deal on three-grave odd lots, you see. When my mother died they had to put her over there, because she wasn't a Waring anymore. That's how much business she was for everybody. They buried her with the transients. Right over there, in case you brought flowers."

"I'm sorry, Anne."

"You certainly are. Goodbye, Arthur." Abruptly departing, they left me standing alone to find a vacant hole of my own I might slip into. I would replay that scene many times in the days ahead, determining my best retort, which would have been to ask how a mother could be buried with transients, if a daughter gave a good goddamn. Of course perfect retorts composed in hindsight are better left unsaid. Why pour gasoline on the fire? No reason at all, except to fan the flames, and frankly, we were all a bit parched from the heat of the thing, though the coffee idea suddenly felt like cold coffee, and the loosened moorings felt as suddenly rusted and rotted through, leaving me to drift alone on the deep blue sea, speechless, with mixed and convoluted imagery competing to illustrate the forlorn solitude and regret I'd come to. Beyond that, my most heartfelt retort would have challenged her to love me still.

Anne walked away, resolute and erect as a few minutes prior but wholly changed, her demeanor still precise but now smooth and sparse as granite. I pondered a coffee date with myself, in which I would pour the cold stuff over my head, so I could douse the fire and drift on out to sea.

Yet the prevailing image was the one most physically apparent, of myself as another statue, one with slumped shoulders and a head hung low and covered in bird shit. So I stood, frozen, as it were, marking another milestone in history, in which the Covingdales were denuded of their sanctity and social grace in a fell swoop. How could she have known? How could she have seen? But then what could she be doing, bluffing? Among that crowd of statues guarding the graves and paying tribute to monumental greatness, I looked up to ponder life and wonder what might come next.

I couldn't return to the office. Nor could I imagine where to bear the afternoon. I considered the yacht club, but it was two already, so the first wave would be there, cheering each other on, any port in a storm, hoo yeah! We'd survived the downpour, requiring the dredge of the great hurricane parties of the past, which any thunderstorm warranted, sloshing up to a beachhead, so we could get this thing established for once and for all.

I watched Anne and the old lady walk toward the parking area past the raised hoods of the several stalled cars with passengers inside, waiting their turn for the jumper cables.

"Anne," I called.

She turned meanly and strained her voice to cover the distance. "A man who hurts his own...." She glared at me, then slipped into her car and left.

I pursued her to the point of reaching my car, where Jim Cohen stood by, brushing away the ding in the door with one hand, holding a set of jumper cables in the other. "Op'mup dem hood, Mist Aht," he said, oblivious to the tragedy playing out around him. I watched Anne as I mustered a call, a plea, a shout, then swallowed it back down and stooped to pull the hood latch under the dash as instructed. Jim Cohen worked the first release under the hood and struggled against the second as I watched the ruins of a happy childhood shrink down the flooded, rutted and pot-holed cemetery drive. Doubt and trepidation compounded on hearing the second latch give way with shrill complaint, and I felt no strength left for a response other than to start my engine as instructed and wait.

Surely a waterman like Jim Cohen knew the consequence of wrong terminals. He must have graduated from a *bateau* with oars to one with an outboard and a battery. He waddled around to the side of my car, scraping himself along the paint and doggedly testing cables to terminals in a shower of sparks and a disconcerting buzz, then scratching his head and changing them. I yelled out that red is negative. He mumbled something to the effect that *dem red be's de one wid de yidda...'n d'other be's...yeah. Aw right...* He waddled to his own car, got in and wound his starter, but got only smoke with sparks and a small fire on the plastic sleeves of his charred cables. So he got out with greater speed if not alacrity and yanked them off, threw them on the ground, shook his head and grumbled more vehemently at the sorry state of affairs over at the Cadillac Motor Company and more or less said, "You be's gwine on a Wadmalaw?"

"Come on," I said. "Why not?" I spoke dispassionately, amazed that nature's power could enable my voice to sound as if one moment led to the next with no repercussion, as if a terrible loss had not just occurred.

It was 1968, and we were keeping up with the times. Forty-three dead in the Watts riots, thirty-eight in Detroit, Martin Luther King, Jr. gunned down in Memphis. In Charleston the brick thrower was consenting to give the Black pallbearer a ride home, so perhaps a continuing buffer assuaged the terrible loss. Yet we served as whipping boy to the world on the issue called racism, which was more specifically the so-called cause of my terrible loss. I'd suspected a nigger in the woodpile all along and lived to prove it. But that insight too would remain unshared.

Except of course by brethren of differing hues. Each of us knew that a Black man asking for something and a white man giving something often as not are two different things. This difference is not a disjunction in communication; oh, we understood each other. No, it was more a practicality of commerce between the two. Jim Cohen wanted the ride and more; he wanted a tow, not so much for the car, which he admitted might be ready for a graveyard, and here we were, so why bother? Except of course you can't leave a Cadillac in a graveyard but have to tow it home to your own yard where you can jack it up onto cinderblocks where the wheels used to be, again in tribute to former greatness. Then again, we do be's ratchere, right now. Then again, he needed a tow on account of the produce in back, "Datuh be's de grocery load fum dem Promise Land," meaning his usual roadside spot out on Savannah Highway, *Promise Land Produce & Root Relish*. He also meant that he was bound for the Promise Land and not *from* the Promise Land as he'd said. Why would he haul produce away from the stand? He wouldn't. This load was his best of the year to date and would bring in some good money fuh true and looked to him like I be's de bestess man fuh hauling him fuh true. I didn't feel qualified to correct his modifiers and wasn't in the mood anyway.

I could have done without the glib rhetoric and didn't mind letting him know that I was not a renewable resource, and a favor requested and then granted would not lead to carte blanche on his personal list of errands for the day, meaning no, he could not give me an itinerary of stops. More to the point, I wasn't about to tow

Jim Cohen's produce Cadillac, vintage mid-50's and looking round the bend of Pork Chop Hill and bottomed out on a fresh load from the gleaning fields, with my Mercedes-Benz of a very recent year. He pointed out the tow ball behind my back bumper in case I forgot it was there, so I reminded him it was for my boat, so he reminded me that many people refer to Cadillacs as boats, so I reminded him there wasn't no way in hell I was about to tow that boat down to Wadmalaw on a rope, because the power brakes on that battleship won't work without the engine be running, which it wan't, and for that matter, neither do the power steering. "So if you want a ride home, Mister Jim, get in the car. Otherwise, I'll be wishing you all the best." I did not say *These people,* but I'll admit to thinking it—but thinking it with an open mind, open and glib, don't you know. That is, we are a nation whose strength derives from self-effacement, I thought, including ethnic humor based on pratfall as pungent as a good point or punch line might warrant. If you care to snidely remark or tell a joke about Tories or snooty snoots or bluebloods, I'd laugh loudest, especially if a vital nerve were touched, I thought. This latter contention was also theory, formulated with data as yet lacking in firsthand experience. Oh yes, I had not felt the vitality or voltage of certain nerves, even at my age, which was only fifty-eight at that time. Who'd a thunk you could live that long and still have so much to learn? Not me, not with my evident success in life.

Jim Cohen ignored my logical position on power brakes, power steering and the general idiocy of towing a junker with a Mercedes by means of a rope. Did I need to explain this? As his kind were wont to do, he waddled on back to the produce load where he rummaged under the corn till he found about a twelve-foot steel pole with tow cups welded at either end. One end went obviously enough on my tow ball and the other fit over the tow ball welded to his front bumper. I didn't bother telling him we'd pull the damn bumper off, because he was so obstinate you couldn't tell him a thing. Besides that, the tow ball on his front bumper looked well-worn, so he must've welded it through the grill to the chassis with steel bars or something, which might take care of having no brakes, but not no steering. He grinned as if reading my thoughts and pulled out an old frayed rope maybe a foot and a half long and looped at both ends. One loop went around a hook on his transmission behind the engine, accessible through a hole in the floor, and the other slipped easily over the niggerknocker on his steering wheel. I know you're not supposed to call them that, and I don't anymore, except here, because I don't believe they have any other name. This one showed a woman in a bathing suit, and the bathing suit went down on hard right or hard left turns to reveal her breasts and vaginal triangle. She was a white woman with a black triangle and red nipples, but I expect Jim would have got one with an all Black woman if anybody bothered to make one, but nobody did. Besides, it was a cartoon woman, and nobody ever cared a snitch around here about things like that, though the fantasized jungle lust for white women was so fervently portrayed in the northern media, as if a Black man might actually fulfill his sexual need over the cartoon white woman on his niggerknocker going naked every time he made a turn. Hell, he'd have to run into the ditch to get a good look at her anyway.

Well, I can tell you it was a day of reckoning and reflection, not to mention gumption and conviction on my part, even attending the judge's funeral. It went from bad to worse with Anne's display of unbridled contempt. I won't say I didn't deserve it, but that didn't make it hurt less. And in fact I'd spent so much of myself regretting my behavior since that ill-advised night, I fairly felt rehabilitated and repaid in my debt to society. I could have made a case, in fact, for those bricks flying through my own window of opportunity; they so forcefully made me look at the moment between past and future and see how futile my ambition had been. We worked every day, nine to five, or put in those hours at any rate, jockeying for position, making our moves, hail fellows getting along by going along, ever mindful of opportunity's ephemeral nature. We live and die in the blissful delusion, that gainful endeavor will deliver us from tedium, some of us, unless we are blessedly transposed, unless catharsis of our own making turns the mirror into a window. Just so, by looking inward we can see, bye and bye, what is what. We may not see it instantly; in my case, it took years to realize who I was and what would come of it, which was this: I was a lawyer in Charleston. The end.

That I had loved Anne Waring in many ways for many years felt as natural as loving a parent or a sibling or, as I can only imagine it might have been, a loving wife. I won't say that I lost sight of her in those years since she'd grasped my fervent boyhood under the covers, perhaps thinking she merely grasped a forearm of equal muscularity, but she hadn't grasped anything of mine since, not that she should have; she'd been a tomboy of sorts, which is far different than a male boy at the age of hormonal challenge. It was a phase for her, leading to the femininity that would thoroughly emerge years later.

It was a phase for me too. They say the male of our species has a penile instinct with a mind of its own. Meanwhile, in those tender, desperate years, the ineffable Eudora did latch on, not her idea, mind, but in utter, disgusted acquiescence after so much pleading, dry humping and urgency. We lie in queasy resignation to the awful demands of romance, her flogging the monkey with pneumatic insistence, me chafing worse than a baby's butt. I nearly reminded her to breathe, till she squealed in horror, as I soiled my pants and, alas, got some on her hand. Such was the nature of radical perversion where I came of age. We became engaged directly, and then married. In a decade I loathed her. That Anne Waring seemed so much more worthwhile compounded my discomfort, but I stayed married another two decades, beginning with a cross burning and brick throwing at the house of my supposed true love. That my life was sacrificed for a hand job is simplistic and inaccurate, except for those recollections in which it all felt as simply worthless as those few minutes of a debutante jacking me off on her parents' Queen Anne sofa, no pun intended, and please, no spunk on the Jacquard.

That Anne and I reunited on a cold, wet and stillborn day felt tragically similar, though this small death was awash in her certain hatred for me that burned no less than acid on flesh. I went to the judge's funeral as an act of humility, as a humble ward by knowledge and contrition. I wanted to see if the love between us had been the real thing, or illusory, as all else.

And like an old fool, not one looking in all the wrong places but one who looked in the worst possible place, I got stuck in the mud, as it were, on humiliation. From there things went from worse to worse yet on mortification, pulling out of the judge's funeral with Jim Cohen riding shotgun and the produce Cadillac in tow. Who looks for love at a funeral? Who tows a jalopy out to the boonies with his Mercedes? These and other rhetorical questions are the stuff jokes are made of, jokes that make people laugh and keep on laughing on account of the imagery so freely conjured; can you picture it? And the laughter sticks, displacing humor with ridicule and undermining everything you ever worked for, until you're no longer a landed, bred and born gentry of original stock who's moved up in society according to its unwritten laws and the dictates of history and the generations begetting the generations that paved the way no less than the cobblestones offloaded from the original ships where they served as ballast, albeit in the bilges, which is where you now reside, figuratively speaking of course, but thrust back and just as far below the waterline, for all the respect you can muster.

We eased over the potholes near the grave as Jim Cohen said goodbye to his friend, the judge, with assurance that Mr. Art be doing fine, that a Mercedes might be small but that don't mean nothing because it really just a different kind of Cadillac is all it is. "Mist Aht, e awright. Mist Aht awright."

On the other side of the grave Walter Snole straddled the siphon as he hand-over-handed it back into the grave, then took two giant steps back in the mud, losing a boot and not going forward for it but proceeding to tease death on the pump pull-rope, pulling and gasping till he and the pump looked and sounded ready to bust a gasket or two. The pump started just shy of beet red and coronary thrombosis, and he stood there living and breathing and hardly seeming to mind the mud splatter flecking him head to toe. He took note of us, looking up forlornly to confide his assessment of his lot in life: "I'll tell you the truth now, a cemetarian's work is never done."

III

An Up and Comer, Don't You Know

It was a day marked with change, the old man's burial heading the list. Our traditional complacency got a judicial reprieve, so it could live free and thrive again with its nemesis safely underground. As if the flesh and blood of a man are all he is, and gone is gone. Which he commonly is around here, unless he left a house in town so his heirs could move up in the world a block or two closer to the hub of the hubbub of memories revered, with a portrait over the mantel and some fine old tales of wisdom and self-deprecation, which humorous anecdotes could best bring out the spirit of the man. They soon remember precious little of the man, settling in to existence once again, rendered lovelier with each passing year in this wonderful old house, thanks be to the forbears.

Such was not the case for the Waring clan, or that branch of it stemming from Waties. Waties Waring sold his house in town before moving north, and when he died the money stayed north, as if he took it with him forever. Still, you could hear the collective

sigh of relief, and nobody begrudged him the Waring plot, so long
as he kept his mouth shut. He'd often made reference to "our little
circle of friends," meaning the great social family comprising life
in town, which was widely held to be the Promised Land, or the
last bastion, or snug harbor, especially after the Great
Misunderstanding, when good manners and polite society were
largely ignored and left us with hardly decent refuge to hole up in.
Our little circle of friends felt an awkward ambivalence when the
judge finally died; we'd won at last, but then we lost as well. It
wasn't your standard issue glorious victory for folks in town, cut
and dried to gloat over and recall play by play like a Clemson
homecoming game. Yet the in-town crowd had somehow
prevailed, with him forever mum in a whites-only cemetery, and
them carrying on as usual, as if to prove their point.

I suppose a part of me died too. For fifteen years my cross to
bear was the one I lit before throwing a brick through the window.
I don't know how the other fellows along for the outing that night
felt, because the topic was unmentionable among accomplices.
Even that word, accomplice, seems so ill-fitted to a seersucker
suit, a blissful smile and a scotch over. Of course that word fit as
well as any word ever had in any kind of suit or bib overalls. But
we enjoyed a certain convenience, saying it was rednecks from the
North who were responsible for such a tasteless, possibly heinous
demonstration. Burning that cross in front of the Waring place;
rednecks did it; that was the word on the street. From that
industrial ash pit came the hooligans and rough-house rabble who
thrived on such demonstration, and that made sense, those half-
wits got so reactionary, and besides, everyone knew *we'd* have no
qualm with integration, given the proper time for adjustment. We
simply didn't want it crammed down our throats, and we surely
couldn't abide the judge's brutality toward his first wife—he
kicked her out, more or less into the street, and Bubba don't play
that way. You hear?

But who cares about an internal explanation of your vile behavior for fifteen years other than yourself? Nobody is the answer, and for fifteen years I'd have paid plenty to get that night back. You don't get them back. I hurt my own kind and was old enough to know better—me, from original Covingdale stock who plain damn didn't engage that way.

I suppose I was young enough to be foolish too, and the judge's fall from grace in Charleston felt like my own, and I lashed back. He sacrificed what was his to give up and what was mine too, so we both lost what we'd banked on and worked toward, all gone to satisfy an old man's delusion. Sixty-five years old and giving up thirty years of rock-solid marriage to a sweet woman with a warm heart who wouldn't hurt a soul, and for what? For passion? Hell, how often can a man that old pump a head of steam? And why couldn't he drive a hundred miles to Savannah, where professional women provide ventilation as necessary so the world can continue in God given order?

That is a simplification but effectively begs the greater question. People talked about the marital problems typically underscoring such a detour in a man's life, and the possible sexual impasse between the judge and his original wife, but putting Annie in the street was just plain damn bad judgment. She was two years older than him and a touch removed from the practicalities. But what could she do, vanish into thin air? Her idiosyncrasy went from a private matter to a public concern, leaving the compassionate resolution of her eccentricity on the street. Annie was rendered a public issue, or rather referendum. And on the street—including each and every block of it, the topic of fair or foul was talked numb and no more clarified after the talk than it was before. But the air clouded with her discomfort and shrinking grasp, and that seemed foul.

Of course the focal point of that talk was Annie's odd tastes, as if they existed in a vacuum with no rhyme nor reason nor similarity to any other oddball behaviors in our quaint little village. Untenable characteristics showing up in your own home were simply not discussed, but this was public and therefore spotlit no less than a cadaver in a learning lab, surrounded by bright young aspirants to the healing profession. Trouble compounded when the new wife got on her soapbox to give us what for on the subject of racial justice, when all she knew about the matter was that her leg was better than Annie's leg, which of course is still conjectural. I think she was more available, which, to an old man is better, but still, the new one was whacked as any leg ever was. She was younger, but not youthful, but then she knew a few kinks, New York style, as it were, and she touched the vital nerve.

That the lovely new couple could no longer live in Charleston was foregone. I, on the other hand, had little choice but to stay. You grow up here, speak the language and live the idiom, you're not virtually unemployable anywhere else, nor do you need to settle for minimum wage. But moving away requires giving up all you worked for and were born into. Some leave and make out all right, but I'd made my commitment and stuck to it. I imagined a need for redemption, which was my wicked euphemism for revenge. It started with doubt, as I smiled and said thank you to the first few lawyers mumbling condolences to me. What? Condolences? *Sorry*, they might say. *Sorry about what happened. Sorry about your friend. Sorry how things worked out there for you. Sorry to hear about your man there. Sorry.*

Doubt thickened and soon grumbled as I realized that the close personal relationship between the judge and me, suddenly ended, meant more than the loss of a friend. It represented a greater loss generating further speculation on the street. *What will Covingdale do now? Bad choice, all right. Shot down just like that. You need to know who you bet the farm on*, and on and on. That is, my future, including prospects for the bench or the big, juicy clients or a partnership or a shot at the Senate or House of Representatives or for that matter the State House could no longer factor in, without the association of guilt. I'd chosen wrong, been in the wrong place at the wrong time and was judged by the company I'd kept. You can't get there from where I stood, not to the legal-review contracts or the state bond issues granted to the chosen legal bubbas for review at one half of one percent, which was not to sneeze at on a billion dollar bond issue. Also fading from view, the bench, any bench, district or circuit or federal, and sure as hell not to an election ballot without a mentor who was himself inextricably intertwined with the original taproot lineage of the original mentors with original roots. My mentor got pulled up by the roots, so all could see the rot and fungus apparently present for years. Who could have known the (pardon me) nigger in that woodpile? I was done, disconnected and disenfranchised in a manner of reckoning, done with what had hardly started. Oh, the condolences and sympathies flowed forth, and I was taken in much as an orphan left on a doorstep, an orphan of evidently normal health and stature but strangely stunted, yet still a good boy, and we do take care of our own. And so my gratitude was forcibly roused, even as my ears burned with whispering on the breeze: *the protégé, the junior legman, the younger stallion....*

Then my brain heated up, and I flushed all over, going red in splotches and breaking a sweat for no reason. We went over between six and seven when they'd be at supper, away from the front windows, so no one would be hurt, or seen. That was our rationale, though I for one wished nothing more than to shout from the rooftops my continuing viability as an up and comer. I wanted to be counted still among the Young Turks as a formidable force, not as a formidable joke, which is what a young stallion sounded like. Be careful what you wish for.

I wrote Anne a year after she moved away with her father and the new woman, nothing heartrending but predicable, thoughtful rhapsody on the changes life requires and the fondness for her that I'd cherish forever, and how I missed her and would surely like to know how she's getting along. I mentioned in passing my regret over the treatment she and her father were made to suffer in those last months. Perhaps I should have included the banshee woman, but that seemed disingenuous, and I, forever the stalwart knight of honor, could have none of that. I remained in my mind undetected, thinking her failure to respond was based on personal difficulty of a different nature. Or maybe she'd found a man.

I wrote again in three years and again in seven more, each time with a bit less of the personal touch but no less warmth and genuine interest in her welfare and our renewed relations. I called on the telephone at the end of fifteen years, a few months before the old man died. The new wife practically commanded my presence for tea. I was in New York for a legal conference, so I went. Anyone could see he was dying. They wanted me back every day of the week I was there, to talk, they said, but it was mostly to listen to the old man's story, like I was Percival receiving the Grail that I'd surely carry home for the enrichment of my people, his people, as though all the lost years and lost love and lost life together had somehow restored me to my rightful and dutiful station as protégé by virtue of time passing. And if greatness had been sacrificed to a greater truth, don't worry; greater greatness waited in the delivery of the Grail. He spoke. I listened, an older protégé if not a wiser one. I was doing the right thing, I thought. Each day they enticed me with Anne's imminent return, as if they knew the longing I suffered, just as I suspected theirs. She'd left unexpectedly for Connecticut the day I'd arrived. Business, you know, the old man said.

I repressed my discomforting sense of detection but could not fathom any other reason for her dogged avoidance. I'd been painfully available, me, her childhood pal and ostensible beau and one, true love. I'd already lost her but sustained my delusion till her father's funeral. I still see and moreover feel the fire in her eyes as she told me her father loved me, not a warm fire but a blowtorch bent on cauterizing the wound between us. I felt it burn to ashes, even as I wondered if she loved me too. She appeared to be done with the love issue, and I could accept that, because I'd committed a mortal sin and deserved the loss for it. I could not accept her denial of forgiveness or any effort to salvage some of the warmth we grew up with. We'd shared a bath and a bed until, for reasons spoken of as beyond our comprehension, we weren't allowed to. But we did comprehend. We did react to nature and the blessed chemistry drawing beings together, and it was not by chance. I have yet to feel anything so meant to be.

If my harm to her was beyond her comprehension, we could resolve that too, or so I thought. I'd disabused myself long ago on prospects of another bath and bed, or I only deluded myself on that score too, that I'd achieved indifference. God knows I needed a hug, one of the old shaggy dog hugs she was so good at and shared so freely in our youth.

Childcare was commonly exchanged in town, where mothers pursued other interests and filled their schedules with solo outings long before the womanly liberation. We traded families and had surrogate siblings. Anne was mine. My mother had the Azalea Society, the Library Society, the Genealogical Society and the Orchid Club, all of which demanded time, dedication and skill, and were dead serious in their goal of making things nice, so when certain dynamic beacons of light and leadership were asked to stand up at the annual luncheon for recognition and applause, the real meaning and value of the woman would be known and felt. Mother longed for the bridge club too and hoped to become a vital, contributing member, as soon as she had time to practice, so she wouldn't look so damn dumb but would appear naturally gifted with nuance and subtlety, keeping score and reading cards in her head, don't you know.

Anne's mother just needed personal time. She was called Annie and was intimate with Sarah Bernhardt at one time, which is not to suggest your lesbian type of behavior but rather that Annie's natural affectation was well-suited to the stage and the dramatic types found there, or near there. Annie remained theatrical long after Sarah died, and that whole dramatic sense of things more or less removed her from mothering. She'd fall into fits of tenderness when she'd grab one of us for a melodramatic embrace, then recite lines from some love scene Sarah Bernhardt had played, and we stood still for it, until she'd run out of lines and ad lib till we wouldn't. Annie sighed over Sarah.

Anne filled in as surrogate wife and mother for her father and me. She wasn't at all fetched like her mother but was stronger than any girl and strong as most boys and kept up, whatever we did. I had to pee before going to school but wouldn't pee at home because the throne room at Palace Covingdale was upstairs and down the hall, where mornings filled with thunder and lightning and the foul moods of the dreaded King George, a tyrant indisposed and worse yet, not a morning person. I had to stop at the Warings anyway for Annie and could pee downstairs and then eat the half grapefruit she'd cut and sugared for her father. I can still see her coming down the stairs ready for school, shaking her finger at me but smiling. Her father got the rind. Puberty came between us, because a girl can't wake up next to a cock-a-doodle-do casual as you please, except of course she could have and me too. But it wasn't allowed. So we adjusted as kids do, and none of that mattered either.

I made amends with her father before he died by lending a good ear to his history of the world, which was the Lowcountry from the turn of the centuries, 19th to 20th. He mostly harkened back to the years the white preacher referenced with "loving father," when he would descend on me stealing his breakfast and grumble sincerely as an ogre and rub my head with his knuckles.

He waited my arrival at the dinette in his modest but comfortable apartment in New York with two grapefruit halves on that last visit. "Master Arthur," his voice opened like a heavy door on crusty hinges. "Two lumps!" With an awful laugh he bade me sit, or he'd knuckle-rub my head. At least he didn't look up my nose, which my friends don't usually do, but Judge Waring was the first man to point out the impracticality of such obtrusive bristles, saying he had a damn hairbrush didn't have bristles thick as my nose hair. Or as long. Or sticking so far out a man's head they didn't leave anybody any choice what to talk about once that man walked off for another drink or something. Nose hair sticks out like a marquee that says *Matinee Today!* Nose hair! Now how in hell can a man make the federal bench with nobody able to get past his nose hair? I was past thirty then, maybe about thirty-two or three when Waties counseled me on nose trimming. Eudora never said anything, and she was in a position at least once every three months to look right up there. But she didn't matter and likely didn't care, as far as factoring one more punishment in the marriage ordeal she was made to suffer. I need not respond to the judge's critique because self-defense was unnecessary and stupid. He wanted to help me in a very big way and for the first time, he plain referenced my nose hair and the role it might play on my way to the federal bench. At home I trimmed the nasal shrubbery and have done so daily ever since.

I might even be compulsive on the issue now; ears too get a plucking right regular. The point is, he had influence, steering me this way and that so I wouldn't trip over myself on the way to what I wanted most. At least the federal bench was what I thought I wanted and was undoubtedly what everyone wanted for me. What I wanted in actuality I'm still sorting out and hope to figure before too long. Yes, I wanted the federal bench, before I was granted the rest of my life to ponder that loss and to come up with something else to want.

In the meanwhile, all was forgiven in New York, or at least set aside. We'd participated in some brutal behaviors and suffered for it. He gave up his society and so much as pulled the rug on mine, considering he was it, on the professional side anyway. He dashed his hopes, cursing our town to kingdom come in the name of justice, and for what? He left me no choice but to draw a line and show what side I stood on. Maybe a brickbat through his window wasn't the most compassionate symbol of my gratitude, or maybe it was a reasonable recompense to killing a young man's aspiration. Except of course it wasn't reasonable and compensated nothing. For years I convinced myself that nobody could be too sure about it, but then I came to know that anybody unsure was a fool, and there we were.

Unyielding love was a delusion, maybe, but it gave us that last interlude of peace. He looked most dead with less pink in his cheeks than you'd find in an ashtray. He more or less insisted that love and flesh are as one and not to be denied each other any more than you might deny what's in store for either one, and that's the fundamental premise of the matrimonial situation—his situation with specific regard to one marriage and another. He warned that love shouldn't be confused with lust, which he also knew from experience.

Yes, Your Honor. I more or less nodded. His reciprocation more or less rendered judgment, as if from the last bench.

He earned the title King of the Tenderloin as a young man, which wasn't so clever but accurately reflected his pursuits and became the gristle on the street in his early, bachelor years, but then those years were rife with potential. Any gristle was chewed with a laugh and a headshake, because a young lawyer on his way to hearth and home and the federal bench fit right in. But you take love, real love, and it doesn't matter how old the principals get to be, and the gristle turns to fresh meat, ripped from an old, familiar victim, because something didn't fit right.

Oh, yes, it must have been the abrupt divorce and remarriage in deference to real love and the few good years a man has left, instead of servitude to a false and demanding society of manners. Bah! I think he'd have banged a gavel if he had one handy. Like I say, the old warmth recalled between us may have served his purpose. I don't know that he died a happy man, yet I'm certain he gained perspective as few in Charleston do.

Anne wouldn't come around that week I was in New York, nor would she answer my letters between then and the funeral. Obstinate as her father, she clung to personal injury, imagining a greater justice. Who knows what she got? I think I'm over her, perhaps by sheer necessity, but that counts, if the pain accompanying every thought of her is gone, or at least subsides. I can honestly say that I did love her and likely could have loved her for all time, beginning with what I more or less obsessed about, which was sexual relations with her, which would have been for me, I think, the only such pairing precisely described by that abused, overused and most often euphemistic phrase, making love. We bonded prior to adolescence, then turned to love. For me, it never died; but isn't imbalance the way of most love?

She married a man named Warren soon after that, and soon after their divorce, a few years after the funeral, she killed herself, her terse note explaining poor health and endless fatigue.

Now that I've been married and divorced and know better than to try that foolishness again, I wonder what people expect in their rush to the altar. Is it the pronouncement of love with witnesses, white lace and a high ceiling? What else but such transitory rhapsody would merit sacrifice of the unknown and adventurous side of life? Then the deal sours, and what you get in exchange for mystery and uncertainty is the chance to know someone so well you can't stand to be in the same room. I would have seen Anne if she'd let me, would have most likely courted and married her and God knows got next to her as often as she'd allow, in time accepting less frequency till we pressed no more and wondered why we chose that path, till wonder atrophied too. Then we'd have gone our separate ways. You live long enough, you repeat yourself. But listen to me; hindsight is the clearest vision, even as you verge myopically on the same abyss.

Maybe I drifted through her thoughts as she wrote her suicide note, but I think not. Soon after the funeral I moved out of my house in town, on Queen Street. I would have sold in a minute, and the market was strong, but I leased it out to avoid the view, review and discussion ad nauseam of the final capitulation to guilt, as Exhibit B in the prosecution's case against my failure to fit in. The simple act of moving out was keenly observed and acutely difficult; college boys more suited to furniture hauling than the arts, sciences or humanities, jostled the furniture with casual aplomb, while the real load was mine to bear. Up and down the stairs on wobbly legs, I trudged under the top-heavy weight of the family burden shifting. I carried on blithely as any task under scrutiny would warrant, cheerfully passing the baton to the next trustee, who could begin directly living the in-town life with care and maintenance as those of us before had done for the past three hundred years. I wouldn't actually seek new tenants for months, but I imagined their presence, eager to take the baton and to learn what I had to tell them, for the company of the thing.

But all was not cheerful in Mudville. Oh, the place had a soul of its own; it talked back, echoing my mumbles and murmurs as if to remind me of my foolishness. That house would outlive me surely as nature would carry on post-Covingdale, indifferently or otherwise, so I moved officially out to what I considered the beginning and the end of what this Lowcountry is, which is nature, so the carrying on could begin while I was still around to enjoy it.

"I'm Arthur Covingdale," I'd tell the marsh from time to time in those first days out, watching the flats rise in the falling tide. I watched she crab and Jimmy snuggle in the mud and whole crowds of oysters pop and squirt—watched them up close like I hadn't seen them before.

I was a white male, fifty-eight, stronger than I'd been in years, hardly affluent but humbly independent on paper. I didn't need to rise at dawn or head out in the freezing salt spray or bloody my knuckles on crab pots or feel my limbs go numb, unless I wanted to feel the thaw by noon, heart and hands. The marsh felt populated with souls, with characteristics, appetites and inclinations. She crab and Jimmy clawed at the detritus and ate as the clumps dissolved. I too reached and fed. It was the climate, I thought, the thick air and slow pace that let the years slip by, meaningless but for numbering regrets. Past and present got fused in the region on a promise for more of the same, dead ahead.

Charleston is still a fossil; time is the Southern glacier. Whatever changes here is first considered for a hundred years. Then the little town grumbles forward reluctantly, its ancient lunacies crumbling to the sea. Then with considerable ballyhoo, we are revealed and reveled anew for adapting yet again to modern times. Don't we?

My floe drifts from the day Waties Waring got buried at Magnolia Cemetery. The distance between now and then seems greater every year, though in the long view the years seem one and the same, evenly quartered by the seasons.

IV

Jim Cohen

The road south out of Charleston even then penetrated a thicket of franchise food lights and traffic swarming like flies on road kill. It didn't feel like the old South or the new South or any South but the one South of how it got to be, going ugly to uglier to ugliest and uglier still, till you'd swear they brought in the ugly consultants from the Great Progressive North to get things going and then pressed a might further for the more, more, more of it, because enough is never enough, unless you're unpatriotic, and because nobody around here could have thunk up anything this dog-ass ugly. The view made me feel ugly just passing through, heading deeper into the core of it, down Savannah Highway past the International House of Pancakes headed toward the K-Mart with plenty of free parking. Jim Cohen pointed to his usual spot for peddling *Promise Land Produce*, across from *Bessinger's Barbecue*, where the produce Cadillac had sat like it was built there and not meant to move ever, until today, when he pressed his luck and maybe proved it wasn't.

Things aired out some in a few miles, back then, and the bridge over the Stono River flattened into a causeway crossing tidal marshlands to the horizon. The causeway became a regular road again at the forest on the far side and ran on south through a long tunnel of live oak boughs down Johns Island to another bridge crossing over to Hoopstick Island that sits in the middle of Church Creek. Hoopstick is hardly an acre of marsh grass on a sharp bend marking the point where the creek changes names; it's called Church Creek to the west and Bohicket to the south, seaward. Church Creek was freshwater, with largemouth bass in the cypress roots and knees until the south side of Hoopstick Island got blown and dredged in 1915 to make a shorter sail from Charleston. The new route cut two hours off the trip. The cypress died of salt intrusion, and the bass disappeared, giving rise to my first real sense of loss. I was a child of six, but you can't underestimate the sudden loss of what deeply impresses a child. One season it was bigger-than-life bass out of Church Creek, and the next year we couldn't go, just because we no longer had a reason.

Moreover, crossing the rivers south of Charleston, you sensed a division between the time consumed and the timeless. Charleston remained engaged in futility, striving for more, even if only more chitchat over things that wouldn't change because nobody wanted them to, not then, not now, not ever. Not a mean place, rarely cruel or gothic and never lynch-mob minded as most Northern accounts portray the South; it was only a village, nosey, dull and proud of its age. What isn't 17 this or 18 that is either English or embarrassing. Time is frozen there, on display.

Jim Cohen may have shared these and other reflections on life and changing perspective on our drive south. I watched the countryside change shape and color, going that late in the day from gray to yellow as the sun broke through a cleave in the clouds, then to orange and gray again as the fissure closed and the river gained speed, emptying headlong to another slack ebb. I watched the scenery, taken yet again by its overwhelming beauty, its marshlands to the horizon asking the most difficult question thereabout: Why has it been so long since you last feasted your eyes on this beauty you were born into? Jim looked straight ahead. They say beauty becomes a common denominator, a baseline from which greater beauty is required, so the beautiful rush may again be felt. May be, and I suspected straight ahead was the direction he most often stared, because it was the direction most integral to his survival.

Another twelve miles from Church Creek is Rockville, the summer village for those who can afford it. No franchise food lights here, only a Negro grocery, deserted, and a piccalo four miles up, *Johnston Baby Grand & 66/Beer, Moonpies, Slim Jims, RC, Penrose Sausage, Can Corn Beef, Pickle Eggs & Sundries.* They got Vienna (vy-éena) Sausage too, and pickle pig feets, but nobody ever bothered with updating the signage to include those delectable extras, because everybody knew. Hell, you could see the pig feets sitting right there on the counter, big old gallon jug with the toenails sticking up just over that white film covering the brown water. People mulled outside among the cars, carrying on, young people mostly, and the stovepipe smoked.

The dirt road a mile before Rockville is easily missed, since it opens between two live oak boughs reaching across from either side, drooping down and arching again back up like thousands of others along the roadside, twisting and groping to close the opening, barely wide enough for a Fleetwood Brougham but with room to spare for a Mercedes, which worked out fine when Jim informed me that the Cadillac wouldn't fit and didn't need to no how, because that's where the produce would be sold, meaning right now, on the road rightchere. So we backed and forthed. He got out for the finagle, so we could signal and yell at each other, ignoring each other and yelling some more until I got it right.

What the hell he had to yell about I don't know. I was behind the damn wheel, so what'd he expect, I'd do it his way?

All I wanted was to unhitch that pile of junk from my car and get home, though the afternoon was sorely beautiful out there, and home waited like a solitary confinement, maybe self-imposed but I plain did not want company that evening and couldn't even go for groceries without running the gauntlet of stares and whispers and the boldest, meaning most compassionate, among them asking in confidence, *How you making out with this?*

So maybe it was easy and natural to give on in and do as I was told when Jim pulled two folding chairs from the produce Cadillac and with one big foot shoved the winter crops from where the back seat used to be to where the trunk used to be, saying he hadn't used them for years, trunk lids nor back seats neither one, and frankly couldn't see much sense of driving a truck when he could ride in a Cadillac. He told me to sit down and enjoy a spell.

Seemed too near the road, practically in it, but then that hardly mattered with no traffic. So we sat much as we'd sat on the drive down, in silence, till he broke into a story, his story, neither solicited nor in the least prompted by me, leaving me to wonder why. Didn't I get enough jabber in town, and didn't I want free of it? But I got to say, old Jim could spin a yarn and seemed to have a load on his chest and seemed to want a man like me, meaning white, meaning town-bred, meaning a man unlike himself, to pour this one into.

So I sat, willing to give him five minutes, or ten or even twenty, and his mellifluous way of telling a thing, spinning the yarn with one hand while at the same time carving up the language like a chef on a turkey with a real sharp knife in the other. I followed him as best I could, not minding what parts I couldn't, feeling easy for the first time all day, fitting in with the time and place after a rough go with something or other I couldn't quite get a fix on. But then I grew up here, so of course I could get a fix on it, that language and way of seeing things as unavoidable as the mud and the tides; I knew the problem full well and heard it round about in a telling of a different complexion from any I'd heard. So I relaxed for the listen. Hell, I had time.

The Lowcountry patois is two similar dialects, Gullah and Geechee, both true hybrids of different languages, both based on English but leaning hard on French with some Gypsy and pig latin and a dash of just right twangs in the mix. An untrained ear can't tell one from the other. Both dialects conform to rules of conjugation, unlike a pidgin or slang that depends on assumed meaning with regular nodding, grunting and snorting by both the speaker and listener. A slang or pidgin has no structure and therefore no precise meaning but rather an understood, or rather presumed meaning, which in most applications comes to less meaning conveyed than what one dog tells another by the smell of his butt hole.

Gullah do, as do Geechee too, convey meaning far more precisely. I can get by in either dialect, but I can't stand in the road in heady palaver like the out-island Blacks do. They'd know I'm from here, meaning way far south of Jersey, soon as they see me, or, short of that, soon as I speak, but they needn't see nor hear either one, since they know me anyway and know they'll not speak a thing past me. But I can't hold my own; or maybe I can, if I redefine my own, disabusing it from the constant self-assertion required in town, both socially and professionally, though the two most often overlap. What I'm getting at is what Jim Cohen felt compelled to tell me, with no need for my opinion, assessment or two cents otherwise.

Once upon a time, way back when, no light shone from either bank of Bohicket Creek or above it. Little bitty waves whispered to the black night. The north bank answered in kind and then some: pluff mud squished between toes till feet sank in a soft spot to the knees. *Ploosh.* A bushel basket pressed into the mud bore a body's weight, allowing the feet up from the suck.

They sank shallower till they didn't sink at all, till they crunched on dull-edged oyster shells. They stopped, and the man they bore bent and reached for the razor edge of good oysters. Clouds rolled from under a crescent moon, and the sliver spilled shadows on the earth. One was man. Two stars fell for his eyes.

Turning the basket over, upside down, he sat on it as if relieving a great burden. Sighing deeply he pulled the knife from his belt and reached again for oysters. He pried the shell open, deftly cut the muscle, slurped it down and nearly sang down the north bank:

Shoooweee! Dem good!

Scooting down the bank, drinking John Allston's brandy from a silver flask, he judged the libation as well: *Ahhh...* Etchings danced around the monogram **A** that shone through the filigree. Gulps and gurgles blended with the creek's babble. *Ah....* the man said, reaching again and eating again, repeating as necessary in a rhythm rote as the seasons and cycles, content as nature's interlude of food and rest, until the crescent set, a billion stars thinned, and a voice called as if demanding order on this, the dawn of civilization:

"Luzon!" Branches cracked from up the bank. The man stooped, pulled the basket out from under, turned it right side up and reached again for oysters, big, single whitefoots that chucked into the basket with a dramatic clunk appropriate to such an effort of gathering oysters like these for the folks, up before dawn to take advantage of the low tide, so these morsels might meet the lips of the chosen few.

The basket filled as the voice drew nigh, as the flood came forth and over it another flood of molten light. Elizabeth Allston stepped clear of the trees onto a limb, breaking it with a snap of authority. Regaining her composure and stopping akimbo, she announced once more, "Luzon!" The man looked up, then down to crown the bushel with three gems, regal individuals that would dare any man or beast to leave things unopened, unslurped and unsavored. Then he raised the basket overhead and let it settle on one shoulder as he faced the direction of the woman now approaching. He would have strode to meet her, but the creek trickling through the oyster beds to the flask at his feet shimmered till both the surface and the flask shone brilliant silver in first, blinding light. Not to worry; with one easy step the flask sank under the big slew foot, mashing it into the mud and removing the evidence of all but the best intentions. The brilliance remaining was no less than sunrise, its magnanimous light reaching across Bohicket and out the Edisto to the sea. "Luzon!" And Luzon's dazzling grin.

"Aw, Missy Bet. Gawt dem awshtuh. Look heah. Dem whitefoots.... Aw, Missy." Setting the bushel down, he straightened, darker still in sunrise silhouette.

"What, you pick up one and eat two and call it getting oysters?"

Mud sequins clung daintily to her dressing gown, golden locks to satin bodice, adorning the lacey abundance. She tapped a shoe, a sure sign of displeasure and key indication the lie was known. He counted on his instinct and her appetite, deftly shucking a notable select from the summit, just as skillfully severing the muscle and presenting the offering cleanly, neither mud flecks nor shell fragments nor Black skin touching the slithery gob. He offered. She took. She examined. He laughed loud as a cock on a fence, "Ha haaa!...."

"Luzon!" But she went mum on the slurp and swallow and stayed mum when the oyster slipped back up for a chew or two and mum still for the slide back down. "Mm! Luzon. You say you fixing to load the wagon by morning. Y'ax for two nickels, you get two nickels."

"Dem awshtuh," he offered another.

"But where you been? Eat oysters all night? Great God, when it come to work, Luzon, you about worthless."

"Gawt dem awshtuh, Missy."

"Git on! And where be my two nickels?"

"Two nickel?" He scratched here and there.

"Git on." So they walked together up the bank, single file, she leading the way and rambling as well over her son leaving for college today and what it means to a young man like John Junior and what paltry little bit a might be expected of the field chattel on such a momentous occasion. Luzon grunted agreement under his bushel burden, so she stopped and turned to ask rhetorically just how much time he might need to shuck this here bushel. Nodding profusely again he assured it wouldn't take but no time at all. She said she'd give him the morning, and it better be done or else. He laughed again across the flooding creek, as if it was good as done.

A hundred twenty years later, a descendant's belly shook with laughter, though only across the flooding ditch across the road from Jim Cohen's *Promise Land Produce* Cadillac. Jim propped his legs on the back bumper for the tell, as if the tell was why we came, or why I came at any rate, or rather why I got dragged out there. We hadn't seen a car in either direction since arriving, but he didn't seem to care, just leaned over till he liked to fall out his folding chair so he could pass gas, then leaned back, setting in with his feet stuck into the winter crops, Jerusalem artichokes and winter corn mostly, piled in his trunk. He said a man ought to take what he knows is his, even if another man thinks it's stealing. He meant this produce he'd gleaned from harvested fields, I thought.

I would have reminded him that the law is the law and does all the thinking in the end, but he was doing the telling, not listening. He said you could call it revenge if you wanted to, but all it is is what it is.

"All what is?"

"Fuh true," he said, pulling a silver flask from his bib pocket and swigging it half empty. He said it was good that I took this time today to join him and give a listen, because he really wouldn't have the time to spare otherwise. I laughed, because the man told a joke with timing, delivery and a punch line that caught me off guard. But I laughed short, out of courtesy, realizing Jim's effort, squeezing me into his schedule like that, as if a country Black's time could possibly bill out anywhere near the hourly rate of a Broad Street lawyer. "'Side dat, you ain' do-een nuffin' better'n watchin' de judge get de shovel, and I sho do 'preciate de han'." That is, he could use a little help unloading, because you can't expect to sell the damn produce if you don't unload it from the car. You got to set it up in a display, or folks won't stop for a looksee. It has to look good, you see.

"If you so keen on a display, what in hell we sittin' around for?"

"Wha' you say? We laxin', man."

I would have pressed him on exactly what folks he had in mind who we were bound to please with a proper display, but he was already tugging a half sheet of plywood from behind the front seat along with another folding chair, requiring me to give up my seat, which seemed timely, since I was due to take my leave. He saw it coming and said don't worry, we'd use the bumper to hold up the other end of the plywood. He motioned me over, because the best way to teach me how to do this would be for him to do it first, while I paid attention. I laughed again, couldn't help it.

No matter who says what about what was or might have been, last year I could bill legal work—my legal work—at a hundred dollars an hour, one of three attorneys in town to warrant that kind of fee. Repeat: one hundred dollars for one hour. He laughed too, reaching for a burlap bag from the shotgun foot well and laying it open to reveal a half-bushel or so of oysters. They smelled all right. "Dey good," he said. "I git a week now fo dey stank. Dey be's awright." That is, he could count on oysters staying alive and fresh for a week out of water this time of year. He went back in for a squeeze bottle of French's mustard, set it on the back bumper, reached in his bibs for his oyster knife, shucked an oyster neat and held it steady as a seventy-three-year-old man can while drowning the sumbitch in mustard.

"Hell, Jim. You like a little oyster with your mustard?"

"Yessuh, Mist Aht. I b'lieve I do." He slurped it down and went for another round and then took a moment to savor the taste and maybe the golden afternoon, looking up and down the road, nodding and assuring, yes, a man got to get even. I didn't ask even for what. He had a burr in his shorts and wanted me to guess what, but I had irritations of my own, and frankly, it'd been a long damn day and wasn't over. Jim Cohen watched my assessment and cracked a smile so slight you couldn't be certain what good feeling it reflected or how much there was of it; maybe I only thought it was an indication of contentment. I didn't need to see a country Black showing me some of the old cliché in the form of eternal happiness, and I knew Jim was past that. But I wouldn't have minded some of the old goodwill.

Jim Cohen smiled often as not. He wasn't old and feeble like the judge had been but showed his age like a soul fermented to spirits rather than vinegar. His smile stretched then, and he said today was his boifday. He laughed, as if his revenge was secure after all, and there we were, celebrating the day on which his survival began. He shucked another oyster, squeezed a tablespoon of mustard on top, ate it and shook his head. "Shoo. Dem moh bettah."

Moh bettah den what was conjectural. He drank again and handed me the flask, confiding it was the same flask his grandfather Luzon stole from John Allston a hundred twenty years prior. I took a drink, to make peace, as it were. "Dem sweetwine," he said.

The flask was monogrammed on the convex side in the center of intricate filigree that had been rubbed smooth where fat fingers had squeezed it so many times, above and below the center. I laughed and asked what the W stood for. "Allston," he said.

A car with New Jersey plates and sunburned faces pulled in, headed north from Florida but detouring for local color in this place they never heard of, or never thought much about at any rate. The father asked for watermelon. Jim Cohen sprang four quarters from his change maker and told me to run down the road to Yolanda's and fetch us a couple of grape sodas. Then he turned to the driver from New Jersey. "No melon," he said. "It too late fuh melon."

He further directed the man to peruse the Jerusalem artichokes, since datuh be's wha' we mos' famous here, fuh true. He signaled the wife to get out and come on over too for a quick primer on root relish preparation, no rush, these ones'll be good till you get home and then some.

I left to run my errand. When I got back the New Jersey family was making final selections on corn and Jerusalem artichokes, and Jim told me to fetch a bag from the front seat of the produce Cadillac and then go ahead and bag up dat corn and dem chokes. The family paid, took Jim Cohen's picture and left. He laughed, as if to say that making money was just that easy, but you did have to put yourself out some if you wanted to make a go of it.

All of which painted another amusing picture in a continuing series, all humorous and distracting, neither of which I'd get at home, but I'd had enough. Yet like a seasoned boxer measuring punches, biding his time and letting his own ring wisdom dictate the pace, he measured my need and me. "Da right. A man got to get eben." I still wondered what he sought from me that he thought was his when I told him it looked about time to head back up the road. He told me to sit down a spell further, opened the grape sodas and handed me one, and he reached back once more as the judge had done. But Jim Cohen reached further back and farther down the river, back before Luzon and Julya to Edisto Island.

A car from Massachusetts pulled in and asked for yams. Jim said no and sold them artichokes instead. I bagged and then went down the road again for coffee, black for me, black with three sugars for Jim.

Business slacked off and mid afternoon turned to four, with the sun falling faster and the chill gaining. He showed me then how to reload the produce, careful now, so's you don't bruise it up, and then you gently shove it all forward with one foot, up to where the back seat used to be so they wouldn't fall out on the way home. I didn't remind him that we were home, or he was home at any rate. He asked if I'd go ahead and give him a lift on up to the house.

I would have said no, it's good for a man to walk a hundred yards, and maybe I stood there a might too long thinking it over, but he stood there too, staring back at me like he would have done, I believe, if I'd stood there staring all night. So I said, "Yes, sir, Mister Jim. Get in the car." He laughed and got in and said I'd done right fine there on my first day of work, adapting right away to being the nigger while he did the talking.

Sure, it was a funny thing for him to say, but it was my turn not to laugh. He had no more place nor manner calling me a nigger than I would have had calling him one, which I didn't. I was none too pleased and let it show, and he said, "Da right. Da right," as we eased up the pot-holed drive a hundred yards through the trees.

Houses slumped in the clearing at the end of the trees, with walls touching the walls of forbears that stood empty, windswept through broken windows and no doors. Smoke wisped from most stovepipes, and a vague avenue ran down the center of the cluster.

Rusty bicycles and broken swing sets littered the enclave, along with assorted debris and a few odd cinder blocks, likely waiting to support the next dead car. A red Pontiac Bonneville, '63 model, sat near one house with cinder blocks under the wheel hubs, the roof caved in and the windshield smashed. Beside it, a grassless patch marked parking.

Chauffeuring Jim Cohen twenty miles to his house on Wadmalaw Island struck a chord in harmony with that sad day and got us warmly removed from the funeral and resurrection so far away. Jim Cohen worked himself free of my car and onto his feet. Surveying the ramshackle dwellings that appeared adequate in providing shelter if not esteem, he swayed side to side till his footing stabilized.

That morning I would have thought cocktails and dinner with Jim Cohen as remote as Cinderella turning out to be a dark-skinned beauty. But he leaned into the car window with another survey, seeing the sorry matrix of that soggy day, or maybe needing a bigger load off his chest. Or maybe, and most likely, I was merely, painfully visible. At any rate he said, "I beviting you in fuh yidda bit moh dem sweetwine 'n some dem muystad awshtuh too." We stared too long a second time, and I said all right.

Who knows where penance comes from or why we seek it, or if we're even slightly cognizant of our drive to reach it, to feel it and have it any time we need it?

A half-spun cast net hung on the porch rail with little lead weights dangling from its bottom hem. A spool of nylon line had unwound from one weight and rolled ten feet down the porch to the ground, where it had sat for hours or weeks. In town such items would appear quaint, a display reflecting our heritage, our colorful marshland, our blah, blah, blah. I asked if the net was being mended and how long it would take and how he came to know net weaving, and if he planned to teach it to his kids or knew the importance of passing on such legacy, and if nylon was so different from cotton.

He laughed short, huffed himself to the door and said, "Shit. Don' know nuffin," and he walked inside. The acrid sweetness of hot lard rushed out as he went in. It enveloped every sense, the coarser along with the finer ones, covering every square inch of essence surely as the mud on the pig it came from. I acclimated with a few deep breaths, adjusting, as we sometimes must. A girl child in overalls and a stained T-shirt passed from the front room with an iron skillet of hot lard in one hand and a steaming bowl of periwinkle snails in the other. She hurried when Jim said, "Shoo!" looking over her shoulder at the white man, making me wonder when last such a breed apart walked here. Her stiff black hair was plastered down her neck, and she grinned, the darning needle used for snail picking and dipping clenched in her teeth.

Jim Cohen pulled a bottle of low-end sherry from the shelf mumbling sweetwine. Holding it in one hand, he brushed crumbs and periwinkle shells off the table with the other. He went back for tumblers and bade me sit. So I sat, loosening my tie and then on second thought taking it off and putting it in my jacket pocket, and then on third thought wishing I'd left my jacket in the car. Jim poured and waddled off again to turn on his TV and turn the channel till he found what he wanted: *To Tell the Truth*. Catching Gary Moore on the tail end of a joke, he joined the audience laughter. When he sat down across from me, I raised my glass. "Here's to better times," I vaguely offered. We drank.

"Moh bettah den what?" he asked, tilting his glass again.

"Better than funerals, I suppose."

"Bettah?" he asked, pouring again. "Dem be's bout de bestess fune-ruh binna rounchea I eb did see." He said he'd never seen a casket so fine, his hands forming the scrollwork inlay of maple on mahogany with all the arabesques down to the curlicues, then showing me on a slow motion grasp how that casket handle had actually been shaped by somebody to match the natural contours of his hand. No doubt about it, he said, the judge must have been as great as everybody said he was, to have a casket like that. Of course the downpour was unfortunate—*dinna bode no good*—cutting the preacher short and leaving no time for working up a good sing.

I agreed that the casket looked fine but assured Jim that an expensive casket has no bearing on a man's virtue. "I'm certain he wasn't as great as everybody thought. Or as vile as everybody else thought."

"Who he? Dat vile?"

"Vile. Wicked.... Bad."

"Nah! Da man wan't bad! E binna tink aw de damn time on dem wotah melum. Da man gawt e mind onum like e do n'en e don' know nuffin fuh save e own soul fuh true. Da man wan't bad. Aw ways e lu-u-u-uv dem wotah melum. Me too." Jim bet that I loved a nice fresh slice every bit as much as the next man, even dem Black watermelon; it good too, fuh true. I poured us again, assuring him I didn't know. We drank.

"Jmetta!" he yelled, chilling me with visions of ultimate hospitality. "Jmetta!" The child returned. "Git dem awshtuh, child." The child brought two oyster knives from the counter along with two paper napkins and set one of each before us. She fetched two foul damp rags from nails over the hearth and began to set them too, but Jim Cohen snatched and tossed them on the floor with a scowl.

She moved forlornly to the shelf and served two fresh rags, stealing another grin at me from behind his back. Jim poured another round as she rummaged crocus sacks on the back porch and yelled for guidance on which sack was right for the white man. She fetched two before getting the right one. "Da right, child," Jim Cohen finally approved, emptying the sack of large, select oysters onto the table and smiling proud. The child left.

"These are some handsome beasts," I allowed, drawing another look of puzzlement on his face for the strange way some white folks talk.

"Jmetta!" She returned. "Dem Frenchies!"

"Oh," she squeaked, reaching under the counter for a jumbo jar of French's Mustard with a push-button squirter on top. Jim Cohen held an oyster in his spatulate palm and shucked it clean as another man might halve a tomato. Setting his oyster knife aside, he leaned toward the squirter. "No," Jmetta said, having fetched another clean rag to swab the squirter free of yellow crust and congealed goo, then swabbing again and again to prove her point and soak up a few moments more of undivided attention.

"Stay with us," Gary Moore said. "We'll be right back to see who is telling the truth, but first...." The audience clapped.

Jim Cohen laughed. "Da right, child." She grinned and left. He severed the bottom muscle, reached and squirted and let it slide. "Mmm. Dem moh bettah."

I laughed too, still wondering more better than what, feeling oddly distant from the gray and mournful funk up the road that had felt far from laughter. I took off my jacket, rolled my sleeves and shucked. I tried a squirt of French's and ate, then chased it with sweetwine, hurrying through two more shucks and drinks so these tastes would lose their disparate tang with immersion, I hoped, and so I too could sink into the apparent contentment Jim Cohen wallowed in. I asked, "Why do you suppose you were a designated pallbearer?"

He smiled that knowing smile, unrelated to humor but kin to incongruous truth. Harkening back, he recalled how things had a pattern, and the patterns held, starting way back when the judge got in the habit of having Jim Cohen row him from one hole to the next while he trolled or jigged for spottails and weakfish. That was forty, fifty years ago and not at all same as rowing a man on to the last fishing hole, "which ain' zacly like binna bestess man at e weddin' too, you know, but den it is, you know, moh less monumentous, so to speak." Still and all, when he got right down to it, "Don' know."

"Did you know Anne well?"

"No. I know d'uddah two, dem wife womens." Elaborating briefly on the pratfalls of watermelon out of season, he said it was demanding enough for a man to have some without it being bitter watermelon, which the judge had a strange taste for.

"I grew up with the family, practically part of it, probably the closest thing to a son the judge ever knew. I wasn't asked to be a pallbearer."

Now he laughed heartily, up next to humor with a double squirt of incongruity and some anomalous sprinkles on top, saying, "All dat son bidness go fly out de window jus soon de brickbats come flyin' on in. Cain't 'spec a man to have you carry him out aftah dat."

"How in the *hell* did *you* know *that*?"

"Ev'body know dat, Mist Aht." He said the same Mary Green who found the bloodstained sheets was the Warings' last housemaid before they swore off housemaids as dehumanizing. Any ways, Mary Green happened to be in the alley between the Waring house and de nexdoe neighba house. Mary Green was scrubbing a pot or beating a rug or dressing a fish or some such when she heard voices and saw flames flare up. She hugged the wall, knowing it be's de debil and fearing fuh her own life, fuh true. She saw. Dinna wan no such view, but she saw. Afterward, when the commotion died down, and the sheriff left, and the federal marshals were on the way but hadn't yet arrived, Mary Green told what she saw, which was four men, three unknown to her and Mister Arthur Covingdale. The judge said she was wrong about that, practically yelled at her, so she cried, describing Mist Aht's mash boots, the ones he got fum de judge fuh Christmas on special order fum the Applecrumbie & Fetch in New York, New

York. She described Mist Aht's hat too and the thin moustache he wore at the time—till the judge broke in, pulling a Bible from the shelf and urging all hands on it, including his own, the new wife's, Mary Green's and Anne's. The judge swore an oath by God that they'd never tell who burned that cross and threw those bricks and made all three them womens swear it too.

I never doubted the efficacy of the prevailing theory over the years, that it was rednecks from North Charleston who burned that cross and threw those bricks. The redneck theory went well with the notion that our outrage had nothing to do with segregation; we weren't racist but incensed over such a breakdown of common decency. Yes, that fit and suited me; you just can't tell what those rednecks will do.

But then my whole life as it had been lived felt like a doubt, like I'd spent the last twenty years with a huge woolly mass hanging out my nose for everyone to see and talk about, but nobody would clue me in on. I felt worse than foolish, like a murderer who beat the rap but then couldn't beat consensus.

I felt low as the dregs, watching that old Black man practically squeeze his bottle for a few more drops of cheap sherry, telling me I was the redneck, known for mortally wronging those close as family, those who yet forgave me, even as they winced from the sting.

"If everybody knew, then the oath wasn't kept."

"D'oat wan't kep, not in de sparit ob d'oat," Jim Cohen commiserated, pouring from a fresh bottle, explaining that Mary Green never was treated that way before, putting her hand on the Bible and all, like God and oaths and such were applicable to her too. So when she told the story to every maid on the circuit, she included the part about the oath like it was just one more part of the story, and she happened to be in the same house the story occurred in, like the tables and chairs were in there too and would tell that story like she did, except that everybody knows tables and chairs can't talk, not like a nigger maid. But oh, if they could. Maids can, and in turn they told the story to every husband, child, parent, cousin and friend on the maid circuit and in the maid sphere of influence, or at least the maid sphere of gossip, all of which spheres happened to co-orbit with the church sphere, where they all went to share in one thing and another until no thing remained unturned. With sparse consolation, Jim Cohen assured me that only everybody knew, and not everybody else, meaning the help and not the gentry, leastways not for a year or so.

I drank. He poured again with a decent silence for a blessed minute or two while I reviewed once again every damn day of the last twenty years lived in smug conviction. I broke the silence with the tough question, "How could you ask me in here? Sit at your table? Drink your wine, after I did a thing like that?"

He said I gave him a ride home, and some sweetwine and oysters were the least he could offer. He looked down as if watching his thoughts line up. When he looked back up, his face drawn between resignation and hard knocks, he said as far as he could tell, nobody cared; nobody outcheah anyway. He couldn't tell about the town Blacks anymore, not since they been claiming what the judge told them was theirs. He laughed again; he didn't much care about all that too, couldn't see where a man with more rights would put food on the table any easier than a man free to run the river and bring home what he could. The judge made a bad time for white people, and that's all there was to it. Besides, he said, "Here be Mist Aht Coven*ton*, drank dem sweetwine and shuck dem awshtuh wid a ole fat nigga afta-all."

A long guzzle couldn't douse my discomfort. I wished he wouldn't use that word.

"Coving*dale*," I corrected. He poured, reminiscing deeper in the Sea Island patois, in and out of the gibberish it can become, as if offering distraction as first aid to what ailed me. I watched his words as I might watch fish in a bucket, following the slow, fat

ones. *Dem fotey fo dollah* was an apparent debt Jim owed the
judge, forgiven suddenly in the recent telegram asking Jim to be a
pallbearer. He'd taken a while to figure where forgiveness came
into the picture; he'd forgot about the debt long ago, minutes after
the judge wrote it down so it wouldn't be forgotten. Jim still
couldn't see where he'd harmed the judge by borrowing forty-four
dollars, but if the new wife saw fit to forgive him, he'd forgive her
right back.

Moreover, the cancelled debt and request to carry the casket
went along with the pattern of contrition established back in those
troubled days, which seemed to scratch the grain crossways from
the former pattern established in prior days of extreme potential,
when folks talked of Waties Waring as a political mover and
shaker. *Dem turkle egg time wid Mist Cotton Ed* reflected the
greatness of those days, if you factored in the sheer, raw presence
of United States Senator Ellison Durant Smith, known in South
Carolina as Cotton Ed. Waties and Cotton Ed snuck up on Jim,
who'd snuck up on a raccoon, who'd snuck up on a sea turtle
laying her eggs. Full moon in July, so you could see the players all
right, her crying and plopping eggs in the hole, raccoon right there
catching most of them and hiking them on back for collection
later, except that Jim Cohen squatted back there like a bigger,
smarter coon, catching eggs from the raccoon, till the judge and
Cotton Ed spoiled the run by laughing so loud.

That was the last time Jim saw the judge for years till the
forty-four dollar loan, which confused hell out of Jim, because he
never asked for the loan. It was simply offered so he could buy a
new bateau for gathering oysters, which seemed a stretch from
guffawing over the whole damn marsh at a man stealing eggs from
an egg thief. Cotton Ed Smith was one of your highly powerful
white men, most likely come on down to discuss the overall
general management of the whole wide world, such as it was,
around here.

A casually spoken yet strident segregationist, Senator Smith hadn't likely lent four cents to a musty hand and owed three of his six terms in the U.S. Senate to the campaign management of Waties Waring. Cotton Ed finally lost and then died, and the next time Jim Cohen saw Waties Waring was so Mist Waties could lend the fohty-fo dollah so's Jim could git dem whitefoot selects 'n carryum roun' de house up to Rockville, fresh and risned, till e debt pay off.

Jim took a bushel by and called it even, and that was that for another stretch of years, till he got invited to Judge Waring's house in town for a sit-down dinner—strange world—with sheets on the table and glasses somehow welded on to these little glass stalks so skinny they like to break just sitting there, so nobody could even enjoy the sweetwine without worrying themselves sick over the dainty handling required by the setting and the occasion. And then you had all these folks talking soft as if somebody be lying up next to dead next door, all making with the *fa fa de blah blah over dem brand new champeen ob dem simple rights like ne'b befo, de judge 'n e new wife woman.*

Back to the old time, aw, me…. Jim Cohen was houseboy for the Waring summer home near Rockville and couldn't even take a samidge on de poach, not de front poach nuh de back poach too. And back to Mist Ned, e be's de bestess white man. Ned Waring, Waties' father, hired Jim Cohen the day they moved their summer things into the summer home on Ledinwah Creek, about the time of the war, meaning WWI, which should not be confused with The War.

From there, recollection was general and confusing but beneficent and providential too, like a eulogy exhuming the unsavory for exhortation, and to call up recollections in warmth and goodness too, lest they be forgotten. He told a good tale, so a listener could follow easy as turning pages on a book that feels like it'll end too soon. I listened over the faint din in my head, which was the clamor of all the people over all the years who knew the crime I'd committed, even as they smiled and nodded at what I'd had to say. How secure I'd been in my little secret. I'd gotten away with it, don't you know.

Jim Cohen reached back as though for cause. We drank through *To Tell the Truth* and *Hogan's Heroes* and two more sitcoms with canned laughter and applause, Jim sometimes joining in like a man who is part of the world, no matter what foolishness it engages in. Between dusk and twilight he stood slowly, measuring his strength and balance, and walked outside. From his porch steps he watched Bohicket Creek through an opening in the trees. "Slack 'm 'up," he said, meaning slack tide, low water. He plucked a finished cast net from a nail and said, "Come on." I said I'd walk down with him to stretch a bit, on the way to running along back into town.

We walked down another dirt road through another stand of live oaks, out to the clearing and parking lot at Cherry Point Landing. The gray dusk darkened softly over the river at low water with a breezeless twilight coming on. The clouds dissipated, and the air warmed a bit, bringing on the night and teasing us with fading warmth. Jim Cohen wound up like a tired spring and unwound just as slowly. The net fanned open, hit the water and sank flat till he jerked it gently in. A single mullet, maybe a pound, squirmed among a dozen mud minnows. He let them fall out three steps back where they'd flip around and die or else lie calm and breathe easy till the flood came in. He cast again, moving down the bank for three more casts and three more mullet. He laid them in the center of the net, folded things neatly, and we headed back up. The dozens of mud minnows flashed silver in the light that lingered from the long day and moonrise. They calmed down and waited for death or flood tide, whichever might come first. I stooped to toss them back in. The tide turned and crept up slow as a watched clock.

Jim Cohen gutted his mullet under a naked bulb at the end of the porch where the planks were hacked and dark and sparkled with scales. Inside, the child tended the iron pot of lard on the fire. In my jacket again, straightened, combed and wondering how the evening might fill in, I strolled out to the cleaning station on the porch for the next phase of departure, which commonly runs in phases in this part of the world.

Jim Cohen scaled and beheaded the fish and cut the guts out and put the heads and guts in a lidded plastic bucket on the ground. I watched him and asked if he was still setting crab pots. He asked back why a man on a creek would not set crab pots. He cut each fish into three sections and set the pieces on a plate delivered by the child. A car pulled up, a Buick Electra with fender skirts, curb feelers, a fur trimmed mirror and a mat woven from six-pack plastics in the rear window deck. On the woven mat sat a fuzzy little dog whose eyes lit up red with the brake lights, as the dog nodded continuing approval. Two boys in shabby sweaters and stiff denim pants with the cuffs rolled up got out, one carrying a load of greens, the other with another bottle of the same sherry.

"Ey," one said, passing me on his way inside.

"Ey," said the other, following the first.

Jim Cohen followed both with his plate of fish. I followed him to complete my farewell ablutions. At the sink he rinsed and floured each piece. I watched him, ruminating on the simple pleasures lost to me but then reminding myself that such things fade in value naturally and must be recaptured by free will and intention. Finally I said, "I want to thank you for your hospitality, Jim. I hope I can repay it sometime."

The idea of him coming to my place socially felt foolish as the mess I'd worn on my face all those years, maybe not so outlandish as a formal sit-down at a federal judge's table, but we both knew the odds on him coming to town for drinks and a visit. I felt like the fox inviting the stork over for some soup but had no alternative but to issue the empty invite anyway, because I felt a rare gratitude for his confidence and hospitality, and there wasn't a thing else for it. I hoped he understood that.

He turned my way and shuffled past. "Come on. Be's good." He moved to the stove, leaving my sincerity and me in his wake. Maybe I recognized a simple pleasure in range for the taking then, seeing where Jim Cohen lived and how he managed to stay there. I was no stranger to casual life at home but felt like a stranger in that home, because it was strange, as close to the earth as I'd ever been and then some, feeling an inch or two below the surface often as not. I walked back out to the porch to watch the sky darken and the first stars twinkle, then went back in, not for curiosity or insight.

I knew how they lived. Primitive and poorly spoken was how, often dirty and maybe less ignorant than they put on but still apart from what held our society together. But look at me. Unschooled and unknowing, they seemed to stay that way by choice, not because anyone kept them from anything, and surely not from smug delusion. They didn't pursue self-improvement but settled in and stayed like water at its own level. Like I say, I knew that and went back in through the freshly acrid sweetness and disparaging gazes of the two boys whose doubt now infected the girl child too. She stared with them at the sorry-looking white man.

The nightly news came on. Jim Cohen turned it off and turned his radio on, covering the knobs with flour. "Dem green!" He instructed the boy with the greens on preparation and cooking. "Fush," he handed the fish to the other boy and took the bottle. He opened and poured so we could get on with cocktails and more talk. I think he knew why I came back in and why I'd stay for dinner, because some things speak the same in any dialect, because I was confused, lonely and hungry.

v

Now How'n a Hell D'at Happen?

The wine had yet to ferment that would have cheered me into staying the night. The mullet filled my belly with a warmth and seasoning of pepper and garlic from the yard. The hospitality fairly fended off the congealing lard soon settling on my chest. I focused on sustenance and the good cheer of the thing to take my mind off the discomforts, chief among them the painful challenges of the long day behind us. The greens had been boiled lifeless with onions, ham hocks, more pepper and garlic to soulful fulfillment. The sherry could only improve, and Jim Cohen's hospitality was Southern as any I'd seen.

The afternoon and evening recalled the severe paucity of rural interludes in my life. We didn't go out to the country like this but rather engaged in a more formal, staged format, in what we called country outings. Like, say, the annual pilgrimage to Camden, for The Cup. That was more typical of our contact with nature, partaking of a continuous tailgate formed of vehicles surrounding the entire track, start to finish, including the clubhouse turn and the stretch. We flowed on around with the drinks, good cheer and buffet to beat the band. I use the nominal "we," though I'd have been hard pressed to fill in the blanks just then with names. The faces too seem to blend on a common bliss, as if this happiness would never end, eternal as the life ever after, as if we, the chosen few, had died, and this was it, walking round the track just up from the River Styx. Oh, I could have easily enough filled in the names and other festive details, but it was as I say, a gray day of reckoning.

Even The Cup, though warm and festive and fun in its time, had come to feel foolish. But it was foolish even then and fun because of it, so maybe I was the fool, finally seeing things straight. The Cup was outdoors and involved horses and racing around a track, so some of the in-town crowd wore riding boots and jodhpurs, for the spirit of the thing. Some wore riding hats or carried crops, perhaps willing to straddle a beast, our beast, bound for glory or some such, in support of our lasting greatness or lingering greatness or ephemeral yet eternal inebriation. And a great good time was had by all. The end. Maybe whatever got in my teeth or sprouted from my nose wasn't so noticeable to my own ilk after all.

This and other reassessments accompanied the drive north from Jim Cohen's, along with my new view of what a country outing should be, as well as a new measure of Jim's merits. He and I both presented new profiles that evening, historically speaking. In objective terms, I could have realized an equally rich history of Charleston's other landed gentry, the dark cousins of similar name who live yonder in the marsh flats. The problem was, I did not see myself or them in that light just yet. Like sibling rivals deign to see virtue in each other, so too was I still removed from perceptions yet to come. Besides, I was too taken with self-loathing.

Overriding my headlights gave credence to the phantoms following me up that long black alley through the boughs. What was ahead came on way too fast, showing itself only when I was already in it. I could have slowed down but didn't for fear of getting stuck in the shuffle I raced to be out of. I feared losing momentum verging on insight—insight that would, for once in my life, prove true. All day developing to a crest of meaning that might liberate my sorry soul, my wave of knowing was easily imagined as fanciful, as gone tomorrow, when reality would resume. Or maybe I pressed the pedal with resignation for the inevitable, that I wanted to get home, where I'd sort things out, because I always had. What phantom, rationale?

A certain decrepitude didn't exactly slow my pace or stoop my shoulders but depressed my mind and body like fatigue. It slurred my confidence. A new lesson had begun, and seemed as elusive as it was difficult. However grateful and warm I was, driving home half drunk and fully doubtful, I could not fathom the notion of bedding down in that place. The smell and Blackness were beyond comfort, whether from chronic prejudice or personal weakness or both; I couldn't tell. I suppose prejudice is a weakness, but a man who doesn't know what he likes and dislikes is a fool. Even as I bathed safely and hygienically back on Queen Street, I laughed and cringed at the great liberal I'd become since morning. I hadn't supped with them since infancy, and then it was one-on-one in the old, Southern direct feed, like many of my generation did but didn't dwell on it. The bountiful Black breast was not allegorical but practical; the Black women were so pregnant, the white women so busy.

Directly to bed, I wanted sleep before the warmth and dullness wore off, before the day's population gained density and kept me up with their difficult questions. The old house seemed particularly aggravated in its creaking rafters and shifting foundation, or maybe that was the wind, turned up a notch to fitful gusts, perhaps realigning the old house, so its chronic lean and slump could reconcile to its earthquake rods and melting windows.

Or maybe the shifting foundation was in me, calling for a bicarbonate to move the pork fat off my chest. I pondered the first of the month, only three days hence, at which time the risk of forgetting to water the fern compounded, or, as I presumptively called it, Fern. Fern, of the asparagus ferns, came as an infant and got hung by a macramé hanger in the same pot of its germination. Too much water; Fern drooped and spotted. Not enough water; Fern browned. Just the right absorption; Fern stretched, reached, angled and cajoled its way around the entire perimeter of the living room with a side trip to the foyer, following the picture molding gracefully as a stroke of nature, hung there with care every foot or two by tasteful hooks screwed discreetly into the wood, and all on the encouragement of short, well-timed drink. Perhaps I identified with Fern. At any rate, I poured the bubbly drink, a single, just for me, and other plain water for Fern, who most often liked company, I thought. Better a bit premature, than no drink at all. Or maybe this round was another attempt to displace niggling thoughts. Hard to say; I was fond of Fern.

Back in bed I followed the standard procedure, eyes closed, breathing slowly on a sea of easy patterns, drifting off like a happy plant reaching for more. Yet I drifted into rapids where Anne the child scurried to tend amorphous needs, scrambling too many eggs and over-watering the plants. Her mother called out meekly, incessant and inane, until those images too joined the pattern and faded to a swirling blur.

Up early, I sidestepped the khaki suit and button-down, blue oxford cloth shirt that more or less made up our uniform. The rest of the world had hair down to its ass, beads, gypsy vests and bell-bottom trousers like the carnival was in town to stay. All that oddball, hippie stuff seemed to sanction our casual formality as a fundamental defense of our way of life. We stayed behind the times by choice, don't you know, as if three decades back might mark us as keen, incisive, independent and sure.

And penny loafers. I stepped instead into my tennies and dungarees and a flannel shirt that felt more like home. Of course country clothing feels better, but this time it itched with apprehension on the questions inevitably forthcoming down on the sidewalk. Taking the day off? Going fishing? Playing hooky again? Ad infinitum they'd ask, pointedly avoiding the old man's funeral that they all knew good and well I'd attended, till it made you wonder where in hell the brains came from, till you knew it was from the same spigot that sired the fools just north.

Not that a lawyer can't take a day off and go fishing, but he can't go without everybody knowing. Besides, I wasn't going fishing or anywhere. It just seemed like time to stop and change some of the things I did every damn day without knowing why but conformed to those things because that's what I did yesterday and hoped to repeat tomorrow. Stop it, I thought. That's life for most people, stable and sane and repetitive, measured in days of enrichment. Move on to something else, I thought. I needed time to hearken myself, back to a young man riled to the point of throwing bricks through his friend's window, because his friend wouldn't be able to deliver a judgeship. I remembered that rash impulse like it was minutes ago, like I just now banged my thumb with a hammer and felt it throb and smart. Waties Waring embarrassed me. But I was my own fool; I didn't even want to be a judge and didn't know that till a few decades after I lost my chance. I had friends all over town who did want it and some who made it and maybe one or two who sat on the bench instead of me, by the Grace of God and Waties Waring's fall from Grace.

All I felt beside regret that morning after supper at Jim Cohen's was gratitude. Every lawyer I knew either repressed the repetition and drudgery of life or honestly recognized the boredom he'd sunk into, so soft and deep. They gravitated to the health supplement of the area, Vitamin S, which is local jargon for scotch. Drinking was cultural and personal and one and the same with all else that defined us. Spirits poured from the bottle if the label showed it was the good stuff, or it poured from an heirloom crystal decanter cut when dollars blossomed like cotton balls if it was cheap.

Genteel company wouldn't delve into ugly talk with words like *cheap* but preferred calling it *second drawer*, which wasn't near harsh as non-white, and those families only two or three generations landed who yearned for venerability but lacked the heirloom crystal might decant to an empty bottle with a notable label, said bottle at one time actually containing the good stuff, and may have been acquired as an investment, such as it was, refillable. This practice was common, discreet and practical, capturing the old flair and flavor, such as it was, as we were forced to do since the Great Conflagration. What else could you do but recycle the bottles with the good labels, as we recycled so much, as a whole damn nation of Yankees comes in and steals what we had? Practicality in polite presentation was the point yet again, and the status of scotch became incidental to the Great Glory we'd known and could more easily remember, four shots down with our own, private victory coming on. Liquor was not an addiction but a tradition of historical stature. But I digress. The greater point sticking in my shorts that rueful and perhaps fateful day was syllogistic, arrived at via a minor and major premise on the way to a conclusion. All lawyers in Charleston were alcoholic. I was a lawyer in Charleston. Voilà.

Don't ask for rhyme or reason. You might ask why the sky is blue. It's blue. Maybe it was genetic or learned or both. We were busy and bored, stifled and gasping for a change of mind that could not muster its own volition without the golden elixir. Just as a lamp needs a rub to free the genie, so were we freed by cocktails, part and parcel to rise and shine, how do you do, lovely, lovely, yes, fine, yes; don't mind if I do. The common supplement to significant cocktails was talk of politics, where you might could find an occasional pulse in our small part of the electorate. A candidate could best recruit over cocktails, perhaps finding an able volunteer willing to spend time away from the family or the law library, which support was never referenced as an escape from drudgery because such reference was plain unnecessary, in the spirit and potential of the thing.

It didn't matter. At a certain point in life, the mirror wobbles with amplitude, and ramification crowds the background. You sense the danger of staring too long but take a good look anyway, because that's what it is, what it's come to and most likely what you're fixing to get a heap more of. I saw myself as a young man searching deeds and statutes, middle age me rummaging the same fine print and me again blowing forth through the same paper. I felt like a kid who got it wrong and says, *Wait a minute; lemme try that one more time.* Life is a game but you only get one go. I charged a decent fee and, goddamn it, I wanted more but didn't need more money and couldn't tell what more of I wanted, till it looked like no way in hell I'd get one snitch of anything better than what I got.

Don't worry. I wasn't suicidal. I suffered severe regret. Then I got drunk, until that daily reprieve went away too, unexpectedly and in its prime, as if my very best friend dropped dead. Oh, but the maudlin recollection still comes so easily. It was hell. My specialty was maritime law, here in the grandest, formerly greatest port of the Old South. I didn't choose maritime law but followed the prescribed path of practical success, which is more jargon for incredibly unearned wealth befalling those who get along by going along and inherit what's waiting for them. In my case the legacy aligned with the fortunes of Waties Waring, a most prominent maritime lawyer in town. Appointment to the federal bench seemed likely for him, though you could never know till it happened. He actually reckoned it to come along much sooner than it did, and once it did, he sat only three years before his fatal distraction. Tommy Holcombe said the old man got his mind stuck on pussy, and that's all there was to it, plain and simple, no matter how many times and how many angles you viewed it from, because once he's stuck, a man won't come up for air till he gets his fill or ruins himself, one or the other. Though bumpkin brutal, that assessment proved accurate. I was odds-on favorite for that same judgeship, given a Democrat for President, but not after Waties got stuck in the mud or the watermelon patch either one.

I don't even care anymore and likely would have run for office just to get out of the office, state senator maybe, spend a few days a week in Columbia, give a nod here and there, get everyone calling me Senator Covingdale, except in town where they'd call me Senator Art. I swear, if I reviewed one ship's document I reviewed a thousand. Chandler disputes, dockage fees, lading shorts; sometimes I'd go aboard, just to get out of the office, to see what the real crews of the real world saw and felt. I spent my time out in the channel too and got offshore now and then, trolling for the big boys. But head out over the horizon to Timbuktu or some such like I dreamed I would as a boy? Not once. And I'm here to tell you I'd have cried like the child I was if you'd told me back then that I'd hit fifty-eight in a seersucker suit with a nasty addiction to liquor and nothing to show for it but small talk.

My first maritime case went to the U.S. Court of Appeals, a mundane litigation over a low-speed collision at the dock, but that case proved to be a channel marker for the career ahead. Judge Waring called a recess and asked me back to his private chambers for a brandy, and then asked what I thought would be fair in this one. He shouldn't have done that, and we both knew it. But we also knew why he did it, which was to show me how things operate among reasonable men, that the law is to serve, not to rule.

We were to share an understanding, that we have a society of manners deferential to a greater law serving civility and society. I don't know who can extemporize on that greater law, except to say it was life the way we lived it. For all I know, and I'm fairly certain of it, my answer did not affect his decision, in which case the question was permissible, but that was incidental. He paid me a compliment of the highest stature. Few attorneys are so flattered, and the only thing higher that night than the stature of the compliment was me, way past cocktails to knee-walking nigger drunk; pardon the indelicacy, but I'm trying to tell a story here about how it was and came to be and what happened after that. I'm still making sense of it myself; so if I stub a toe here and there cut me some slack.

I don't mean he was warm. He wasn't. From the beginning of the fifty-five years I knew the man he was known as a tough sonofabitch among the kids. He never begrudged me his half grapefruit, but the knuckle rub wasn't playful; it was corporal punishment, hurt like the devil. Last time I saw him up in New York he looked older than Methuselah, his face drawn worse than taffy at the end of the pull, hardly a spark left and his eyes too tired to rise. I suppose they couldn't do much to make him look different for the picture in the *Times*, page two, with the caption telling how he was "cast out by lifelong friends and colleagues who could not accept his liberal views on segregation."

They didn't run a single quote from him, but the blithering bitch he married gave them what for. "You can't keep a good man down. The crusade will go on until we have freedom and justice for all." You look at the two dried out olives hanging out his eye sockets and the jaw hanging slack as a gate with no hinge nor springs left; you know damn good and well who's running the show and pulling the strings, who got cast out by whom and still ranted to set the facts her way if not straight.

I don't just say these things conjecturally, though that's all it was, before I went up there to New York for a visit. The place smelled like flesh no longer restoring itself. The new wife greeted me with a toothy cavern she must have thought looked like a smile, though it seemed shopworn and past its useful life. Her overbearing joviality may have been the New York, New York version of what's imagined to take place in the hustle bustle capital of the cultural world as seen from way down yonder in Beulah Land, but it made my teeth itch.

We had our tea and grapefruit for old times' sake, as she ranted all the while on justice, freedom and courage on the one hand, and sloth, ignorance and malice on the other. He gazed my way out his tired eyes, trying his best to keep breathing. She was very old. He was ancient. Their sense of vindication sparked like bad wiring, a short circuit, draining normal current. So how in hell, I asked myself then and ask it to this day, could these two account for my fortunes?

Her teapot whistled. On her way to calm that noise she said, "I know which way the wind blows."

"Of course you do," I said.

"I was wronged," he said. "It grieves me still. That may not surprise you. You still enjoy the benefits of polite society in Charleston."

"Some of those benefits left with you," I assured him.

He laughed, maybe gratified that misery had some company. She called from the kitchen that the judge was a champion of social justice. He and I shared an eye roll. Or maybe I only imagined that; his were so droopy. Maybe they only looked like they rolled because I wanted them to. He insisted that I hear the whole story, that I be the judge, reminding me of the time he asked what I thought was fair in this situation, as if a little slack cut once warrants a little slack cut again.

Back with hot tea, she poured over her passion for the truth and told me to move so the judge could see me better. She called him the judge, then blushed, or something like it, excusing herself so we men could talk.

The white walls, white ceiling, white rugs and white drapes made for a glaring light that would have been called tacky then in Charleston and served no purpose but to complement his ashen pallor. Or maybe the white on white was to simulate the white tunnel opening on the moment of death, like his New York parlor was a practice room or something. He stood crookedly as a time-lapse weed, leaned precipitously and poured another cup. My own was still scalding hot, and I realized he'd gone ahead and drank his down, maybe trying to feel something. Maybe old people lose their nerve endings, I thought at the time, knowing now that nothing of the sort goes away. He only wanted a more immediate pain to distract him from the one inside, which I also learned since. Then he wilted back down to the imprint on his leather chair, even into the lightened spots under his drumming fingers— tea sloshed over the arm to moisten the tracks of former spills. He downed the second cup and wrung his hands like a wizard conjuring a spell. I waited.

"Separate but equal is not equal. Open primaries.... How long do they think a man can live on that island?"

"Well. Which island is that?"

His color rose dangerously red. "The island no man can live unto alone by himself!"

"Oh. That island. I'm sure I don't know."

He waved a hand, knocking the empty cup onto the carpet, over old stains to a familiar resting spot. "No!" he finally sputtered. "You can't...." He stopped trembling by grasping his chin. Turning toward Central Park, he whispered, "The place...."

"I beg your pardon."

"The place. You know the place as well as any of them. People don't affect history, which a place…a place they know…in them, a place that is them. Mark my words: they can see its shortcoming. You try to change it, if you love it, or else…." His breathing became labored.

"Or else?"

Eyes rolling as if scanning the room for an imminent arrival, he said, "People in hell want ice water." His eyes fell on the empty cup. "They learn to drink it hot."

"I see."

He shivered slightly. "Do you?"

Well, of course I didn't, or couldn't, or wouldn't. The only thing I could or would do was sit and listen to him drag eighty years through an hour and a half and only get to 1892 after shuffling through so many births, marriages, deaths and more profound departures from the Lowcountry. He blended into the street noise below, dates and names intermixing with brakes, horns and, good Lord Almighty, the sirens. What the hell use is a siren if you got more sirens in your ear than silence? I mean, goddamn, they might ought to have figured that one out. He didn't even hear the sirens, as I suppose you don't after a while, a long while.

In 1892 he was twelve and fought with his brother on his birthday on a beach outing. "Rice pudding," he recalled, as if to note his penchant for ancient detail. His voice congealed, "And my ma's cornbread," and so on, listing historic niceties that shored up an enduring society, as if recollection was tantamount to original enjoyment.

He remembered prep school as a waste of time, and I don't think a case could be made otherwise. The College of Charleston was marginally better, though it "treated young fools as young men for growing hair on their faces and paying tuition, and the only requirement for admission was a ride to town on registration day." No matter what kind of sonofabitch I thought he was, or which side of the battle I saw him from, I still admired his wit and incisive assessment.

After college days he jumped back to antebellum and reverent fantasies of the Republic—the Republic of South Carolina, that is, as if delusion long forgotten still factored in his personal history. He recalled the world coming to Charleston by way of ships, and the earth-shaking transition from sail to steam. His first advent in dockside law was learning the rules of the road as a boy, when he hauled fresh fish and oysters by the bushel down to the ships to trade for trinkets. Like when he and his chums traded oysters to Chinee, a cook, for flowered vases, and everyone bowed, and Chinee had the boys sit on a galley bench so they could watch him spread grain over the counter with one hand while wielding a swayback cleaver with the other.

The old man leaned forward tensely, holding up a shaky finger as Chinee had done and mimicked the chicken walking from its wood box to peck across the counter, his old head pecking like one tired chicken's, till he stopped, his hand slashing the air, his little chicken coo-cooing to an abrupt choke and gurgle, head severed. Opening one eye and the other, like chicken never would again, he more or less smiled. A carefree bloodletting and youth made him laugh and cough and swear to God, "like to scare the daylights out of us...."

Now I wonder if he got those oysters from Jim Cohen, but no; Jim wasn't even born till '00 or '01, and it didn't matter anyway. He gained color on the retelling, easing on back in the chair to recall Chinee making the boys drink whiskey in honor of Chicken. He looked up, smoothing a temple. "It's an easy place to miss, some of it." In '94 he nearly killed his brother Ned Jr. and vice versa. For years after, knives flew out of nowhere, and anyone standing under a second storey window was subject to a flowerpot on the head. Ned Jr. died in '36. "He'd moved down to Florida for a company that sent its salesmen around by car. We were friends then, when he died."

He never admired his father but liked him a great deal. "How can you admire a man who stays with a losing business year after year?" His father and brother both worked for the South Carolina Railway till it went bankrupt and Southern Railway took over. Ned quit working then but Ned Jr. got on with the School Board of Charleston, "which never went bankrupt but made some young minds insolvent." After working on the school board, Ned Jr. got his traveling salesman job but apparently failed to share any jokes with his brother. The old man stared glumly.

"Archives are given over to basic existence in Charleston. Whatever happens between birth and death is largely unrecorded, I believe, because it's largely insignificant, unless you count the decades of easy living with the bubbas." The Waring genealogy does note Ned's time at Tulifinny, elevating the family name to the revered plateau of those who served, who defended life as we'd known it again the northern incursion. Unrecorded is Ned's work with Daniel Chamberlain on the railway merger. Dan Chamberlain was the last reconstruction governor of South Carolina and lived up in Connecticut in exile after Wade Hampton beat him in '79. "Heroes everywhere. I suppose Wade Hampton was a gentleman. For all I know he humped his horse." He smiled again, perhaps at imagery that soothed his grief or distracted it. "Dan Chamberlain was a scalawag—a white man who worked with Republicans from the north to exploit the spoils of war. Chamberlain came home to Charleston in '94, stepped off the train to a waiting crowd and said he'd been homesick for fifteen years and was mighty glad to be back. So everybody said welcome home and called him Governor Dan to the day he died. Fifteen years." The old judge smiled grimly and said he'd go home some day too, horizontally.

Wavering from historic dates and events, he went reflective, as if to show what could be gained with proper perspective, watching the gray rain out the window for days on end in New York. Ned the father often opined that expectation was the downfall of the South. Ned accepted his menial station in life with assurance for anyone who asked, that he had no expectation, and that makes for easy living of a different nature. Ned claimed it was recorded lineage that gave rise to expectation; otherwise folks in Charleston wouldn't have had the gumption to start The War. Everyone has lineage. Hound dogs and geldings have it, and The War, like most wars, was for money, for King Cotton and the free labor to pick it. Nonetheless Lowcountry lineage made for expectation. The original Waring in South Carolina was buried outside Summerville in a swamp near Givhans Ferry. "Pa called it a mush hole in the pluff mud out between the Ashley and the Edisto, but folks had expectation, so they called it the Old Waring Burial Ground, but you can't go gawk and sigh, because Ben's the only one knows where it is, and he ain't talking. Original Ben died a hundred fifty years before Ned was born, but Ned spoke of his forebear like a brother, like a century and a half didn't mean squat where blood was shared. Ned said they shared a temperament too, he and Ben, and he always claimed to feel a part of Ben in himself. I believe we did too, me and Pa."

The judge leaned over much as an old tree in a gusty breeze, creaking up next to toppling but then easing back with the bottle in hand. He poured us each an inch and pushed mine across the end table. I don't drink, or wasn't drinking at the time, but took the glass to finish the exchange and let him proceed with the load off his chest so as to avoid the load on my chest, with the drinking issue.

Declining a drink in town doesn't require an explanation but warrants pleasant diversion at the least. On that wet, gray day in

New York it seemed best to keep moving along the bumpy road to the fork, where we went our separate ways.

His diversion was plain to see. He stared at that little snort of courage that could be his last and lifted it for a pass under his nose for the fumes and memories therein. Setting it down, he topped us off to an inch and a half like a reformed smoker who misses the ritual as much as the drug, tamping the pack, knocking a fag out, taking it to the lips but not lighting up. Neither one of us ever smoked, because that was filthy, expensive, unhealthy and stupid, unlike us, hugely successful men of the New South sorting out our path to greatness.

Jumping from his father's military service to the future once more, scanning a few decades in the next breath, his boyhood gang was known for jumping horse cars and then street cars and leaping off without telling the driver to slow down. "It was quite an adventure."

I must have nodded off. He took it for agreement and backed up thirty years to The War as thunder rolled outside on cue as backdrop for the Battle of Tulifinny, where his father fought for The Cause. At the end of the skirmish he belched. "I don't sleep anymore."

Lightning popped through his mumbles over the free and open life so available in New York. He choked and hocked into a handkerchief, convulsing briefly and whispering, "We're memory as we speak. Then nothing." He slept.

The downpour cushioned the silence. I sat a few minutes more and was getting up to leave, when he opened his eyes and asked, "Later?" I stopped. "Later. We'll walk. My wife and I...." She slid in smiling. He said she was a beautiful woman once and still is. "My critics call her my weakness. I call her truth. Truth and beauty. My Grecian urn. She let me see. You might could see along with us...." With four eyes on me I fidgeted into a weak smile of my own. He drifted. "My critics and their children take tea at three and sniff flowers in March. I watch the rain and wait. Sit down." The wife backed out.

You can't recall a gray day of fractious recollection like that without seeing the life once lived and sorely missed. Hardly a pulse remained in him, yet the slogging blood could not restrain the passion that surged like a last flood bucking a cold breeze from up the river. He said he couldn't tell what happened all those years in Charleston, socially speaking, except for sipping scotch from one garden to the next, agreeing on a particularly appealing shrub, a unique arrangement of flowers, a crumbling edifice, new blooms, an apparent ambition or a notable humility, a new arrival in town with apparent charm and the manners to match. These and other trivialities were the stuff of life, serving as background and context to interpreting *the law*, so the building blocks of society could rise in a warm and orderly atmosphere, not with an air of detachment but in service to the root core of society, which was us. His wry, possibly vague implication was that right and wrong were accurately discerned in Charleston, just as those two notions may have been clear in Booneville or Timbuktu, meaning the town and its residents and all who came before were deluded, an affliction imposed by self.

"So it damn well didn't matter whose garden it was, because the whole town all fed the same damn grandiosity and blissful ignorance commonly suffered by criminals, especially those who got caught and did their time behind high, masonry walls. Go to the federal slammer and see for yourself. They got barbed wire on top. We had broken glass from historically significant bottles, don't you know. Ha! The temperate weather just made delusions more sensible. We had it good, better than anybody we'd ever heard of. Southern cordiality on the rocks made for a special feeling, a bland but pleasant inebriation facilitating the passage of time. Those of us in control assured the status quo for the rest of the, shall we say chosen few, born into it. None of that *accident of birth* talk around there; we wouldn't have chosen anywhere else, not even anywhere in the South, because Charleston was who we were, born into and carrying along."

He needed not condescend to me in this way but rambled on with feigned humility, as if this interpretation was not his but a historical record, to be sure. "See that hutch. That's what it comes down to. Not...that hutch, but the....

"No place in the history of the world has offered a greater collection of inanimate objects to adorn such a poverty of imagination. Oh, hell, I'm bitter. What would you expect? I think of our eccentricities and the unique personalities among us, and it doesn't matter that they were emotionally unstable or disturbed. They at least achieved realization of their fantasized selves. No, I loved the oddballs and quirks. Still do. It was the gardens and scotches and how-you-doings, the arcane expectation derived from the accident of birth, all of it cut from the same cloth—that's what got to me. The glorious past. We were raised to it. You never outgrow that old feeling, until one day you do, if you're lucky. Sure, it was a terrific place to live, I guess, except for the general consensus that we'd never judge a man by the cut of his jib, except that one day I realized I'd been judging all along and couldn't have been more wrong about it. Ignorance is bliss, and I was a happy man too. You too, I suspect. Still are, maybe."

I'd sat nodding mindlessly until then but stopped short of agreeing with him, that he and his and me and mine and everything in between was illegitimate, reprehensible and wrong. I couldn't agree because I had not come to visit in order to take my rightful twenty lashes. Maybe he read my hesitation; he didn't dote on it but hearkened on back to recollections of young women by name and brief description, responding, I think, to the indictment of decades past, King of the Tenderloin. It was a nickname originally coined in youth and great good humor, a well-intentioned come-uppance for an up-and-comer, a mover and shaker with youthful vigor and Broad Street connections. Such a profile seems oxymoronic in perspective. Nothing moved on Broad Street but the heat ripples; nothing shook the place but the earthquakes every hundred years or so. Rearranging anything required a tremor or a hurricane, after which, folks could continue as they had done. King of the Tenderloin went from a nickname to Exhibit A for the prosecution, exhumed as if to damn the defendant.

Tenderloin was as racy then as high thigh might be now, not exactly over the top but easing up to it. Putting virtues of the fairer-sexed at risk was risky business. Most debs had daddies and brothers and matrimonial prospects to factor. Cracking a horrible grin, he called young lust and its attendant pursuits the most harmless of habits. And who hasn't chased or been chased? Nobody at that age or any age, because a man is not naturally celibate but in fact considers the human vagina what, once every seven minutes or something?

I glanced at my watch.

"That doesn't make him evil, which is what every normal man knows and any man will admit to in private."

I'd had no sexual relations in six years, give or take seven minutes, but I saw his point, though it seemed tortuous and self-serving. I didn't object, because he squeezed his hands, pressing blood to his face so it could open on his scornful voice: "King of the Tenderloin." Derision twisted his grimace, as we approached the meat of the matter. "Young buck is all it was. All the fellows had names. Rube, Wop, Duke, Slicky, Hominy, Coondog. Didn't mean a thing."

She entered again, holding her finger in a paperback copy of *Cry the Beloved Country*, cheerfully ready to serve up further proof of salvation, like a missionary complacently satisfied that the Truth is irrefutable because it's written right here. She left me no choice. "King of the Tenderloin," I repeated, twisting the knife for her benefit.

"I love the developing cultures," she ignored me, her great big shrillness somehow amplified in her own withered posture. "You can just see them taking form. We've talked about a trip to Africa. Maybe next spring." He nodded or maybe only succumbed to a palsied twitch. She left.

The wind howled and blew the rain away. "Blackberry winter comes along," he told the window, referencing the cold snap occurring in the middle of spring but to what end I could not tell. "Before you know it. I can hear them sustaining each other with the weather forecast and analysis."

"Them?"

"Yes. They'll be agreeing right now, as we speak, that home is where you want to be, wiping their noses and heading that way, for the prudence of the thing, with the same old joke about vitamin scotch." He wiped his nose. "Party season coming right up. You'll be there." My personal presence for festive times sounded accusatory, but he eased up. "Flowers in two months, or maybe three. I'd like to see them one more time."

My second nature tongue-tripped me on an invitation down in the same moment he spared me.

"God sends the flowers to Charleston, don't you know." He stared out the window at what God gave New York; screw-faced he struggled through the gray, fitful scene outside as if for surer footing. "Lucille LePrince..." He lingered on those syllables, perhaps seeing her on the windowpane or just beyond it.

"I don't know her."

"Fifty, sixty years ago. Her goal in life was to have the first party every spring, but her luck was rotten. Every damn year she'd spruce her garden and send invitations and land right smack in the center of blackberry winter. Lived on Tradd Street, with the ivy-covered archway and the tunnel. Talbots live there now."

"I know the house."

"Of course you do. They buried their family there, just off the walkway toward the garden, the Pringles, I mean. Lucille's mama was a Pringle; more money than a bank or the Cogswells who printed Confederate Currency down on the corner of East Bay and Broad. Lucille's daddy was a LePrince, original family but on to hard times after The Conflagration, depending like they did on slave labor. But name is also currency down there, so it was considered a good match, and then Lucille's daddy's brother up and died without a place; leastways they claimed he had no place, likely so they could make a case for burying him right there on the LePrince walkway, to show how they felt about the two families being one or some such. I don't know what those people were thinking, burying a dead man in the garden in modern times. Lucille's mother liked to drive you batty with her simpering over the headstones, all chipped and worn down to nubs—damn kids used to play checkers on them—leading to the garden, which could have been over the Jericho and on into Canaan, and we got to enjoy that place both before and after we died. My God, she'd go on over good cheer and good times and good company and good funerals, and that's what Pringle always meant in Charleston, and she meant all ways, and so did LePrince too, because, just look. Damn Walter LePrince wasting away not three feet under on account of the water table and all. I don't even know if he got embalmed or they just laid him under, not twenty feet from where they sat down to breakfast, chattering happy as mockingbirds, like it didn't make a difference between where you lived and where you lay dead, because the house was the thing, marking family greatness for all time and with a rock solid address too, so those folks from out of town who might not know could look up and see how it was."

He'd got worked up and eased back for a breather until a new angle pushed him back up. "It was lovely, you see. For two hundred years lovely, with the flowers and headstones and the scotch and parties, didn't make a damn if it came out blackberry winter. Trouble was, Lucille's parents died one day in '03 when the lot of them ate about a half bushel off a bad load of oysters picked too near the wharf. Typhoid. You ever see somebody with typhoid? Typhoid twists you up, won't give a care about your address or a few hundred years or flowers or how much money rolls off a printing press. Typhoid knows you ate a ball of poison and need to die. That's how civilized and quaint things were. Dropped damn dead."

He sat back and would have sat up again but raised a wobbly hand instead like a fighter asking for a moment's reprieve so he could cough up from way deep the vicious hock generated by so much excitement. He did. I looked away as he lowered this one, so big, into a makeshift cuspidor, which was an old tin cup appropriately dinged and dented.

"So you...had a sexual liaison with Lucille LePrince?" I didn't mean to touch a nerve but to help an old man regain his place in a story interrupted.

"Hell, no!" But the sudden denial got him coughing again. His point by point enumeration of Lucille's skinny body, nervous airs, shaky voice and altogether unattractiveness kept him coughing, till he stopped and found his pace. With another smile for a scorn refreshed and ready for another crusty derision, he whispered: "Daddy Ancrum." He waited.

"Daddy Ancrum?" I asked.

"They stuck a silly name on me and called it Providential a long time later. King of the Tenderloin was a joke, don't you know, till it explained my undoing years later, or so they'd have you believe. But they had Daddy Ancrum. That old Negro stood behind Lucille's punch bowl all those years, pop-eyed and grinning, because he knew that's what we wanted to see, and we did, though we'd never reflect long enough to realize why we wanted such a thing. Daddy Ancrum poured the punch and scooped the ice cream for the children of the right families. Oh, it was a hospitable crowd with a welcome for anyone new, except that none of them were ever dark-skinned, which begs the question of hospitality, if you ask me.

"You think Daddy Ancrum had a wife or children or grandchildren who might would have wanted to come to one of those parties? Hell no, you don't know. Nobody did, didn't even think about it or care. Wouldn't have made a difference anyhow. They were Black!"

He took a drink, deterring another spasm, or maybe bracing for someone to step in with a reference book showing further evidence on the essence of right thinking and the glory of defending it. When she didn't enter on cue, he eased up. "Lucille LePrince was gangly as a stork, couldn't get a boy's attention to save her soul, and no wonder. She'd stand in front of that old Black man, like to shriek till the birds flew off: 'Don't stop, Daddy. Don't stop now, Daddy. I want to fill it up. I want it running over the top, Daddy!'"

We both laughed at his shrill rendition of Lucille begging for more.

"I liked Lucille; she was sadly awkward and bound for a single life. She never did come out, what with her parents dead and then there wasn't much reason to anyway. They say there's somebody for everybody, but then they said there wasn't anybody for poor Lucille. Moved away when she got to be about twenty, few years after her parents died, and nobody knew why, what with the money and the house all to herself, but that's another story. The real picture emerges when you take a minute to look at the so-called ladies of the society, who near took each other's heads off, squabbling over who had rights to Daddy Ancrum with Lucille's mama and daddy dead and gone and no longer in need of such services. They argued like women at a rummage sale, like he was a piece of equipment. It was a tribute to his strength of character that he didn't care a hoot who he worked for, but the ladies made it a process to behold, because whomever he worked for had him till someone came and *borrowed* him, and then that someone was beholden to the lady who had him before. It was what they call a package deal nowadays, Daddy Ancrum and the ice cream machine, since nobody could remember who it belonged to, though I suspect it was Lucille's, and her little show of generosity was to let it go with Daddy, so his employment opportunities wouldn't be compromised. Daddy Ancrum hardly ever said a word, except to excuse himself for every little task he performed and say how he loved the children."

"I think I remember him. He worked for a time for Miss Annie, didn't he?"

The judge ignored my reference to his former wife. "When he died, well, all those ladies were very sad. They had their own little memorial for him, nothing formal, just a shared grief over losing such an important cog in the social machinery. And I swear I didn't give it a second thought till I heard the most profound eulogy delivered by Elizabeth Allston over punch to a few of her cronies. She said, 'Old as Daddy was, he gave me a better day's work than any of the younger ones could. It's sad, them dying off like they do.' Verbatim, after all these years. Those ladies had a little nostalgic humor among themselves after that, making reference to AD punch, which was After Daddy, which just wasn't as good." He stared for a minute.

I stood. He watched, empty-eyed. "Well," I said. "It's getting late, isn't it?" She slipped around the corner and leaned on the doorjamb in a pose you could call suggestive and unnecessary, with the hour upon us.

"We could have given him more," he said. "He could have given us…." He paused, uncertain what old Daddy Ancrum might have held back.

"The gift of native intellect?" I ventured, hat in hand, looking past her, down the hall to the coat closet.

"Elizabeth Allston," he told her. "Now there's an institution. Do you realize how many Elizabeth Allstons they've had in the last few hundred years? And how little she's actually done?"

She ignored him to better escort me out. "Tomorrow then?" she asked.

I recoiled. "Tomorrow?"

"Yes. Tomorrow." She pre-empted my surprise and possible declining with a flourish, striding to the coat closet for my coat. "Say, three o'clock?"

"I don't know." He watched. She held my coat.

"Anne is expected," she said. "Wouldn't it be lovely?" She smiled, effusing loveliness as best she could, as Elizabeth Allston might have done.

The old man nodded and said, "Oh, sure, she could throw a party. What the hell good is that? None. I mean none that's...lasing, don't you know...." I nodded, turned and left. He called after, out the door and down the larger hall: "Nothing. That's what. As much nothing as any of it...them...nothing.... You'll see."

Lovely?

I'm amused these days at the different forms it can take. For years lovely meant linens and silver, crystal and china. Now I sit on a bank still as sawgrass till the fiddlers think I'm another bump in the mud and ease on out their holes fanning the big claw to show whoever's looking who's top crab around here, sidestepping up the bank, taking for social contact as they find it and tiny nibbles as they may. They surround me in a few minutes with their clicking, dancing and posturing and make me feel at home. The bull china-back has one small claw, and a big claw going about two inches. He waves it slowly over his eyes, cocky as a ringneck kingfisher calling from a half-rotted piling across the creek, though he'd run for a hole to duck into if that kingfisher swooped on over for some fiddler crab cocktail.

A bull china-back's shell is unique from other fiddlers, filigreed with purple pin striping in a perfectly lovely family crest. No mud sticks to this dandy; he saunters, clean as the Black fellow I saw on TV who washes cars in a tuxedo and doesn't get a speck of foam on him. I waited fifty years to pick another fiddler up for a closer look at the artistry on him. Anne didn't come by her father's apartment that next day of my New York sojourn, not at three or four or five.

I don't know if he ever found peace in his heart, or if the path down memory lane stayed open, without the flowers and warm scent he took for granted for so long. But I think he approached peace of mind, and death came easy, a dark appointment that lightened up bye and bye. It helped him on his way. I sit in the mud watching little crabs, wondering what kind of lovely path I'm on, accepting for once that this may well be it.

VI

A Quaint and Sheltered Life

The morning after the judge's funeral and dinner at Jim Cohen's, I stopped for coffee on King Street for two hours till the Library Society opened. I had the good sense to bring a pen and a legal pad, because a lawyer doodling on a pad is considered billable and best left undisturbed. The coffee eased the effects of Jim Cohen's sweetwine, and since I had to write something, I wrote a list of questions on the general wonder of life, turning like it does to stare you in the face and damn near dares you to make sense of it. Two hours over coffee seemed like a stretch with so much foot traffic and all of it careful not to disturb a lofty pursuit, but that time passed too like another dream, fitful, fleet and solitary, decocting thirty questions in the end to one lone interrogatory, Your Honor. Why do the good suffer? I had a few more questions, like the number of seven-minute intervals required to fill eternity, but that was just foolishness.

Moreover, I watched people, casual friends and close friends, pass in my periphery, careful to avoid disturbing the important work at hand. Maritime law, like much of our society, was one more ship in a bottle, antiquated and preserved, no longer mobile or exposed to the mutable influence of nature but rather protected for all to see its once-impressive splendor. That I would not be missed at the office was given. Maritime legal billings had gone further south than, say, commissions to the chandler's boys, who used to race out in sailing skiffs to meet incoming ships when the world moved by sail, which was only a hundred twenty years prior. Fact was, the last chandler in town remained in business for two reasons: all the others had gone under, and the real estate the last chandler sat on was paid for about two hundred years ago. So it was only old man Harris tending the till for walk-ins and his ancient mariner father, assumed to show a pulse but not checked too frequently, tipping to the left or right just as infrequently, most likely to free the gas.

I pondered retirement in deference to self-respect; I might have considered extinction just as well, which contemplation led to the most logical and pleasant transition that morning, down the lovely boulevard in the chill but sunny radiance of a brilliant winter day. I've often wondered if the women working the hallowed halls of the Library Society can actually speak, or if a career in the stacks atrophies vocal chords down to whispers. Did they whisper at home? Who knew? I never saw any of those women at a party or anywhere. Maybe they got together after hours for a good, personal whisper. I asked for Annie Gammell's letters, realizing for the first time the anomaly of a daughter named Anne after the mother, with the mother as the diminutive Annie. Did those who named the child anticipate that the daughter would be mother to the woman? Anne filled that role; had to.

I'd known for fifteen years those letters were bequeathed by Annie's estate, or delivered to the Library Society at any rate by her last housemaid. I don't know what drew me to those letters, except for the company a person might seek in the attic after a death in the family. I sensed that Annie took comfort in those letters, and her ended marriage, bereft of love as it must have been, ended whatever meaning remained in her life. Divorce in those days was scandalous, indicating a failure of wifely proportion.

The bundle felt casehardened by time, conforming to itself and rigor mortis. I cut the binding to spare the pages, brushed off the dust and started through the ruins. I can attest to the warm heart Annie was known for, both in the conventional sense of welcoming strangers to her house as well as keeping an ear open to whatever tale or question needed a sympathetic listener. She was easy to be around, and I often was, with my own mother far busier than Miss Annie was crazy. We didn't call her crazy back then or think it; nor did the more acceptable profiles, like eccentric, unusual or peculiar stick to her. She was Annie, an original, who chose our town to be born into. Fifteen years after she died I could feel her presence, largely a stage presence, but the curtain rose as it always had, with a warm greeting at the top of the bundle in her undying persona:

I am dying.... It is a sad life that I am leaving.
Pardon me if I do not write longer, but those who say
they are going to cure me wear me out with blood-letting,
and my hand refuses to write anymore.

It doesn't sound warm, unless you knew Annie Gammell. She wrote that farewell in two letters, once to her mother and once to Sarah Bernhardt, thirty years after Sarah died. Alexandre Dumas wrote it first for *Camille*, and Sarah Bernhardt, the premiere actress of the Western world, played it over three thousand times.

Annie and Sarah Bernhardt, oddly enough, got to be very close friends, not exactly like a mouse and a lion, though the probability seems the same. How they met is conjectural and unlikely, but it happened. I think they were lesbians and Sarah led, Annie followed like a bee to honey, but like most intimacy between dead principals, this one engendered more speculation than consequence and in context doesn't much matter. Annie was peculiar but in the fold, the lovely fold of grace and hospitality; she had such lovely manners. She wound up in the eye of the storm, unable to alter inertia, simply warm and wonderful as her place and time but no longer fitting in, until she made no difference in the surrounding chaos.

She was born in '78 in the heart of Charleston with an excellent view of the harbor. Under her two farewells was a small, crumbling note in a childish scrawl addressed to Dear Miss Sarah. It briefly thanked the star for coming to Charleston and being so good.

> *Yours very truly,*
> *Annie Simmons Gammell.*

Beneath that note was a newspaper from 1892 folded back to an ad for Sarah Bernhardt in *La Tosca*, two shows, in Charleston. The rest of the paper covered Ben Tillman's gubernatorial re-election campaign. He personified the South then, having lost an eye as a boy on the farm, unable to reach a cow's teats without pressing his face to the bovine hindquarter. Infection set in, requiring surgical removal and rendering what was locally described as a permanent wink, though in hindsight, it probably rendered him truer to his cycloptic nature. The socket stayed empty, squeezed shut with no patch, so it trickled when he ranted, which was often, either at a coastal blueblood exploiting an inland farmer, or a Negro, any Negro doing anything. Defiant to a fault, he filled a collective need, post-Reconstruction; you voted for Pitchfork Ben Tillman so that defiance could represent you and your hardpan, hardscrabble, hardhead life up at the statehouse in

Columbia. Some said a veterinarian performed the eye-removal, but like so much liberal quip through history, this too was a whisper in a freshet. Ben Tillman was an original pedagogue, hateful, loathsome, fear mongering and stupid.

He became Pitchfork Ben from his campaign promise to go to Washington and fork their guts out. His targets were general, though he once threatened President Grover Cleveland. Nobody seemed to mind. He won a second term as governor in '92 and three terms as U.S. Senator, where he initiated a rare first for South Carolina legislators on the floor of the United States Senate: a fistfight. But it was only the other Senator from South Carolina who caught his Sunday punch, so a second Civil War was avoided. Skirmishes did ensue, however, between the Red Hills and the Lowcountry.

Years later, in 1947, the Red Hills produced another governor in the same piss-and-vinegar tradition, Strom Thurmond, who seceded from the Democratic Party in '48 to run for President as a segregationist on a third party ticket, the Dixiecrats. Strom bellowed, "All the laws of Washington and all the bayonets of the army cannot force the Negro into our homes, our schools, our churches." Nor can the written record capture his drawling, slurring repudiation of Harry Truman's position on civil rights. Strom sounded something like: *All a de laows o' Washntn 'n de baynets o'de ahmy cain't foce de Nigra inna ah homes, ah schooz, ah choiches....*

Strom carried South Carolina, Louisiana, Mississippi and Alabama that year, folks who mostly thought and talked like he did. One more electoral vote from Tennessee gave him a total of thirty-nine, which brought the country to the verge of Dewey Beats Truman but in the end couldn't tip the scales. Strom shook things up but never threw a punch in the literal sense. He made amends with the Democrats, as politicians do, and became U.S. Senator in '56, urging defiance against desegregation as it had been ruled by the U.S. Supreme Court. He filibustered on the Senate floor for more than twenty-four hours, the longest tirade in Senate history. He broke from the Democrats again in '64 to help Barry Goldwater become the first candidate for President from the party of Lincoln to carry the Deep South.

Strom Thurmond was U.S. Senator for fifty years by virtue of good manners down home and the fundamental values of the average grit with a pickup, a few good dogs, two TVs, a washer and a dryer, who begrudged the feds dollar one and didn't want nobody telling him what to do. And don't forget the door to Strom's Senate office—open as a back porch to any man or woman from any part of the state, Black or white, because Strom understood the critical need to show that it wasn't personal, those things he represented. He moved on from racism, his new voice stronger than a bleeding-heart liberal's, by then budging a might further than the proverbial inch. In '77, he enrolled his daughter in an integrated public school and was among the first Southern senators to support Black candidates for the federal bench. The daughter was six, born when Strom was seventy-five, so they called him Sperm Thurmond in Charleston, as if a man should outgrow certain needs.

But that was a joke. People appreciate a man who sees the light if that light won't raise taxes. Strom saw it, proving that his former stance was merely political, for the good of the nation at the time. Oh, the South changed on the racial issue, way too slow to please the NAACP, but then the pace would have been inadequate to them at any rate.

The Democrats took Senator Thurmond back into the fold because of his bedrock constituent base, and then the Republicans welcomed him with open arms, further demonstrating his adaptability, though most political parties would welcome anyone without a rap sheet. Strom was the original Southern Republican, and when he signed off to me: *With kindest regards and best wishes*, I felt his political skill deftly applied, even as I imagined his nasal rendition.

Strom mended fences between the dirt farmers and the la-de-dahs, who were us over in Charleston with our worldly airs and so-called culture looking down our noses for decades, when everyone knew we were too poor to paint and too proud to whitewash. I heard him criticized for his failure to initiate anything. But you see an original fire-breather put his child in an integrated school and then endorse a few Black judge nominations with nobody's pond showing a ripple, and I'll show you some initiative. Strom Thurmond single-handedly took the red hot baton handed down several generations from Pitchfork Ben Tillman and stuck it right in the pond, where it sizzled a bit and then cooled off. Since most events of consequence rise to the surface sooner or later, we came to learn what else Strom stuck and where he stuck it and the little sizzle it made. But given the nature of things, nobody was all that surprised. Strom Thurmond was not a man to pass up sexual opportunity, and so another daughter came to be. The end. Maybe way back then, we'd have spurned such a distinguished patron sending his nappy-headed yard child to college. But I jest yet again. *Yard child* was euphemism for mixed-race spawn since way back, said children commonly left to play in the yard, finding amusement and education in a chicken bone, a coat hanger, an abandoned car. But not Strom's progeny, no sir, and by the time that news bubbled up, we were all more intimate as well with a hard fact of life: it's full of changes for some of us, and we best not stare impolitely, lest we be gawked right back.

Sarah Bernhardt's arrival was second section, entertainment. A reporter rode the train all the way to Conway for no good reason but to ride back to Charleston with the great actress. He revolutionized journalism in South Carolina, where many reporters to this day ride trains in search of exclusives, or "scoops" as they're still called here. Miss Bernhardt wore a silk robe in Nile green, flowered in Parisian Gray, with a feather boa around her neck. With her nose pressed to the window through the hungry outback of Charleston she said, "Voila, Negre!" Her insight was keen; more Blacks than whites lived in South Carolina then, underscoring our difficulty. The Black population was one more unavoidable niggle of our charmed life, like death and taxes. Sarah's first reply to young Annie Gammell was torn in half with the bottom half gone. It greeted:

> *Mon Petit Choue,* (my little cabbage)
> *I am promising teach you Français....*

That was all that remained. The rejoinder was prompt:

> *Merci, Madame, Ça me plaisait bien.*

And so on, down through the pile. They corresponded two years, until Annie left Charleston at fourteen for Miss Peck's School in Philadelphia. Sarah sent her a train ticket from Philadelphia to Washington that year, '94, where they finally met. A sweet exchange preceded their first rendezvous, in which Annie expressed anxiety over her appearance; she'd been "out" socially so briefly in Charleston, and social intercourse wasn't allowed at Miss Peck's. She looked so plain, she said. Worse yet, Miss Peck hinted at canceling the trip in spite of its fabulous opportunity, or maybe because of it. Such were the times, in which a young woman of uncommon spirit was thought best constrained. I found no evidence of Annie's social debut and wouldn't be surprised if she hadn't come out. Just as Lucille LePrince was non-viable in the matrimonial field, because her family's considerable wealth could not override her physical shortfall and neurosis, so too did Annie seem bound for the singular with her disjunctive outlook and matching curiosity. She was past thirty when she married

Waites, damn near over the hill back then, though now it seems the age of just warming things up. At any rate, she wasn't rebellious; she simply didn't conform. Of Miss Peck, she wrote:

> *She has grave reservations. Very grave. She commonly says grave. Very grave. She worries I'll change. I would think that would please her.*

Sarah responded:

> *Non, non, non, non, non! You must change nothing. Glamour, it is like the snowflake falling on you, it melts. But spirit, it is a diamond that will last forever. You are my little Miss Peck.*

I think no one loved Annie Gammell like Sarah Bernhardt did, and it began long before they met. Next came a tattered greeting signed by all the girls and Miss Peck, wishing the World Famous Sarah Bernhardt the best of luck in breaking her legs. Playbills from *Magda* and *La Princesse Lointaine* lie crumpled randomly through the bundle.

They wrote over the next ten years and planned to meet again in '04. Sarah sent another ticket that remains uncancelled. They were to meet in New York, but Sarah contracted influenza; the tour was cancelled, and she went home to Paris. Annie made overtures of coming to nurse her but was forbidden.

Two years later another ticket came. Annie wrote that she was a woman now and could pay her own way. Sarah responded with her longest letter in the collection; her heart would break if Annie were ever else than her *petite choue*. So take the ticket, because she, Sarah, was wealthy, not in money; she had so little on hand she didn't know what to do, but she would make much more, as you will see. She and money were occasional lovers who kept the passion fresh, because money is cavalier, but an actress who is wise with money will be blind to the truth between her lines. She was wealthy but would have no money when her time came, because she wanted none. So come, help me live.

> *Money? Money is nothing.*
> *Ça ne fait rien!*

So Annie accepted the ticket, and they met again in New York. Annie wrote home that Sarah proved her point by pulling a hundred dollar bill from her bosom and burning it. Annie cried; Sarah laughed. *Voila!* It was stage money.

> *Sarah told me that an actress who is foolish with*
> *money will starve to death. I don't know what to make*
> *of her, honestly.*

They dined on *canapés et Champagne*. Sarah paid in hundreds and told the maitre d' not to worry; all the world is a stage. Had he not heard? He had not, so Sarah sat him down and introduced herself to the little (but high) café as Marguerite Gauthier, the lead in *Camille*. The maitre d' was delighted, of course, to forego a dinner tab in exchange for a bit of history. The patrons cheered, as Sarah died:

> *I am dying…. It is a sad life I am leaving….*

On a champagne label's crumbling arabesque, Annie wrote:

> *Dear, dear. How shall I ever be normal again?*

Sarah played New York for a week with Annie as valet and companion. *Angelo, Esther* and *Pelleas Mellisande* were played again in Philadelphia, across Pennsylvania and into Ohio. The last letter of the trip was gone, except for the bottom half of a single page. Annie complained of reporters ruining everything. Sarah said she loved the newspaper crowd and cured them of being boring by releasing her pet ocelot, Etienne. Near the end of the tour, Sarah bought a poodle pup named Genevieve that she gave to Annie.

Annie reported the next few years on life in Charleston from her house on Meeting Street. She spent time with Genevieve and described the dog's moods, as people alone with pets will do.

Genevieve had her muzzle trimmed and looks so pretty when she blushes.

The poor girl was in need. The dog too; it whined on hot nights, so Annie read to her, Henry James. Annie turned thirty in 1908, when her letters first reflected insight to Charleston Society. She took to the little world bounded by the Ashley and Cooper Rivers, those letters revealing her emergent humor, warmth and tolerance. Never priggish or stuffy, she remained unimposing, friendly, well matched to her station in town and revered. Still a recluse with sparse and polite social contact, she learned etiquette as a way of life, as our substitute for all else. Passion, whether unguided, misguided or absent, was compensated by cordiality, in service to our small-town need. Worldly was as worldly did, and frankly, we didn't travel much, on the whole.

I remember Annie's classic features and flawless skin, a woman who lived with a dog and books till she pulled her head from her burrow and stepped into our sidewalk society. She wrote of self-awareness, conscious of her family's image as peculiar. Stephen Crane might have written a different tale from the Battery, *The Peculiar Badge of Courage*. Oh, we love our oddballs, maybe in compensation for our pickled dispassion.

Annie compared our society to a self-tending abattoir, gossiping itself into sausage. She described Miss Edmunds as

Queen of the meat grinders,

recalling the day Miss Edmunds visited Annie's mother to say:

The Gammells are different, my dear, because you were a Simmons and not a Simons, don't you know. It's common understanding that a Simons is somebody, and a Simmons ain't. She said we had no genealogy at the Library Society, nor at the Genealogical Society under the "proper" spelling. She'd looked us up and dropped by to make sure we knew who we were, or I should say, who we weren't. You'd think no genealogy was pert near no lineage, but then we wouldn't exist, which we obviously do, because we think, some of us.

Trouble was, Miss Edmunds only presumed the née Simmons. She deduced it from Annie's middle name, Simmons, which must be the mother's maiden name. Musn't it?

Of course Mother said, 'Now aren't you sweet to pay us a visit when you have so much to do. But I'm not a Simmons. I'm an Ancrum. One m. Mother's father's mother was an Ancrum, too. We have but one Simmons in the entire family, and that's Annie's middle name. I feel terrible, giving in to a lark and misleading you like that. Isn't it lovely, though? I felt it would keep the common touch. Look us up again, Dear. Ancrum.'

Miss Edmunds was mortified. She said, "Oh!" and was on her way, though we invited her to stay and visit a while.

Annie told this story in hindsight as backdrop to a development some years after Miss Edmunds' nosy house call. The development was a new friendship—with Miss Edmunds. They became close, two single women with days to fill. Miss Edmunds was old and withered, still sorting the affairs of others. They passed on the street. Miss Edmunds said hello. Annie was curt, replying that she was living with Genevieve Bernhardt, first generation landed, Paris extraction, possibly Huguenot.

Genevieve scurried about like a mouse.

Or a rat. Those yappers outlive you on half a chance. They watched the dog find the right spot to relieve herself. Then

I thought something was about.
Miss Edmunds touched my arm and smiled.

Annie took it for instability, but Miss Edmunds said,

'It's time for tea! Won't you?'
It was quite unexpected.

Miss Edmunds lived in Bedon's Alley, a major pinnacle on the social range. Not an alley in the conventional sense. Bedon's has no stray cats or garbage cans and certainly no bums. Bedon's Alley is an enclave of houses buffered from pedestrian byways. No street leads to Bedon's Alley. To call it landlocked would sell it short; it's protected. It must be born into. Its wooden houses lean from age and brittle crust. Its masonry dwellings droop their roofs like children daydreaming on their feet, gardens rising like knee sox, pressed and laced in fuzzy beauty. Twisted spearheads on iron fence tops and glass shards topping garden walls deter any burglars left over from the Eighteenth Century.

Miss Edmunds' house still needs paint, and a tricycle and skateboard clutter the yard now, sixty years after that invitation to tea. The stained glass in the corner alcoves show matching bucks on hills, but the windows sag from age with beer-belly bottoms. The drapes are still open so the curious and envious can look inside. The windows, shutters, dormer and furniture lean askew as if drunk or tired or both. Breathing walls meet rolling floors. Pictures hang aslant. Cracks scurry, the dinette slumps and the chandelier hangs aslant, or so it seems. A gilt plaque out front announces: *Miss Edmunds' House.* And a would-be original woman narrates each room's notable anecdotes; who slept where and who his cousin was, all leading to someone who signed the Declaration or perhaps watched it being signed or was alive then and likely fished nearby, both before and after lunch taken from a brown bag on the Battery, where, of course, The Great War began. Sixty years later, nothing remained but the shell of the former self, and tourists came gawping on the Tour of Homes, a common format but nowhere served with such certitude, fortitude and magnitude.

Meanwhile, back in circa '08, Miss Edmunds served tea and sugar cookies. Annie described the event to a woman whose life was an international adventure. They walked through the garden, Annie and Miss E, though it was February and barren.

> *She squeezed my arm, Sarah. I feared a fit. She said, 'It will madden you in March! The riotous azaleas are near too much to bear. The wisteria, child, is more than I can stand, alone. But you know that.' She has guests for weekends, or weeks, March and April. She touched my heart, so far past her prime and her foolishness. She set her table for two and kept it that way.*

So I accepted, for Genevieve and myself.

Annie and the dog crossed the great divide in April for a few days to visit among flowers and tea in blue oyster demitasse, and to share in Miss Edmunds' radical, perhaps revolutionary experiment—monogrammed doilies! Unseen and unheard of in Charleston till then, these doilies were momentous proof of trust in her new confidant. They were printed out of town for security. Miss Edmunds served tea and asked,

What do you think? Are they Dutch? To which I merely replied honestly, but I suppose it was the perfect thing to say: 'You do set the standard here.'

Bingo. Next thing you know Miss Edmunds is suggesting that two can live far more efficiently than one and have more friendship than living alone. Would Annie like to sell her house and come live in Bedon's Alley? Annie declined, proposing regular luncheon instead. She wasn't ready to take up with an old woman but couldn't help love the old woman for that most sympathetic characteristic, her vulnerability. Miss Edmunds couldn't hide her loneliness and put it on the table like an honest woman. Their first luncheon was planned for a select guest list. They said nothing of the doilies, nor did the guests, but by May the local printer was swamped with orders. It was a smashing success, on a level in modern times with a major detonation in town followed by naked abandon.

So ended the Miss Edmunds interlude—ended but lingering in warmth and love, the two key ingredients added frequently over the years, rendering dismissal a heinous crime committed in genteel society and providing reason for the backlash. Annie said Bedon's Alley was too confining and described herself physically, bursting like a blossom, perhaps for the vicarious pleasure of her pen pal. Taller than most women, she called her figure complete, its contour and firmness a complement to its complexion and hue. Miss Edmunds was recalled forty years later in a series of letters with the greetings torn away, letters to Sarah, long dead. Beside herself by then with scandal, divorce and dissolution of her life's relevance, Annie was easily forgiven her raw behavior. The old poodle joined the haunt thronging her last days. She wrote:

> *The past seemed infinite, once upon a time. Now I can measure it by the number of friends left to recall it. So little remains. Miss Edmunds had a story to tell for each chip in her Blue Oyster Service, each blemish episodic, so tea time was good for stories. I heard them a hundred times. The teapot handle was broken in unloading from the boat in 1764. God bless it. The day before she died I chipped her creamer lip. 'Don't worry. You make such a lovely story. Now you're part of my service.'*
>
> *Oh, dear, dear, dear. I wish she could join me for tea now. What old fools we get to be.*

On Fridays Miss Edmunds fetched the bourbon if things were getting on, casting fate to the wind or sultry heat, naughty girls. Drunk again on memory, Annie addressed Miss Edmunds:

> *I could spend days on end with Genevieve with nothing much to do, but your house was always there with tea and good time, so I never had to wonder at all....*

And in the same letter, back to Sarah:

> *You would have liked Miss Edmunds. She had such a lovely way....*

Maybe she was past realizing these letters would never be posted or received, or past caring. She drew on the only company remaining, which was that of memory. Apparently out of chronological order near the center of the bundle was Sarah's response to Annie's most provocative letter, in which Annie teased with romantic innuendo, hinting love for another, a man, the first man mentioned in all the letters from her first childish thank-you, age twelve, until 1911, age thirty-two. She wrote that he'd called. He was a handsome young fellow she believed to be known in town as the King of the Tenderloin. She then mentioned other young men expressing interest but easily dismissed them as

...part of all that crowd. They're so silly.

Waties Waring was different:

He's quite present, not in the conventional sense
but with profound strength, angular in his facial structure,
handsome in dramatic terms. I'm not so sure about him. He
has trouble remembering which line comes next, and he seems
an awful typecast.

A most available bachelor with youth, a decent appearance and steady income, he boldly strode through Charleston's young womanhood. She thought him unsatisfied because those women were cast from the same mold as the silly fellows, as if she alone could provide what he lacked, namely substance in a woman.

Those other women are social. They're in vogue.
They keep up with the styles and make up their faces.
I'm not sure what he could see in me.

Annie made herself up, but the rouge made her cheeks too red, so she drew grease pencil tears and a big black frown.

I'm pretty but plain, and I'm content with that.

He happened by as she came out of her house with Genevieve, an obvious coincidence. Exchanging hellos, he sputtered; she couldn't quite get what, but it sounded like an invitation to spend the weekend at his father's creek-house.

His bordello in the woods, he should have called it.

He gave her a rose and rambled over a fire in the box and plenty of quilts and fresh shrimp from the creek. When she remained speechless, he said it might rain, might not. Eventually she laughed, in his face, as it were. She told the same story forty years later in another letter:

He was outlandish from the start, but it could have been his greatest charm.

She remembered him as awkward, tedious and boring otherwise. Sour grapes notwithstanding, her last opinion was no different than her first impression. She told him there on the street when she finally found her voice that he was

a rake and a scoundrel.

She left in a huff. It must have stimulated the young stud. Sarah's reply was the first in several years:

Come, let us reason it out. You love me, do you not?
And you would gladly spend two or three months alone

with me in the country? I too should be glad of this solitude
a deux, and not only glad of it; my health requires it. I
cannot leave Paris for such a length of time without
putting my affairs in order, and affairs of a woman like
me are always in great confusion; well, I have found a
way to reconcile everything, my money affairs and my love
for you, don't laugh; I am silly enough to love you! And
here you are taking lordly airs and talking big words....

The sentiment is yet another Marguerite Gauthier soliloquy, suggesting that Miss Sarah rarely existed between her lines. She pulled out near the bottom, though, for a brief personal note:

L'experience serait a tenter, petit choue.

Experience is good to try. This phrase too is idiomatic to the French and clearly encouraging. She advocated the outing.

I am coming to Charleston. Adieux.

Chance meetings on the street compounded Annie's panic. Waties would tip his hat, half bow and mumble Miss Annie.

No thank you, I told him again.

His pressure was synchronous with Sarah's impending visit, announced by her first letter in a long while. That letter spawned a frenzy from Annie, most of it pleading for help. She said a big difference between Waties Waring and Marguerite Gauthier's French lover was in the two dialects. The Charleston brogue is curious. Annie Gammell called it

a great security blanket most people here carry into
adulthood and then to the grave. They walk down the
street with it. They suck their thumbs with it as though I
can't see what they're doing. It's not a difficult thing to
escape. I have none of it. Most others here hide under it,
though I do wish I wasn't so harsh. I know some who can't
come out from under it. But even if he were one of those,
still you see the difference.

The dialect is hard to write. It has a few notable words but is mostly a nasal patois derived from the Gullah of the islands. House becomes *hoose*, three is *shree*, boat is *bawt*, the center of a word stretched over a diphthong to make it melodious like *bo-awt*, thick as molasses with a *dash o' de mash mud ona tawp.*

There was no solitude a deux suggested. It was more
like Hoo boot some a dat foress frolic, Sweetie Pah! He
wants to sleep with me in the bushes! He's so indelicate.
Come quickly, please.

In another chance encounter he blocked her way to further plea for assistance in relieving his hormonal crisis while droning over culture, the stage, the arts in general, because Charleston was always one of your, whatchacallit, major foundations of culture. And art. The contention persists. This was a new tack, perhaps a last resort, appealing to a more sophisticated and perhaps more lenient nature. He spoke with civic pride and his rapture over Miss Bernhardt's performance on the weekend of the seventeenth, for which he knew she was engaged, because, after all, *dat's show bidness,* so

'Hoo boot de twenty-fote?'
That's when Mary McGrew walked by.

Mary McGrew was a vamp, the type later known as a slut and later yet as comfortable with her womanhood. In kinder terms, she was a girl about town. Recently returned from a divorce in Boston, she was tolerated in Charleston, undefined and unmentioned. She'd been seeing Waties Waring, and it showed.

> *She is pretty. She makes herself up. They were so*
> *Calm when she walked by. They said hello. I blushed.*
> *I could practically hear the branches cracking and her*
> *shrieking for Mercy. And more....*

Mary McGrew was

> *a bitch in heat. God shouldn't extract the ordinary penalty*
> *from the poor child but rather let her die in the midst of*
> *her beauty...and luxury.* (more Dumas)
> *He longed for her. I could see it in his eyes even as*
> *his mouth chewed on culture. I walked away. He looked*
> *so confused, like a lost boy. If he followed Mary McGrew,*
> *it would have looked bad. He could have followed me but*
> *lacked the stamina. I wish you could have seen him*
> *standing there, telling himself finally that it might not*
> *rain after all, then crossing to safe passage up Queen Street.*
> *He does seem vain and self-serving.*

Nature had revealed its fundamental drive, and Annie was clearly enamored to be part of it. Sarah came mid-May and played two shows in one day, the ineluctable *La Dame aux Camelias* for matinee and *Proces de Jeanne D'Arc* in the evening. A review from the local paper is flecked with dark brown over the decaying medium brown, like it was spat on. The review lamented Madam Bernhardt's age and waning greatness, then spewed the compulsory parochialism over art and who we are. Penciled in the margin in degrees of fading emotion was:

Lies

lies

lies

Though the emotional response came decades after the review, the words grasp a failing woman's desperation. The playbills reflect Annie's unique fragility—and the tenuous, artistic soul we've claimed since The Great Loss. Inside the back cover of the evening program, Annie drifted like a milkweed seed on a spring breeze. Doodling in the margin here too, she wrote:

Ambition Love
Romance Sarah
Sarah Bernhardt
King of the Tenderloin
Loin Tender
God should be merciful....

VII

Our Crosses to Bear

A standing joke in town was that time could be measured in fifths, and that didn't mean musical interludes. As I recall, this self-deprecating but face-saving humor emerged around '64 or '65 of the century in question, about the time Johnny Carson pointed out that distance in LA was no longer measured in miles but in minutes. Soon after Johnny told his joke, someone in town retold it for those of us generally sleeping by the time the *Tonight Show* came on. Someone said it's just like time around here, measured in fifths, and don't you know it became our little joke. How late did such and such a party go? Oh, about three fifths. Ha, ha, ha, ha, ha.

Everybody laughed in deference to our pratfalls and addictions, because you had to laugh—or die sooner or later without. It wasn't funny but hit the bull's-eye that was us from such a precisely skewed angle that we overlooked our epidemic alcoholism for a better view of our humanity. After all, Johnny was talking about us in a way, making our little Paradise a worldly place, hardly different from LA. At any rate, nobody complained, so the joke got told over and over, legitimizing us as fun-loving people. Another standing joke was the nickname the town went by, the Holy City, because of all the churches, though the devil couldn't be happier with available vices in a mannerly setting anywhere. We were not evil, but the converse—that we were holy—held as little water. We had our crosses to bear like everyone else, yet our particular burden, the booze, was unique in its magnitude and consequence, as was our dependence on it to nurture our little garden of eternal nicety. Community alcoholism surrounded by temperate weather, polite society, beautiful flowers, hospitality and history thicker'n a skeeter swarm is not your average fare up the interstate.

They say excessive drinking doesn't hurt you nearly as bad as it hurts those around you. I suppose I should remove myself from judging that one, and if I had my druthers, I'druther recuse Miss Eudora from that bench too. I won't say I didn't make her suffer the ill will and hurtful behavior a drinker pours freely from a liquor bottle. I will say that a woman never warranted more abuse from an alcoholic. Even if there are no good drunks, that doesn't make all drunks bad. Some pass out prior to hostilities, while others abuse everything around them. I was an abusive drunk, letting the hurtful truth rise from subliminal consciousness and sputter all over anyone nearby. Eudora would have been miserable in any event, because she was not a happy person. And a more boring woman never lived. Sober, we worked through it, as they say. Just add alcohol, and I'd enumerate her blind spots, tracing them to genetic shortfall that rendered her so goddamn pigheaded and dumb.

Her mother Betty named her "Eudora, in the rich tradition of Southern literature." That was Betty's set piece for her daughter's gothic greatness, whether literary or social or cast as a statue of the mother and daughter displaying monumental poise and grace. I wanted both of them cast in stone all right, or concrete better yet.

Yes, that talk was ugly, but it fairly captured the sentiment of those decades. Not to go too far out on a limb here; suffice to say that neither mother nor daughter owned a single volume by Eudora Welty or ever checked one out of the library or the Library Society or spent five minutes reading a single story there or could quote a single phrase or cull an idea or concept from any paragraph ever written by Eudora Welty. Betty got the gothic part right by dumb luck.

Betty and Eudora Summer often claimed historic antecedents, stalwarts for whom Summerville was named, but they never spent five minutes there either; it was so gauche, Betty said; and tacky too, Eudora chimed in, her finger on the pulse of modern times. Much less did either one let another five minutes pass without running her mouth like an oscillating fan, in case any quarter needed filling with words of sheer, numbing stupidity or mean-spirited gossip or idle talk of no avail to any man or beast. You spend twenty-seven years with a woman; you know the ins and outs. The mother's dead. The daughter took up with the first man who paid her any mind, God grant him the liver to withstand her.

I don't mean to pick the parts of my road-kill marriage up off the pavement and jam them into place to make sense of the greater picture. I only point out that my name is Arthur, and I am an alcoholic. That I have good reason to drink excessively is of no matter, nor does consequence derive from the years that woman drove me into such a funk. The salient point is that I never went regular down to the AA, because it's a misnomer, because you can't scratch your hind side left-handed in town with anonymity much less stand before a roomful of drunks and admit you're one of them, as if they didn't know, whether you showed up or not. I'm on a regimen now, based on nutritional supplements, which people here laugh at and say I'm too lazy to attend the meetings and only fooling myself. I know I spared my gut about forty gallons of coffee with sugar and a few pounds of cigarettes by not going down there. I did go sometimes when it got tough, to take my mind off things, even if only to displace my troubles with the drone of other people's troubles. I believe those people are well intentioned. More importantly, killing a little time is sometimes all you need to do. Next thing you know it's the next day in a series, one at a time.

Maybe the relevance of these iotas was that I was one thousand one hundred and fifty-two days without a drink the day Waties Waring went six feet under. Jim Cohen poured my first drinks in all that time that same afternoon, and I didn't think twice about down the hatch, because a funeral warps your perspective no less than a lifetime of gravity slumps glass.

Not one person at that funeral, including Jim Cohen or any of the white people, would attend my funeral if I had dropped dead that day. Some things you just know. You wonder who might turn out for you, telling yourself that it makes no difference. I believe it doesn't, once you're dead. But I'd wondered for a while who would interrupt their lives to pay respects, because I wasn't yet dead and sensed that very few people would muster more than a sigh and brief eulogy, something like, *Oh, old Arthur; well, I wonder what's for supper.* It made me think twice about the social motions I went through every day. That contemplation was not what drove me to drink that evening, but it contributed to the cause.

One thought led to another, and I wondered what might happen on the day I die—that notion got stuck in my craw. Nobody wants to think about it, as if not imagining it makes it less certain. I don't want to bog down on verbalization over strained meaning when it makes no difference to a thing if it's spoken or not. Nor do I dwell on the world's willingness to get along so well without me. Why shouldn't it? What got me wondering were the deaths of friends who passed day or night, and I knew they'd died, just plain knew it before anybody told me. I don't think psychic phenomena are extraordinary, but I had other friends who died and nobody told me for a day or two, and I was surprised to hear the news.

So I wondered if my death ripple would find a shore to roll up on where someone would sense my transit, or if the wave would roll eternally out to sea, unlanded, unbroken, unfelt. A dream recurred about that time; it was morning, same as all mornings, but standing in front of my dresser where I put on my watch and rings, I didn't bother, because I was dead. As a matter of fact, I wasn't going to the office, because dead people don't do that, starting with no watches or rings or claim to any material possession. I was clothed in that dream, which ought to have told me it was a dream, because you go out like you came in, buck naked under a scrim, but I didn't see it logically because I was dreaming, and dreams don't always add up sensible. It was knowing not to bother with my watch and rings that got me stuck there in front of the dresser all night, realizing I was dead.

My aunt gave me that watch thirty years prior on the occasion of my first promotion to associate partner. One ring is a gold horseshoe with diamonds around the top, and the other is a signet with a star sapphire. Eudora called those rings tacky as a Vegas card sharp, but she was like that, rendering all things either tacky or lovely in direct correlation to her view of creation. If something made her look good, it was lovely. If it didn't, it was tacky. She taught me my deep distrust of Southern women with her chronic accusation of any being, object or event as being tacky. She wouldn't castigate the watch for fear of my Aunt Florence's disapproval, which she and God knew could lead to the outside, where a woman can only look in, which is commonly viewed as tacky. I always felt better wearing my horseshoe, call it lucky if you want to, and I loved star sapphires since the first time I saw one. Moreover, Eudora never went to Vegas. Hell, she never made it down to Disney World, what with the overwhelming situation in Florida, which is full of nothing but crackers, don't you know.

Anyway, it was quite a few nights I had this dream of standing in front of my dresser, realizing I was dead till morning, time to get up and go to work, which felt about the same. It wasn't a nightmare, where you bolt up in a sweat, breathing hard, but it weren't no walk in the azaleas neither. I stood in that mirror knowing it was all over but the crying, only to wake up to a more somber reality, another day of statutes, precedents, political stratagem, social talk, obligatory chuckles over the same old jokes and cocktails stretching way past sundown as necessary to balance life with the other, whatever the other might have been, which I couldn't quite grasp but knew it came closer every day.

I stopped drinking so I could attain the healthful benefits of sobriety, which benefits I had to review every afternoon like one last precedent or statute, because I forgot.

I got that dream to stop when I stopped wearing rings or a watch. I'd practiced for years, accepting those things I could not change or wouldn't try any rate. Both consciously and subliminally, I let things go, lest they linger. I'd adapted to an imperfect world, allowing life to proceed on simpler terms. Maybe I did die in the small way of the French, not after sexual relations but in marking life from day to day, like an alcoholic anonymously. I'd had no sexual relations for a very long time, including the time of Eudora, which relations seemed like a chore, like taking out the trash or relieving pressures with bowel movement. My dream of death in the mirror was not satisfying and made only for fitful nights and days at the office. Once I got the dream to stop, I slept better and accepted more and began to wonder at odd moments, about people I engaged in normal conversation. *Would you feel my passing?*

Well, the road to knowing what the hell is up is full of potholes. I didn't worry over who'd show up at the funeral.

Funerals are social. Folks show to say goodbye and see each other and tally your score, so you want a good turnout. Hell, I didn't care but wanted to count a few close friends while I still showed a pulse.

The worry over mortality or the end of days or whatever you want to call it went away too, mostly, and that's another good thing, leaving me peacefully mindful of the day I'll die. Or the night, and I suppose passing on between the witch and the cock is preferable to the daylight struggle. I don't know but feared the reckoning I had coming and figured I'd caused the dream myself. I feared as well that I'd be served up as one more doughy centerpiece for a few hours of chitchat. Or maybe that fear faded like a dark night at first light, and I only anticipated as much.

Now I hope the dream and mindfulness are part of my personal liberation, starting with my jewelry or continuing with my jewelry after starting with scotch, giving it up, that is. Few people alive or dead would have believed what I would come to give up.

I read so much about alcoholism and feelings of well being, and the judge's funeral turned out to be a milestone and certain death of me too when it warped badly on the reckoning issue. The truth had festered in me fifteen years, my secret, even as everybody knew what I'd done, and I needed a drink, a long one, just to chase myself down the road. Things got worse as they will do after a good self-loathing, making my obsolescence as a professional man as plain as the nose on my face.

You got to die to get to heaven, and I did, hitting purgatory like a boar in a wallow. I thought I was cured of the sauce. Feelings of well being did not derive from that bottle of cheap sherry. The edge of a most peculiar anxiety was dulled, and for that I was grateful, but that dullness was temporary. More importantly, I saw that, as I felt fine the next morning, no need for a bit o' the hair o' the dog what bit me. I could ease back into the world with manners and a stable disposition. I felt sober and strong and not likely to fall off the wagon, but the road was bumpy, and the bone in my craw wouldn't swallow and needed something to wash it down. My embarrassment flared on so many levels, in a town so narcissistic that one level can do you in.

For starters, I was guilty of vandalism. Next, I'd turned on my friend, presumed guilty by circumstance and consensus. These infractions of the moral code were acceptable as long as nobody knew. Or at least they'd seemed manageable. We all carry secrets and indiscretions into the pale, and that's what I'd planned to do, as usual, for practical convenience.

Third, my spurious invitation to Jim Cohen wasn't really an invitation but an empty sentiment of reciprocal hospitality, when we both knew I was blowing smoke. The smoke didn't matter, because the courtesy of the language and the manner counted. It's never been important for white folks and Black folks to mix like kin the way Yankees insist we should. Hell, we mix better than they do every day. The Blacks have their way, and it's enviable in some ways just as our way is enviable in some ways. You mix everything together and you lose the character and charm and flavor of the delicate spices. It's risky. Take the time Jim Cohen came to town for sit-down dinner with white folks back in that phase of the judge's conflict. Sit-down groceries with the help in the formal dining room was supposed to show the whole damn world what for. Hell, everyone saw that dog and pony for what it was, Jim Cohen most of all. What could he say? No? You put Jim in a suit with a collared shirt; he'll squirm like a late baby, sweat like a mule and shake his head over groceries that would otherwise draw him in two-handed.

No, I didn't mean to offer that kind of showy hospitality, where country Blacks dress up like white people and come to my house and sit at my table, as if that's what they wanted to do all along, as if they and I would have had drinks and dinner years ago, if not for our demanding schedules. I meant the real hospitality that's anywhere for the giving and taking, like I had out at his place on a night of personal confusion clearly visible as a time of need, into which he stepped, like one of those friends I'd hoped to count one day. I didn't mean to suggest that he should come over in his time of need, but that the door was open, and it was different at my place, orderly and nice.

Maybe it was that notion of order that stuck the whole empty day in my craw, and nice for that matter. I'd felt plain miserable at the funeral that morning, easing on down to uncomfortable, sitting roadside in the cold that afternoon, easing on into relaxation and warmth at Jim's table that night. Never mind; I could kill two birds with one stone, shrinking the liquor stock I'd walked past three years now and repaying a social debt at the same time by carrying a bottle of the so-called good stuff out to Wadmalaw to share with Jim Cohen. I believed he'd like that, and I'd be a bottle closer to clean.

Sitting in the Library Society all morning was good for historical perspective but left a man hungry for some fresh air, and if a thirst could be quenched with a social call, we'd both fit in, which tends to be a daily objective here. How else besides trying can you hold a show like this together? Besides that, I viewed my number of days without a drink as one more thing to let go of, lest it get a swelled head of its own and suffer the local ailment of self-righteousness. To be free of that and freer still, I took initiative on this phase of realignment. I sat and stared, as if at realignment and the country road ahead.

It was mid-afternoon, when the breeze slacks up like time standing still, taking a break, and recollections come out like gnats. The old gals at the Library Society damn near twiddled their britches with me nosing into Annie's letters all day. I needed out before they closed in. Annie Gammell's poor performance as a heterosexual wife may have been the original source of integration in the South. He was insatiable. She felt bothered. He went elsewhere for the hootchie cootchie, and another Civil War started on a local scale, just like the last one, except this time it was Yankee snatch lobbed at the heart of old Charleston instead of cannonballs, and this time nobody outside of town paid much attention. Annie could have been a spinster, deluded on passion and lost love. Waties saved her, and then he dumped her after thirty years of marriage, spending his final years in the frozen north, listening to the tick-tock clock and parsing *the stuff that justice is made of*; his words, not mine.

Approaching a man of Jim Cohen's experience, removed from the nuance and subtlety of town, for an opinion on history or affairs of the heart seemed anomalous to say the least and laughable to say the worst; we'd laughed so often at our Black neighbors. But I could make that approach and followed my instinct on that approach because I needed it. I anticipated honest answers, removed from polite society.

Speak o' de debil; I rolled carefully into his place, barely bottoming out on the deeper pot holes, crunching a yard toy but missing a chicken, just as Jim looked up with a half nod and waited for me to stop and get out and fall in line behind him, back down to the river. I caught up where the path widened and said, "You know, Mister Jim. I'd like to talk."

He looked over with a smile on one side of his face, leaving the other side noncommittal, or committed to a further knowing, as he summed up what he knew of what happened all those years ago and the result, that it didn't make a pinch o' shit difference.

Well, anybody can dismiss anything with glib brevity. The brevity too was dismissible. "Hell, you might as well lie down and die if that's all you think things amount to." At the bank, he looked left and right and walked left twenty paces or so and sorted the net and his relation to it for a cast. "It's a situation," I said, sinking already into that nonspecific language, soft as pluff mud and just as viscous. He cast the net, let it sink, jigged it in, shook out a mullet.

I sat a few feet up, drier. I'd driven out from town on a weekday afternoon, after having dinner with him the night before—after not seeing him for quite a few years. I carried a brown bag with two bottles of the best Teacher's Scotch money could buy, aged, not that the price ever mattered. It just felt odd, that I'd thought myself way past caring on the higher cost of better scotch for myself when I bought it; I was just that oblivious to life and how it might play out. I never in a million years could have seen myself carrying that bottle out to Wadmalaw as a gift for a Black man, an old fat Black man of no more consequence than any Black at any time. He was longstanding, colorful, cheerful and friendly. The end. But that million years ended the prior morning, and there I was, on my way, trying to arrive.

"I need to talk, Jim." I mulled. He cast for mullet.

The critical point of my presence there was the incumbency thrust upon me, of getting him beyond glib summary of my misdeeds. I needed more by way of details, people, talk and, yes, insight. I had a few blanks needed filling in. Sitting too near the marsh mud, I waited. He waddled up the bank for supper, mullet again, after ruling on my motion, that it didn't mean shit. Case dismissed. I wondered how many mullet he'd eaten in his life and figured it must have been a few.

Moisture seeped in through my pants but I stayed there, enthralled with late sunbeams glittering in points of light on the concave faces of tiny waves, here and gone and here again. I could not remember a single moment in life so fulfilling as to render me selfless in solitude with beauty.

Pro bono work is not required and is rather frowned upon for a lawyer of stature, as measured in years with the same firm, especially if said firm dates back with appreciable depth in proportion to all else in the preserved scheme of things. But I took some pro bono the last few years; God and I knew why, and a few other people must have known why too. Nothing dramatic; I provided counsel on a few juvenile delinquency cases and a domestic abuse case.

Maybe this visit was working out, making progress already in conversations with self. What I'm coming to long way around, which is the general route in this region, is a report I read about that time, '68 or '69 or so, as part of an appeal on funding denied to research general health among Blacks in the rural South, in particular the Sea Island Blacks. They get more protein than urban Blacks, oysters, shrimp and fish mostly, right there for the netting. They get less cancer too, with less access and less cash money for Slim Jims, pork rinds and processed lunchmeat, which they fairly subsist on in town. Jim Cohen looked fair to middling, in spite of the fat, for a man of seventy-three, which age I could only hope to reach. My father died near ninety, which felt like another challenge, one way or another. It seemed easier to go on ahead and croak sooner rather than later, needing continual realignment all the way. I thought of my years remaining as the stretch. I would round the turn as a new man, physically, mentally, emotionally and financially. Those characteristics would grow stronger, if I could liquidate a few more former assets that had aged to the point of liability. The future should loom different from the past, though that's not often the case around here.

I wondered about Jim's lineage and figured he might not know; that's how it was. Blacks got born and died every day, casual as I might scratch an itch. I felt foolish, thinking I might free him up on some inside skinny on what I needed to know by way of some top drawer scotch. But I needed to start somewhere to free something up, to ease the discomfort taking form over many years to the point of culmination, one way or another. I'd wandered from the great, gossipy desert to the north, seeking relief. I sorely needed to leave a qualm or two in the arid past and get on while I could. I sensed a reprieve from old constraints, not so much a lasting bond with a man I'd never taken the time to know, until he took me in. It was nothing more than cheap wine and oysters and recognition of the trouble on me, like he could see it coming out from inside. I asked about his father.

Who knew? Maybe he had a yarn, and I needed a closer knit. Whatever Jim lacked in social nicety, he compensated in well being. He seemed unflappable, till I got the rise. Even then, he rose slow to the bait. He seemed testy but waddled on up to the house like I wasn't there. I brought two bottles of scotch for the generosity of the thing, and because they were the last of the Mohicans. Maybe those two bottles felt to him like a *nolo-contendre* or a sad white man's attempt to adjudicate. As the tide went slack, I watched the creek to see who might stick his nose out of the water.

For years I'd to suffered very heavy drinkers arguing over the best scotch and what might be better, like it was high protein feed for our thoroughbred race horses, all serious and concerned. The best was Dewar's to most of them, because Dewar's spent more money on advertising, and those fancy ads out of New York conveyed worldly sophistication by osmosis or saturation to those who drank Dewar's. That might sound simple, but they declined the effort if of thinking for themselves any farther than an oyster can spit.

Dewar's is to scotch what Old MacDonald's farm is to Tara. You got your snooty toot toots who'll swear by Glenlivet, because Glenlivet doesn't advertise as much. Advertising is so public, and Glenlivet is more discreetly top drawer and a certain cut above Dewar's. But it wasn't Glenlivet either. I could go on, making a case, till excusing myself to top my toddy with Teacher's, which is, long story short, the best scotch God made available to our little town.

Didn't matter once it was whiskey on the mud, which was a might different than the rocks. I took a long last pull as requiem for a maritime lawyer undermined by progress, and as farewell to the sauce. Didn't need it, could live free and easy without it, and there in the guzzle was my proof. I could feel the goodness and well being that bottle had to offer, because I'd learned to see the good. I could see the good in sharing with Jim Cohen and more good in scotch being gone forever.

It flowed forth, an offering to my best bubbas on the marsh, the oysters, who gave so much over the years, sacrificing kith and kin so I might enjoy the bounties of nature. I poured out that first bottle, and don't you know those thirsty devils drank it. Better them than me. Some went tight-lipped, likely minded to start an association of clean and sober oysters who might take a tentative look at the others and say, "I'm Oyster, bivalve filter feeder. I'm an alcoholic."

Well, you can't blame them, living the life they do, ebb and flood every day the same and nothing for it but to sift what flows by for something to feed on. You get perspective out here without the clutter and distraction that blinds you in town. I think about what happened, not in historical relevance of a few key personalities who were part our pickled society but more focused on what a person might consider sooner or later. That would be the difference a life will make and what will be left behind. What happened in town was no different than a dream of death, fading when the dreamer finally figured out how to leave his jewelry behind.

Time and its segregation of hearts unto themselves simply sent each player to personal resolve. We record our births and deaths in town in great detail, though the years in between summarily condense to gossip. I wonder if self-assessment is a requirement of evolution, an innate burden we chew on like cud. Or if Jim Cohen was nature's metaphor, dying and regenerating with the seasons, as somnambulism prevailed in the little village to the north, even as the sleeper seeks the light blindly. There is no new South and hardly an old one, just white people continually reconstructing their sense of defeat. You could see and feel it in town and out here too. The Blacks didn't shuffle and scratch nearly as much by then; didn't need to.

The report on nutrition and protein intake of rural Blacks compared to the Blacks in town wasn't all roses. They got more protein and had less cancer out in the boonies. But they had worms too, because of shallow wells dug too near the cesspool, so for decades internal parasites factored in infant mortality and general health. I'd thought those people incorrigibly stupid for drinking from a hole next to where they shit, so stupid you might well have called it genetically deficient. I realized that genetic predisposition can take many forms. I realized that some cavemen were white and nevertheless carried clubs and didn't drive Chevrolets, much less Mercedes—not even used Mercedes—but nobody called them stupid, because they needed time and a few dollars to achieve something more. We walked out of the mud and cleaned up all the way to doilies, impeccable manners, failing livers and gossip flowing like a flooding tide.

Maybe cavemen were a bad analogy, because I doubted that squalor out on Wadmalaw hinged on evolution. I asked Jim Cohen about his well when I got there. He laughed without breaking stride to the river, presumably replying that his well didn't make a shit too.

I wonder where society came from, how it started and how it came to get so full of itself and so way the hell removed from this twilight peace. I sensed personal progress or fatigue, looking up at the cloud closing in. Jim had come back down to fetch me. "You gwine eat? Uh sit in de mud?"

My turn to laugh; I came to eat. "Jim. Who was your daddy? How long did he live?"

He offered a hand, taking the unopened bottle with a nod, not reading the label. It felt strange, a man fifteen years and a hundred pounds my senior helping me up, and God forgive me; I felt the amebic microbes move from his hand onto mine. "Dan. My daddy Dan. He dead."

"Well, I suppose he could be. If you're seventy-three, he'd be what, eighty-five anyway." We walked slowly up the bank in silence save the mud sucking, on up to where the gravel crunched and then into the hissing grass and on up the creaky wood steps. Jim Cohen shook his head and mumbled something, sounded like *de fuck you thank*…. Maybe he did the math, but here again I intended no insult in my speculation on biological potential.

"He dead fo' I born. My real daddy Luzon. My mama die too, jus' soon's I cry. Juya be's my mama fuh true."

"Who were they, these people who raised you? Friends of the family? Kind of people you could count on?"

Stopping in the failing porch light, his half smile changed from tolerance to pity, maybe for a man of my age still ignorant of the drama playing out south of town. I needed to sort things out as distraction and contrition for my act of cowardice, but I stayed out at Jim's place for something more. I didn't know what, but staying seemed likely to provide, and leaving did not. And I didn't ask if I could stay, didn't need to. I still felt cured on the sauce issue, though Jim wailed in the wee hours on learning of the first bottle's sacrifice.

"Da's awright. Dey say you binna drank de good stuff foist." Then he yelled for the girl to wake up and get us a bottle of sweetwine, because it was too late, and we were too old to get up ourselves. She rose like a robot, obedient and uncomplaining, fetching two bottles to spare herself another wakening, and on second thought fetching a third to be sure.

It seemed like a long time later that I lay down on the blanketed mattress as directed. I could easily imagine the microscopic migration taking place, as I gave in to gravity, could easily feel the Blackness creeping in at cellular level and me, in my daze, defenseless. Could amebic microbes infest blankets too? Well, I was half asleep but not yet half stupid; no, they could not. No, this was a different cootie creeping inward, call it fear of what we suspected all along.

Then I slept like the living dead but not in a mirror. I fell deep for the first night in any I could remember, free of dreams. I did not wake up wondering where I was. I knew, because of the girl observing clinically the struggle of a white man in first regret long after first light. I did not attempt good cheer to cover my pain because it hurt too much. She saw and winced along with me. So I explained: "You know…. They say severe hangover is the greatest deterrent to drinking, but…it doesn't work with me. I've been depressed. Years now, more or less, but the one time I feel really good, well…your father…or, I suppose he's your grandfather…."

She ran off, one lap around the kitchen and out the front door, letting the screen slam. There wasn't a thing for it but to move, with the synapses, the blood and finally the bones and muscles, or remnant sinews at any rate, seeking coordination so the unified whole might rise and improvise as necessary with personal hygiene. My God.

VZZZ

Julya

Sunrise lit the coiling mists, so an early bird could see the river break where a mama porpoise pushed her calf up to breathe. A thousand egrets broke into flight. A raccoon broke an egg and a cooter cracked a periwinkle. Jim Cohen cast his net three times, shook shrimp from it and flung the net to the high bank. On an upturned bushel basket in the mud, I continued the waking process too, sipping cowboy coffee I'd carried down from the house. He flipped the heads off the shrimp with his thumb and ate them raw as the heads and front feet scratched in vain for the river. You can't know much on a morning after nights and days like those just behind us, but among the small truths available was the certainty that I'd not eat raw shrimp first thing, not then or ever.

The next few days swirled like marsh mist and disappeared. Morning to evening we gathered, ate, and talked over the TV. Mama and baby dove, coming in on the flood to surface downstream, little fish fleeing fearfully before them. I'd come back out to Wadmalaw with a few things, a change of skivvies and socks, a few shirts folded in the trunk, a toothbrush and hairbrush. I hadn't meant to stay but to retreat, which is short of surrender. I didn't know if I'd stay the night but just in case. I needed a break from things, before things broke me. The workaday world and sociable streets, the Library Society and yacht club felt like the special kind of pluff mud out on Bloody Point, innocuous looking and willing to take a man in. I didn't sleep any better on Wadmalaw after the first drunken, comatose night, still preoccupied with my hard bed and hygiene, yet I woke lively. Jim Cohen was up before me, arranging things on the porch.

We walked to the narrow cut below Bloody Point in the lee of a palmetto stand. The still water looked shallow but wasn't. The pluff mud there would sink a man to his knees, or Jim Cohen to his hips. So the morning ritual began in the sawgrass tying ten-foot strings to four yardsticks. The far ends got tied to chicken necks, *dem fonky biddy biddy*; the chicken stank. Poking the sticks in the mud, he called over the water, reminding Bruh Jimmy of the good times shared. Jimmy crabs are bigger, meatier and sweeter than she crabs. Sometimes Jimmy goes deep, maybe to ponder his hazardous yen for rank chicken, maybe to get some peace from she. Maybe she runs him off. She's meaner, smaller, faster and harder to eat. Jim Cohen told me these things like I didn't grow up same as he did, up next to the crab disposition.

He sat on his crate, and soon a string twitched. So he leaned in to finger-by-finger, drawing his namesake closer. With the net in place he drew Brother Jimmy to the last good time, dead ahead. Scooping the crab, he laughed at the puzzle part called breakfast, fitted just that easily into place. Grunting up and tilting his basket, he pushed the crab under. He caught five. I got two, because he had a flatter bottom to crab on, and I had to drag mine over a ledge, where your smarter crab will drop off every time. I used to catch two dozen at a go but gave most away.

I couldn't say when I'd last crabbed. It felt good, but I got restless, like this was it, day in, day out, grubbing for breakfast before grubbing for lunch and then dinner, sleep and repeat. Pastoral and idyllic seemed best from a distance. A way of life is one thing but this seemed tedious. I'd topped off on simple wonder and flowed over on heat and skeeters. I was ready to roll, like maybe another forty years lawyering in town might feel different on another go-round, given my refresh and a few cocktails.

On his last pull, Jim got a fair-sized shrimp to hang on while he pulled it over the net. He flipped it over to me, so I pinched its head off, peeled and ate it. I tried not to wince like you do over cheap liquor and raw shrimp, and I wondered if Jim Cohen knew I never ate one raw before. Why would I? He glanced up to see for himself, so I looked casual but tipped my hand with a frightful smile as I chewed and chewed, breaking up the sinews like boiling water usually does. And chewed.

Maybe that shrimp is what kept me there, stuck in the mud, chewing grubs first thing. I suggested we fish that morning, to see if Jim could back up his stories, but he said no, too hot; the bass go deep to stay cool. I reminded him it was winter, and the water didn't fluctuate but half a degree twixt January and April. So why in hell wouldn't Brother Jimmy go deep too? Impatiently he said, "Jimmy dumb." So we crabbed. I asked if Waties Waring caught thirty-pound bass like he said he did, and if the old Waring creek house had lunker bass under the dock like he said it did. I asked if Jim thought big bass had worms in their flesh, but Blacks smoke big fish in an old fridge smoker and eat them anyway, because smoke kills the worms, so what the hell. I asked why he thought so highly of the judge's father Ned, and if Ned fished like the judge said, hooking up with huge spottail and black drum, playing them slow as a turning tide, then talking to them while he unhooked and released them.

Was Ned nuts for fishing or plain nuts, advising the fish he caught that they'd best detect and avoid hooks in the future? He was said to listen too. Near the end Ned put away his fishing gear and sat on the dock calling the fish. He'd whisper back and forth with a few favorites.

A marsh hen squawked bloody murder, likely getting pinched by a fiddler—and why in hell shouldn't we shoot some and then go try for some big, wormy bass under the old dock? He could smoke them. A great blue heron tip-toed down the flat, her neck cocked to aim an eye at a wiggle by her ankles before shooting her needle beak and coming up clamped on a silver shimmy. She took off over a sudden eddy nearby. "There!" I said, pointing a lunker likely feeding, and us without a rig.

Jim Cohen shrugged, explaining that we already got breakfast, so what sense would it make to get lunch too, before we eat what we got? Man, the ignorance of some people. On hands and knees, bushel basket upright, he grabbed the crabs scrambling for the river. I tossed one in by the back fin but grabbed another too high and got another wakening. Tears rolled, as I grinned over the crab dangling from my bloody hand. Jim grinned too, squeezing my wrist, freeing the crab from its claw and tossing it into the basket. Then he crushed the meaty part of the claw between thumb and forefinger, gently removed the pincers, carried the basket in one hand and dragged his fly-swarming baits with the other. Wiping my eyes and holding my wound, I followed. I'd been out three days. In another week I'd call it a leave of absence, which seemed redundant, which made me smile after all at my compulsion for proper usage.

Jim boiled a pot of grits so we wouldn't starve to death picking crab for breakfast, on the whole a tedious project first thing but a good start for any day, savoring that which is given. So we picked, ate grits and eased out toward noon. He felt that his grandfather Luzon suffered a dual onus of slavery, the first being for sale at any time, which was tough if you had a family. The second was being on sale, like ripe tomatoes late season. Luzon got discounted because his aversion to slavery was frequently manifest and required additional upkeep. Compounding his lower value were his shiftless reputations for stealing out at night to eat select oysters up from Rockville and drink expensive brandy that he stole. So he was tired in the mornings, returning with a bushel for the white folks, who yelled at him, especially Miss Elizabeth. Luzon left the Allston place when he'd had enough of that racket. Then it was time for dinner, fish, if I wanted fish, but first we'd rest on the porch to let breakfast settle and give the flood a chance to come on in.

Okay, Isaac Mikell liked the brown sugar and favored the woman Cloe. I doubted I'd find this memoir at the Library Society, but Jim Cohen's story rang true, as it was told to him, detailed down to a phrase or jumping thirty years in a sentence. Isaac Mikell humped Cloe on the bluff in view of the half-built house that would be Point St. Pierre. His cock-a-doodle-do could be heard in the cabins on the periphery at first light. From there, he'd march up the bluff and across the yard to press on with construction, likely wondering if his next wife would endure. He'd had three, none surviving the rigors of the place and the man, but he'd get a new one, because a man needs a wife.

He'd bring her in once the house was done, so she could walk the marble steps to the piazza, where she could entertain like a planter's wife. Here was the luxury of Charleston, along with pastoral elegance among pines, palmettos and live oaks. On the greensward, a woman could show off the plantation, simply pointing and telling. Superfine cotton could not keep up with French market demand, and with crops sold prior to planting, Isaac Mikell was a wealthy man. Charming speculators in tights and lace brought gifts for Isaac's wives, who seemed pretty but frail for a season or two. The wives were buried out back as the gowns became a renowned collection, until the collection was also lost in the evacuation of '61.

But on a satisfying morning twenty years before the exodus, Isaac Mikell stuffed his cheek till drool ran with sweat, on down the neck to the chest. It was hot. Never mind. Isaac's own private Eden shaped up with abundance. Wiping dribbles from his chin, he wagged his head at so much sweetness packed into one blessed morning, hardly spitting distance from home.

Sweet Cloe, slave queen of that little Nile, got no French gown but lasted longer and was loved dearly as a night wife could be, not in the do-as-you're-told-till-death-do-ye-part sense but in the poetic sense. Isaac bestowed the comforts of life upon her in gratitude for pressure relieved and sharing his joy. He never overpowered and remained open to a substitute if personal reasons prevented a tryst. He matched his great need with great manners, though revisionists would mar his name in spite of the style he brought to plantation love. Isaac Mikell took care of his assets, in sickness and in health, for better or worse.

He courted his dark women as if they'd blushed at high tea. They giggled like debs, like Pinckneys, Rutledges or Middletons, which many musty women came to be. The wenches had no family names but didn't need them, not with deeds of ownership. Isaac traced his vigor to steady work, sultry air and fine Black women. They moved languorously, like ripples on a sultry afternoon, as the master drifted through the fields watching them pick, hoe and bend to the common fortune, glistening with grace. He watched them idle, eat, laugh and sleep, until evening, when he sent an invitation through a nappy-headed child.

On arrival, the evening guest got a flower, wine in a glass and a walk to the bluff in starlight. This heaven on earth was God's gift to Isaac, who chose daily from his box of chocolates. A humble man, such as it was, Isaac Mikell saw his lot in life as Divine Mercy. Moonrise over the creek glimmered out to the sound as the corn shucks rustled and whispered nothings drifted, and the old ramrod pumped steam till the whistle blew. At some time prior to the big house being built, Cloe bore a daughter, Julya, who achieved maturity, just as the big house was done.

As the master aged, the Negro women coveted his invitations because the gifts were greater for the greater task at hand—lamp oil, molasses or sugar tits—butterballs mixed with sugar, wrapped in linen squares tied with a thread. Auntie Riah, the cook, measured the master's vigor by his need for sugar tits. "Maum Jane jus foal, Riah. Reckon I fetch her a box a sugar tit." The gooey balls pacified the babies, ten minutes to a tit for a twilight hush. The master went to French candies and perfumes, silk in bolts and, near the outset of The War, money. So they lie with the master as he expounded the virtues of seminal relief as supported by recent studies in Northern journals. Oh, those Yankees had time for that sort of thing, and before you knew it, it was time again for love, the elixir of youth and health.

Isaac's happiness was challenged when the fourth wife denied him her bed until he gave up his vile habit. She died directly, and a fifth wife followed, along with a syphilitic sore on Isaac's lip that grew instead of shrank, until it matched the one on the donkey short-tethered by the cabins on the periphery. The new wife died directly, as the chancre vanished, never to rise again, except prior to the master's death after The War, when he cursed from the bluff to the sound, "God damn you, Margaret!" He demanded dark women by then, but they wouldn't love him after The War; he was so old and had that nasty lip. He died in '65 with naught but heavenly memories.

A social class had evolved at Point St. Pierre between the white class and the Black class. High yellow was not white but felt equidistant from Black. The tawny mulattoes scorned the darkies. Among the oldest and lightest was Julya, a full-fleshed, big-boned woman with round cheeks, sloping nose, high forehead, a big butt and thick lips. Yet she strutted, chin up, chest out proud, even as her peers sniggered, twenty years old and yet to find a man. She wore crocus sack sleeves to protect her fair complexion, but pushed her sleeves up in the company of white men or pulled her shift down to reveal her ocher bosom. She stood apart, declining miscegenation to keep the line pure—her line. Pride became buffoonery, but she held out, wondering what could take her white prince so long.

In November of '61 the Confederate steamboat *Beauregard* landed at Edisto Island, carrying a courier from Charleston: Yankees and freedmen will land directly; the only course is evacuation. White women cried and wondered where to bury the silver, china, crystal, jewels, linens and lace, what to pack and what to leave. White men mulled over brandy, the fleeting nature of greatness and the end of civilization. The men packed weapons, drank what they could of the liquor and ordered the crops burned to minimize the spoils. The Negroes packed a rag, a shirt, a dull knife for shucking and whatever else got grabbed in the hurry of the moment. Edisto scurried like an anthill under a boot, leveled and revealed.

Rude as the Yankee threat, some slaves remained recalcitrant, sauntering, sleeping or sitting on porticos, on the marsh or in the yard. Most of the young mulattoes eased through that day into a niche newly opened, in which they would inherit the earth at last. They watched the changing of the guard. Julya waited in the yard, explaining to herself why breakfast was taken as it had been for a hundred years, but dinner was on the wing. To those fleeing, she admonished, "Jus' run off." The small federal force found her brewing tea the next morning in a three-gallon kettle, her morning chore. Cold and tired, they hailed Miss Julya Mikell in accordance with the new order. She poured carefully. Time had come today. With the federals and freedmen, she wandered the big house, sorting the finery, trying the divans and beds. In the portraits of the Mikell forbears she sought insight and the family likeness.

The soldiers recalled the fried mullet, shrimp and grits, cornbread and molasses of the last plantation up the coast, but Auntie Riah was gone. So Julya brewed more tea and told a sergeant that if a pig was caught, she'd cook it. The Yanks were city boys or dumb, chasing the pigs till all parties grunted, and the pigs scattered into the copse. Near dusk she remembered the old boar behind the curing shed. He'd do; the tumor on his neck could be cut out easy enough, and though bad legs had left him lying in the wallow wet or dry for a year or two, he'd hardly need to stand up over the coals. Fatback was a fondling who loved melon rinds and fish heads and grunted for a scratch or some greens. But time had come; her mentors must be fed.

Pleasantly facilitated by Isaac Mikell's brandy, the federals slit and hung the venerable swine by the hind feet. A few Black children came out laughing at the city boys with bayonets, ignorant of dressing a pig. The federals decapitated Fatback and hacked away till Julya stopped the carnage. Scolding and snatching a bayonet, she removed the nuts and returned the blade with the pork balls dangling. She knew what bohog trim could do for a man's spirit, but alas, the soldiers laughed. So she cursed the fools for opening Fatback before dipping and scraping. Once dipped in the boiling cauldron, Fatback hung again. Julya scraped bristles and asked who else needed a shave. The Yankees laughed again, and so she glowed. Gutted and trimmed, the old boar got staked over the embers, and evening settled with soldiers by the fire watching Julya tend the coals. At sunrise she poked the crust. The soldiers and freedmen who'd finished Isaac Mikell's brandy stirred and rose to the scent of seared hide. By noon Fatback's revenge was secure, his sinewy flesh tough and sour as shoe leather. So the federals left Edisto to the pace of yesterday.

Amazed and landed, the new gentry moved to the big house to begin life in earnest. The French collection was adorned, but the dresses constrained and affected the normal stroll to the creek, where the former slaves sat on the bank as paler ladies did that very moment by the Seine, albeit with less mud.

Daily life became a mission of gathering food and, with winter, staying warm. Mahogany and rosewood burned well through December. Hand hewn and hand crushed, it blazed, celebrating the liberation. That old furniture was too bulky anyway with so many folks residing in the big house, and it burned like a gift from the forbears. By January, unfurnished, the new residents had to haul dead wood in from the yard and chop it. Still, bitter cold seeped through nooks and broken windows that were covered with journals that had warned the master on the hazards of seminal pressure. Tawny hands now tacked those pages over drafty openings till the house matched its tenants, who moved through the dark like shades, though this afterlife was hungry and needful as that of the former flesh.

Net weaving remained with admirable skill in some. Gleaned cotton got spun, and lead weights were forged from pewter mugs. Some weights showed a sword hilt or a horse's head or a man's nose or a ship's bow, now ready to sail gracefully again, this time to settle in the mud around a few shrimp or mullet or crab. When the shrimp ran, a man could net a hundred pounds in an afternoon. Then all gathered at the cauldron.

When the planting families came home to Edisto in '65, squalor was in the air. The kitchen had been used as a cesspit and closed, once full. The new gentry hadn't needed a kitchen anyway; cooking was such a fuss, and anyone could do without. So don't complain of the stench since it was the formers who accounted for slavery in the first place. The new gentry solved hunger more efficiently, eating at the point of acquisition, felling palmetto trees for the bittersweet cabbage at the top. Downed trees lay strewn around the greensward thick as dead soldiers. Palmetto cabbage staved starvation till the tide ebbed for a shuck in the mud. The cloakroom was next closed, then the upstairs.

The worst of the filth showed up as smallpox on all who had stayed, so all were banished on the day the Mikells returned; banished from Point St. Pierre and Edisto Island, forbidden ever to return on pain of death. The Mikells sat among their mildewed columns and debris on the chipped steps. The women cried; if good help were hard to find before the Great Pandemonium, it'd be impossible after. The men spoke on the portico of the diligence that would be required for restoration and drank nothing.

The banished Negroes shuffled aimlessly, until Isaac Mikell's son, the unblemished, half-brother, cousin, uncle to the poxed minions of presumptive Mikells, called them down to the crib by the creek. Townsend Mikell told them to leave Edisto as they'd come, not as Mikells. Most Negroes who left with the family in '61 and returned to the old order in '65 would be allowed the name of Mikell and a wage, factoring expenses of course, because no man nor woman gets free room and board, no more, no how. Stipends would be minimal, but times were tough.

But with the tawdry yellows of Point St. Pierre, it simply could not be. Defeat was one thing, but releasing such a sordid tide upon humanity as Mikells would be worse. Yes, they would need a name and could call themselves Washington, Jefferson, Lincoln or Green. But they pressed Townsend to grant a name, to make it official, since Townsend, after all, was white.

Townsend Mikell said, "Cohen."

"Who?"

Townsend said it was all fixed with the man in Charleston, and he wrote it on paper: C-o-h-e-n. The Cohens were cousins from Beaufort, or close as cousins anyway, who'd moved inland after the Great Misfortune. Townsend asked for objections and a few new Cohens glanced about to see if dem jections was a good thing or a bad thing. Townsend laughed; assuring their fortune was changing for the better. The Beaufort Cohens had allowed their own slaves the family name, so what harm? An infected band of Negroes wandering about with Mikell on their lips could not be endured. Cohen, on the other hand, seemed convenient, acceptable and apropos. So Townsend Mikell walked over the bluff and back to the old home. The Cohens also turned from the creek and headed north, mumbling uncertainty or crying or simply falling into rhythm.

Walking to Babylon, they stepped free of bondage and this place that was, as far as they could see, used up. Northward seemed the right direction. A few died soon. Some quickly culled themselves from the mortally infected and moved apart. Some spoke of Johns Island, two islands up the barrier chain. A factional group veered off for Yonges Island to the northwest. Those remaining went for Wadmalaw, due north, since convenience and hospitality still seemed joined at the hip. And it would be easy, hardly a few days walk, if you don't count the river.

Two days tramped sadness and confusion into dust. Julya Cohen, née Mikell, had a few doubts but felt the peace of movement. Too many dead babies proved the damnation of Point St. Pierre. At the south bank of the Edisto River, only dark splotches remained of the pox. Festering up and down her arms and across her chest, it had eased out, leaving scars and a change of heart. She stared across the water without pride and not much to show of hope. Time had come and gone with nothing for it but the river, the river, the river yet to cross.

Strewn along the south bank, the refugees scanned. A current closely watched moved more swiftly than the distant surface had seemed. The tide was high, so they waited for ebb. But ebb revealed a hundred yards of mud between the migrants and the water. It oozed knee deep and deeper. They forged west, up to a narrow bend and rounded that to a thicket. They forged back to wait for the flood, knowing the flood would sweep them in, unless it was slack. Slack tide would last forty-five minutes or maybe an hour. Ebb tide would sweep them to sea.

Little waves lapped beyond the mud over an oyster bar and gained momentum to high water. They waited two hours but should have waited five. Holding hands, they stepped into the flood, the mud and current. A voice rose, *Walk me wid dem Jedus, you gawt a walk me....* Some sank in the mud. Buoyancy plucked some of them free. Some moved through the water more readily than others. The voice failed when the soloist sank, pulling two more links of the chain down with him. Grasps tightened to the end of the line, and the soloist emerged as another voice rose, *Yeah walk me...*but the chorus couldn't follow, because no seas cleaved for these wandering Cohens. It swallowed. Breaking up as the mud thinned below, the chain drifted apart. Some links disappeared, hands and feet flailing on the bully tide.

Julya sank but then crawled in the direction she hoped was up. At the surface with a gasp, she saw near the middle that the river was a lifetime wider than it seemed from the south bank. Choking and gasping all around her calmed, as she alone pulled for the far shore, making progress as flood slackened and stopped sweeping. Slack tide lasted a long time but not long enough, before the ebb gained momentum. Bobbing seaward, she pulled for the north bank till the water broke beside her with a great, toothy smile. But a porpoise, not a shark, chirped a brief hello, not to worry, except for choking and sinking.

Fifty years later, an old woman would dream of crawling from the river on hands and knees. Up the north bank, cut and bleeding but still breathing, up to the scatter of half-drowned Cohens. A few more arrived within the hour thoroughly drowned. The rest were not seen again. A man staggered east. The rest followed, this time sinking only ankle deep, as if the promise was holding with sawgrass. So they slogged east, as oysters hailed their passage, popping, squirting *hallelujah!*

At Ledinwah Creek the wandering Cohens sank again knee deep but pulled through and across, up and into the trees where night fell and they slept, up from the mud, too weary for weeping.

IX

Luzon

Mud sucks feet like sugar tits with a squish and a gurgle. Jim Cohen trudged down the bank and dug a dozen chowder clams to dice and cook in milk, pepper, butter and French's Mustard and call it clam chowder for dinner. That left supper unaccounted, so we lifted his bateau by the sides and slid it in and waded a bit deeper and climbed in. I sat between the oars but he ordered me forward; the bow seat was too small for him and would have nosed us too deep anyway under his weight. So I sat up front.

Never mind; I asked if the judge knew mullet from a surf trout, the small dogfish shark abundant in the tidal creeks, along with toadfish, catfish and stingray, none of which white people would eat, if they knew about it. Did the judge know scallop from stingaree? Did Jim? He laughed, umphing us farther in till we floated. I suggested we try for spottail bass under the old creek house dock, but he spun us the other way and kept us shallow, out of the current. Upstream a ways, we crossed and drifted as he rigged a fresh shrimp on a hand line and jigged off the bottom. He gave me the line and steered us over some eddies where a fish took and tugged till my fingers stung then came up like a dead weight—juvenile hammerhead, two feet. She rolled over and bit the line in two with a grin. "Yeah," Jim said, handing another hook as shells clawed our bottom.

He pulled seaward near slack ebb out to where the Edisto River joins Ledinwah Creek. Near the bank in slow water, he reached back for a rag so I could wrap my hand in the wet, smelly thing before dropping the new bait over. In a hundred more yards we snagged the bottom but kept moving till I yelled for a knife, and the fish dove and hung tight as a snag. So we sat. Jim worked the oars easy, explaining, "Dem drum."

The fish towed us a stretch till I wrestled it in. Jim estimated forty pounds and chopped the tail off to show the squigglies in the meat, worms or veins. He didn't give a shit; that fish was three bags of groceries, or four. We drifted home while the black drum died, silver and black bars all going gray. It was a day like the old man described, fishing in shallow water long, long ago, when a snake dropped from a bough overhead between himself and young Jim Cohen at the oars. Jim grabbed the shotgun the judge carried when fishing for sharks, in case of a shark too big to manage. Firing both barrels from the hip, he shot the snake in two, thereby sinking the bateau. I asked how the judge took the sinking and the close call on his nuts, and if a Black man's nuts really do turn to jelly at the sight of a snake, because he thinks every snake is a rattler.

Jim Cohen went screw-faced as the old man, focusing on so far back. "Dey I be. Dat rattuh snek wid dem cawton in e mouf…." And so on, the thrashing fear of the snake's head, fangs bared, till it drifted out and sank, tide turning, moon rising, and through it all Jim keeping the shotgun dry. I couldn't call him a lying sonofabitch in his own boat, so I didn't point out that a man treading water couldn't keep a shotgun dry. He said, "Shi…." and spat overboard. He said any man who thinks a snake isn't a rattler is a fool or white one and waddled up the bank with the clams, as little waves washed his tracks away behind him. On firmer footing, he stopped to watch my struggle with a twenty-pound fish and nothing for it but a hug against my last clean shirt. He pointed yonder and said: There. There the first Cohens crossed Ledinwah Creek; up under the trees is where they slept, and right below that, where oyster shells barely show over the first of the flood tide, is where they went back to the river at dawn to eat.

Back up at the house, he opened and quartered the clams and a few spuds and onions into a pot of milk with a stick of butter and peppered the mix like pepper was a vitamin supplement, recalling that one man forged the river with a hatchet in his belt, which he used to knock the sharp edges off the oysters in the shallows so the others could pick, pry and eat, a tedious task but better than none. Reasonable people don't eat summer oysters. So Jim walked to the door to spit past the front stoop for the foul taste his forbears had endured. He asked, "Y'eat dem summa awshtuh?" I assured him I did not. He pressed on: You ever wonder what you might eat? He poured in more milk and a cup of French's Mustard. For the occasion he laid on some fatback. He scaled the last six inches of that forty-pound fish, cut it off, filleted it from the backbone, cut it to one-inch cubes and tossed them in the pot. We simmered with another taste of sweetwine.

Bellies full, they lay in the shade, digesting hardship and miles till dusk cut the heat. The hatchet man climbed a palmetto, hacked out the cabbage inside, and dropped it to waiting hands, but it was eaten before he climbed down. So he climbed another and hacked and ate it in the tree, calling down to the others below, *Eat dem awshtuh.* So they did.

Dawn cut the mosquitoes. Some shuffled down for oysters. Some ambled into the forest in a refugee tide that scattered along the north bank of the Edisto on the south side of Wadmalaw, then elbowed sideways like crabs claiming bottom. Their clearings sprouted lean-to shacks that would grow into four-wall shacks with roofs and sometimes floors. But time moved slow. Julya stayed with Nat the hatchet and his woman Bet, the last three of the original band to remain by the creek. Eating summer oysters and palmetto cabbage morning and evening, they agreed to set out again tomorrow to meet their fate. So again, they slept under the trees, until a squall woke Julya. She huddled into a live oak crook, hoping *Mist Cotton Mouf won' be feelin' hongry in dem rain.* She couldn't sleep but woke at first light, wet and alone. She sat and waited, without guidance, short on hope, waking the fifth morning unmoved. Hunger moved her on the sixth day, not knowing what to eat, heading north and then east before turning back south, her path springing up behind her.

Tired and bruised, she lay down at dusk, hungry and forlorn but soon sleeping deep. She woke in pitch dark, the forest slinking and buzzing until dawn, when the morning birds called the all clear. In the shallow mist she wondered how far away were oysters and which way. She walked southeast. A yearling pine in her path, dead and brittle could easily be stepped on, but she stopped on a whimper, wide-eyed at the creature moving toward her. Big and fearless it grumbled, "Hareehaa!"

She jumped back, and the creature spoke, *Wha fo you tek dem yiddah tree'n stompum down? Dis heah blong Luzon! Who you be?* Thick as an oak but smooth as a snake with muscles like a panther, he shook his head and raised a fist to claim dominion over all this and the weaker forms. She turned away but a Black hand turned her back as a calmer voice grumbled, *Wha fo you mek fuh leave?* He jumped around her. *Wha fo you go? Whea be's fuh you? Wha you gwine eat? Wha fo you go?*

Julya peered into the thicket. He laughed, *Ha!* He curled an arm around her shoulder, squeezed too hard and asked again, *Wha fo you go?* Squeezing again, he led her to a clearing with a shelter in the center and into it. Two rudimentary walls of palmetto fronds bound with vines to a live oak were roofed with fronds too. Over a mound of dead coals sat a black skillet and beside that were a dozen tins with no labels and many spices spilled from their linen to mix in the bottom of the box. She stooped in and looked out. Two walls and a roof and a man with a knife now stabbing a tin— beans—made sense, even if he wasn't light skinned. He laughed, adding beans to the pot licker. She lifted the spice box and smelled gentler time, well fed and happy in the big house kitchen. She sniffed, nearly tearful. Luzon saw joyful acceptance and pounced again, this time with a silk pouch of life everlasting, also known as rabbit tobacco, a favorite smoke for youth and poor people through the centuries, or it could be steeped for tea called life everlasting. He pulled a sterling pot from a dark recess. Mud crumbled from it by exhortation and his hands. He added water from another pot, though she hadn't seen fresh water for days. In exchange for a home, she gave Luzon a name. He neither wanted nor needed one, especially not the Allston one, but after saying Cohen aloud for a week, he would not leave the shelter without it. Julya and Luzon remained bonded for forty years, not what was known as an item in town, or what was also called shacking up or common law, but bonded in the more biblical and most holy sense.

Luzon Cohen was blue black, and thereby was able to leave the Allston's home at Rockville, the summer village on Bohicket Creek. Known there as the most shiftless darky a family could ever buy into, he could bare his teeth to prove undiluted lineage from Africa, the only source of blue gum Negroes. On a few nights of waning moon, he joined the darkness and became free. Near the end of The Great Calamity, the Allstons stopped using the Rockville house as they had before the war. Leisure time was less available in a civil conflagration, with decent help so hard to find. Luzon couldn't see much point in staying, when he could starve to death well enough on his own. So he crawled under the portico one day with his box of tins and spices and waited for dark. The creek flowed green to silver. The sun dipped in, sizzled pink and set. The flow went silver to gray and then black and so did the night. Sitting cross-legged, naked, palms down, mouth shut with the box sat behind him, sheltered from stray light, nothing remained but his eyes, which he closed. He'd not hoed nor repaired the rotten risers on the back porch nor gathered vegetables nor chopped wood. The porches remained unswept and the yard cluttered with windfall.

Miss Elizabeth got sorely shrill at one so shiftless, mean-spirited and downright worthless as Luzon, sticking her head under the porch where he liked to hide. He held his breath. "Luzon! You in there?"

No; he had only to breathe with his eyes closed, even as they ached to open on the mocking white faces and pointing fingers surely waiting for the crazy naked slave under the porch. She yelled again, "Luuu-zon!" She saw. She knew. He felt it. "Git on out here! Git out here right now!" He stayed shut until tears rolled and he feared they'd sparkle, but she stepped back and said, "I swear, he's suh damn black you couldn't see him in there any how."

She walked away, and soon he crawled out from under and walked into the woods, as she and a few neighbors and other Negroes pursued in a half-hearted hunt. When they thought they heard something, he stooped over his box and closed his eyes. Backing into the trees like a commoner taking leave from a king, he turned and ran the last hundred feet when the torches got lit.

Luzon often told of his private emancipation, filigree gaining length and stature until his hair turned white and wouldn't fit under his hands. Till he was long past apprehension, he sat cross-legged, palms on knees, mouth shut, eyes closed, more of a meditation on his exodus than a practical defense. Luzon and Julya would share forty years before Luzon's eyes stayed closed. Forty years marked their walk from the mud to what they knew as civilization. When Luzon died in '05, Julya recounted the years for whoever might listen or the breeze wafting across her rocker.

The first year brought *de sparit*, as the anomalous virgin learned respect for her husband's patience and compassion, learning thereafter that Luzon's greatness as a man came mostly from his benign indifference. She slept outside, three feet away. Luzon left and returned the next day with a live coal wrapped in a frond. He'd gone to Rockville, invisible in daytime, now the war was done, and he plucked a coal off the fire easy as you please. He stacked oyster shells in a circle around it and lay kindling over it, topping off with Spanish moss and faggots. When flames rose, he threw her tattered smock over her head, wrestled her to her stomach and spared her the view of his sincerity. No longer anomalous to her age, she squealed. He heard rapture, and they were wed, such as it was, man and wife, to love and honor and do as you're told till you're dead. He stoked the fire and kept it burning through the night.

The second year brought four walls, a door and an iron pot with four feet, so she brewed again from sassafras.

The third year brought Rozetta, who died that year, as Luzon built a bed and began an addition that would be the main dwelling.

Near the end of the fourth year Asa was born. She grew strong, and before too long, the shack was done, and Jefferson came along, first child born in the shack.

Mose was born in the sixth year and lived.

In the seventh year came a child stillborn. The father named him Luzon for his perfect stillness and held the dead baby up and closed his own mouth and eyes to show the likeness. Julya wept.

Soon after baby Luzon, newspaper went onto the walls of the shack as it came available, layered into the next century until the newspaper and marsh mud and sometimes flour paste held the shack up. The covering stopped with color comics, whose beauty defied covering.

In the eighth year, Dan was born, one of three brothers and two sisters to reach maturity from eleven starts. When Dan was two in the tenth year, Luzon ran a stovepipe for a hearth, and the Cohens were warm in winter. Julya made a kitchen and learned to cook. Luzon built a table in the ninth year from wreckage planks hauled from the river.

Cora was born and died.

Tyra was conceived and born in the tenth year, the last child to survive though three more were born: Oree in the eleventh died that year; Dessie in the twelfth died that year; Lila in the thirteenth died in the fifteenth of yellow fever. The other children fevered but survived.

In the eleventh year Luzon carried the benches to the yard and set chairs around the table, ladder-backs also built from planking. Julya gathered spices, blending garlic and wild scallion and called it biddy tea, since it tasted like the chicken broth Auntie Riah once brewed. She found bay laurel and gagged on berry tea but then hung the pungent leaves from the eaves for thirty years. She found basil and planted it near the shack. She was given okra in the fourteenth year and planted it too in time for okra gumbo on Christmas at the end of the fever.

By the sixteenth year the gumbo lost its slime when she learned vinegar and planted apple cuttings for two years before one lived and became a tree that bore fruit in the twentieth year. She picked rabbit tobacco, stripping the leaves from the stems with thumb and forefinger for a tea that took the place of sassafras and was called life everlasting.

𝓍

Dan and Lena

By the sixteenth spring Luzon sold oysters and learned that cash currency was no different than the handwritten scrip he got from the man at the Rockville Store. Two thousand feet of quarter-inch line knotted every three feet cost the two-dollar scrip the man had written for ten bushels. Another fifty-cent scrip bought the bull tongue, or what the man called bull tongue but was more than buckets of bull tongues. It was cow tongues too, and lips, eyeballs, noses and spleens looking to crawl out the buckets braying stink like an ass, whose tongue and gizzards were likely in there too. The Cohens then saved their cooter guts, chicken necks and feet, possum bellies and snakeheads for wrapping in cloth that got tied onto the knotted line.

Night fell on the fetid reeking buckets as the Cohen clan gathered round. Luzon unwound and passed seven knots of longline around the circle to Julya, Dan, Mose, Tyra, Asa, Jefferson and back to Luzon. They reached for the bull's tongue and wrapped a hundred times seven lumps of bait and tied them on.

At dawn, he loaded the bateau, rowed out Bohicket to Ledinwah to the Edisto River and floated the ebb out to where the crabs still stayed in early spring. He anchored the line and buoyed it with a hand-painted jug, then drifted two thousand feet, hand-over-handing overboard. He buoyed the bitter end, then rode back easy on the first of the flood and out again near dusk, ebb again. He pulled in a crab or two on most knots till the crabs scrambled ankle deep in the bateau, and he laughed out loud at the rising moon. The next day he traded crabs for another longline and twice as much bull's tongue.

Sharks took three lines the sixteenth summer. But Luzon had money and sat up late, thinking, sometime till sunrise.

In 1886 he became a farmer. He bought plowshares and a coulter and laid out rows, a hundred-feet long. He squared the field and cleared it and stole a moldboard and made a harness from old hides. He traded two rows' yield in advance for the use of a mule and planted more basil and okra. The crop was blighted and infested, but he bought his own mule in the twenty-first year. Asa moved to Charleston that year to work domestic for a dollar a week at the Pringle house in town. They vacationed at Rockville and knew Asa to be as dependable as could be expected.

Mose sailed the next year on a Connecticut shad schooner to Savannah. He was sixteen and fished forty years before coming home in '28, three days before his mother died, then went back to his family in Guadeloupe, in the French West Indies.

Jefferson picked tomatoes the year Mose first left, then followed corn to Johns Island. He picked melons inland till they played out, so he bought a machete and headed out behind the long sugar cane harvest the next spring and never came home.

Three years' toll of three children left the shack quiet. Luzon gathered less and farmed eight rows instead of twenty. Still, by the twenty-sixth year he had more money than he needed, so when Dan proclaimed his yen for Lena Hope, Luzon planned a wedding. Julya boiled yams. She cut onions into collards and field peas, cow peas, black-eyed peas, snap beans, butter beans, lima and string beans. She cut fatback into parsnips and turnips and blended okra gumbo with cooter soup and served it in the cooter shells. Diamondback terrapins were plentiful in the area then and had no future in the long term because of their availability, their protein content and the convenience of their shells as soup bowls.

She baked cornbread and bought a keg of molasses for the cornbread and then again for the boiled yams. Luzon fried mullet, whiting, bass, shark and a dozen eels in the yard cauldron. Two hundred people came to celebrate. The spirit of generosity and abundance made Dan and Lena's wedding a social benchmark on that side of Wadmalaw. In appreciation and reciprocal generosity, Dan gave his father two blue tick pups that began Luzon's coondog business. Dan also crafted a sign that hung out back for the proverbial coon's age:

CONeDOg FOr SALe FOr reNT WILL TrADe

Dan walled in his sleeping area and re-planked an old bateau half again bigger than Luzon's, which economy of scale was plain to see. He sank it again to swell and seal then rowed to the best beds over on Edisto. He went early or late, timing his effort to the tide, pulling hard against the ebb to gain time up the creek, where he picked two small mountains of oysters fore and aft. One mound filled his needs and the other was pure gravy, so to speak. Such industry could get a man ahead but left him a hard row back to the fork, against the flood. He rowed harder yet to swing deep, into the stronger current, to clear the shoal jutting from the point. Once rounded and centered on the tributary, he could relax on a sweet drift home.

In a single season Dan's back stooped, and he hunchbacked down the street, by that time lined with shacks, from where Luzon first bound fronds to a sapling. Dan walked like an old man, his arms bulky with muscles to twice their natural size. He sometimes twitched, itchy to engage their horsepower on a heavy oar.

By his second season, Dan was legend. White buyers from Charleston in shirts and pants waited to pay cash money for Oyster Man's select whitefoot oysters. Prosperity rose as a measure of bushels, his for the picking. His father smoked rabbit tobacco on the porch as Oyster Man described wealth like a far-away place. Dan reckoned oysters more dependable than crabs, because *dey be's whea dey is, widdout no running 'bout it. Dey be foun' money, layin' deah fuh de pick'um up.* He shared his insight, that success means money flowing free as water in a creek. In anticipation, he prepared for success with a new Dutch oven for a dollar and a dozen pre-packed spices for another dollar and two calico dresses on the installment plan for two more dollars owed, plus interest. Lena prepared for birthing.

Oyster Man paid what he could to the white man in Rockville for boards, nails and tin sheets. He hired two men and began his own house on the far side of the garden. He stopped for oyster season and Lena's miscarry. She urged him on, and the house was done by mid-'94 in time for oyster season.

Tyra turned nineteen and moved to Church Creek with her new husband, John Bohne.

Dan and Lena moved across the garden and soon had enough money for a pot-belly stove from Charleston, half down, and only two bushels a week on the balance. They bought new clothes and pondered a new wagon, so Dan might carry his own oysters into town, where surely they'd bring more money on a direct sale. Lena swelled again. They talked of what to buy and the new way of buying, in which you don't have to wait till you're old to enjoy a thing. Julya sat up late, watching the new house across the garden.

Oyster Man rounded the bend pulling hard against the tide and the load that grew with each trip, his stroke often licking the last inch of freeboard, which made him laugh in fear and reverence; that last inch representing the fine thin line between buoyancy and sinking. And he rowed homeward on faith and goodwill for the power flowing beneath him. He could beach easy on a reverse current, but on two occasions a late ebb on a westerly breeze bucked the flood and kept him out overnight. When bigger waves came in, he chucked the load overboard and knew that a smart man lives longer.

But an ambitious man will take a risk, and he might as well chuck dollars overboard as ditch whitefoot beauties. In his fourth season, soon after acquiring an eight-place setting for four dollars down, Dan gave back a load so he could get home. Dropping these oysters in a pile in water as close to the yet-exposed bank as he dared, for easy re-gather, he bought back five inches of freeboard, but alas was already too deep in deficit spending. Five inches could not fend those waves, so all debts got settled on waves breaking three feet and coming over the gunwales with foreclosure. Dan learned about caution and downside of risk with his mouth and eyes agape. He drowned.

Oyster Man's body floated up the creek on the flood and back down a mile before snagging near the Ledinwah confluence and stayed aground with the falling tide. Marcus Seabrook found it and towed it home to the loamy landing on Ledinwah Creek and called out: *Tell Luzon e boy e drown. Tell Juya she son e gone.* When his bateau rasped sand he pulled the body in by its towline, and in minutes Wadmalaw knew: Oyster Man be dead. Julya walked to the little landing, saw her son, looked down Ledinwah Creek, looked up to the gray sky and fell to her knees.

The body was carried home, where Luzon cut up two benches for material to build the coffin. Neighbors brought more planks to finish the job. He nailed to nightfall and bade the neighbors go on home, so he could be alone with his son. In the coffin, Dan's knees rose above the gunwales. His feet curled over and the arms squeezed out too. *Dan be's layin straight. Be's layin straight.* Luzon repeated these words to make them come to pass, until lo and behold, Dan fit into place, once Luzon broke the leg bones with the blunt side of his ax, smashed the knees and broke the arms too. Dan looked more peaceful, fitting in. Luzon stood in the doorway to say Dan be's ready. The women carried their chairs outside. They helped Julya to sit out near the fire and the coffin, and the vigil began on low moans.

A mourner spotted Oyster Man in the smoke; the others saw him too, just there *twix' dem flame* tumbling to Hell. They lamented the fall, giving voice to the dead souls gone before, who spoke now through their children. Seeking a common timbre but avoiding harmony, their discord eerily scored the misty chaos. Some bayed. Some shouted what they saw. Some called out at Oyster Man coughing up oysters he'd taken from their homes and eaten—*Puke! dem awshtuh.* Oyster Man gave up his life's fare of cooters *'n dem rattuh snek 'n all dem fush 'n stingaree 'n soif trout and all dem po misfotunate crab 'n clam folk too.* Then came the others, possums to periwinkles, squirrels, rabbits and shorebirds, all purged, so Oyster Man could get his name back. Julya spoke it softly.

Dan locked spirits with the devil and looked good, young and strong. The devil was tricky, so they grappled to the wee hours, the mourners finally hooting at the turning tide. Dan stood over the fallen one: *E whup de debil! Whup um, Dan!*

Near dawn, the vigil and fire played down to embers, moans and groans. At first light a woman ended the bout with a song:

Angel roll de stone away.
Angel roll de stone away.
On a bright new Sundy mawnin'
Angel roll de stone away.

Oh, yondah come de Angel
By de breakin ob de day
E bring good news fum Heab'm
Angel roll de stone away.

The women sang in harmony at sunrise, except for Julya, who wept. Dan was ready.

At the funeral, Luzon closed his eyes and afterward shuffled the street wearily, till he sat on the porch and smoked. Lena whimpered like the young girl she was, not yet eighteen, but her grief before the funeral gave way to fear after, facing her last month of pregnancy alone. She feared solitude and hardship. She feared the omens.

Don' bode no good, Julya murmured, sorting those omens to better sense how things might change. She boiled water in the big skillet on the hearth and added rabbit tobacco so life everlasting could steep and steam. *Don' bode no good*, she told the empty cup, filling it, carrying it out to Luzon, who winced again.

Formal condolences gave way directly to birthing preparation, on into Christmas. Callers brought sympathy and birthing aids. Most brought linen-wrapped spider webs taken from hearth cornices for warmth and from rafters over the bed for potency. Spider silk would hasten clotting, as necessary. A few brought ergot tea to induce labor. Julya arranged these things near the swathing.

Luzon walked to Rockville for laudanum in a vial. He dripped it onto his thumb, still swollen from impacts suffered on coffin nailing. He drank the rest to feel good. He returned to

Rockville for a bottle of laudanum, the tincture, pledging to pay bushels as necessary, because this was a critical time. The man at the Rockville store stared at Luzon and granted a half nod, making history by issuing credit.

By New Year, Lena showed no sign, which was a sign unto itself, and so she remained in a purgatory of her own. On January third, the sun rose in a cold, blue sky. Ergot tea would be given by the rise of the new moon. It couldn't get any clearer. Haggard and weak, Lena moved little and spoke less but assured that little Dan would come home today. Julya poured a teaspoon of black tea, ergot, down Lena's gullet and held her jaw tight against the spew. Lena bolted, fading dull as the iron pot, but anyone would; this was no convulsion. By dark she weakened. Julya wept into full throated sobs, pouring another dose of tea and another, stroking Lena's neck to make her swallow. Lena shuddered as the sheet moistened and turned red.

With her ear to Lena's mouth, Julya felt nothing. Like a sorceress conjuring one last spell, she crawled under her own bed for the Mason jar that held the goose quill and snuffbox. With a pinch of snuff on the back of her hand she held it behind the feather and bent to Lena. Inhaling softly, she blew the snuff so it sifted through the feather onto the Lena's face. Lena moaned. Julya blew harder, and with a sudden, voracious inhale interrupted halfway by a sneeze, Lena sneezed again and again, eyes open over a whimper and a squeal. The mattress flooded. The great mound moved, and Julya moved down to receive. In short order, it was free, breathing gently beside Lena, her comatose face beaded with droplets of melted frost fetched by her silent father-in-law.

Luzon spoke at last after a dozen trips to the frosted grass. Pulling the swathing to reveal the infant as male, he said, *Dis yiddah beeby look like Dan. Call um Dan.*

Lena quivered, perhaps with approval. Then she died. *No*, Julya insisted. *Call um Jim.*

XI

Jim Cohen

Jim Cohen laughed; to think, he could cause such a fuss and not even be born yet. I concurred, especially in view of the fuss he caused for the next seventy years, meaning the whole Negro commotion—I meant that to be a joke, which seemed obvious to me. He didn't laugh but looked up like a duck in a downpour, saying he caused no fuss whatever after that first one, and the commotion I alluded too *wan't nothing to do wid dem Black folk. It wan't no mo'n a passel o' white folk sortin' dey trouble.* That's how he saw it, because a Black man minding his own business out on Wadmalaw had no reason but to get on with folks.

I hadn't intended the tar brush and regretted my ill-timed and obscure jocularity. I was one of those folks who depended on the foibles of others to explain personal trouble, but then no clan is ever free of picking its way through the mud and sharp shells.

I pointed out that next to his history, mine seemed uneventful. And there I was, rendering mine simpler still, moving from the urbane to the rural, or from the paved area surrounded by circled wagons back out to the bush. But simplicity is a delusion. I suffered social fatigue; the place I came from was mannerly, polite, well groomed and alert.

I was a top-drawer representative of those things till they turned on me, or till I realized who I was, or maybe what I'd inherited, or the source of my discomfort or some such. It wasn't the town's fault. I'd made my own trouble, first in life, then in marriage. Then I closed the show with alcoholism. But I was done with drink surely as I was done with living in town. Eudora was a bump in the road ten miles back. And my saturation at that moment was merely a phase, a swan dive into a ditch before climbing back onto the wagon for the long ride home.

I knew what underscored my migration to the boonies, even as I would have denied my flight, even as the seed germinated, its threadlike roots cracking the foundations of my heart and mind, finding at last something to quench my parched soul—something tangible, way past scotch. A man may well need deconstruction down to rudiments prior to a rebuild.

I returned to my place on Queen Street to see what might draw me back or what had held me there or if any iota might inform the bond I'd so believed in for what had been my entire life to date. Those quiet rooms with their tall windows, drafty as a sieve, and ceilings high enough to accommodate a passing squall, seemed to echo my wonder. I'd spent hours outdoors on Wadmalaw engaging in life itself, unmindful of the cold. Yet for two days back in town, in the presumed security of the family abode, I chilled to the bone. My joints squeaked and creaked along with the floor joists, unless I stood still, looking out the windows to see if I hadn't missed something. I gathered a change of clothes, some toiletries, my rubber boots, a hat and some odds and ends along with the rest of my booze, which was the ready reserve and not the private reserve, because the Mohicans rarely ever go away. I gave Fern a drink and headed back out.

Hauling the rest of the booze was only practical in my view, given the practicality of the thing and recognizing Jim's soulful appreciation in that shut-eyed blissful moan of his. I didn't feel generous but once again reciprocal, unable to say what he'd given me but feeling things change. After a few days on the island, I was struck by the convenience available in my own bathroom and kitchen, so simple and clean. Yet relieved and sustained, I could also sense the greater difference between the rural and the civilized; one was set in stone while the other changed every day in beautiful patterns.

I would call my return to town rigorous and occasionally chilling during those two days. Wearing the hail-fellow happy face, if not the khaki suit, the wing tips and the sky-blue, button-down, oxford-cloth shirt, I assured friends and associates in passing that no, I had not "gone native on us," explaining as necessary and then some that a man needs a reprieve now and then. I responded in the tentative, bordering on affirmative, when asked if I'd found whatever I'd been looking for at the judge's funeral. Smug sonsabitches; as if they'd know what that might be, whether I told them or not.

Mr. Hughes Boyd Thomas asked if it was true, that I was staying out to Wadmalaw with the niggers, right in their damn houses and such. I hadn't known Hughes Thomas other than to exchange gratuities at the club, but I filled my eyes with the stocky little man, taking him in slowly, head to foot. What could I do, be angry? He'd likely never burned a cross or thrown bricks through windows. I suppose he got an eyeful of me too, allowing, "Hey, man, you do whatever you want, don't mean shit to me. I just.... You know."

So I told him, "Yes. It's true."

He served up one of those half-lit smiles to convey his mournful wonder, as if to say, *Aw, bubba....* And he walked away. I wanted to call after him but couldn't muster the energy or skill to summarize what I'd learned, that two shabby Black boys in a jive car were in fact descendents of a survival saga to make your hair curl. He knew what they were and wouldn't be told otherwise.

Little dramas played out, some calling for my opinion, as if to challenge the point I'd more or less put forth, for my own good. That is, my friends expressed concern those days over my, shall we say, peculiarity. Peculiarity is a catchall ailment in town, diagnosing them for whom eccentricity is innate as well as them who may swing precariously, on the verge of unhinging. But if a man of recordable background has a phase of doubt and confusion, he might ought to know that his friends are right there to call on in his time of need. I appreciated the sentiment and took the sincerity at face value, yet hearing this pledge of support, I wondered why I hadn't called on them but instead found solace in the old Black fellow who sold gleaned produce from his car out on Savannah Highway.

I did not know the answer to the questions of peculiarity and friendly support, except that I'd failed to imagine what support might be offered in town that could be significantly different from what I'd experienced there in the prior fifty-eight years. I'd be a fool not to value their assurance that I remained among kith and distant kin, despite my unannounced and indefinite removal to the marshlands. So turning the happy face inward, I resolved to keep that assurance in my pocket, in case I might need it sometime.

And in a mere matter of moments, I pulled it out, confiding in a chance encounter with Peter Maxwell, of the Greenville Maxwells, but still a sterling fellow in spite of his parents' relocation to the Holy City only fifty years prior, that yes, I may appreciate very much the support of friends in this time of, shall we say, retreat. That is, Peter Maxwell was one of eight or twelve men who maintained the Wadmalaw Hunt Club, a wood structure painted green with a tin roof, twenty by twenty with a wood stove, four bunk beds, a sink, a water closet and two electrical outlets.

Four or five times a year these men would spend a long weekend there staying drunk, smoking Cuban cigars and trying not to shoot each other in their staggering efforts to shoot Bambi's mother, or, into the second night, Babar's wife. But the cabin had remained unused since Orian Hale took his secretary there for what he called some private dictation. His wife Helen (a.k.a Helen of Coy) followed him, flat out picked up the scent a day in advance and sniffed him on out to the cabin and waited outside right up to *de moment inflagránte, Yo Honah*, then walked in snapping photographs, providing happy grist for the mill in town that grinded it out for weeks in juicy speculation of what Helen was thinking, taking pictures, which was better for Orian than shooting him with a gun. Further speculation rose on the question of whether her shots were vertical or horizontal format.

Orian lost everything in the divorce proceeding but was allowed to keep his print shop in town, which he called his job, claiming she'd never want that. What would she do with it? Work it?

He rose in general esteem in town that Christmas. In self-deprecating and glorious gratitude, he raised a toast among the already-toasted at a brimful Hibernian Hall, regretting he had but one wife to give for his country. Orian Hale proved that a man's dexterity can turn the tide of public sentiment on a good one-liner. Moreover, the Hunt Club was tainted evermore as a trysting spot and therein became off limits to those members with a keen instinct for discretion, making it right for me.

So I asked Peter what he thought about me using the place, say for a month. He didn't say a word but smiled warmly with a half nod as he reached into his pocket for his keys and removed a small one and handed it over. He said it fit the Master Lock on the door, and don't worry; he'd tell the fellows not to go out there without making some noise or something. I begged off as required, insisting that you can't keep people from their place. He said,

"Nah! You make better use of it anyway. You might want a cooler. Don't have a fridge."

So I threw some sheets and blankets and a pillow in the car but went back in for some books and my house slippers and a few more shirts and my tennie pumps. I drove on down to the K Mart for a cooler but then realized I had no easy access to ice, so I sprang eighty dollars for a small fridge and set it up for a delivery, though I couldn't really say how to get there other than go to Rockville, hang a left, a right and another left along the creek and look for a green cabin. I hoped the Hunt Club wouldn't mind my contribution and doubted they would.

Back at my place for a final tally of needs and supplies, I had to pause over the finality of this purview. I was headed maybe forty minutes out of town. So why did I feel like tomorrow I'd cast off for parts unknown? I marveled once more at my discomfort on the verandah, with nothing to occupy my hands and mind, like a drink or some chit chat. So I had a beer.

You still get a beautiful sunset in town along with songbirds, though fewer in winter, and clean air, though nature's blessings seem abruptly pre-empted by buildings and pavement and the man-made veneration that goes along with that sort of thing. I pondered chitchat and thanked my stars that day for the only dialogue audible on my own verandah, which was a friendly exchange in question-and-answer format between Fern and me. You want to go? It's small and has a wood stove. I didn't go so far as to hear him answer, but I figured his preference. Next thing you know it's looking like the Wadmalaw hillbillies, save the rocker on top. I draped Fern around the rearview and damn near felt like a family on the go together.

Maybe I had gone native. I wanted to get back out there, like something waited for the finding, but I wouldn't find it unless I went. I stopped off for some candles and a lamp and some wood for the stove. And a sleeping bag, in case it was too cold. And a coffeemaker and some groceries.

I got back out there with an hour of daylight left, in time to see that the marshland stays busy as a boulevard in rush hour, if you gear down and see it. Soon enough, you look up to a weather pattern as something more than the basis for prognostication at street level as prelude to cocktails. Out yonder, free of interruption, I could watch the clouds cleave in deference to an overbearing squall line, with presumptuous thunderheads moving in. That felt refreshing, once I learned patience and stillness, country style. I could wake up to the ion charge in the hair on my arms followed straight away by a chill popping head to toe. It was only stray static charging up a conductivity conduit but felt more like myself changing, molting, bursting forth and shedding the old carapace. I wondered if a soul can outgrow itself, but I couldn't sit there still for as long as I wanted to because of the greater want to feather the nest and get comfortable. Didn't take long.

Amazed again at the expedience of a man's change in life, I took to the flats the very next day, sipping a tumbler of Teacher's for the prerequisite expedience, which was getting rid of the last of the liquor so it would be gone forever and new times could begin in earnest. I told Jim Cohen I was an alcoholic in recovery, explaining that the nature of the ailment is that the alcoholic diagnosis has no cure, because nobody ever found one, so recovery lasts as long as the alcoholic lasts. But I'd decided with a clear mind to accept this brief regression to facilitate the current transition, so I could sort out what else ailed me besides getting rid of the liquor. Jim stared at me until I offered two fifths, which he took with a tick of the head, either in gratitude or to underscore his assurance, me that if a mind was clear, it was already sorted. *If a man be clear....* Clarity in this case defaulted to *his* dictate.

I enumerated the variable complexity between mud grubbing on the one hand and more evolved social, political and career matrices on the other. I mean, one may be clear, so to speak, for sorting and the other not. Of course that analysis echoed the sophistry I'd suffered for decades in equal measure to the sauce. Still, his superiority in our mutual understanding could be a bone of contention. I tried not to be generous as antidote to my own superiority (not to be confused with supremacy, though deriving from similar distortion). Then again, why shouldn't I challenge *his* sophistry, if all things were equal?

I frankly wished him a clear view on his insistence: "Dey ain' no two way bout'um. " And I told him so. Oh, but he knew about recovering alcoholics; they were only recovering as long as they laid off the sauce; otherwise, "dey be's relaxing."

"You mean relapsing."

"Yeah."

Make no mistake, Jim Cohen could tell the difference between screw-top sherry and premium scotch, and therein he recognized a phase of his own, in which top-drawer liquor was pouring for the drinking hardly a step and a stumble from his porch. He joined me often as not but could not hold pace with a conditioned toddy tipper such as myself. No shame in that; a novice needs time and practice to achieve journeyman skills—this glib assessment was more accurate than might be perceived from afar. The age of realization brings certain tastes, commonly called acquired tastes, though they seem to compensate life's general demeanor so concisely that the acquisition may be automatic to many. You age; you drink. The reason our Lowcountry region is so absorbent on a historical basis may be conjectural. Some hold with the alcoholic gene theory; others say the sultry air and slow pace demand fortification if not courage. Others pshaw all theories, saying that a place so social will drink more. Jim Cohen disproved this social theory. No less social than the next man, his society was that of a country man bearing warm tidings to all things met, including the next man he met, though that man may be a few tides and some time since the last man met. He was thirsty and outside the daily flow in town.

One more theory I felt held water was that of abundant beauty; with such a high baseline of aesthetic pleasure, a person needs external stimulation to get higher. Whether this was merely alcoholic rationale doesn't matter; it worked. But the real cause for so much drinking was a blend of all these theories plus any others you'd care to conjure. The place is sultry, egregiously social and aggressively hospitable, with so many house-and-garden showplaces open on a regular basis to show what the habitants have done, that you get drawn in and handed a generous libation as part of the show, with audience participation required.

Forty miles south, on the other hand, with such beauty abounding, a man could take his leave from all that falderal and repetitive spew of words without end. He could go home and drink alone on his own veranda, because solitude was never so warm and friendly as nestled there among the live oaks and Spanish moss with the scent of wisteria turning the mind to sweetness and nothing but. Jim Cohen shook his head and shrugged. *Da's what I tryna tell you!*

So we drank the last of the good stuff, Jim and I, sitting out by the flats, enjoying what we loved in equal measure, meaning the hooch, the sea and sky and all the creatures in between, among whom we played our part. The sauces loosened him up, I thought. I didn't then suspect ulterior motive in his relentless tale, yet perceived the yarn spinning out and piling up at our feet, as it were, until I could only wonder: What in a hell *he* fixin' a weave?

On just such a social afternoon maybe two weeks or two months into my Wadmalaw sojourn, we neared the end of the booze. Only a handful of bottles remained. It wasn't a binge but a diversion in those days of pleasant survival. I would have thought it barbaric and wasteful to guzzle this stuff straight from the bottle—in other places, at other times, that is. But there never was a meal so good as one taken in the rough, over the fire, and we'd arrived at that same natural goodness.

Jim was jumping around, narratively speaking, moving to major world events and their impact on those people who seemed to summarize the evolutionary process in a generation or two, crawling out of the mud like they did in '66, but instead of taking the Pleistocene or Neanderthal ages to invent wheels and discover fire, they were forming up the Gullah Air Force hardly fifty years down the road, around '18 or '19.

I suppose the military has always imagined efficiency, succeeding about as much as the ugly step sisters squeezing them bunion dogs into some dainty glass slippers. The Gullah Air Force was designed by the U.S. military via the South Carolina Militia to utilize resources, meaning the Blacks, on the islands south of town. A couple of trainer biplanes got painted up camouflage, except for the stars and bars predominant on the fuselages, which was meant as a joke, don't you know, sending a special signature gift from way down here up to what was still called the Union Army.

Oh, we knew we could count on the island boys to send our sweet revenge airborne on that moth-eaten fleet of swayback nags. It would have been a laugh for the ages too, had not those nappy-headed pilots turned revenge back on us, crashing both planes into Church Creek shortly after take-off, after one lap around the pylons. Jim Cohen laughed softly telling the story, maybe underscoring his appreciation of the resources available south of town.

Hardly a cynical man, he turned quickly to happier days, circa WWI, or maybe it was a time before that, on account of his being only fourteen when he first hung out at his aunt's piccalo. You give two or more country Blacks something to drink and eat and a fire to stand around or a radio to jive to or some gossip to chew on, you got the basic rudiments for a piccalo. It's a place of social gathering, more or less, devolved now to gas, beer, Moonpies, RC Cola, Slim Jims, bicarbonate, Goody's Powder, combs, rubbers and breath mints and maybe some hubbub in the parking lot on the weekends. But back then those places could swing, most often the only places for miles around with a radio, meaning music, which was the meaning of swing, or bop or rag, which was to music what cursing was to polite company, in town; you plain didn't do it in town, so sometimes the town Blacks would come out too.

A piccalo gave a pulse to what needed ventilating in the social wilderness. Jim Cohen's aunt was Tyra Bohne, though he never called her Auntie, maybe because she facilitated the good times available then to a healthy young buck. That is, she got him his *first taste*, meaning she knew whom among the teenage females was willing but not too willing, who she liked or considered hazardous, unhealthy, whether from poorly chosen partners or unmanaged proclivity or otherwise ominous indicators. It was a Saturday night, Jim Cohen said, a night he'd remembered fifty-five years already and believed the imprint leastways good enough for another fifty. Tyra Bohne came out to the house the week prior to encourage her nephew to come out to Bohne's Piccalo on Saturday, because she had something for him.

He went. He'd been before but had yet to penetrate the periphery, passing through the observers and otherwise constrained folk who mull outside any social gathering like flotsam whirling near an eddy without ever easing into the whorl. Again he lingered on the periphery, until she spied him and came out and took his hand and led him into the rhythm. He knew right off something was up; his aunt Tyra looked so different, disheveled, like she'd danced to abandon or slept in her clothes after a wrestling match. Sweaty and fanning her blouse, she grinned in that crazy way of women who throw the reins aside and let the spirit run.

He'd sensed that such things took place and remembered his apprehension, approaching the mysterious pulse. The radio supplanted his own heartbeat with a downbeat through loops and dips, swirls and dives, joining every person there through the plaintive sax, piano and bass of Jellyroll Morton, Lester Young and Robert Johnson.

Jim Cohen wagged his head like a pendulum, regretting that such a time was so long gone. And he went to a nod on the rhythm and swing of Fayreva, call her Fay, the only girl recalled by name from those years, his *fuyst tays o' de tang, you know.* I suspected her thirty-fifth taste and an insatiable appetite, even as she skewered his heart with the power a young female can wield.

We guzzled again for Fayreva and the power; *mm mm!* I did not ask where she is now. Better to let him savor what he'd dredged from the years. The memory seemed rare, possibly hearkened for my benefit, so I stayed mum, passed the bottle and let the show unfold in Jim and the sky above. A few gamboling clouds, six egrets winging home on the five oh two and a first twinkle of the evening star, one more facet of the invisible gem Jim and I cut there on the flats.

I mean, you got to love the sauce for the good it does sometimes, like infusing brotherly love between a stodgy white lawyer and a fat old Black—sure we were tipsy, not quite seeing double but feeling single and moreover numb to the parasites passing on the bottle—hell, the liquor'd likely kill them or me first anyway. Sharing a bottle with that Black man raised no more compunction than double dipping in the punch bowl on the way to knee-walking downtown with your so-called "professional types." That is, Jim Cohen was my friend, not that we weren't friends before, but it changed with stories and meals, the binding behaviors of most species. Not sex; sex is divergent, not binding, at least not within the clan, so procreation enhances the gene pool, avoiding the inbreed. Jim and I were not brothers, but we'd made our way to brethren, though I paused internal on that one to ask myself what the fuckin' difference might be.

We had so many stories to tell, and it didn't mean squat, who shared a bed or a bottle. More important were the souls that touched in the most unlikely ways in this veil of tears. I'm not sentimental and never considered what motivated Jim Cohen to go gather his meals one at a time. So I stepped up that bank for firmer footing and asked man to man: "First taste? You mean you ate de watahmelon?"

I laughed so he'd know the question was merely playful, but he scanned the river, squinting at a break or a rip, then smacking his lips my way. "Wouldn' you?"

Well, hesitation can give a man away and lose ground on the masculinity issue, depending of course on the venue of the cross-examination. I didn't believe I'd eat the local watermelon on account of the hygiene issue, though my personal position of recent decades on this tender issue was not based on hygienic practicality but rather on the hazards of a man touching his tongue to ice cold steel.

Hell no! I would have spewed forth in great good humor in the professional crowd I ran in, no need to explain practical survival in keeping a tongue safely distant from Eudora's swollen rectitude. Those men understood practicality and feared ridicule and so declined such notions altogether, in public. Not that the wives seemed unsavory, if you could wrap some duct tape over the talk hole, but that seemed unlikely as unconstrained passion or those women shutting up. Eating Eudora seemed inappropriate, because she wasn't that sort of woman. Look who she'd snagged on the rebound: a fellow with a questionable pulse, much less a yen for crotch pie. I think she'd scream bloody murder, demanding to know where such vile behavior came from and screaming again on any expectation of reciprocity. Given such perversion, how could she look her friends in the eye?

Jim waited for my answer. I finally lawyered out on equivocation. "There was a time...."

"Mm...." he said, waiting to hear when and what, finally nodding and allowing, "Might yet be."

I let it go, uncertain of his meaning, though I speculated, because all species are slave to hormones, and I had a few stragglers. Perhaps it's only our species that contemplates individual prospects for certain acts. I ruled out the white women I knew, most seeming prohibitively similar to Eudora, and the Black ones for obvious reasons. The young of either color were easier, flaunting their wares, daring the hazards of house arrest.

I'd hungered for sex the last few years, till Meredith Montague got divorced about the same time I did and was still fairly preserved. She presented herself one cocktail hour with a suggestion of some private time together and a body accent to boot. I suggested a date for the following day, just before lunch, when I really am at my best. She never came by and maybe that's why I still think of her as my last chance for a last taste.

Maybe that pall on the marsh made me realize that no woman wants mere sex but needs romance, and it doesn't happen before lunch. That moment also marked my rebirth after so many small deaths. I hoped so but wondered if I'd ever get laid again and shrugged off my base anxiety as typical to a man in the wilderness. I felt good with nature abounding but could not forget the you-know-what and thought I might ought to head up to Rockville and call Meredith Montague on the pay phone, see if she might want to come out to the Hunt Club. Then I laughed, certain I'd never get laid again but hoping she might think this far out of town would be discreet. Besides, what could she say? No?

Jim Cohen scanned for weather or recollection. I scanned him, curious to know what happened.

"Oh, man, dat Fayreeva; si'teen yeah ole 'n like to ruint me fuh walkin on dem feets uh dem knee eida one." So they danced and drank to optimal aerobic range, out to the periphery among the older folks and on out, toward the trees, where she led him by the hand up the path to a lie-down he realized later she'd arranged in advance. But ignorance was bliss at the time, and so was Fayreeva, sweetly tapping the vein to free the mother lode.

Proud as a cock six days running, he sought a second taste and found her on a casual stroll in the trees with Henry Seabrook, an older, taller boy who worked maintenance with his father and had money in his pocket for sweetwine. She granted Jim Cohen greater insight on the tough row to hoe for a fellow with more oats to sow than fallow fields lying ready for seeding.

As I say, this drunken recall of youthful romance into twilight was another bonding, and I marveled at the scene of us reviewing vaginal vicissitudes over a guzzled bottle on the flats. I hadn't questioned his motivation on friendship; hell, I was a novelty. Besides that, he led the way with facility and soul baring and nothing left to question....

Until he said, "A niece be's same's a daughta to me, though she ain' but Mose grandaughta. Tek care like she do. You know? Fohty yeah ole. Ha ha. She fine."

Accent notwithstanding, I pieced together this obscure detour to his niece, whom he cared for like a daughter, who turned out to be forty-one and (oh, dear) fine. Jim Cohen a matchmaker? I felt like a shrimp on a shallow bottom, minding my own business, gnawing on some medium grade detritus, sensing something settling from above. I twitched. "Wait a minute. Mose's granddaughter?"

"Mm hmm...."

"Mose was your father's brother?"

"Mm hmm. E sail ob de Guadeloupe, in de French Windies."

"Then she's your cousin."

"May be she a cuz too."

"You said your niece."

"She Aníse. Her name Aníse."

"Like the spice?"

"Da right. She de licrich stick."

"I see."

"Hmph. Don' see nuffin. Gimme dat bottah."

"Jiss whatchou gittin at, Mista Jim?"

"Ain' gittin a nuffin. Jis spec a man oughta see what e see fo e go sayin e see wha'd is."

"So you want me to see her?"

"Don' wan nuffin." He guzzled too long for comfort, like he needed the extra time to think and the extra sauce for courage. Lowering the bottle with a gasp, "Ah," he put it back on me. "How bout'chu? Wha'chou fittin a want?"

"Aw, man."

"It good."

XII

The Fulgent Light of Knowing

Robert F. Kennedy got shot the second week of June that year. Or maybe it was the first week or the third. Didn't matter hereabouts, since we were predisposed to the Hump anyway without much need for review. RFK got shot in the head, winning the California primary, so maybe he'd have beaten Humphrey. I suppose we'd have backed Bobby too back then when the South was solid. Seemed odd, after they killed Martin Luther King in Memphis two months earlier. Not that he mattered around here either, but for looking like Jim Cohen fifty pounds lighter with a different articulation.

Jim knew Cirry Seabrook since childhood but saw her only when her daddy brought up a load of greens from Seabrook Island, namesake of the emancipated Seabrooks. Jim paused at the telling, still struggling with her absence ten years after her passing. Or maybe he only took a moment to bring her up, as if indifferent, such as I strove to feel for Eudora, instead of feeling bitter.

I savored the image of Eudora under her new husband and would have paid plenty to be the fly on that wall, watching her anxiety for the pulse of the man inserted into her. But surely they didn't.

But I digress. Jim's wife Cirry died ten years prior, influenza. They had three boys and two girls, all but one grown and gone down to the south end, closer to Seabrook, where Cirry's family had land. The two boys staying near Jim's house were Jim's grandsons, cousins to each other. They wanted to start a salvage yard and garage, inspired by so many cars here and there jacked up on cinder blocks and left for dead, most wanting no more than a belt or a generator, regulator or battery. That and new points and condensers; hell, a fellow'd hardly bust his knuckles billing forty bucks on an easy fix, and the folks would pay it gladly to get a car running. A new distributor or even just the cap; you talking pure gravy, and that's on parts in inventory and didn't even count the salvage parts in the yard!

One daughter died of the influenza with her mother, leaving an infant daughter, Jmetta, who was sent up to Jim's when her aunt fell into the bottle, exposing Jim to alcoholic consequence with a child to care for as well. I assured him that older parents have more mature children. Jmetta seemed normal and was easy company. She watched TV to the point of numbness, but her manner was to please. Supper with the Cohens had become a habit, not so much for the Black-and-white-together issue but rather from two men striking up a friendship. Maybe that's what integration advocates had in mind short of browbeating the thing till it had little chance of surviving beyond conceptual analysis.

I set hygienic anxiety aside. I washed my hands enough to draw stares from Jim Cohen and Jmetta. And I kept a bottle of Pepto Bismol at home at the Hunt Club, along with the physic of those days, which was mostly vinegar. I retired to my cabin afterward to stoke the fire so we (the fire, Fern and I) could ponder and shed light on the situation. In no time the cabin flickered its own magical interlude. I put a pot of water on the firebox for Fern, who loved the extra humidity. I'd brought a few books out with me; most I'd read years ago in school with no reflection. With age and no distraction, I could see a common rhythm and motif in those older narratives, that nothing is free of purpose in the great scheme. I wasn't so naïve to assume that life held the same sense but knew that it could, with some luck.

I gravitated to the so-called classics, mixing what I loved with what was good for me. *Lord Jim* and *The Beast in the Jungle* were like chocolate cake awarded for finishing my beets. They balanced eath other, with a few hours of adventure on the high seas after a long spell of navel watching, down to a hair's interaction with each hair to the north, south, east and west of it as well as the collective hairs' potential realm of feeling as it related to the lint living in the mid to deep recess of that navel, all casually yet acutely aware of the wrinkles surrounding the rim and possible residual trauma to those wrinkles from what may well have been a less-than-delicate excision at birthing, with remnant trauma lurking in the ever-present form of umbilical wraiths, who drift still, sustaining their torment as stoically as the downtrodden ever did, even as a careless, non-thinking finger might ream out the entire cavity with no care whatsoever but to scratch an itch.

I'd usually save Henry James for last, so we could savor his gifted cure for insomnia. I could rarely finish a James novel, though I was taken by *The Beast in the Jungle* at nineteen when it was force-fed and again at fifty-eight, when I sipped at it leisurely. John Marcher knew his life was marked for something extraordinary and seemed to me painfully similar to the society I'd aged in, whose collective ego knew damn well it was something else. James touched a nerve when he killed May Bartram and let old John have it right between the eyes, and then John dives on to her grave, his face in the dirt, as he realizes she's gone forever, and he'd missed the greatest love a man ever missed. And so a bigger, fatter zero than a man ever came to was the extraordinary summary of John Marcher's life, pouncing on him like a beast in the jungle with the realization that he *was* special insofar as his extraordinarily gray life in a vacuum. *Finis*. Roll credits.

Zero ain't an easy number to reach after years of endeavor but is a thing that must be nurtured just so with the devil's help till the days add up to a huge, life-devouring beast. It was enough to make me wonder what I'd missed. Not Eudora, certainly, nor did any woman enter the review, so I was safe on romantic love. I'd had none, which wasn't as bad as losing foolishly. Yet I read parts of *The Beast* over and over, looking for what I sensed as missing right before my eyes.

Lord Jim was no walk in the park but got me way out of town to a world attainable to a lawyer only through books. The exposed nerve was young Jim's act of cowardice in light of all the breeding, training and career advantage a fellow could want; in a single moment, jumping from a vessel of helpless refugees when it looked like the *Patna* was going down, his own honor sank. Conrad shored him up with an overdose of guilt, which can't be healthy but seems redemptive in the endless task of comprehending the sin committed.

I went way past midnight on that note; guilt gnawed at young Jim and redeemed him marginally, which wasn't enough to absolve his cowardice. So he gave his life in order to erase it, to rejoin the history of men and honor. It seemed rash, but I got stuck on the logic. What was I doing hanging out in the boonies? Waiting for something to go away? No, I was merely enjoying life, recalling now and then something that wouldn't go away. Maybe I was truly lazy, but Tuan Jim wandered the South Pacific in my mind, as I drifted the creeks and oyster flats, his compulsion lingering, drawing me round the next bend, even as I knew what waited there, which was more of the same.

Jim Cohen rattled on with tales of the judge's alliances prior to his epiphany. Jim was comfortable in his presence, though others were made to feel like children in the principal's office. He felt protected too in the company of renowned segregationists, like United States Senator Cotton Ed Smith, who regarded Jim or any Black as he might regard an umbrella stand or a hat rack. Cotton Ed's private rant was a notch down from the public version. He might tell a darky to go fetch him some more tea. But he wouldn't yell like he did for the crowds. He flat didn't see the coloreds nor care what they might see or hear. Cotton Ed's travel valet was Franklin Hines, who had one cardigan sweater, moth-eaten, and who chewed on a stogie till it looked like swamp pulp, because he wasn't allowed to smoke indoors. Franklin's brand was *El Estanco*, known for economy and Cotton Ed's summary: *Them El Stanko's like to kill a white man to death soon as not.*

Franklin's father was bought from a red hills farmer who liked the idea of slavery but soon realized the great convenience was meant for cotton and not food crops, and he honestly needed to free up his capital and get clear of the maintenance. The father came to Tanglewood, the Smith Plantation near Lynchburg, where he married Franklin's mother, and they had a child, Franklin Hines, born like Ellison Durant Smith in '64 as the Great Confusion wound down. They would spend their days as U.S. Senator and personal valet at Tanglewood Plantation. Franklin minded the home fires when Cotton Ed went up to Washington, D.C. While the one learned farming and politics for eighty years, the other worked the fields, a-laughing and a-singing with his needs met. Franklin Hines and Ed Smith grew old at Tanglewood, peas in two pods, spitting distance but worlds apart. Ed Smith swore on Franklin's durability. Franklin mumbled ablutions to the affirmative. I met Ed Smith once and heard him: "Look at that old sonofabitch. He could outwork the lot of the young ones. Here, Mr. Hines...."

Jim said the Senator's habit was to pull a bankroll from his pocket and peel off a single for Franklin Hines, who'd say, *Yahsuh*, as a Pavlovian pooch might drool on cue. Franklin's accent derived from the Piedmont, free of Gullah inflection, making communication between himself and Jim Cohen idiomatic, deriving from common experience. For example, Franklin would stand there nodding and mumbling so anyone could see his admirable traits. He'd tug on his sweater and more or less reorder his general dishevelment for anyone's further insight and amusement. One particular dollar was granted in the third week of May, 1940, when Cotton Ed came to the coast to lay low or hobnob with the Bourbons. That was the week *Time Magazine* called him *grumpy, walrusy, tobacco spitting, the senate's No. 1 mossback* and, worst of all, *a conscientious objector to the twentieth century*. He had a bone to pick, contending that all his political opponents to date were far more vociferous on white supremacy than he was, as he reiterated the dire need for segregation, if a race war was to be prevented.

Franklin Hines may have understood that his mentor's stand on the racial issue was merely expedient and not personal. Franklin took the dollar and headed outside to smoke his cigar with Waties Waring and Jim Cohen in audience. Jim watched Franklin shuffle to the wood stove on his way out, open it and reach in for a hot coal, barehanded and casual, turning it for the best angle to light his cheap stogie, demonstrating his durability as the Senator had claimed and showing as well what a man could bear up to. Franklin Hines set the coal back in the hopper with a nod of another understanding and smiled *Yahsuh* yet again. Who knows? Maybe old Franklin didn't know shit.

Jim Cohen said Franklin's fingers didn't burn because of cotton picking, because the bolls fluff over the thorns, and you can't pick a boll without hooking some flesh, which hurts like the devil a season or two then calluses over like anything will. But a man with fire fingers picked his share and then some, and you won't see any but the old stock of cotton pickers handle coals like Franklin did, fingertips hard as wood. They'd burn in time like anything will, but not in the time he needed to light his cigar. I'd met Franklin Hines, so maybe I pictured him more easily than others Jim told me about. I considered Franklin Hines late one night, when I tried to feel what he'd endured. Ember handling seemed easy, compared to old age as a valet to a master of questionable imagination. My own imagination was fertilized that night with the last few pages of *Lord Jim*, in which every character set the stage for resolution. I was never so wide awake in town as out in the boonies past midnight, alone in that cabin, when the great Tuan stepped up to face hatred, revenge and death, grateful for a chance to right his wrong and end his torment—stepped up to the evil and weakness of human behavior with no fear. Lord Jim had grown free of fear, clear in his heart and mind at last.

Hell, for all I knew, Franklin Hines thought it was the best deal a man ever cut. A dollar could buy a sit-down dinner in any restaurant in those days, and he had only to show the old durability. Franklin couldn't take dinner in any restaurant but likely loved every production of that show.

I didn't have a cigar but leaned over to open the stove and reach in for an ember. I held it up with some difficulty at first but then got resigned to searing nerve endings that had never hooked a cotton boll. I heard the sizzle and smelled burning flesh but ignored the pain and tears; hell, that was physical, what every man and beast leaves behind, sooner or later. No, I wanted to hold that ember just as Lord Jim stepped up to hold something at last. I don't know that I ever thought myself a coward; I was more a young fool than anything, yet I watched that fire in my fingertips to see what truth might be there to see. You can't just get what you want through self-affliction. I knew that and dropped that ember on the floor and hurried for the dustpan to get it back into the firebox. Then I sat with the pain, which cannot be conveyed in words. Maybe that ember facilitated my rural epiphany by revealing a truth other than what I sought. Pain feels like contrition but will not absolve the lasting hurt. In the end they're not the same, pain and contrition. Pain distracts attention from the greater regret but cannot counterbalance guilt; no, physical anguish might provide a dramatic change of scenery, but that's all. In the end there can be no substitute for good deeds in nature, as a body seeks the greater absolution.

I never held with the Christian dogma; and here too I saw life as a series of behaviors with less than optimal results and a continuing source of regret, balanced in the end by compensatory behaviors, maybe.

Solitude, silence and order had become my bunkmates, and for all the truck I hauled out to that cabin, I didn't bring a tube of antiseptic ointment. So I bore my pain alone, except for Fern, who heard about it plenty. I did find a big brown spider in the hooch box and carried him outdoors, though he wouldn't ride on the damaged hand but only on the unburned one. I don't know that I hoped for a spider bite to top things off, but my indifference was profound. I returned to the box for the liquid antiseptic, reckoning on my first guzzle that the drink's cash value came in between a dollar or three, which seemed a great bargain, things being what they were.

XLII

Aníse

You can't make a long story short covering centuries, honing on decades and going macro on a few select moments. Suffice to say Aníse's arrival on Wadmalaw occurred near the time of my own immigration. That she'd remained unseen was due in part to personal difficulties in her adjustment, which were not exactly parallel to my own but similar in a broader context. She moved directly on arrival down to Seabrook, where accommodation seemed more plentiful and in closer proximity to her own age group. She moved northwest, up near Rockville, when distance from Jmetta's troubled mother seemed propitious.

Her specific ailments stemmed from a broken heart and shattered nerves, both of which compounded with the shocking difference in culture between Wadmalaw "'n dem French Windies;" Jim Cohen's prognosis, not hers. Coming home to blood family is one thing, while crossing hundreds of miles of open sea, moving to another country and finding yourself single is another. I knew.

I could only speculate on the depths to which Jim Cohen's manipulative stratagem could be plumbed. I couldn't help but wonder, despite his fundamental approach to life on an hourly basis, to what ends he was capable.

Aníse had changed her name from Claudia some years prior, after her Grandfather Mose enlightened and amused her with tales of his mother's, her Great-Grandmother Julya's, magical ways with soul food, beginning with the spices, anise among the favorites if not the foremost. The most favored and certainly most consumed was garlic, but a girl can't very well call herself Garlic or even Garlíque, not when her boyfriend insists on calling her his own licorice stick. She resisted to the point of conjuring a name more suitable to her style and context, Aníse, which was acceptable to both her and her former boy, or man, who promised she would always be his licorice stick, even on their last encounter, a sad one for her.

Aníse's physical bearing seemed inextricable from her recent past, in which she'd ended the love of her life (her words), an eleven-year, live-in relationship with the most notable disk jockey in Guadeloupe, a man so known and, if you will, powerful, he had only to schedule a dance party to have it sold out in no time and a full head of steam pumped to the rafters or the stars, depending on the venue, by the spin of the first disc. The man was essentially energetic, bordering on vibrant; he was, in a word, anticipated. That is, she was bereft, slouched, slumped and otherwise personifying depression.

To me, the boyfriend was pumped up beyond the magnitude or fortitude innate to any man, and so was the so-called bliss she still swooned over. How could she miss someone with the personality of a Tesla coil?

No marriage and no children led nonetheless to undying devotion on the one hand and insatiable sexual appetite on the other, which would have been fine, or at least comprehensible, or short of that, something plausible for working through, as they say. But Aníse's boyfriend suffered extraordinary libido to begin with, and that burden compounded with so many volunteers to assuage its demands. Said libido led him astray in behaviors common to most stories told of men. Not a bad man, she said, nor unlovable nor significantly changed from when they first met, except of course for his growing appetite, unless he'd been philandering all along, but she didn't think so, or at least she hoped not, not that she would have cared, not really, she said. At any rate, she had no recourse in time but to leave him, or else engage in the ménage he longed for, which wouldn't work with such a steady change of players, so she moved out. That didn't work either but led to a further reduction in recourse potential, coming down to her removal to distant shores.

She didn't fault him or the shameless girls, hardly old enough to be his daughters, offering him sweets of marginal quality and questionable freshness but with such easy access and, she supposed, youthful vigor. She turned forty and sought refuge and salvation for the good years left to her, coming to the place her grandfather had never ceased calling home, though he'd left it seventy years prior.

I'd seen the Lowcountry's homing effect on people who leave, but never over such a span. But then nostalgia is among the easiest of human emotions, things always seeming so much better back in those days and places. The summary was hers, warranting doubt in the details, once observing her general state of anxiety. She seemed naturally nervous, not knowing what to do, down to sitting or standing, looking out the window or out the door, or walking over to either one for a better look, or away for perspective, not knowing if she could ever love again. I suspected the hormonal imbalance and mood swing common to the change in life. She seemed young for the menopause, but then physiology varies from one race to the next in certain things, so maybe that was one of those things, except that it wasn't. She was plain damn lovesick.

This had nothing to do with me. That Jim Cohen had maneuvered me into meeting his cousin was surprising and a bit disappointing. An ambush with a blind date at the end would be unwelcome in the best of circumstances. To set me up, as it were, as a likely suitor to a woman of darker complexion than the proverbial ace of spades left me with critically less recourse in the realm of polite interaction than she'd been left on her island in the middle of the ocean. She'd migrated elsewhere to be with family; but where did I fit in?

Letting Jim and his niece down easy became the task of the hour. I had a mind to put on my khaki suit and oxford-cloth, button-down shirt and penny loafers to underscore our common ground, which shrank quicker than a sand bar in a storm flood. I did not change clothes, having come to see that former mode of dress as depressing, post partum or mortem either one.

Aníse's charms were apparent in any light. Her broken heart and culture shock could not hide her fundamental happiness, which often defaults to stereotype in her race, but not in her. She was not predictable, though her curiosity and opinion were incessant. I understood in my open-minded, magnanimous view of the world and its lonely seekers that a woman with a spark and appetite for life, leading, perhaps, to dinner, intrigues most men. In the past, dinner could be taken out, with table service and atmosphere.

As it was, we met at Jim Cohen's for a supper of fried mullet and okra gumbo. Aníse filled the room with an energy unlike what I'd seen thereabouts, understandably anxious over her instability. Busily arranging and rearranging her few things, she rearranged them once more, anxious to get it right. She smiled cheerfully and attempted social nuance by saying her move was such a "hassle," a tiresome word so common to hip language then that it flared up and died like a struck match.

Yet she was different, young, compared to me, and enjoying the mysterious characteristic common to many Oriental and Negroid persons, making her look younger still; I guessed early thirties, or late twenties showing some stress, but she happily proclaimed that she'd "made forty-one already," as if her years were a source of pride by virtue of survival. That was a switch from what I'd been accustomed to, but freedom from self-consciousness was in keeping with her family tradition.

Whether her values derived from her forbears is conjectural, but I think they did. I found her straightforward, engaging and refreshing, compared to Eudora's apoplexy over birthdays, questionnaires, driver's licenses or any of society's hateful ruses to pry a woman's age from her, when she doesn't look nearly that old and doesn't have to be that old if she doesn't want to. Eudora was sixty-one but looked only fifty-nine and swore she was forty-eight. Near the midpoint in our marriage I developed a sustained embarrassment for her vanity. I warned her that in time a forty-eight-year-old woman looks foolish, married to an eighty-year-old man, which was the predicament we were headed for if she didn't fess up and grow up and old with grace. She assured me we'd cross that bridge when we came to it.

But I dabble in the stream at the foot of a bridge ready for crossing. Aníse suffered a vanity or two, as most people do; a person weighing in at two hundred will admit to one-sixty, like she and Twiggy are peas in a pod. Aníse did not weigh two hundred but looked svelte and curvaceous. She wore a wig when I met her, medium-length, wavy brown hair that blended well with her other features. I saw it was a wig right off, though she seemed more natural with it than the local women of complexion.

I'll concede that I counted her figure prominently among her charms, her body language a fluent articulation of the universal tongue. Assessing her sparkle, shape, and apparent happiness, I found her curious. My curiosity seemed a natural response to her interest in me; we are often drawn to what we draw. Getting acquainted was easy; she had fun in the kitchen and seemed comfortable explaining how things should be, as far as she could tell. She was exotic, not strange, and equidistant from the local Black women and the women I'd known in town, more open-minded and lyrical than either even hinted; quixotic and elusive with a salacious savoir-faire that a blind man would have sensed.

I mention these traits and behaviors as typical requisites, what is common to many relationships between men and women, which this came to be. Given the social barrier, we couldn't pass square one without some natural magnetism anyway, so the flirtatious aspect shouldn't seem surprising. What she saw in me beyond stability, I can only speculate. Did she wonder what in hell I was doing out there? She seemed preoccupied with her own situation, but I cut a decent profile of urbane demeanor, which must have been exotic for her as well, or at least different from her recent fare. She liked that I presented a difference, I think; I didn't even own a Hi Fi, much less know how to work one, and I could have called a dance party to the four winds with no response. She told me in the way that private thoughts are shared, once intimacy is achieved, that she'd been drawn to the way I looked. At average height with even proportions and my hair mostly intact, I thought she merely liked what I liked, which was something and someone to engage there in the outback of midlife. An unlikely proposition loomed between us, with a dare, an act of rebellion and a fantasy as well titillating the air. She assured me no, no, no—make that yes, that she liked what I liked but was moreover taken by the high cheekbones and firm chin, by the silver hair combed back regally, the square shoulders and flat stomach, but mostly by the steely green eyes offsetting the warm smile. With each accolade I responded, chin out, gut in, hair pushed back, eyes steeled and so on, till I couldn't move, and she laughed, perhaps at me, before making amends as only she could, perhaps assuring me in her way that she was putting me on, or maybe she wasn't.

The first time I saw her without the wig was our second meeting, by chance, in Rockville, at the store. I browsed pharmaceuticals for some antiseptic ointment and perhaps to discover a holdover inventory of laudanum. She was out and about, such as it was. I didn't recognize her so I didn't look twice, beyond my general smile and hello for anyone in passing, but then I looked again when she gazed at me. Did I know this woman? I didn't think so, until the eyes caught, and I saw what several bulky layers could not hide, that yes, I knew her, or had met her at any rate—"Ah! Aníse!"

"Arthur," she moaned, offering her hand in another unimaginable gesture, or at least one thoroughly unpracticed there between parties of the first and second parts. Transcending taboo with practiced momentum, she took my hand naturally, lifting the bandaged fingers with alarm and continuing curiosity as to the source of my injury.

I explained how I'd carelessly grasped the firebox handle when it was too hot. So with a headshake and renewed warmth she shook my other hand on the great chance of our meeting again. She proceeded directly to chitchat, like it was Broad and Meeting or Queen and Tradd Streets. And wasn't it grand, out shopping and running into old friends like this? With any other woman I would have called romance forgone, but this was different, not yet shocking because of the overwhelming denial. This could not be.

"I need a pain reliever," I said, making conversation as I might have done in town.

"Oh, yes," she gushed, "I am very interested in that sort of thing, you know, pain and relieving. In my home of lately, I make a study of the tincture and the herb. Do you know these things?"

The mini-drama here was not so much a common interest, which was my pain and her study of tinctures and herbs, but the absence of the wig. Her naturally kinky do was like the Afros popular then, but she'd cropped it closer so it fit her head like a wool cap. Distinctively Negroid, she was yet again dissimilar to the local women, most of whom were scraggly-headed or wore their hair forcibly straightened so it hung stiff as quills on a hedgehog. Hers seemed groomed. Sensing her discomfort with my scrutiny, I said, "You did something with your hair."

She touched her hair and blushed, yes. "Yes. I…. I let it go." She ventured a timid glance.

"It looks good," I assured her. "You look good." She cast her eyes downward, sparing me the embarrassment of my deep blush. Had I just signaled game on? She never wore the wig again, more from her own embarrassment than pride, I think.

At any rate, her natural hair was so different from wavy brown that I hadn't recognized her. The store was warm, so she removed her sweater, reminding me otherwise of what she looked like. So we took up where we'd left off, in animated dialogue with no direction or point but with apparent vigor. I blushed again, feeling flattered.

She didn't know why she'd come out, she said, or what in the world she could buy at that little store; she just needed to get out, you know. So she joined my search for old laudanum. I told her that her great-grandfather had likely bought the remaining inventory of that very constabulary in the prior century. She said, "You know, that is so interesting." I wondered what Luzon would say, to see his search continued by his great-granddaughter and a surly white lawyer from Charleston.

She patted her hair frequently, caught out, her first impression undermined, displaced. I told her she should have no concern because she looked quite nice. I risked patronization, but she beamed, informing me that she was still influenced by cultural trends from the continent. That wig was an experiment, a silly thing to try, to see if she might like it, you know, because it was something different.

We managed a pleasant exchange that led neither to lunch nor supper, nor to any suggestion of further engagement. We actually by-passed any mention of a next meeting by agreeing that the place was so small; we would surely meet again in no time, and until then, see you later, goodbye, ta ta, *au revoir*.

We met again that night, subsequent to my decline of supper at Jim Cohen's, the invitation to which was delivered by Jmetta, the child. I stayed home in everyone's best interest. I mean, what was he thinking? She was nice enough, and easy company by any standard. But her egregious availability was plain damn inappropriate and poorly timed. What did he expect, a romance? Or a one-night stand?

Aníse showed up at the Hunt Club cabin with a covered dish, which seemed unsubtle yet appreciably discreet and even touching. She also carried a thick stalk of aloe vera, wrapped in a paper towel to soak up the viscous ooze, commonly known to remedy burns or skin disorders of any kind, and known by me too; but who thinks of such things? I suppose the evening livened up, as perhaps things would have done in any event, when she squeezed the stalk that emitted the goo and squealed at the awful, soothing mess. She dasn't look up from her tender ministrations of my wounds, so sensual was the exchange.

In that softer, kinder light, she was a woman alone in a foreign place seeking friendship. That she came to me with first aid and something good to eat could only feel warm and generous. If I put self-interest, self-loathing and social conscience aside for once, nothing remained but hospitality and female charm. That she was Black and a bit neurotic became quickly incidental in the privacy of my own home.

We sat by the stove with two colas she'd also brought, having learned from her uncle of my disease. I assured her it wasn't contagious, and we let it drop, because further discussion of my personal condition was unnecessary. Yet she filled the little cabin with observation and curiosity on the strange turns life has in store. I was reminded of my letter to Anne Waring on the subject of changes in life, but only briefly, before advice on nutrition, doubts on Wadmalaw society and the paucity of dance music thereabout took over. Not that she craved dancing all night, not anymore, or not like she used to, recently. She stared off, speaking her mind on the difficult adjustment to anyplace new at this stage of life, and the abounding beauty of this place. The beauty made adjusting easier, but not entirely easy, but then life is never entirely easy. Is it? And so on, sounding her stream-of-conscious opinions off the backboard, who was me, wading in the stream, in a dazed sort of way. I corrected her English when a word could squeeze in edgewise. She rambled like Topsy (no wig), grateful for each correction, though I assured her I was no authority on the language. *"Ah! Mais oui! Vous etre!"*

My observation went beyond accent and content to the comparative level. I imagined her naked, as men will do, though I hadn't done so with Anne Waring, my fantasized love. Not that Anne was beneath such fantasy; it was I who failed to indulge, though she did carry the genetic code for burdensome rectitude and was never so playful, even as a child. That didn't deter our childish bonding. Our chance moments of intimacy were more awkward than thrilling, but comparison remains unfair; with Aníse I was making up for lost time, a sentiment unique to the Holy City. Imagining Aníse *au naturale* was tantamount to watering and feeding the anarchy germinating in my soul. Well, it germinated mentally at any rate. I didn't dwell on it, or wouldn't allow it, because beyond the mental realm it may as well have been Timbuktu, where I could not go, because you can take the man out of the society, but you can't take the society out of the man, or some such—this I firmly believed as I backed away in my mind.

Yet there I stood at an appropriate distance, peeking under her sweater, so to speak, whereas my ideal love had remained fully clothed for decades, as it were, in my mind. Anne Waring and I shared a bath and a bed as children, and what I felt as romantic potential could have stemmed from surrogate sibling bonds that merely compensated for my loneliness. I don't know; Anne was a tomboy, and I'd seen her plenty in a t-shirt and dungarees and more or less assumed the body she'd grown into and accepted that as a vague concept, simply never considering the ultimate contact. I only pondered love, true love, the way most people ponder the future, with its house, children, nice cars, lovely things and a daily schedule spinning tirelessly as a wonderfully ornate carousel; *and the painted ponies go up and down.* That song was on the radio just then, Joni Mitchell singing about the seasons of life and so on, and it was a time of reflection on life and values for most of the world. But this too was rationale. I merely wondered what Anne was doing that moment and felt regret and gratitude that she couldn't see me then, as I imagined this Black woman naked; oh, God, now on her hands and knees, crawling over in predatory dominance.

Most men are weak for the female form; so women present what drama they can, to draw men's attention and test interest and manners as well. Aníse reminded me of school days and our raucous glee over the first real breasts we saw in National Geographic, but Aníse wore a black dress in a scant, French cut beneath her fuzzy sweater with no spear or face plates. Her delicate hands with long, painted nails contrasted to spatulate, work-hardened mitts. Her social dexterity was simply, like her dress, French. She was nothing like what I'd known but different in every way, except of course for her black skin, thick lips, kinky hair, flat nose and blood relations.

She pressed on, her curiosity driven by a need to fit the greater puzzle. Oh, but it was difficult, so recently arriving at such a beautiful but primitive place. Was it not? And then it was difficult *aussi*, not knowing how long a body would stay, before, perhaps, needing to move again to somewhere else. "Do you not think of this?" I nodded, yes, though I knew this was it. Where would I go? Yet I commiserated. What could we ever do, two people like us? How should we feel, she and I, here and now, with and without, trying to make do and keeping our minds open to discovery but still not knowing? Her mode and manner were not shown in National Geographic or anywhere I'd been or imagined.

I absorbed her as I had not apprised a Black woman. Her Negroid features were typical, but the French nuance rendered her uniquely foreign, a bit tedious but pleasing in her playful accent and impish eyes, or, in a word, complex. Well, I'd denied racism my whole life, insisting that my sole distaste was for ill-mannered, unclean and ignorant people, who, coincidentally, happened to be Black around here. And there I was, proving myself true to racial neutrality, adhering instead to hormonal integrity, which likely proved nothing but was good to feel.

With regular frequency in town then you could observe that species known as the great liberal snowbird, who in time would vanquish our town as no Yankee general had dared dream of. These advance scouts often spoke aloud on things, things done wrong, things done far more intelligently in the North. The snowbirds audibly deplored the "blatant stupidity" of the customer lines in our post office that ran as lines should, with seven separate lines cuing from seven windows, instead of one main line cuing to the next available window. The reason for this antiquated lineage was unspoken but understood, since a street-sanguine postal patron would not choose the shortest line but rather the line with the fewest Blacks. One Black could require food stamps, welfare registration, welfare checks, welfare renewal and/or replacement documentation, assistance with food stamp forms, questions and translation to the surface from the muddy, rocky bottom, taking as much time as nine whites, or thirteen.

Aníse was obviously not of that world and proved my cleverness besides, though I thought best not to run my observation up the flagpole for a salute. I felt satisfied that she was different and had my attention. It was harmless. Where could it go?

Her lipstick and, yes, eye shadow, complimented her natural mystique, her general allure rounding out with lustrous skin, perhaps more dazzling in firelight. Her good posture went prouder still when she caught me sizing her up, and I thought to ask if I might check her teeth. But that wasn't funny either, and she'd likely ask back why I would want to check her teeth, leaving me to explain another obscure, ill-timed joke at someone else's expense. So instead I imagined good manners in myself and said, "Sorry. I've been sizing you up."

"Sizing you up?"

"Not me. You. I've been assessing you. Appraising you. Seeing how you are."

"Ah. Yes. I'm fine. Thank you. And you? How are you?"

"Yes. I'm fine too. Thank you."

"Ah, Arthur." She touched my hand with cool fingers and overflowed with brimful warmth. "You are welcome."

I mean like that, taking a potentially awkward moment and turning it into the greater communion. Meanwhile, her teeth were perfect. I suspected dentures, but she smiled and caught me again, looking closer; but she held the moment of good cheer and proved me wrong again by displaying mottled, blue gums, inherited from her great grandfather Luzon. Oh, if the venerable membership of the Wadmalaw Hunt Club could see the courtship underway!

I sensed directly that she didn't mind my inventory, as she began her own, as if such measure for measure is natural and acceptable at that phase of what arced between us, the voltage of which was apparent to all parties by that time. I assumed her scrutiny would be less rigorous, on the physical side anyway, since women are more flexible there, scrutinizing more keenly on the security, stability and financial-fluidity issues. Besides, I wasn't fat or slouched. What did she see? What did she seek?

Let her look. In the meantime I struggled with the cost/benefit ratio of the evening's endeavor, weighing hormonal return on the one hand and practical liability on the other. I repressed both with moderation, polite conversation and gratitude for dinner and company.

She'd heard that I was a lawyer, besides being an alcoholic. I disabused her of the lawyerly notion, assuring her that I'd practiced the law for more years than were good for my health, and the law was likely a causal factor in my drinking, given the stressful nature of a career in law and, moreover, the habitual drinking of my peers. My occupation and its hazards remained in flux, I said, though for the time being I preferred the occupation, or avocation at any rate, of oysterman and crabber, like her Uncle Jim, more or less.

She laughed like a deb at a ball on hearing this comparison of myself to her uncle. Her mirth was contagious but made me wonder; was I so obviously removed from elemental viability? She laughed on, promising that it wasn't me but rather her uncle; imagining him as a lawyer. I doubted her ruse, it was me on the mudflats she found amusing. In any event, she either saw Jim as something less, or saw me as something more, neither of which was fair.

Yet she laughed, heartily and uncontrollably, covering her mouth and failing, till she took her sweater off and said something like, "Oh, my, my," and laughed again. I hoped she hadn't been a loose woman, which should have told me what else I hoped for. She was clearly primed for spontaneity and fun and would likely consent to a casual romp, a friendly fling, a one-night stand or whatever a bit of the cure for heartache might be called. I knew from my infrequent visits to the bars in town that this practice was called sport fucking, which sounded vile, meaningless, seductive and convenient. She proceeded, flirting doggedly as a waterman jigging over a known hole.

I assured her that her solitude, if continuing, would be self-inflicted; she could attract company at will, including men her own age. I avoided further profile of those she could attract; that she would be better matched with a man of similar social strata seemed obvious. I further assured her that wealth could assume myriad measurement on Wadmalaw beyond financial security, and a dance partner who might keep pace was no doubt available thereabout, or certainly within range.

She stopped laughing then to tell me she was forty-one and practically an old woman. Unless you happen to be fifty-eight, I did not say. I constrained my response, because anything I said encouraged her, recalling my longstanding theory that a man does not achieve sexual dominion but is simply chosen, and whether he's chosen or not will determine the disposition of his evening, which has nothing to do with his best or worst but reflects only ambient female appetite. I too sensed the deep hole; I was in it, resisting the bait bouncing mere inches from my every sense.

The old, inhibited sense raised its long snout then, with images of family and friends and a chill up my spine. I'd been decades since engaging in a significant flirtation, and I understood that the difference between a normal young man and a dirty old man is the tally of their years. Nothing changes.

We took a reprieve for dinner. I was indeed famished, I said, turning our talk to daily regimen, her family's history as I'd recently learned it, the changing times and again, as talk in the region must, returning to the beauty abounding and oh, the weather. It was in the sweet digestive aftermath that she moved to make the place tidy, cleaning up the dishes, utensils, napkins and soda bottles. I moved to tend the fire in the box, sliding past her close enough to warrant a head turn, yet we felt each other's breath, pausing as we knew that a pause was good as a leap; and just like that, we closed the distance still, until nothing remained.

Just like that, I pecked her on the lips. "There. I did it," I said, as if to show something or other or make another obscure point about clearing a hurdle. She came on in, responding as a lonely woman in gentle embrace might do, and, truth be told, we shared a kiss with a gravity field of our own making.

She did not say yes, yes again, yes; I only imagined that too, having just that day read Joyce's last paragraph of *Ulysses* several times. She did say, "Yes. Arthur," which I presumed was the answer to the thumping loneliness, dissatisfaction and disenfranchisement between us. What else did we have in the whole wide world but the moment and each other? I'd been called dispassionate by those presumably in a position to know, those who failed to arouse that which they lamented.

Aníse had no complaints for the duration of the evening, from arrival to departure, or for many evenings to come. She merely murmured assent, that I follow the step of the dance she could show me. Mutual needs notwithstanding, I think our secondary motivation was also mutual and significant, and that was a dash of adventure in the face of so much loss. Because, Ladies and Gentlemen of the Jury, the dash of this and pinch of that was precisely why we'd come to Wadmalaw in our ignorance and bliss, and so we spiced something to serve up together. It was about time.

We'd been too long without, years for me, weeks for her, and I for one gained sudden insight and perspective on life and its converse dimension, in which a soul might regret those aspects of a great wide world that were missed, beginning with a kiss. A sweeter, more succulent exchange I had not known.

She held me, moving quickly through embarrassment to her own realization of the impracticality between us. What if? She stepped back, flustered, to sort the implements for re-bandaging my hand, to proceed awkwardly in this new expression of caring, leading to yet another kiss and from there to the greatest expression yet. I could not help comparing this woman again, this time to the one most recently known in the so-called biblical sense, my former wife. Impracticality aside, Aníse rose in my esteem, beginning with her skin, its color like all skin in the pale flicker. Liberated from the nuance and ache of clothing, we moved past visual to tactile, her softness transcending what hurdles remained; if this wasn't practical, then a lunker won't lunge at split shrimp on a three ought hook with a rising barometer at slack flood and run like a bull.

To share my intimacy with Aníse further would be indelicate. I will annotate here for further comparison, however, not so much to analyze the physical or behavioral difference between two people, namely Aníse and the ex-wife, but rather to show variable sugar contents thereof.

Eudora's lament of our waning years was uttered infrequently but all too often as a means, I suppose, of explaining the terrible predicament our marriage had put her in. To think, she could have done so much better; why Rutledge Reid himself wanted to…blah blah blah. The specific charge of the plaintiff here was: "You *nevah* could stack up to nobody I know's idea of a lawyer."

Maybe my deficiencies grew; God knows Eudora stayed as ignorant of my work as she was of the English language relative to grammar, syntax and usage. What could we share in sweet embrace? That's what it came down to, descending deplorably to zero. The spirit between Eudora and me didn't matter in the beginning, what with the mere thrill of her lying prone and naked instead of posing in one of those Villager outfits with the ruffled blouse, the tweedy skirt, the unspeakable bobby socks, the tediously predictable green muffler and oh, my God, the virgin pin, all of which made her look like a school girl who skipped down the street in a sci-fi thriller and stumbled into a diamatrix and got spit out of the crazy old-lady machine. She signaled receptivity with a reluctant parting of her knees and a marginally reduced tremble, I think, but subtlety was lost on both of us. I was allowed entry to the royal chamber only as long as appropriate to make the necessary discharge. No loitering, please.

I didn't realize while serving time with Eudora that the female partner in conjugation does have the option to squirm and verbalize. I'll grant her a degree of responsiveness the first few years, when I took longer than good taste warranted, till her heavy breathing signaled the stretch for her. It went something like, *Oh, Awthuh. Oh, Awthuh. Awthuh. Oh.*

Of course I had no choice but to resolve my personal crisis with an earful of encouragement or rapprochement, one or both, as if it hardly mattered to a bestial man like me. Likewise, I won't detail sexual relations with Eudora, other than to point out her rare and constrained orgasm as a mixture of gratitude and accusation. Oh, the things I made her do. What? Breathe hard and fight the release?

I can still hear her baritone indifference, needing to know, please, "Are you done yet?"

In the last ten years or maybe twenty, past the point when the spirit between two people must compensate the dilution of so much, she dropped the *Awthuh* part and crossed the finish line impersonally: *Oh. Oh. Oh.* Imagine an orgasm on a doily, and there you have it, Eudora's sweet embrace. "Excuse me; I have *so* much to do. Be a dear and clean this up? Please?"

I shitchu not, and I would have considered her behavior normal among all women for the duration of my life, had not free will and circumstance steered me to Aníse.

Aníse, on the other hand, enjoyed the benefits of exposure to international style, fashion and presentation. She grew up in a popular tourist destination. Unlike Charleston, arrived upon by the teeming refuse driving down the highway, Guadeloupe was a poor but exotic Caribbean island, popular with European tourists, mostly the French. She wore very little, all cut to advantage, whether an abbreviated blouse with no sleeves or a dress with a daring, taunting neckline. She remained equally attractive without garb, and though I had to request repeatedly that she please shave her legs, because the nubs were like eighty-grit sandpaper on my skin, she failed to comply only because she forgot, not to prove her will or anything.

Remembering, she made herself as smooth to the touch below the hips as she was above. Factor that with continuing sparkle and warmth, then discount the equal level of anxiety afflicting both women, and a fair comparison is still precluded by the judges' decision that women of two different leagues cannot be compared.

That is, "Don't stop, Sugar. Don't stop, Sugar," may sound impersonal, and as well suited for one sugar as another, but that sort of thinking felt negative and unnecessary to my peace of mind. Besides, I didn't sense her to be promiscuous but rather neglected and lonely—and oh, so new and different from what I'd known. Maybe that perception too is a terrific convenience. I didn't care. I'd taken fifty-eight years to get there. She was monumental, a woman I loved looking up to, a profile I would store away and cherish forever, and the view available from the summit or the valley was vast and clear: I thought Aníse would have felt better than my ex-wife, both physically, mentally and socially, even if she were white. That she was not, only felt like cream gravy, delivering me from what ailed me on many levels, including stratospheric removal from town. Make no mistake, the Covingdale patron had gone to orbit.

Aníse was a classic in whom beauty grew. She drew me in as we became more acquainted, her idiomatic charm and mannerism expressed in every gesture, her brief, nervous looks my way and her knee-jerk smile whenever she could manage one. Her visage would have lit the face of anybody wearing it or looking at it; beyond that, she was simply beautiful. Suffice it to say that the question of a repeat performance was not grounds for equivocation. That we avoided equivocation as necessary was perhaps nature's greatest good deed toward me to date.

Then too, her nervous glances and sundry other symptoms of anxiety went away, signaling progress on a personal level, moving beyond hormonal gratification and the uncertainty a recently rejected woman might feel. Her womanly wiles were proven as soundly as John Henry ever drove a steel spike home. I won't say she represented mere sexual release, because nothing was mere about it. Rather it was thorough as the drubbing Sherman pounded from Atlanta to the coast in '64.

These and other images delved into hyperbole to the gross extreme, serving to justify, rationalize and perhaps encourage my inability to curb our habit. After all, service seemed the order of the day. The impracticality would not go away on one level but then the deed could only seem ultimately practical on another. Talk about convenience. The thrill of the thing compounded with our first go in the clear light of day, and another first go outdoors. Adrift in a bateau was good for another first and good for making waves, gentle waves, which were easy to see as a good thing, even coming home with only a single select gathered up. Another first go came spontaneously on a Sunday, when silence ruled Wadmalaw, save the chorus raised in song at the African Methodist Episcopal Church. "Hep me, Jedus," they called, as our righteous refrain warbled on cue from the Wadmalaw Hunt Club.

Then came all night; she didn't stay that first night and not for what seemed like many nights to come, until she did, by which time we were known as an event, if not an item, by which time an attempt to control our pace could only be conjectural, because neither one of us mentioned the wisdom or even the purpose of attempting such a thing.

It was a trick of nature between us.

I've had unusual liaisons before, once in my mid-twenties. I was courting Eudora at the time, which process was ostensibly a formal stage of career development taking two years for respectability and, here too, practicality, like an escrow, where claims against title or insufficient funds can come to the surface if in fact they lurk just below. Eudora kept her so-called virtue intact, in deference to presentation of good title by the party of the first part to the party of the second part, who would in turn bring honor and income to the close of the deal. She offered to jack me off for the second time in our epic courting one New Year's Eve in a sweet gesture of caring, but then begged off when I asked for lotion this time, as if avoiding the chafe was sheer, utter perversion.

Miss May Steadman's husband had died the prior year from a brain aneurysm and might could still be hoisting cocktails, had he not passed out during that happiest of all hours. Falling on one's face was hardly *de rigueur*, even in that crowd of two-fisted drinkers, or maybe especially in that crowd; sodden behavior so shockingly declared what could otherwise be denied. That the fall was tolerated was the death of Peter Steadman, who failed to attract help and called no more attention to himself than a gasping titter, "Good gracious!" The men were bemused that Peter had once again soaked up too many toddies; ah, well. So he lay there, peaceful as a happy man taking a nap with a smile on his face. They agreed to this peace and happiness later, after Peter was pronounced dead as a doornail, which nobody had reckoned for a good many more rounds, which must have pushed another hour or so.

Peter Steadman dropped dead at forty-two. May Steadman was forty-six when she told me, not three months after Peter's death, that she favored younger men for their vital energy. Their vigor. Their stamina and staying power. I got the picture; it had been a few months, and a woman had her needs, but I had a full agenda at the time, developing the honor, reputation, potential et al ad infinitum, representing the party of the second part in its betrothal proposition to the party of the first.

Peter Steadman was safely planted a mere three rows down from the Covingdales, which gave the two clans a certain neighborhood affinity, or something or other of a warm-hearted nature that motivated Mrs. Steadman to up and invite me over for dinner hardly six months after the fact. I went for the greater good of society, to discuss the weather or politics or the common interests we shared and the lovely disposition of life and thereafter, and that was that, leading directly to dessert, which included pie, ice cream, liqueur and hootchie cootchie with hot sauce. It was fun alright, I suppose because forty-six is old enough to have been all grown up when the young man was hardly old enough to figure what his tallywhacker was for besides peeing out of. I remember myself trying to look down Mrs. Steadman's blouse and then again up her skirt while picking up my pencil— oh, yes, Mrs. Steadman had been my teacher, and both the blouse and skirt had seemed aggressively ventilated even then. And there I'd come to enrapt in one of life's rapturous surprises, having my way at all points and intersections with Mrs. Steadman! She seemed amused. I know I was. I went back once but then let it go, though I often regretted letting it go. I assumed she needed romance, marriage and love, which goes to show how young I was. She only wanted a good time and viewed me as safe, all but married and firmly niched with enough spunk for Eudora times ten, but I wasn't so receptive to practicality back then.

Victoria Lee Cordet was a lesbian, and everybody knew it, living with her girlfriend, and them going out and about all lovey dovey for the benefit of anyone who doubted their daring. She took me home one night when her girlfriend was out of town, said she was using me but didn't think I'd mind, no offense; she just had a yen for lawyer, or at least a downtown fella who wore a blue oxford cloth shirt with one of those cute collars with the extra little buttons and a khaki suit every day of his life out of plain damn fear, no offense; but she was curious. Bi-sexual is what she was. I didn't go back for seconds on that one because she was crazy, insisting I do what I didn't want to do and keep on doing it, you hear. She wouldn't have me back either.

Then I married Eudora and got to have sexual relations once a month any time I wanted. Horny as Eudora rendered me, she was at least consistent, so in time normal libido atrophied or adapted, if such a thing is possible. I considered intimate congress unnecessary for myself in the big picture, thanks to adaptive chemistry or genetic predisposition or, once again, repression, meaning denial of the truth staring me in the face.

I did not view Aníse lustily when we met, except maybe for a covert moment, when it hit me like sunrise that it was lust in a strong surge, as I angled myself strategically to better ogle her breasts. Oh, things change, all right; they die for decades to resurrect down the road in the hope and light of life. I had suffered unrequited demand, pent-up. I knew it but repressed it, until it flowed over the levee, and the levee breached.

I believe most women want to turn a man's head, especially if he ignores her. I didn't mean to ignore her that day we met by chance at the Rockville Store. I didn't recognize her. She was a Black woman with keen insight to an advantageous cut of her blouse and what she wore beneath it, which was nothing. Her lapels unfurled like a whirlpool, drawing eyes adrift from the backwater into the swirl. At forty-one, her view of life was magnanimous, sizing up a situation with warm simplicity and a positive outlook. Yet moving into whisper range, she proved complex as a deep draft hull in shoal water with shifting ballast, iffy caulking and pumps keeping up but barely. These aspects of two fools fumbling to stay afloat on romance, we shared concurrently on one pillow. I watched the ceiling, listening to an exotic woman from Guadalupe, of Lowcountry and French extraction, a woman whose fate was to lie beside me.

I don't know that I suspected her direct approach as anything but a lonely woman seeking company. I felt cured straightaway of those things afflicting a man in emotional and mental crisis. Ramifications remained, but for the time were easily set aside. Then came the addiction, which appeared to be the most immediate problem to solve. We solved it as we could, as if a bite made for an itch; we scratched and scratched to end the itch. That was the trick nature played with this casual gift of convenience and release with no consequence, even in light of our utter failure to moderate, maybe because of the relief and convenience or because of something else. That is, nature threw a fit of chemistry, feel and scent—yes; sweet and soft, it went with the skin, the accent and the rest, including the company we shared, which was easy, fun and stimulating, all of which hallmarks of social contact with a sex partner I'd yet to experience. She was the world of adventure, mine at last.

That first night was blessedly brief and shockingly sweet. She walked home in the dark after pecking me on the cheek and whispering that I wasn't so bad, and she really needed that and wouldn't mind going again but not tonight, because it was late; people would talk, so maybe again soon. "Yes? But people will talk soon enough, will they not? So maybe…tomorrow, maybe. Or the next day. Who can pretend to know? Maybe tomorrow you will feel so bad. You won't like me. I think you won't…."

But I did—like her, that is. She eased me farther south and way outa town, making my first fifty-eight years seem like a false start, or that I'd arrived at a middle and an end and a fresh start. I exaggerate; that was the hot flush of the heavy action talking. I don't know what else I could have done with my first six decades and really didn't think I'd done wrong, not in the moral or professional sense, except for a night of weakness way back when, which seemed more sinful now than ever, seeing the reward of a different form of weakness as so superior to the former. Throwing a brick through my friend's window in childish tantrum still burned, and so did my failure toward my rightful love. But who's to know. We take things for granted on most speculation. Anne never saw me as a sexual being, just as I failed to see her that way. I saw her as my perfect love, another accessory in a matched set that could be admirably showcased in the hutch we called life. I loved Anne along with a concept of life with Anne, yet her reciprocity may have led to a great mistake similar to the one I actually made. Never, ever in her or my wildest dreams could she have trounced the restlessness and dissatisfaction like Aníse could do. Some things are known.

I suppose I'd known for a while as well that my professional life could not serve me to the end of my days. I changed. It didn't. I became an outcast, self-banished by tedious practicality and then by choice. I wasn't depressed enough to kill myself or talented enough to take up art. So I stepped off the deep end to the south of the causeway, out yonder onto Wadmalaw. Then I found Aníse and wasted a little more time parsing fate, like a starving man presented with a sumptuous meal and wondering what to do. She opened my eyes and my mind to clear thinking, and it felt like my lucky day and night.

She hid nothing from anyone but spoke the facts without speaking around them. She stole my heart with a different and French type of innocence, in which behaviors were freely conceded, and why not? Are those behaviors that harm no person not natural? She held back on public displays of affection, deferring to my acute sense of discretion. Small anxieties surfaced between physical contacts, as if things built up and needed continual ventilation, and any less would prove her fear of further rejection. I could only speculate briefly before signaling that it was time for the remedy with a wink or a nod, to which we scurried like kids to candy.

Jim Cohen laughed short and shook his head, perhaps at the loss of an assistant, though I joined him on the flats as usual, when I could.

That is, our love was neither premeditated nor expected but evolved incidentally, a by-product of familiarity, mutual drive, repetition and need. We leaned on each other. Aníse was exciting; I took that to be the basis for love. I awaited her arrival, savored her presence, coveted the next go and wanted her around.

So there we were, conforming to social standards till after supper, or sometimes before, when personal drive transcended community consciousness. We lived a fantasy, deferring to her goal of having fun, wallowing in what was soon known as our private jungle boogie. *Old AC and some Frenchie spade gal down there whooping it up to beat the band, don't you know, carrying on like he lost his plain damn sense, which any man might consider doing, but he went and did it, just threw it all away. And for what? You tell me.*

Um, er, uh…. Have you seen her?

Threw what away? It was all gone, save remnant fondness here and there, a potted fern whose reach and radiance underscored my contentment. I commiserated with a potted plant and felt grateful for it and more grateful yet for the heart and eyes opening to that gratitude. Beyond that, my pastoral boogie wasn't perfect; Aníse complained frequently of no dancing.

Nevertheless, we were a headline, then an ongoing event, soon to be idle gossip, relegated directly to one more eccentricity, hardly notable so far out of town. Like a flash boil cooling to a simmer and then to room temp and finally to the tepid flow of days, we had only to live happily ever after.

On Down the Road

The end, however, was no more concise or neatly delineated than it turns out for anyone. She was not Sleeping Beauty and I lacked Prince Charming's riding skills, so we had yet to forge the bogs of every life ever lived. Oh, they deepen and widen and suck you down. She wanted to move in after a week. I declined, explaining briefly the difficulties of moving too fast, facing the peril of untangling a knot too quickly tied. I elaborated on the rich, rewarding goodness of biding our time, savoring what we'd stumbled onto.

She protested tying a knot. "You think I want for marrying you?" She swore she did not and asked if I thought we were teenagers, who should wait before the cootchie coo.

I did not think we were teenagers or that we should wait but it seemed unnecessary to mess with what we had. What was the rush?

The rush was bunking at Jim's place, with no privacy and hardly a bed of her own, much less a bedroom. I reminded her that the Hunt Club cabin wasn't my place. She harrumphed, as if knowing of the resources a white man of means brings to bear on whatever problem needs a solution. And don't worry, if the Hunt Club members don't want a Black woman staying there, their old bubba Arthur could explain that she keeps the place clean, beginning with his tubes, if he wanted to. Her playful French approach could verge on the indelicate or mix caustically with resentment. We agreed for the time to the status quo on my assurance that she was welcome over anytime, though I chilled on issuing the invitation. Call me typical or psychic.

Sho nuff, complexities emerged.

Take for starters our first social outing. We didn't need to go to town; I could have lived well into the future without crossing the vast separation or either river between two worlds. A man knows he's getting old when he cringes on telling his girlfriend to come by anytime, but eases up, knowing she won't walk in on anything compromising, because nobody is left to compromise with. She was it, the sum total of what lay over my horizons. Did that mean I could have picked oysters, shagged shrimp and crabs and gone fishing every day and cooked up with some vegetables and a few friends, give or take? Could I live in a beautiful place, in a warm, loving relationship with Aníse indefinitely? Well, yes, I believe I could. She showed me the exotic thrills I'd missed, moreover showing that racial differences come to zero once it's dark, and nothing remains but the sigh and small death so similar to the big death in its perspective, that nothing will survive this life but love.

I thought such insights were positive gains that would round into the stretch to the finish line. What could be better? I was a new man, born again and more; I felt redeemed, having fun, with a purpose and love. But change comes on, whether you know it or not, or want it or not, or plan accordingly, and it rarely ceases right where you want it to.

To her credit, she didn't care about wandering aimlessly among the commercial byways in Charleston, looking at frilly things to buy. Hell, what I called French tailoring, she called homemade, which was French in a way. She had a knack with fabric and a body to make the cheap stuff look good. But she felt no need to go shopping otherwise, no need to prove mobility or anything to any man or woman. She knew what they said about us. I think she liked it. I think she realized that without me, they'd have said little of her, as if her spectacular charm would warrant no attention at all, had she not snared the likes of me. I think her assumption was correct, but it led to no resentment. She felt certain somebody would have come along for her, and that assumption felt correct too. She saw me struggle with that potential and assured me that it, like all else, was only natural.

But the dancing bug stuck like a burr in her shorts with only one thing for it. So we settled on a casual reconnoiter of Folly Beach, to see what pubs or honkytonks might have music. Who knew? I didn't know. She'd never been. We freely discussed the hateful potential, but she thought it was a myth. I assured her I'd not been to Folly in twenty years, but even at that I'd bet her instincts to be correct. I'd plain never seen that sort of thing around here.

Yes, I said that, believing it as I said it, feeling it lump in my throat in the speaking, as if I'd come so far as to forget. Fact was, I didn't consider my own past behavior to be racially motivated but rather an ill-chosen prank, a personal frustration airing out with hardly a thought for race, creed or color. At least I'd forgiven the principles, though I still suffered remorse for the perception of others, and I accepted Aníse, in her darkness, as my penance, my redemption, my puzzle to solve.

This too may have been sophistry; she was such an easy price to pay. More importantly, I didn't see any reaction in her to my comment on the absence of racial hostility, so I doubted she knew about the old Arthur Covingdale, the button-down, suit-and-tie, brick-throwing, cross-burning sonofabitch. Not that it mattered; those events, people, places that feel too personal are also natural, bad or good, and only by airing out can things change. I wondered if all of France was so cavalier, or was it only Guadeloupe, or just her. I determined to tell her of my misdeeds, one day, so I could be the source of her knowing and spare us the rude surprise.

We headed to Folly Beach on a Thursday evening, and since it was thirty miles each way, we planned to stop for dinner at Bowen's Island, on the way to Folly. Jim Cohen got wind of our plan and said he *spec dat be's igna't as igna't be's*, paying good money for oysters you could have for the picking.

Aníse hushed him with her happiness, telling him she tried dancing on the oyster beds, and it didn't work, and besides, it was the picking she wanted free of, and besides, she needed to get out and about to see if she wanted to stay around, you know.

I gave her points for subtlety and couldn't blame her for wanting to get out, but a man feels the screws tighten, no matter how exotic the woman or the situation. I wrestled with the advisability of Bowen's Island, the pros and cons grappling to a draw all the way there. We pulled in to the parking lot as I clearly saw that where we ate in public, like so much else, didn't matter. In a hundred years we'd all be dead anyway. Still, I repressed the next forty minutes for fear of the living required to get through them—and the stories arising from them that might be told for another century or two.

Bowen's oyster-shell parking lot would have cost upwards of ten thousand dollars anywhere else, but the Bowens got it free and took care of the trash-hauling to boot in laying down those oyster shells; this interesting iota I pointed out to my date, who stared at the oblique plain, reflecting concerns equal to my own. So our adventure into the world proceeded intrepidly, against our collective instinct.

Bowen's Island is an island only technically, bounded to the north, west and south by the Intracoastal Waterway and to the east by the Folly River. But Bowen's was clearly an island in the cultural sense, home to the Bowen clan for eons, those people deriving sustenance from the creeks and marshes with a bare modicum of social etiquette, like the Wadmalaw Cohens but different; the Bowens were white folks. Their island remove was unpolluted, their oysters sweet as ever, served roasted, sit-down, for money. So it wasn't a restaurant with dishes and menus and such. It had tables covered with fresh newspaper, changed from one party to the next. And oyster knives. But the chief characteristic was its refuge from a world picked clean as a piglet in piranhas; this certain raw remnant of Lowcountry color we'd held back for ourselves. Bowen's Island had no signs. You had to know where it was or know someone willing to give directions. The real reason for no signage at Bowen's was the nightly sellout. The Bowens declined signage, which was okay by us. We didn't want outsiders stopping in for oysters, shrimp and crab easy as that; next thing you know, it's packed and gone.

You couldn't get oysters that good anywhere else without the boots, the mud, beer and whiskey, the rain, gloves and knives, ebb tide, bushel baskets, the truck, the fire, sheet metal, burlap, picnic table, rags and cocktail sauce. A demanding schedule made Bowen's the only option, if you wanted to scratch that itch in an hour or two. Oh, it was our essence and inner sanctum, insulated by the hail-fellow ballyhoo popular with the seersucker, penny-loafer crowd. So why did I pick Bowen's? What else could I do, take her into town? Like I said, I didn't think it mattered.

Yet town seemed better as we neared Bowen's. At Bessinger's Barbecue, the cracker crowd wouldn't know me. That was twelve miles farther but made more sense on second thought and third as we shuffled across the lot. "Maybe barbecue'd be...."

"No."

As we walked on, I nearly felt my membership card to Jimmy's Social Club, nestled in my wallet like an anthropological artifact, claiming my right to socialize with friends in a private club. Jimmy allowed no Blacks. When did I change? Would I ever taste fried chicken so good again? *Have you heard? Arthur Covingdale been hitting Bowen's for sit-down oysters with his new squeeze.*

Man. Whatchou thankin'?

She looked over, so I explained there was no menu. It was oysters, crabs and shrimp with corn bread, coleslaw and a sidefly, your choice of okra, collards, field peas, succotash, lima beans, green beans, summer squash, rice or potatoes. They serve the oysters with a shovel. She didn't see the mirth in Bowen's serving folks of certain crust and genealogy from a shovel. Or any novelty in that same gentry bringing a brown-bag bottle for a most efficient dinner and drunk. "Maybe we might ought to go get us a bottle."

"No." She hooked her arm under mine so the charm could work its magic once more, for a few more paces anyway.

You can walk into the Valley of the Shadow whistling Zippity Do Da, but that won't lighten your prospects. Sho nuff, Aníse and I walked in like a modern couple to see my longtime friend Hedley Rice having dinner with Ashmead Montague, whom I'd met on several occasions socially and worked with twice professionally. I didn't know Ashmead Montague beyond the niceties, but he seemed wanly predictable, meaning he wore his trousers low and entered a room with a happy, tired face plastered in place. He had the high forehead and swayback common to the area and appeared to be programmed since infancy on what to wear, how to walk, what to say and how to say it. I sensed that Ashmead Montague had lived the proverbial low profile with deliberation and method since early adolescence. He strove for expertise in estate settlements with no surprises. Constraint with grooming was his choice, his plan, his life, conforming to the blue blood coursing damn near purple in his veins. His two bubbas, Ashmead Pringle and Pringle Montague, unrelated by blood, unless you count the roots ineluctably intertwined to the point of inextricable tangle under the family trees, also practiced the law, making for a complex cluster of salutations.

All the Ashmeads and Pringles germinated from the same conjugation back in the 17th, with the Montagues tying in around the turn to the 18th. To suggest inbreeding was plain rude, and reference to a shallow gene pool would have flown over that pond like a goose at midnight.

Ashmead Pringle also practiced the law, like Ashmead Montague, but Ashmead Pringle sold real estate too, specializing in discretion on pocket listings, so a transaction might close before the gossip got underway. Pringle Montague was known more for civil litigation with a focus on outlanders failing to measure up financially, ethically or any which way. The three had no choice in daily encounters but to call each other bubba. They redirected calls from folks looking for one of the other two.

The devil was in the details; calling someone bubba and actually bestowing bubba status were not the same. Ashmead Montague waited with something pithy on his tongue as the distance closed between us, both of us knowing the challenge upon him. That is, his bubba and cousin long removed, Pringle Montague (*mah cuzzin Prangle*), had kept his man Marcellus in twenty-four-hour service for the past eighteen years. Marcellus was personal valet, hand and foot and then some, avoiding scandal, because everybody knew that reciprocity is a fundamental tenet of homosexual society. Loyal service in this application, predicated the two-way street, going and coming. In a nutshell, Pringle and Marcellus were a novelty, an amusement, in time, a familiarity, another eccentricity called colorful in town. Marcellus was Black; never mind, *because* they were homos, passing transcendent in the spirit of social parity. Pringle Montague was one of us by birth, and that was that, just like a particular judge had been a cousin and bubba hardly removed before he defiled our historical values and ageless decency, don't you know.

I sensed that the jury was still out on my new honey and me. She was Black, along with strikingly beautiful and worldly, so maybe we'd slide in there easy as Pringle Montague and his man Marcellus. I knew, however, that personal history might overrule the eccentricity argument to favor the prosecution.

So we strolled, Aníse and I, toward two colleagues of my former life, the sight them rendering me fatigued with the ritual before us; *hey, bubba, how you gittin' along? Whatchou fittin' a do? Jeatchet? Whassissear?* Ashmead Montague was tedious and boring, a royal pain in the ass by birth. I anticipated his pithy retort to the peculiarity among us as something along the lines of, *Well, now, lookaheah; Mist Awthuh finally got him some comp'ny, huh?*

He dispelled any notion of the peculiar with regard his own appetite, lest anyone confuse him with Pringle Montague, the homosexual. His tiresome reference to the smutty side of women provided safe haven, he thought.

Just prior to my retreat, I'd entered a conference room at the office as he reached terms with two of our young attorneys on a divorce settlement. Our boys represented the husband, Rutledge Reid, candidate for the Congress of the United States of America, an office that could bode well for our firm. That's why he got two attorneys instead of one, up-and-coming hotshots who billed out good too.

Ashmead Montague represented the wife, Mary Ellen, whose morals had loosened dramatically in a last ditch effort to make Rut jealous and win him back, or so the story went. Said loosening was rumored to include a series of blow jobs for Bubba Loomis in the back seat of his Mercedes sedan. The failure here was Ashmead's. He set his client's best interest aside to serve his own interests, at

Mary Ellen's expense. I walked in at the tail end, so to speak, as Ashmead Montague confided like the bubba he wanted to be. On Mary Ellen's last visit to his office, she'd worn no underpants, which she was also rumored to do, as she was rumored to yen for orgiastic intercourse with couples or women or out-of-towners, because that's what gossip comes to in a village so bored. Mary Ellen crossed her legs, he said, not modestly like a woman but ankle over knee like a man, so when she rocked back in contemplation of the terms they would seek, "why, she aimed that thing at me like a Gatlin' gun, and I'm here to tell you it was the most terrific beaver a man ever laid eyes on. I mean to tell you that thing was big!"

The young attorneys present were not fully developed on gentlemanly constraint and leaned in for a good pussy story. Oh, Ashmead had their attention. But their professional affiliation was my own. They grinned on cue, and Hastings Bayden said, "Ashmead, you don't mean a Gatling gun, do you, Bubba? You mean, like a elephant rifle, don't you?"

To which Ashmead Montague rejoined like a learned barrister, "No, I mean a Gatlin' gun. It was big enough for a elephant rifle, but the breach was warped, indicating repeated overheating as a result of rapid fire, Your Honor."

I walked out on the raucous guffaws. I can appreciate an off-color story, but this went beyond lawyer-client to defamation, to abusive tedium, rendering me sick of the entire charade, sick of grown men of no real stature sustaining each other in mutual edification. And the deep brogue used to seal the bond also made me sick. *De mos tuhriffic buyhva* (the most terrific beaver) and *Ah muyhn a tellyu at thang was big!* (I mean to tell you that thing was big.) Ashmead clarified the sexuality issue; no homo there, not like that other Montague.

And there he sat in our path at Bowen's, beaming with good cheer, cordiality and impeccable manners, adherent to the rules of our road.

Hedley Rice sat at his table. Far less predictable and in fact a practicing intellectual, Hedley avoided the local brogue as he could and reflected on purpose and meaning where he could. A physician trained in orthopedic surgery, he gave over early in his career to emergency room medicine for the set schedule of the thing. He said the ER's fixed schedule, freed him up to fish and be with his children, without suffering *totalus interruptus* every day, which is a doctor's cross to bear. I believe he'd pick the ER again, though it embittered him over the years, applying his education and skills (his words) to humanity's dregs. Day in, day out, he complained that a certain segment of the population was out of control, haywire, without resources, without hope. That is, ninety percent of his emergency room patients were Negroes suffering what only euthanasia could cure, his thought.

He'd complained about a long shift given over to a Black woman, age fifty, with a stench, fecal and regurgitated. She'd come to the ER because she "don't feel no good," with nine children in tow, promising to pay for part of this visit next Tuesday when *de ADD check posed to come in de mail.* That was then, when ADD meant Aid to Dependent Children instead of what it came to in the age of sensitivity, Attention Deficit Disorder. Then she puked down her front, over the dried puke already there, dribbling onto the examining table and the floor.

Diagnosis: pregnant. Hedley's diagnosis: repugnant; "Don't ask. Man, oh, man, you would not believe...." And so on into a bottle, he'd soaked down what ailed him. Hedley admitted that euthanasia would never fly, on account of resistance from liberal quarters, but he could not figure who in the world would not benefit from sterilization. And he shored up his case with personal commitment: "Hell, I got my tubes tied" But he knew that wouldn't fly either, on account of God-given rights and the sanctimonious nature of human life. "They dredge and fill marshlands for condominiums, so the money can flow where it has to, and there goes what ought to be sacred but ain't. What about that?" Hedley swore he was no racist, because he hated the bastards who built the condominiums and the bastards who moved in, every damn one white, proving his equal opportunity disgust with folks in the area, and I liked him for that. He could go on.

Suffice to say the stage was set for drama of a delicate and personal nature when my new date and I walked through Bowen's.

Tension came to us from the outside world, people thought, but there we were. I'd made an effort in recent days to sort my life into what I loved and what I'd sooner live without. That is, even as I wound up my serve for the upcoming volley, I strove to keep this passing light-hearted. I would not factor Ashmead's homosexual cousin or Hedley's wife, who left him on account of his drunkenness. She moved north seven miles to Dr. Lattimer Smythe's Isle of Palms beach house. Latty Smythe had been a longtime associate and friend of the Hedley Rices. Dr. Smythe was willing to help a woman in need and plug the gap in her love life. But that's another story, and nobody begrudged Latty Smythe. The Smythes were not original but climbed up from Smiths for heaven's sake, or the Elizabethan ring of the thing. Those extra letters made the difference between soda bread and baguettes, the change occurring late 18th, sorely recent in social sway and like much else in our place and time, discussed only in private.

Hedley had been celibate before his wife left, and the last two years living on his own were worse. He wasn't the first man to consider sex more frequently than having it, but this was Hedley Rice of the Georgetown Rices, a physician of eminence, income and family history, but he couldn't for the life of him tame a little leg. His deprivation was not widely known. I was made privy at odd intervals, advising as I could on his roster of candidates for the sexual act. What did I know? And he was stuck, afraid of sexual harassment, afraid of the gossip line and the womanizer epithet. But he couldn't score dribbling; never up, never in. His image and reputation fairly intimidated women, even though his propriety and turpitude were bullshit. I urged him to visit Beasley Barrineau's Blow Job Parlour out on West Ashley (no signage there too) for the magical interlude known to cure what ailed a man. He feared that too; stuck bad.

I couldn't begrudge his eyes opening steamy as two oysters. Still, I hoped we could get by on a handshake and hello, bubba. Already causing a buzz, Aníse and I would be part of table talk around town in no time and on the street a good three days quicker than a direct feed to the local paper. I wanted past these two stalwarts, but on a strange tick in time, I wanted to savor as well the summary conclusion moving over our collective consciousness, such as it was, like a squall line. I wanted them to see Aníse and feel her presence. She was French, hardly Huguenot but then hardly African too, in the sense of what we thought we knew. Hell, we were all Goths and Visigoths, if you went back far enough. But I doubt they saw things that way.

Aníse's artistry was essential, not like the artsy fartsy we saw too often in town but the real McCoy, exotic, graceful, gifted. I wanted them to know I'd done well, much better than Hedley Rice, who ran his mouth like a wood chipper over one woman and another who might want to lie down with him, if he could only figure out how in the world he could, you know, get her there.

Tackle her, goddamnit! That was not my advice but a measure of my exasperation. Was he the only man with a libido challenge? No, he was not. My sexual life was a similar failure, in which an aging man doubts that a woman could see what was once there, much less want what's left. The difference between other men and me was that I had the cure. Better yet, the cure had me.

I wanted Hedley and Ashmead to sense my good fortune and to know I'd fared better; me, a man of the world, if not for all seasons, at least for this one.

I should have anticipated what came next in a kinder, softer light, but they'd set me up to be defensive. That is, Ashmead and Hedley saw Aníse as exotic and beautiful, and as men of great good sense, they would stay on the high road. They stood as one, effusing honey charm in synchrony. Ashmead slipped sideways to block our path and pull a chair for Aníse, as Hedley said, "Please."

Ashmead concurred, "Won't you join us?"

I know those two nosy bastards wanted firsthand dirt, maybe pick up some stories to share with the crowd down at the Hibernian or the club or group lunch, but they neither smirked nor tittered. Rather the old warmth flowed like warm molasses, ready to pour, like Aníse and I were regular folks out to dinner. "Oh! You are so kind," she tittered, casual as a lady running into old friends, who bowed in chivalry, as they waited for the lady to be seated.

I made the introductions. "Aníse. Hedley Rice is one of our foremost...." I checked myself and relaxed. "Hedley's a doctor. And Ashmead here is a lawyer, like me."

"Like you used to be," Ashmead sniggered.

"Yes. Like I used to be."

So it was time to sit, eyes sliding into the whirlpool, down Aníse's bodice. Shadowy surfaces sorely tested their night vision, the black dress blending with her skin, so a man had to stretch his neck and squint more than good taste could warrant.

Nobody's fool on a tit shot, Aníse eased us into this unusual gathering with a suggestion. "Why we do not share the oyster as we wait for...ah...*plus encore*...ours. And then we share those too." Oh, a topping suggestion indeed, agreed our old friends, now brimful and spilling forth, yet tongue-tied in the face of the world suddenly arrived. Aníse signaled the waiter and ordered two more shovel loads of *oy-stérs*—letting a *merci bien* slip softly at the end. She retained control of situation, picking a steaming beauty and handling it deftly in her fingertips.

Ashmead presented opening comments for the plaintiff: "You not from around here. Are you? I heard you weren't. I heard you were from…way out."

She explained that her family was not entirely from Charleston, because her Grandfather Mose, sailed away at an early age and wound up on Guadeloupe, which they, Hedley and Ashmead, well knew as part of the French West Indies, where the balance of her family remains. "I am a Cohen by blood. You may know my Uncle Jim. My family name in Guadeloupe is Coquelin." Unable to resist its scent any longer, she brought her oyster to her lips and eased it to the chew, to where staring any longer would have been rude.

When the boys caught themselves watching, Hedley blushed, but Ashmead went to local tactics, back-quoting the facts as surmised. "You're Aníse Coquelin, then?" *Yo Ainus Cokelin, den?*

"No. *Ce n'est pas ay-nus.* Ay-nus is, how you say, ass hole. Aníse. Like the spice."

"You mean the…licorice one?"

"Yes. That one. Do you like it?" The boys couldn't keep their eyebrows down on that juicy tidbit, that AC's new squeeze was black as licorice and had the same name.

"I am Aníse Monfret. I was married once before."

Ashmead queried further, as if seeking clarification for personal edification, yet I sensed dubious motivation, to be spokesman for the whole. "You're…visiting then?"

Aníse favored me with a suggestive, though ill-timed sparkle. "I don't know." Her exquisite self pulsed in soft allure and French flair, even though she hailed from a small island likely as parochial as our own. Her social ease felt familiar, though we knew what was different here, what was changing in our hearts from taboo to something else. It changed in their hearts from naught to envy. They knew about charm, they thought, as if personified our little town. Yet they saw dimensions in Aníse as yet unanticipated.

"You staying with your family here?"

She ate another oyster, taking her time, savoring the taste and the tension. It broke on another smile. "I was. I am staying now with Arthur." *Ah-tuh,* she said in a sweet blend of accents, Guadeloupe with a Gullah underbelly.

Hedley's eyebrows rose again, though Ashmead managed to keep one down as the other rose.

"You staying out there with Arthur? At the place?" Hedley back-quoted again, like a cross-examiner eager to pin down the facts, so the court reporter could get every juicy bit.

"Mm hm," she hummed. "If the place is where he is, then that is where I be," she cooed, nodding sidelong at the cooling pile of oysters, which the boys and I proceeded to eat.

Ah, nothing like a good meal to ease a conversational impasse, and so we ate, muttering and mumbling sounds of goodness and appreciation for the delectable morsels before us. "You don't get oysters like these over there, do you?"

"No. We do not. You are very lucky here. But you know that. Do you not?"

"What sort of.... What do you.... What were your days like over there in Guadeloupe?" Hedley asked.

"Oh, you know. The same as anywhere. You try to enjoy life. Guadalupe is very warm, you know."

"Yes," Hedley affirmed.

" But did you have a...you know, a job?" Ashmead pursued.

"I was assistant in an office of legal affairs," she said, which got them nodding, giving them something to approve of at last, something tame and not so daring. "But that was before. The last few years I live with my boyfriend. He was a dj, you know, a disk jockey, but not at a radio station. He works at a club, where I help. It was quite nice and very popular. We often dance all night."

"You danced all night?"

"Yes." That harsh reality rounded the table in silence, until Aníse asked the follow-up, "You never dance all night?"

Hedley and Ashmead shared their first glance across the table; no, they had not danced all night.

"Drank all night, maybe," I injected. "But these two haven't danced since they did the shag at Folly Beach before the pier burned down."

"The shag?"

"Another holdover habit," I explained. "It was a dance popular in the fifties. That was a safe time, so we preserved part of it."

"Ah, so you never dance with *Ska* or *Zuké*?"

"Who?"

"Island music."

"This boyfriend. He wadn't da former husband, was he?"

"Oh, no. I was not married for years."

Ashmead moved, unfortunately, for the summary judgment. "So you worked in a night club till you broke up with your boyfriend the dj, who was not the former husband, and now you out to Wadmalaw with Arthur Covingdale?"

"I think you are a lawyer too," she said. "Tell me something. Have you been married?"

"Yes, Ma'm," Ashmead said. "Both of us."

"You mean both you and the woman who was your wife?"

"No, no. I mean me and Hedley here. We were both married." Ashmead enunciated clearly, for the record.

"But no longer?" Ashmead shrugged and shook his head. Hedley grimaced tentatively.

"And you have no girlfriend?"

"You got any girlfriends for us?" Hedley asked, pressing the har, har, har to diffuse the sad truth. Or maybe Hedley meant to suggest the ultimate laugh over those two professional white males dancing all night with musty womens. Unless Aníse might have some girlfriends…like her.

Aníse apprised him. "You are a man of not bad looks. I wonder why you have no girlfriend."

"Well," Hedley mumbleded, picking another oyster to allay what he knew. "There's more to life than dancing and having fun, darlin'."

"What? What could be more? Are you homosexual?"

That liked to brought an oyster back up.

"Arthur. I think you got yourself a spitfire here."

Ouch. I'd read that word not long ago in a crumbling local newspaper, describing Judge Waring's new wife. So much of what I'd sorted through those last few months surfaced in the tingling on my skin. I wanted to tell Hedley and Ashmead that this woman was no spitfire but my girlfriend, plain and simple, a more charming, more spritely, more worldly girlfriend than they could hope to find. As it was, I only said, "Hedley…."

Aníse intervened, wiping her fingers and settling them on Hedley's arm. "I want to enjoy life to the maximum. Don't you? I have hear that you do. Arthur, he may be not too bad for dancing. I hope so. I will teach him, maybe. He's got none of the rhythm *naturále*. Oh, but he do show me a rousin' good time, you know." The boys could only stare down their empty shells and ponder. "I think he is in love. *C'est vrais. Aw-tuh? N'est-ce pas?*"

She had us bound and gagged, relieving the boys of any doubt remaining on the bliss of my island days, but perhaps burdening them with further fantasy. I suppose she liberated me too, rendering me free of my inordinate elaborations. I kept this one brief. "Fuh true," I translated, in case their French was rusty.

The boys declined her invitation to join us for dancing after dinner, down at the beach place Arthur knows. But no. Hedley had to, uh, er, work early in the morning.

Ashmead Montague shook his head, presumptively over the principal of the thing, and said, "Sheeyit. You crazy? Us? At Folly Beach?"

xv

What Was I Thinking?

And that was that, completing our first and, with any luck, last effort to penetrate civilization. We gained clarity on the stereotypical notion that I lacked the natural rhythm gene. She marveled at the disconnection, heart and mind failing to recognize hips and hind end. I was able, however, to compensate this disconcerting disconnect with demonstrable aptitude in horizontal application. She praised my grace and style. I suspected flattery but took it like a wise man, because it worked, serving us both, inspiring anew to reach deeper in energy and love for a personal best. Such was the difference between this year's *Beaujolais* and the vintage dregs of my past.

To call the early segments of that memorable evening enjoyable, however, would have been a stretch. The oysters were excellent, and surviving dinner with the boys was a relief, as was the brevity of our sojourn to the single bistro open for business on Folly Beach. The Hog Call was dark and dank. The place smelled of stale beer and soggy butts. A handful of hippie types at the bar looked us over, and one of them voiced approval, "Right on, man."

A tired old jukebox took my quarter on a dull clang and played three tired tunes to complete our dancing experiment. I hoped she was only discouraged and not demoralized. Enjoyable it was not.

Relief restored us, back in the car, insulated from social challenge, cruising south on a beautiful night, over moonlit causeways and marshes, gaining distance on what seemed tolerant and tolerable at best. The ride home felt meditative, with sparse dialogue but apparent communion in mutual enjoyment of the scenery, the movement and cushy warmth of my Mercedes sedan. The serenity of home filled in as we neared the Hunt Club.

We ended our adventure on a mutual sigh and closed the evening on a high note, initiated by Aníse's lively gratitude for my willingness to go along, including dinner on a spirited volley, an awkward go at dancing and a plush ride in a luxury sedan, not to mention my gentlemanly aplomb. What else could I do but assure her in kind that the honor was all mine? I too was grateful for her soft skill in taunting my old friends without their knowing it. Her salacious lilt and suggestive eyes seemed like cream gravy.

Or else I presumed her gratitude; she may well have shown me nothing but love. Or her motivation could have been hormonal; she seemed persistent on that level, and maybe a wooden baton cut from excellent timber by an English manufacturer of repute could have sufficed to fill her need. Perhaps I only reciprocated the physical fervor of the luscious woman in my bed—I didn't know but thought the situation was not so devoid of feeling.

I'd reached a happy point, at which underlying causation was incidental to the moment, and the moments were sweet. In any event, she soon snored gently beside me; she was forty-one, or two, after all. And I, old guy on a lark, followed suit like a chain saw, clear-cutting the thicket around us.

In the eighth month of our first year, Aníse Monfret, née Claudia Coquelin, of the Guadeloupe Coquelins and the Wadmalaw Cohens, swelled with her first child, causing her pitch black skin to glow eerily ruddy, like an *aurora borealis* much farther south and closer to the ground. Her eyes also shone with the popularly construed warmth of encroaching motherhood, though on her it looked more alert or alarmed than warm, like the gaze of a wild creature suddenly sensing momentous change in the forest. She looked a little crazy, which I, for one, rather enjoyed, considering the essence of our attraction as that between the known and unknown worlds. She seemed more exotic and mysterious on each approach. I could only speculate what I must have seemed to her, but I think it was bolder, with fewer compunctions and inhibitions than she'd sensed early on.

She confided her condition with trepidation, rambling in and out of English and French, that she understood the impracticality of an established white lawyer fathering a Black baby, so if I could provide a few dollars to help with the birth and childhood, she would take over from there. She understood this to be a common arrangement, and though she'd been plagued to date on the money bother, she didn't anticipate such a problem with me, after all, since it would be nothing to me but a few dollars here and there. She did not mention childbearing at her age with regard to complexity and potential.

As I digested the news, she eased alongside on the ratty sofa that so many of the white gentry had relaxed upon. She raised an arm tentatively, as if to rest it on my shoulder but held it aloft, where the fingers dangled but soon settled onto my head and stroked my gray temples. Again, by design or chance didn't matter; she eased the burgeoning realization and acceptance beneath her skin and mine.

Stunned with what should have been no surprise to a more grounded, stable man, my mind turned circles like a tiger chasing its tail. Little Black Sambo Covingdale watched from overhead, dressed in knee breeches and a natty shirt with lace trim, on his way to private school. He strolled happily with other children of recorded ancestries and in-town addresses, all with two-digit street numbers....

But wait; Little Black Sambo was Indian, not African; how else could he have watched a tiger instead of a lion? No, change that to, uh....

So my distraction took form. Why would my child lack a highfalutin genealogy or a two-digit address? What African mythology or joke could portray the burgeoning reality pressing my skull and her womb? I stared off, though my eyes gave in to gravity, as her fingers had done. She caressed my face, her fingers far softer than those of her forbears, whose hands grubbed and hardened like wood and gnarled like cypress roots; hands that had gone palms down to secure total blackness. I took her hand in mine. She sensed affection. This hand had not worked cotton or oysters, not for a living, not with those long fingernails painted red, a stylish holdover from the dancing days, or should I say nights, when she shook her booty (her words) till dawn, then entwined wildly (my thoughts) with her former...what? Boyfriend?

I held her hand to ponder her grasp. I could call her deft or devious but chose intuitive; she'd won the moment and the hour on wit and wisdom and what felt purely motivated. That left the questions of me.

How could I lean on sixty as a new father? How could I have a Black woman as mother to my child? Could she assuage the repercussions abounding with repeated dalliance, like I was nineteen and couldn't get enough, and love would conquer all?

Well, she seemed game for a try. So I put the tough questions aside and rode it out, as it were, one go to the next, or, more generously put, from gathering to prep to taking sustenance and sleep amidst the natural beauty abounding. We drifted downstream as if nothing had changed in a month or a century, taking as necessary in those ever-mutable marshlands. With historical perspective and a sense of tradition, the niggling doubts so common to this veil of tears were held at bay. It wasn't bad. Hell, it was good.

By the eleventh month of our communion, the third month of gestation, the paved village to the north reverberated with Eudora's vindictive glee, "She's preggers! His Black bitch is preggers to beat all get out!"

What is it with former wives who get everything they demand yet retain the bitter bile? Well, of course they don't get everything. Nobody gets the time back, and a bitter woman will pounce on a scapegoat to blame for her loss, to facilitate lunch with friends. I had given her a place to go, conversationally.

Eudora didn't get the house either, because it was in my family five generations, and she moved there from a dump on the back end of Society Street, and her case for restitution was presented to a judge residing two doors down from me.

Given, however, that Eudora's cerebral capacity was similar to that of a smallish legume, the question still niggled: Why would a mixed-race infant of unwed parents generate such foul anticipation among small-minded people? What could this child do but learn potty training and how to dress itself? What harm would this child cause in going to school, playing outdoors, growing up and contributing to society, breaking no major laws and living happily, as our Constitution warrants and several amendments, proclamations, caveats and annotations serve to shore up?

More to the heart of the matter, I'd match my Black bitch to her Jeffers Rutledge on the auction block any day, figuratively speaking of course. Not a bad fellow, if taken substantively, Jefferson Rutledge was among the handful of lawyers whose word, intention and standard was every bit as straightforward as he was. His word was called currency, because of his cut on state revenue bonds. He couldn't afford not to be honest, having secured contracts with the State of South Carolina on legal review of all revenue bonds issued since 1934, at a fee set of one half of one percent, which comes to some big dough on two billion dollars annual in bond issues. What did a man of stature and wealth need with Eudora? Company? Comfort? Solace? Insight? What?

Jeffers Rutledge was eighty, that's what, owning up to seventy-eight, insisting on the two-year difference, like Jack Benny but pathetic instead of funny, disappearing under fleshy folds, wheezing to the edge of apoplexy. A man so wealthy and wizened worked out well for Eudora too, providing context to a woman beyond her years. She'd taken to smearing her lipstick outside the lines, to look like a vamp, red hot, so Jeffers could anticipate some pecker juice extraction, tired as he was. My God, that's ugly. Boring enough to numb anybody, Jeffers wasn't a bad man, kind to friends and strangers, an original practitioner of our brand of charm.

He only needed to ask me, to know what he was getting into. He didn't ask but wouldn't likely have married anybody without the prenupts. Even at that, he likely offered her more money than I ever hoped to have. Whatever arrangement or romantic rigmarole drove Eudora and Jeffers to matrimony was conjectural, and doubts were rampant on the consummation issue, though sordid speculation took the form of great good humor, contained to privacy among the men of that polite society. Jeffers Rutledge required more maintenance than a sports car, a rickety old collectible hardly up to daily driving. Eudora deserved a needful husband, and he must have had a spiritual debt in the shadows too. Knowing her practical side, I savored her accounting, balancing dollars against time, short time maybe. Harsh again, I only proved what marriage can come to, and hoped Jeffers a long life. He had the means to pay for the very best in comfort and care.

No doubts came our way on the consummation issue. Aníse was a knockout, and I wasn't yet sixty, giving us a leg up on Eudora and Jeffers, speaking of whom, I sorely wished I could have joined the manly palaver in town, in great good humor, don't you know. I reckoned Eudora on top. Who could hold Jeffers up? Not him or her. Besides, she preferred the upper hand and better view. His jowls would surely look best lying flat instead of swinging like an old hound's. The moles and liver spots would come at her either way, but her breasts would benefit from the dangle. On the bottom, they'd slide sideways like batter on a griddle tilt. Yes, unkind and ugly made that talk suitably responsive to the thoughts and dialogue aimed our way.

Aníse shone on a few facets, from certain social skills to natural love out in the marshland. She required a degree of stamina too, but it seemed a blessing next to what looked Jeffers Rutledge in the face. A woman has an effect on a man, and Aníse loved hers on me. Eudora should have been grateful, but I didn't wonder why she harped; that's who she was, a harpy, which vile creatures of half-female form were actually thought to be the original cunts, or so it went in Greek mythology. Or so I longed to postulate among the manly segment. Eudora likely overhead the common consensus of that same segment, with regard to Aníse, which collective perception came down to a rhetorical question: "Are you shittin' me?" It triggered envy in a different shade of purple.

Aníse hadn't thought of children, she said, immersed in freedom and enjoying life to the maximum. When life changed, delivering her to beauty and stimulation of a more serene nature, she felt ready. She'd fantasized travel but feared being a fish out of water. She craved a more rounded resume, with London and Paris, but feared she might be too provincial. "Compared to what?" I asked. "Or who? I've seen you out and about. Any more confidence and you could get in trouble." We ventured down to Beaufort for the close proximity of the place and endured the stares. On up the road to Greenville (*Grainvull*), a similar interlude provided a change of scenery and relief on coming home. Hilton Head Island wasn't much better, stares there accompanied by liberal grinning and nodding, as that place too failed rapidly under the yoke of Yankee imperialism.

In 1969, the world watched three white men touch down on the lunar surface and pray, raise a flag, claim another colony for the mother country, play golf, pray some more and cruise in a dune buggy. Their lunar frolic included many important experiments for the betterment of mankind. Womankind still deferred to the master gender and appeared only in commercials between the scenes, where women in kitchens or bathrooms praised detergents, dish soaps, disposable diapers and douches, digestive aids, degreasers. Cross Your Heart brassieres went black as an option about then, or colored, or Afro American. African American came later, as Black faded from *de rigueur*. I point this out to underscore the depth of my situation. I felt farther from home than the Pop'n Fresh boys on the moon. I felt farther out than the proverbial far out, banished to orbital eternity. Can you imagine the street-level murmurs burbling up on my casual return to the byways of my former life? The question to me was whether apparent fulfillment could last, or would it become something to endure? I could feign happiness in a charade, like Eudora, but a few doubts took form. For starters, Aníse gained weight, far more than the weight of a fetus, any fetus, anywhere, any time. The doctor called weight gain inevitable and variable, depending on genetic predisposition, diet, exercise and, oh, yeah, age. She could hardly tote the load. We were miserable.

But we came to learn that confinement was what we made of it, and reawakening daily took our reality vacuum to the simple pleasures in easy access. We reached for society too, a different society to be sure, the heart of which was the society we made between us. Talk about getting to know somebody.

Life was fraught, and I welcomed a practical distraction. Rumors of AC and his new darky family out at the Hunt Club were not surprising but triggered a new concern. I'd anticipated long-term logistics, which is not to say convenience to church, schools and shopping. I was done with that and comfortably so. But a man senses responsibilities.

Peter Maxwell had issued the original invitation to stay at the Hunt Club, and then he solved our fundamental problem once again. He drove out unannounced, not that he could have called. We had no phone. The Hunt Club could have had a phone since '67 of that century, and the Hunt Club boys wouldn't have minded me putting one in, so long as the phone came out, once AC came back to his senses. I opted out. I wanted no calls, because a cut should be clean and decisive, I thought, lest is fester. And I could predict the calls incoming. I suspected Peter's motivation in coming out to see us but couldn't fault his curiosity. After all, with Ashmead Montague braying like a Philistine over the red hot mama ol' Covindale's bangin' like a drum out at the Hunt Club, what man wouldn't want a look-see?

But Peter was more cordial than curious and sincere as always, greeting me and then Aníse, as if it was my old house in town, and she was my new better half, and the sun was shining on our special world, and everything was lovely, and we were all white. I paint this scene in mockery, even as I task myself for failing to take Peter's goodwill at face value. What more anyone could want from a scene, except maybe for the part about us all being white. And, I suppose, if idylls were real, urban or country, and we were all accepted, I'd get itchy again for the wild side. But maybe not, getting it regular at home.

At any rate, Peter Maxwell spoke freely as a friend, one of the true variety. "I don't know why you got yourself into this, Arthur." He checked himself to make sure he hadn't stepped out of bounds, smiling at Aníse with the unavoidable once-over, likely surmising the before and after of pregnancy. "Well, I do know—I mean, I understand. We all need a change, sometime or other, and the restlessness.... And so on.... Doesn't matter. I want you to know I respect whatever decisions you make." He let his approval of my life sink in, but not too long, before proceeding to the practical reason for his visit, lest I view him as superior in his approval, which superiority remained an exposed nerve in our crowd, because we were. "Fact is, a man needs a place to live."

He paused again, as if to allow for hope, so Aníse and I could share a brief, anxious glance. Did he come to offer up the Hunt Club at a reasonable price, given the color and complexity of the situation we'd found ourselves in. He cut that idea short with: "You can't stay here."

He paused yet again for another eyeful, this time of the ramshackle but venerable Hunt Club, home of the tallest tales yet risen from the Wadmalaw mud, as told by white men. Again, my eyes settled downward on a loss, down to the vast space beyond the question: Now what? I stared at the ground, waiting for notice and timing, recalling the new little woman's great-grandfather, feeling just as shiftless, with nothing to say for myself or my unwieldy behavior.

"Unless you buy it," Peter said. I looked up, suddenly grounded, back home among associates of the realm and real estate, buy and sell, terms and conditions, parties of the first and second parts, aforementioned and by all parties witnesseth thereof. "I mentioned it to the other fellows." He seemed uncomfortable at this point, as if our friendship had fundamentally shifted like a rift in the earth's crust after a tremor. "Nobody's coming out as long as you're here, and none of them want to ask you to leave. I proposed we sell you the place, and if we want to come on back out some time, we'll get us a new place maybe on the creek. You know, with a dock and all." He paused, so overlying concepts could line up for proper absorption, beginning with the tolerance and understanding of old friends. He went from there to generosity, because established white men do not give each other charity, and from there to the future and deeper needs of the Hunt Club, which might well go to the Hunt & Fish Club, given the natural proclivity, affluence and sporting skill of the membership.

I looked at him and waited, and he said, "Thirty thousand. We figured you'd have the cash, but if not, we'll carry you for eight years."

"Why eight?"

"We all gettin' on, Arthur."

Truth be told, Peter and I had both taken a look at what might be available on the creek. Those places didn't come up too often, mostly because they didn't sell back then; they were so far out of town with nobody to talk to and nothing to do. They'd just sit there with a *For Sale* sign on them, growing mossy on the north side and the southside and the other two sides too. Besides advertising the most abundant crop thereabout, which was mildew, *For Sale* signs looked so commercial, which was tantamount to tasteless, or, in some quarters, tacky. The old Chace place was up for sale, though, for thirty thousand. I knew it, and I knew Peter knew it and would have bet he reckoned I knew he knew it too, unless of course he and the hunt boys were banking on the idea Billy Whitehead suggested to the group, which was that old Arthur Covingdale's got his mind stuck on pussy, and once a man.... Blah, blah, blah. The concept here was me, happily deranged and thereby an easy mark for engagement in anal intercourse of a commercial nature, which I suppose is what charity *cumma* generosity gets around to, once the other fellows reckon the mark is getting all the select gash, so nobody comes out a loser.

Moreover, there was a time when the old Chace place, with its deep-water dock over a known spottail and sheepshead hole, would have put my heart in my teeth. I'd pondered the difference between two times, which weren't exactly the best of times and the worst of times but were in fact the former time and the right-now-this-minute time. I'd taken a look at the old Chace place about a week or two prior and finally gave in to necessity, determining to buy the place; that is, the old Chace place. Fact was, in hindsight, however, with two bedrooms, a big porch, living room, dining room, kitchen and two wet bars, it was too much, an audacious display of country formality, landed and gentrified in the urbane, Caucasian spirit of things. The thought of fine furniture and that whole dog and pony couldn't but lead to the next thought, which was entertaining and house guests, and damn it I'd just absolved myself of boorish living, so why in hell would I boor again so soon? Moreover, I'd grown attached to a certain something in the rickety, soulful place of my redemption.

The Hunt Club domicile, that is to say, was perfectly marginal, lush, close to the ground, reclusive and suitable to a misanthropic old fool who had no notion whatever of what tomorrow might bring, much less next year, and I felt fairly happy with not knowing.

"It's a acre," he said, which was a rare and desirable parcel size, since most places were far bigger, meaning more liability, more insurance, more maintenance and more tax.

"You mean the Hunt Club or the Chace place?"

Peter blushed red as a sugar beet, more or less proving that he'd figured on my ignorance of the Chace place, busy as I must have been humping my Black bitch. Or would that be my bitch

Black? I'd need more time getting the hang of the thing. He recomposed admirably though. "No. Chace place is two acres."

"Two and a third. I'll give you fifteen. It ain't worth but twelve."

"Fifteen?"

"I got the cash."

"Well...." So the deal was done, and we both knew *that*.

Credit to Aníse; she neither wide-eyed nor glanced my way, proving her poker skills and her worldly knowledge of what an aging white lawyer can do, if he had the cash to solve the problem. I did, and that made her smile—with pride and love, don't you know.

Peter Maxwell looked away, shook his head and looked back with his own smile of resignation, as if old friends like us had to take care of each other, or what was the whole damn point of a thing in the first place? He spared us the burden of saying how many dollars the members would need in order to secure the Chace place if they only got fifteen for the old place, but I could see him thinking, as if half down might get eased on up to sweeten the deal and the prospect of acceptance by the membership. I would have murmured, "Fuck me, Peter. Half down is sweet enough." But I'd learned the better part of race relations already, so I said, "Ten down. Five years on the balance. That'll get you in and down the road."

He nodded. He would not divulge the lowest price pre-approved by the members but offered his hand, which, in that blessed region was contractual as a signed document. To appease the devil abounding, infiltrating the leaves and shimmering in their magical green tint and slanting sunbeams, we would move next to a document.

I looked down at his hand and nodded. We would remain friends in spite of what life had put between us. I shook it, though

I doubted the gesture held the same obligation or promise it once had.

Aníse cut the tension, inviting Peter to come in for some tea. He laughed short, maybe thinking she'd offered some o' dat tea the country darkies love, meaning life everlasting or sassafras. He begged off, a hell of a schedule and all that. His girl would work up the papers, so we could sign off in a day or two, or the following week if I needed more time to, you know, get the money together or think things over or any damn thing. I assured him I was ready any time the docs were done. As we shook again, I sensed constraint, as if he felt something on his hand, jumping onto it from my own. Well, he could wash it soon enough.

So we settled in to nesting, me and mine. Aníse wasn't a bad cook but lacked culinary aptitude. I, on the other hand, had always enjoyed cooking as a form of repose. Maybe she resisted cooking because she'd done so much of it or wanted to avoid that traditional role, though our traditions to date were as far gone from Elm Street as I was from Broad Street. I told her to read a book; I'd cook.

I used the phone at the Rockville store to call the J.C. Penney's and the Montgomery Ward. Both had delivery, even to the boonies, and I got us a new bed, an easy chair with an ottoman, a few lamps and an end table and an oven with a range top. We stayed busy and grew closer for it, as nesting couples will do, till her skin color was incidental and then invisible. She was no longer a foreign language that I translated into English on my way to comprehension and response. I processed her front and center, literally and figuratively, till I dreamt of her, both physically and essentially, heard her and spoke back with no intervening process of translation.

She was Aníse. I was Arthur.

XVI

What Came to Pass

Aníse had the further sense to avoid the question of marriage, knowing full well my awareness of legal aspects underlying such an event, including but not limited to our impending event.

We had a TV, 12", black and white, but soon tired of *The Honeymooners, Sgt. Bilko, Ed Sullivan* and the rest. I cooked supper and read what I considered to be classic novels. She read modern maternity magazines and made lists. She sometimes filled me in on what would happen, when and why. And, as if in context to who we be, she reviewed what had come to pass, enumerating our unusual courtship, our budding romance, our blossoming love and marriage of a sort. I did not back-quote these concepts but smiled, allowing these evenings to pass in pleasant contemplation of the past, just as our neighbors to the north might have done. Still I wondered: courtship? Marriage?

She filled me in on the balance of her family's rich history. Mose Cohen arrived in Guadeloupe in 1905 or '06 and kept on sailing and fishing out of those islands, more or less returning to

Guadeloupe between trips. Luzon died in '05, but Mose didn't learn of his father's death for another twenty-three years and didn't imagine it, as the tale goes, because nobody knew Luzon's age, neither in exact years nor in approximate years. Time was measured for Luzon only from his departure from the Allston place in Rockville in '64, when he was likely not younger than twenty or older than forty-five.

Mose was said to have turned an eye west in longing for kinship and home after his first few years of fishing the Caribbean, but then he gave in to the distraction abounding in Rochelle Goussard, who ran a café there at Basse-Terre, located to attract fishermen from both the Atlantic and Caribbean fleets, though they weren't fleets at all but men fishing alone or in pairs from small, open boats.

Mme Goussard held an attraction for Mose far greater than the warmth and sustenance of her beans and baguettes. Her husband was presumed dead on the common variables of the time and place, sea faring and longstanding absence foremost among them. He returned some years later to claim his share of the café and cause Mose no end of trouble but got nothing but a divorce decree by law for his effort.

In the meantime Rochelle Goussard had let Mose know that she needed help and a man. He must've been close to thirty-five and feeling every day of it, given the rigors and solitude of life at sea. He settled in to café work for brief periods, heading out behind whatever schools were running, thereby keeping the café afloat with supplemental income while keeping himself buoyed on Rochelle's charms.

Mose and Rochelle bore a daughter named Julya in '11, so named for the mother he missed most of all.

Julya was notable in childhood for precocious conversational skills. She practiced daily with tourists, mostly French, and with fishermen, also French, with a few Hollanders in the mix. All too soon, at age sixteen, the age her father had left home, Julya fell for Antoine, whose last name was lost or more likely discarded. Antoine, a Parisian, was well into his thirties, nearly the age of Julya's father. Antoine came for a week but stayed an entire month, leaving with a pledge to return post haste to that island paradise, once he'd arranged his affairs back in Paris. Antoine's departure was remembered for passion, crying and vows of eternal love, though it could have been only the time they'd spent together that he would forever cherish.

Julya was inconsolable, to everyone's dismay, especially Mose, who couldn't trust a Frenchie of such affectation, so many demands and ill manners—and who stank worse than a bilge, unflushed. Rochelle, the mother, was neither disappointed nor surprised, having seen her share of tourists and sailors over the years promising one thing and another, for ever and ever, on their way home to arrange affairs, so eternal love could begin in an orderly fashion. Perhaps most dejected of all was Claude Coquelin, Julya's amour and peer and apparent betrothed since childhood and through adolescence, with its hormonal complexities. The story sounded like a parallel universe, like the one Anne and I bonded in, to a state I thought of as love. The big difference was that Claude's and Julya's infatuation solidified at age twelve or fourteen, given the sultry air and sensual inclination of the place. That is, they had sex, as children, more or less. We have sultry air here too, but the inclination is more social than sensual.

At any rate, Julya broke Claude's heart, just as her own got broken in her head-over-heels tumble for Antoine. Both hearts seemed crushed more thoroughly, when Julya woke up retching soon after Antoine's departure. The bilious noises rising from the small house of the pretty young girl was evidence for all to hear. Julya had symptoms of the ultimate love sickness. Though never to be seen or heard from again, Antoine's lingering presence grew obsequiously in Julya's swelling womb.

Claude pined, but Julya vowed to wait her man's return from Paris.

Yet even a child of sixteen knew the score, after six months with no word. Wiser still after three more months, she gave birth to a blue-black baby girl showing mottled gums to match. Self-evident and to everyone's relief, the baby girl was Claude's after all. Antoine was pale and skinny as a baguette and just as soft. And so old. Never mind; the child was Claudia, who soon charmed the tourists. It was 1927, and the world seemed bright and sunny, surrounded by gentle seas of crystal clarity, cooled with balmy breezes.

Mose sailed west to Wadmalaw the following spring, arriving at the Edisto River mouth after ten days reach under steady trades. He hung out on a slack ebb for six hours before easing in like driftwood. Julya Cohen expired soon after hearing from her son Mose that her granddaughter had been born and grown to become a mother as well. The baby Claudia promised another generation. Nobody knew at the time that baby Claudia would become Aníse, whose eyes welled in the telling, grateful that her great-grandmother heard her name. Julya passed as Mose spoke of warm, clear water and little fish of amazing color and grace.

Aníse cried, either for her great grandmother trying to see the little fish or for herself seeing them again, or for something amiss.

Was Julya banging Claude at the same time as Antoine? Or after Antoine left? These questions seemed indelicate in the face of such emotion. I came from a place hell-bent on genealogical detail, but who cared anyway? I was sixteen in '27 and imagined those teeming schools of garish color and profound innocence as she described them, because I'd visited those reefs in my youth. That was long ago, and there I was, arrived at shores as yet unanticipated.

Claudia married Jules Monfret in '44, when she was sixteen. A dear man, he couldn't keep up, and he died in '51. She wiped her eyes, as if his passing was not grounds for mourning but rather as a consolation of nature and life.

"Couldn't keep up?"

"Yes. He want to and try so hard. But he could not do well at all without his sleep. Now he get all he need."

"That sounds dispassionate."

"Yes. I did not love him. I was too young. You can't tell a girl anything, you know."

"Seems uncanny, all the girls and boys got married or left home at sixteen?"

"Yes, we have our pattern, but everyone do, you know. I think I marry Jules because his name is Jules, like my mother and my great grandmother. I think it is meant to be, but it is not. Yes, it come to be, but I force it, not the same as meant to be."

Claudia worked the café a few years after Mose died in '56 and took over when Rochelle passed in '59.

Julya and Claude separated then, love and life having run its cycle, and both had many good years remaining. In their mid-forties, life seemed long after such an early start. Instead of twelve years taken by school, education had come to them more naturally from the wide world, visiting in many voices.

Claude farmed and fished. Julya worked the café with Claudia, who stayed on till Etienne Gaulois showed up for variations on a theme. Etienne brought records and a record player and a vision of himself as the disk jockey. His rhythm rolled steady as waves on a beach. He could not stand still but moved, irrepressible as a downbeat with a scat or loose lyric trickling from his lips. So too, nobody stood still in his presence. His step was contagious as a head cold; Etienne sneezed; soon the crowd was juking. Or so the story went, his mystique deriving from his rhythm. He'd played trombone in a *Ska* band, could play trumpet too for a lighter touch and sometimes went to tuba that could sink a tune into your bones. What was a girl to do?

I hated the imagery, trombone, trumpet and tuba…and bones. "Girl?"

"Yes. Would you not call me a girl?"

"You were what? Thirty-one? Thirty-three?"

"I'm still a girl. What you think sometime. I don't know."

"Gaulois?"

"Yes, but it was show biz, you know. His real name was Picard, I think, unless that was show biz too, you know, last year's production."

"How old was he?"

"How old? I don't know that too. Why you ask, how old? What difference, how old? Old enough to be a man. Not so old as you."

"Thank you. So he was younger than you?"

"Yes. Not by much. A few years. Not more than ten or twelve."

"I'm getting the picture. He's thirty years younger than me. So you feel safe with me."

"Yes, I do, Arthur. You do make me feel safe."

"That's not what I meant."

"What do you mean?"

"So he was the great love of your life?"

She looked away. She gave it time. She looked back. *"J' ne sais pas."* She didn't know. "Not yet. I think it could be you, but I don't know that either. Not yet."

Oh, yes, Aníse's lawyerly skills were impressive for impact on few words; she could turn the screws on very few syllables. I think she needed great love and age was incidental, if he could measure up. Most women nurture this fantasy and think it reasonable. They don't call it a fantasy but an ideal or a value system, or something more accessible than what Sleeping Beauty had for Prince Charming or Cinderalla got from that other cartoon character. Some men try to conform but don't adhere nearly so easy as they do to football and pornography.

"So he was a white man, Etiénne Galois," I deduced.

"No. He was Black, not Black like me but Black as any Frenchman. Nobody knew his first name either, the real one. Abdul or Aziz. Something like that. He was Algerian, much worse than native French."

"How's that?"

"Arabs. They are different."

"You mean from you and me?"

"Yes. Jules Monfret, my husband; he was white."

"Oh, boy." I hadn't had a drink in weeks but needed one to melt the shadows cast late in the day over my woman's past.

"Why you say, 'Oh, boy?'"

"I don't know. Maybe it's the same for…. It's that I…."

"If you must know, he was quite beautiful. I would do anything for him. Anything."

"You mean Jules, your husband?"

"No. Jules was different. I mean anything for my boyfriend. So? Whatever you imagine, now I would do it for you. That make you the winner. *N'est pas?* Come. Let me show you something."

"Oh, please!"

"*Non!* You want to torture yourself? Okay. I will help."

So she showed me what I'd won, a jackpot of sorts, beyond my own wildest fantasy at seventeen or fifty-seven. Or was it fifty-eight already? Never mind, because the mind won't work under certain stresses. Besides, I was too dull to imagine at seventeen anything so fetched from what we knew as safe and sane, and maybe still too afraid to admit it at fifty-seven.

Well, I'd arrived at a front row seat and paid dearly for it. But isn't that how it goes with love, removed from rationale and tidy progressions and safe suppositions, and spurious frills, like doilies under tea cups or a virgin pin on a villager blouse, or.... That would be true love, which most often comes after saturate seasoning of the principles, realizing what's been lacking in life to date. Drink? Not necessary, not yet. Maybe in a minute or two.

Meanwhile, I recalled a trip to town recently, my hat pulled low on a surreptitious route to the tasks at hand. I took the back streets and alleys less trafficked than the gadabout byways.

I'd stepped out of Maiden Lane onto the wider sidewalk but stopped short at the invisible wall, bouncing back around the corner into cover. Closing my eyes and calming my breathing, I waited for the unpleasantness to resolve and move on. For there, standing by her black Mercedes, demonstrating her proprietary interest and quacking disconsolately at Elspeth Pinckney over Helen Lachicotte's God-awful she-crab soup, was my own ex-Eudora. "That soup was based in heavy cream! It near stopped my heart and liked to run me something fierce!" *It laktuh roo-un me sumpth'n fee-iss, Ah sweah't did.*

But the fat was naught, next to the sherry on top; "I mean to say, that if you want to have a drink, then you ought to have a drink. You don't sit down for dinner and pour your damn drink into your soup for heaven's sake!" *Ah muyeen, ifya wonna hayuv a drank, yota hayuv a drank....*

Eudora most often wanted to have a drink. Besides, what could she do, not eat the soup? Which she couldn't. "I mean to say, my God. And the horrendous difficulty of finding a parking place these days. It's enough to make you wonder."

I didn't mean to eavesdrop but only to make life easier for all parties concerned. What could we do, make small talk? Assess soups or air out some issues?

"Yes," Elspeth said, looking down her nose in her officious way at the teeming refuse yearning to be free. They lurked everywhere, just below the radar. She affirmed the fatty soup and it heinous consequence, then digressed poignantly: "Well, it's like you say on Arthur's little escapade. Birds of a feather do flock together. He is reaping exactly as he's sown. To each his own, because you can never forget that a man is judged by the company he keeps." *Buhds of a feathuh do flock togethuh....* It wasn't easy, holding my peace, and I verily trembled at the voracious satisfaction within reach, if only I had the courage to step forward with a simple declaration....

Yet as I mused on my dream retort, Eudora asked, "What *was* he thinking? I know a man his age wants to be a young buck again. I can assure you, he isn't. But I can't get over his carelessness, out there humping that Jemima. What'd he think? He wouldn't get a...dis*ease*?"   I lost an audible laugh on duzuyeez and feared detection.

She covered with vigorous exclamation, "God knows where she's been! Did he think she was immune from preggers, just because she's convenient, and he's white?"

"Yes, well," Elspeth said, "It has been my experience, that the male of the species...."

And so on, back to Eudora, who cheerfully speculated on a yard child named Covingdale, which, of course, "...he'd nevah, evah allow, even if it meant taking up lawyering again, which he wadn't much good at in the first place, but my Gawd, you'd hear some Covingdale bones roll over on that one if he did. Allow it, I mean to say...." Firmly agreed that I would assuredly avoid the legacy issue, they proceeded to amusing visions of a pickaninny in the living room. They giggled, asking each other if social standing would be better with a high yellow rather than a blue gum, which, by the way, Eudora understood the wench to be. She further wondered if Junior would become a partner in the firm. Ha!

I backed up Maiden Lane as Luzon had backed into the forest a century or so ago, gaining distance from the shrill titter on every step. That I was more reflective than he'd been is conjectural, though I felt redeemed at long last, like a man stuck in a mysterious funk, ditching it at last. I had sinned a long time ago. My time with Eudora was no less confining or debasing as penitentiary time. I had paid my debt to society and not even realized it. I wanted to shout hallelujah and click my heels. I knew what an epiphany was, and this was.

I strolled in the opposite direction, feeling freer than in decades. I'd done my time! I was paid up on my debt to society!

Aníse would no sooner call Eudora a white bitch or make casual reference to Elsie Borden than she would cross a road to pick a fight at random, or call out bad tidings. Aníse was superior, more evolved and more compassionate. Not that I needed superiority, but there it was. Some people are blessed in life with charm and intuition. Eudora had none. Aníse was superior.

Eudora seethed with vindication for the social wrongs she'd been made to suffer, bad marriage to bad soup. What could ever benefit by me telling Eudora the difference between Aníse and her? If they met face to face, Eudora would remain blind or even hostile, because that's who she was, a cold woman in blinders. Eudora would see nothing but Black, as a variation on a theme.

I didn't mind walking the three blocks extra, long way around to Johnston's Feed for some chicken scratch to feed the biddies near the boxes I'd built, so they'd lay us some eggs. I also needed some new dungarees and gloves. Then it was four blocks more, long way around, back to the market I used for frozen lima beans and Brussels sprouts. I stopped for olive oil and lemons on the way back out at The James Island Piggly Wiggly, known thereabout as the Jim Island Pig. That stop was tedious, thick and gritty, gridlocked on traffic and that honky-tonk ugliness called the New South. But cold-pressed, extra virgin was more than a luxury; it separated me from angina on a daily basis. And I stocked up on produce as well.

Those menial tasks captured the difference between Eudora's rancor and my contentment. Blissfully humble, I felt the joyous potential of fresh eggs in the country, soon to be laid. Residual uncertainty lingered on the trip home and most other times too. I didn't give a fig about social standing and laughed, eating figs from the bag beside me. Aníse would bear a blue gum child in keeping with genetic patterns, maybe not so blue as her gums. But why would that bother me, if I loved her, her essence as I often recollected in those brief times we were apart. And I loved her presence in the moment. It was the common sense of the thing, or lack thereof, that buzzed in my ear.

What was he thinking? If Eudora could script thoughts for others, especially the lesser beings most in need of her wisdom, my foolish thoughts might have gone something like: *Shoowee! Poontang! Ah want some!*

Wrong again, sweet thing. Frankly, my most blessed state of being in those months was characterized by no thought at all.

That's what I was thinking, free and clear, and I sensed progress. If I'd had a telephone, I might have called Eudora to answer her question on what I might have been thinking, because that question had preoccupied me too, till the answer practically erupted. Nothing at all, Sugar Tit. That's what I'd thought. I'd merely let a thing flow, ebb and flood and then again.

We simply be, Aníse and I, and a good time was had by all. The miles south from Jim Island were simply thoughtless, a pleasant syncopation from hubbub discordance and strip-mall clutter to clean and green, harmonious as the transit from one life to another. I won't wax rhapsodic on sugar plum fairies dancing in my head, though I did look forward to some lima beans, Brussels sprouts and fried fish with lemon and salt, just as soon as we finished exchanging pleasantries and savoring our love, me and my musty woman. I'd worried about who she was and where she'd been and so on. Soon we'd have dinner, and she would expound further on her longstanding interest in nutrition and feeling good to the   maximum.

XVII

A Long Row to Hoe

Nine months is a long time to be pregnant in the best of conditions. Given the tenuous new world of our making, the seconds ticked off one by one. But nine months would soon enough prove incidental to the years ahead. Nothing would change for the better after the birth, not for a long while; our days and nights would thicken with sleep deprivation, baby shit, bawling and the end of romance. Fatigue would surely factor in many things between us.

That's how it was, peaches and cream one sunny day to cold porridge that night. I knew the score: Aníse was nearly a generation my junior. She could rouse a head of steam I'd thought long gone, but I knew her skills would also come to no avail, bye and bye. Wadmalaw women were fat, some of them waddling fat, and they bore none of the salacious charm I'd been drawn to. What could a woman her age do to get her shape back after a pregnancy?

Well, Aníse was different, drawn from a gene pool with a French undercurrent. She'd held up physically into her forty-second year, so maybe her health and charms would hold to the future too. I considered asking if she had a picture of her mother. But that's a tough one, because she'd see my ploy, so I asked if her grandmother or mother had stayed active. She said no, her grandmother Rochelle couldn't, once she got too fat. And her mother Julya blew up like a house even younger; she was so depressed with one thing and another.

I said it was good that we ate sensibly and maybe ought to hold off with the lard, bacon, fatback, pork butt, ham and chops every damn day, maybe ease off the cornbread and cancel the hushpuppies. She cried and called me a cold-hearted man.

Judging a woman by physical standards is harsh and reflects a failure to evolve on the internal beauty issue. I was guilty in part; I loved her within, but the social challenge would be tough enough without Aníse going native. Then again, I had the cash to set her up comfortable in a home of her own, and like Isaac Mikell, her great-great-grandfather, as the story was told, I could better abide a yard child on the creek banks if our our private time could retain its rich and lovely spirit. My woman's physical shape should make no difference in a perfect world. But we'd adapted to a woefully imperfect part of it.

Most things do make a difference. Isaac Mikell came to rue his bit of heaven on earth. But that story had no bearing a hundred twenty years later, nor did Jim Cohen intend it as a warning. Isaac Mikell got his come-uppance in syphilis and a lost war. I'd already absorbed my losses and hadn't yet considered sexual relations with animals. But the biggest gap between Isaac Mikell and me was in hearts and minds. He viewed his slaves as subhuman, good for free labor and convenient relief. I didn't want to hurt Aníse or Jim. I counted them as friends. That was the dilemma; I didn't want to hurt myself either. I felt exposed. I felt that bearing the responsibilities of fatherhood would ease things to the point of birth. Money would clear me from there. I did not originate this solution; Aníse suggested it as she informed me of her condition, our condition. What does fat have to do with it? Not a damn thing; I worried about it, couldn't help it.

But no matter how a story unfolds, every good plot thickens. Of course Aníse gained weight; she was preggers after all. The average baby runs what, six to eight pounds, and then all that other stuff adds weight. Aníse got big in the legs and arms. The midwife said it was mostly water, not fat, not yet. It jiggled but didn't look too bad in the dark. Her breasts got to XXL, and stretch marks broke through her perfect blackness. Near midterm, she lactated, changing the nature of our intimacy with breast milk freely flowing. She made a joke one time, squirting me across the room. I'd left the prudish side of life behind, but that was disgusting. Moreover, I felt more like Isaac Mikell and every other satyr, as reality gained weight and emotions got hormonally charged and constraints closed in.

Seeing my restlessness, she strove to keep things fresh, rearranging furnishings, trying new recipes, bringing in flowers. She also planned outings but often cancelled from fatigue and the unbearable heat.

Beany Seabrook came around to Jim Cohen's one day to see if anyone wanted a bushel of beans, late summer, harvest time, when all the green-bean growers in the region hauled their beans to auction out on Savannah Highway. Beany was buyer for a supermarket chain across the southeast and a bunch of smaller stores as well. Beany could judge beans in four quick steps: color, complexion, snap, and taste. He'd pick up bushels at three dollars wholesale after the auction, and offered to drop off one or two on his way home.

Aníse said we ought to go along. I could not share her enthusiasm but agreed to the ride and the change of scenery. So the four of us headed up the road on a beautiful evening, clear with a chilly tinge, feeling better already, pulling into the biggest bean auction for a hundred miles, many farm trucks full of beans and semi's waiting to load and haul away, many people browsing the many samples as many farmers chatted and buyers browsed, eyeing, snapping, tasting. Beany's arrival sent a stir in the crowd. He bought big. The auction could begin.

Childlike in her wonder among the growers and truckers and farmers and buyers, Aníse browsed the samples, walking the rows, picking her favorites based on character in the farmer or his pickup truck. The auctioneer and buyers moved down the rows, as the farmers watched their season's fate. Aníse followed to see how her favorites would fare. Still a sparkler, albeit roundly and significantly slower, she baffled a few farmers and truckers with her flair and accent as foreign to Savannah Highway as shrimp 'n grits would be to Paris.

The evening proved to be a pleasant interlude, except for its challenge. We hadn't discussed marriage or continuing cohabitation or terms and conditions or anything, and the topic loomed, not on my part. I thought no discussion was necessary. I did love her and loved having her around. A case could be made for commitment, with my feelings for her so much greater than what I'd felt for my ex-wife—or so much more positive at any rate. Aníse understood my dilemma, or at least tolerated it, I thought. She could have known my true feelings for the asking: I'd tried marriage and hated every minute of it. Aníse to Eudora was like ice cream over crap, thank you very much, but I would decline another go. But she didn't ask. She rather put something in the air, a question pursuant to our liberation from society, such as it was. That is, could we display affection in public? Or would I find that…embarrassing? Oddly, she'd posed that question as she eased into the perfect position for me to lay an arm over her shoulder. I felt her glance and that of her uncle. A man of few words, Jim

Cohen looked puzzled. Now that I knew the quality of the issue, how could I fail to care for it in the easiest way?

I sought a proper response, like explaining affection as something similar to what a man might feel for his truck or his dog, which sounds cruel, even as most men loved their trucks and their dogs. A trucker might drape an arm over a side-view mirror or scratch his dog's head. I couldn't tell if she looked confused or deeply hurt. She had no mirrors and wasn't a pooch and didn't want her head scratched and grew impatient. Resigned to a shoulder squeeze and whatever else it took, I leaned in but looked up as Beany called us over. He'd bid successfully on the beans he needed and said he'd be another while making sure everything got sorted and loaded, don't worry about him; he'd get a ride on back to his truck. He pointed out three bushels to carry home and walked away. Jim followed. Aníse drifted.

I finished carrying and loading the green beans and looked for her so we could go. She stood watching some trucks, holding her chin. I came up behind and put an arm around her, and she looked up, tentative and a bit anxious. I pulled her near and kissed her forehead and turned her to kiss her face and plant a sweet smooch on her lips, which felt monumental and world wide. A hundred eyes seared in, I thought. Steam wafted wistfully between us, I thought, and as I looked up to meet those eyes with a smile, I saw them all looking elsewhere, at the trucks or the beans they'd just sold or bought, or the twinkling stars. A few smiled our way, at a man who works the dirt and his woman. It felt as good as those fresh green beans would taste, and I longed for a dog and a truck.

At home in bed I wrapped an arm around her, trying to get it right.

A few more weeks into pregnancy, playfulness gave way to the ominous event. We stayed busy, repressing the pros and cons of true love and fatherhood. Jim Cohen came by one day with a bottle of Teacher's, spending what he'd never spend on himself, seeking to comfort a wayward attorney from town, out here in a bind. Aníse made it worse, insisting that we enjoy that bottle of scotch directly, so Arthur might come home.

I begged off, no more needing a bender than a blue gum demented yard child. We didn't know as much about alcoholic fetal syndrome then, but we knew enough. Jim Cohen took his scotch home, to drink among easier company. Aníse and I settled back in to reading and thinking and the tick-tock clock until I walked it down to the creek and tossed it in.

We got by on cordiality, helping each other through this strange and rigorous time.

In the ninth month, neighbors and friends brought gifts, mostly pickles and relishes put up the prior year, though some brought packets of spider silk and spiders to spin in the eaves. One brought a slice of moldy bread with a strain of ergot, advising caution on the dosage. The midwife seemed relieved to have spider silk on hand and doubted she'd need the ergot to jump start labor, but it too was good to have on hand. She visited regular, diligent but calm, and since she lived a good ways out and could stay with a cousin hardly a minute's walk from the Hunt Club, she did. She never mentioned downside potential of pregnancy at age forty-one, though she rolled her eyes now and then.

I arranged with Hedley Rice for standby medical service and reserved a hospital bed in town, though that was thirty minutes away. Aníse felt good, despite frequent flashes and spells. Hedley said not to worry but keep an eye open. She was healthy, but at forty-one you can't tell what might go squirrelly on you. I hated having this dialogue with Hedley, but to his credit, his pond showed no ripples. My anxiety attacks put me hip deep in dissatisfaction with what I was headed into. Sire of a mixed-race, bastard child, I did not relish the subjective dose coming on.

I wanted to culminate the difference between what I'd been and what I'd become. I felt different, until social dread rose like a tide. I wanted up. I wanted out. I wanted a fresh start at my fresh start. What would we name him? Or her. Arthur Covingdale, Jr.? Queen Elizabeth III Cohen Covingdale?

Aníse sat by one evening, staring, thinking, moaning occasionally. I struggled through *Ulysses*, perhaps comforted in that tangle of equally elusive comprehension. Here too I persevered, sensing self-improvement as compensation for something or other. Joyce's flagellation distracted my mind and salted my wound. I'd read the last page a hundred times, though I slogged through the first two hundred pages only once, leaving four hundred pages and the rest of my life in the middle to get through. At any rate, she sat nearby, uncomfortable with the load between us. She smiled sweetly, more in courtesy than affection, assuring me softly that she would ask nothing of me that I didn't want for myself. Surely she had not suggested a round of hotdogs and watermelon to distract us.

She did not refer to short-term needs but rather the future of the child, who would gladly bear the Cohen name, unless I wished otherwise, meaning Covingdale. She may not have realized the legality at play here, though I think she did. The child would bear her name, unless we married, or I officially adopted it. Oh, she could have my name on the birth certificate, but that could be contested. In any event, she nailed me neat, sooner rather than later, as if asking: Does your mother know you're queer? Of course, Mother didn't know. Don't you see? I had no reasonable response. I couldn't win and still viewed the situation as a win/loss. I avoided pointing out the dilemma she put me in, because stridency was best avoided.

"Would you mind terribly if I give this some thought?"

"Oh, no! You must think it. Take your time!" So we resumed our reading, staring, thinking, briefly, before she asked, "What is it you are thinking?"

"I uh…. I want to research a few things."

"What thing do you want to research?"

"I want to see if, uh, if a name like Covingdale…. I want to see about adoption."

"Adoption?" She laughed briefly, harshly, giving vent to the frustration running both ways, reflecting the mockery she must have felt. "You do not need adoption for anyone. Maybe you could have adopt me. But that would make you illegal, you know, having the liaison with your daughter, and now, well, as you see, you will be the *père* of the baby. So what is for adoption?"

"No, I mean, with the uh, name."

"I understand. You must think about having a baby with skin like me and a name such as you."

She concisely summarized for the jury, whose lips sealed in a slow nod; yes, that was precisely what warranted some careful thought.

"Would you like for me to eat you?"

"That's ugly."

"Do you think so? Why you say it is ugly? You did not think it ugly before. You say, 'Oh! Oh! Bay! Be!"

"That's ugly too."

"I want to make you happy."

"I want you to be happy too."

"So?"

"So. I think we can have a right nasty argument here if you want to. Or you can give me some breathing space, so we can see how this thing might play out."

She eased back into the sofa, giving in to the burdens and relaxing with the deal on the table, knowing the deal with the

Covingdale baby was secure, just as I'd known the house deal was done when Peter Maxwell said, "Well...."

We let it rest, sitting there as if content, as if all our evenings would pass on such peaceful resolve, with young Rufus or Rastus or whatever we'd call him on his way to Harvard, which appeared to be receptive to that sort of thing. I continued reading my book, though it could have been upside down. I scanned the same line twelve or twenty times before sliding down to the next line. Nothing stuck. I glanced over to see her eyes closed, her tired and puffy face, and there, as if between the lines, was pain. I took it for emotion; the task upon us was bound to give her a headache too.

I loved her spirit, I thought, thinking myself a pedantic windbag, trying to distinguish loving a woman from loving her spirit. I hadn't felt either one for a woman. I loved her and didn't care if she was Black or green or purple, because we lived in nature, free of social pressure. Yet I felt the challenge; nothing is simple. I didn't want a baby, not a Black or a white one, but there we were. At regular intervals I'd warmed to the idea and wondered where the fuck that came from.

I saw the short and long term. In ten years I'd be pushing seventy. She'd be nigh on to fifty-two as junior would first ponder the thrill of grand theft auto, teen pregnancy and drug abuse. Surely, I exaggerate; let's say junior turned out to be a normal child who merely needed braces, private tutoring, psychiatric counseling and modern pharmaceuticals to take the edge off, new clothes and regular check-ups. Nothing wrong with that, if parenting happened to be a priority for the golden years. Any picture changes value, depending on the skew. I did not foresee peace or contentment for me and did not want to see an apprentice in the seafood-gathering trade.

I saw decrepitude encroaching with a potentially obese wife and a dark child calling me daddy, a child who would be heir apparent to centuries of family history and stability—scratch that;

call it wealth, including real estate, heirlooms, the works. Those things meant nothing to me, but the ghosts of Covingdales past raised a hue and cry in my mind. Where else would the assets go? To a foundation of course, the Covingdale Trust for the betterment of something or other, perhaps the preservation of Ledinwah with a lovely obelisk at the confluence, admirable at low tide.

Patterns emerged all right, aligning with my former mentor, slinging mud in the eye at the town we called home. Difference was, he had a vendetta. I didn't. He chased some game leg and left his wife of thirty years out in the cold and got called out himself.

I, on the other hand, merely retired to the country and consented to some convenient leg with no chase, repeatedly and without prophylactic protection perhaps, just as men and women have engaged since time began. Convenient hell; she drew me in. Now she had a case for patrimony and child support, and I did not doubt she could find representation in town. Talk about fat and juicy; the Covingdale target was about succulent as a bull's eye could get.

I doubted she'd go legal. She wanted security with affection, which seemed straightforward and honest, and I could provide, in my way, taking on those parental responsibilities deemed appropriate for a man of my age and situation, and in monthly support to include the basics and then education later on. I'd take care of her.

I felt absolved on what should have been a brighter note, yet my practical assessment felt gloomy as fog on a marsh at first light. My legacy in and out of town would be similar to Strom Thurmond's, known for two strokes of the tar brush, for a cross burning—or what seemed tantamount—and a yard child. Strom and I would be lesser known for underwriting our dark spawn's higher education.

A mixed-race baby results from an act of love or carelessness or both. The baby would not erase that other behavior but might open a man's eyes. In my case, impregnation was an extension, so to speak, of my feeling for my woman, but it proved no more than what Isaac Mikell proved. I was guilty of lighting a fire and failing to tend it.

She eased back an inch and slept. I covered her with a quilt and watched. I felt the gap between us, taking me away. I would come to realize a few months later that nature controls motivation no less than a puppeteer pulls strings. It's all a ruse, designed to facilitate nature's way. She looked distraught, serving out the sentence.

Jim Cohen was complicit but natural, devious but well intended. I laughed, recalling my thin sincerity toward him. It didn't matter any more; he was my kin too, or good as.

I sensed the years remaining, the easy days and beauty abounding, the oysters, crabs, shrimp and fish. Throw in some beans, cukes and relish, some leafy greens, grits and good books. Some decent repartee might compensate in candor and wit what the boonies might lack in formal erudition. With any luck, Aníse would return to whatever she had that drew me in. And a little door cracked open on the light behind it just then, twinkling with the idea that maybe it was only my eyes that took her in as a woman to behold. Oh, she got heads turning, but I wondered who else would have gone this far and figured I had on account of love. That's how it went in my mind; hot and cold, yes and no, lucky me and horrors. And love?

A faint tap on the window was speak-of-the-devil himself, half nodding at the door. He shushed me when I opened it, as if to warn against waking the baby. I nodded back, as he huffed and waddled in with a burlap bag of oysters, scrubbed clean, a half dozen crabs, two spot tails and a whiting, dressed out. And the same bottle of Teacher's as yet unopened.

I shushed him back as he clattered things onto the table, as Aníse eased down flat on the sofa, going sideways and pulling her knees up under the quilt to join her bunkmate in a fetal position. Jim took a seat and nodded up that I could go ahead and prepare dinner. I didn't mind and in fact enjoyed the culinary pursuit as an easier distraction than *Ulysses*, especially with fresh fish. The scents soon changed the atmosphere to yes again.

You lay the fish in a baking pan along with onions, peppers, tomatoes, potatoes, lemon, basil, garlic and a little cayenne; hell, I'd add a dash of anything in reach, and there it was, the chef's special, in the oven in ten minutes. Bake at 350° for forty minutes or so, and in the meantime, relax. Jim nodded up at the tumblers on the shelf and opened the bottle. Maybe he sensed the struggle going on at the Hunt Club, or the tension of such a time at any rate. Close as we'd been over the months, we'd mostly talked history as a means of sorting and seeing how two roads converged in the woods. He'd manipulated Aníse and me, played us on light tackle with what he knew about the woman and a man's drive, any man. Now he worried, like me, kind of. What could go wrong? Oh, brother.

I thought he came to ease things along. Dialogue remained sparse, until the presence between us, our common ground, felt like a shoal at ebb tide. We'd wait it out until the flood could float us out. I thought he aimed to sort things out but couldn't figure.

He poured an inch in each tumbler and sipped half his and said, "Mm.... Mm." He sat back. I followed suit. We waited for dinner and Aníse in perfect harmony, early evening, low light, silence, scents, scotch whiskey. That was Jim's play, to improve the situation of being. The place got right damn cozy, making me wonder if a man ever really knows what he's up to or up against or nestled in the center of, if only he could muster the sense to get out of his own way.

He capped off the exercise with, "Mm.... Mm. Dem good."

XVIII

A Time for Every Purpose Under Heaven

I had a dream much later that night, a vivid enactment starring those figments who populated my troubled mind. I dreamt that Aníse gave up the ghost in her sleep sometime between midnight and morning. Morbidity, as Hedley called it, resulted from prenatal complication, a breach with umbilical strangulation compounded by uterine hemorrhage. That was Hedley's summary of the autopsy report, as required by the coroner.

Jim Cohen put it more concisely: *She dead.*

Earlier that night, Jim and I had slogged through a random hundred miles or so of his journey across the tidal decades, wading concurrently through the bottle of scotch that loosened tongues on troubling truths. I put it to him to say, if he would, what in hell we should name the infant. He said it wouldn't make a pinch of shit's difference *dem yidda enfant be's a high yella like he great great-grandmama uh one dem blue gum like he mama. Twix't one of anovah you still gwine have de nextes pres'dent ob de Unated Steates ob Merica, mebbe, neb know.*

"What? And you'll be the Ambassador to Uganda?"

"Neb know."

The problem with too much liquor is that you don't remember much, and what you do remember is often dubious. I'm not certain what we actually covered and what I merely imagined. I asked Jim if he'd dress up in military regalia with orange and green epaulets for reviewing the troops in Uganda, which an ambassador would not do, but he thought it over for a while and finally said, "Who?"

But a drunk thinks he knows what's real and what's not, both in life and sudden death. Aníse's passing in the night was both a painful loss and a release. She'd been so forlorn; I'd been so torn. Her spirit departed with stabbing pangs for her and me. Relief seemed vaguely obtuse, suggesting that things work out for reasons of convenience.

I drifted aimlessly in my dream, back to my place in town to fetch a better lamp, a rug to keep my feet warmer and some odds and ends for minor improvements in personal comfort. I'd made a mess of things and stood at a crossroads, with rural seclusion up one fork and a return to the fold up the other. Maybe I wandered back to town for familiar faces and friendly voices, to hear a few opinions on which fork to take. I couldn't tell; a fellow I knew in passing grasped my arm and confided, *Welcome home.* He smelled like failed preservation. And there I was, critiquing again when he might have been warm and friendly. And sincere.

Maybe I wasn't ready for polite society. I'd known Marybeth Rutledge for ages in pleasant context. She didn't grasp but came in for a confidence. *Don't you worry about a thing,* she said.

Don't worry? I asked. *I loved her.* Yet in my declaration, I wondered whose benefit I served; Aníse's or my own. What difference could my love or lack thereof make on anything that would pass for truth in town?

My God, Arthur! Marybeth replied. *I'm aware of your feelings for her. You went through some changes, Honey. Some of us still call you friend and admire your career and want to return the favor for your contribution. Can you understand that?* Marybeth made me cry, right there on the sidewalk in the middle of a drunk dream, because I hadn't understood and still suffered a few doubts.

I woke up numb and dragged my legs off the far chair and waited for consciousness to catch up. Jim Cohen slumped on the easy chair, snoring like an engine, as a greater discomfort took over. Aníse grimaced, as if chagrined. That's okay, baby, I thought but didn't say. The sofa was wet beneath her.

Stumbling out the door on adrenaline at first light, I ran to the Rockville store, calling to the midwife just yonder on the way. I called Hedley on the phone, then huffed it back to the Hunt Club, where Jim stood in the door with swathing and birthing stuff, stupefied as an old man with staggering hangover, at a loss. The midwife hurried along, goose stepping through the scrub weeds in her nightie, and I yelled, "Don't just stand there. Do something!"

He looked back in and back at me, nothing for it but to let life take the next step toward everlasting. He shook his head, too labored to speak. Aníse lamented as the midwife came in, and in a short while it was over. Or rather it began. Julya Cohen Covingdale came in at seven pounds four ounces with infantile features in high yellow and mottled blue gums, wailing for the tit. Blue gums on a high yellow had not thereabout been seen, and I laughed, imagining the murmurs flooding in on the brand new tide and the end of apprehension.

I held her, amazed at my paternal drive.

So it came to pass that the Covingdale line went over a line. That we lived happily ever after remains to be seen. Our future felt bright in the eyes and smiles abounding. We'd had our tears and would shed more but had yet to wear them as a veil.

Aníse and I exchanged vows of one heart shared (her words) down at the brackish pond where many Cohen forbears rest. I'd grown to depend on her counsel in the new life of our making, so the vows affirmed us. She did not blow up big as a house but got back to turning heads, a seasoned woman who seemed no different than any loving mother with a loving daughter.

The flame lived, though romance took a turn for the more civilized, with less frequent congress and rarely with the old, wild spirit. The magic thinned, as it will. Comfort filled in, as the child grow up and went into the world, and the parents no longer sought each other but drift together now and then like a lazy hand casually scratching a vague itch.

Those things came a few years later. A few years sooner, Aníse went to town on a notion and knocked on the door of my house on Queen Street and told the tenants how do you do, this is it, thirty days notice; thank you very much. Our controversy had gone to scandal, in some quarters born of shame on a direct heir to Covingdale pride. Not to worry, in hardly any time at all, our scandal collected dust in the hutch in town, the one reserved for scandal, also known as eccentricity, or character or color or something beyond the humdrum pace of every day. By then, the world had come a long way as well.

We'd settled in as the Covingdales, another family from the islands, so far removed from idle gossip that the tenants on Queen Street had to check on Aníse, to make sure she was the landlady.

She practically moved to town after that and called it efficient, sparing her the drive back and forth every damn day, because she sure as hell wouldn't trust the subcontractors to get things right on the remodel without herself to oversee. She and Julya stayed at the Queen Street house for in-town pursuits as well, exposing the child to street-level stimulation, lest she not see and feel and know. I joined them for dinner once in a while. Aníse and I went dancing, such as it was, when the homosexual disco opened on King Street, where nobody looked twice if Puff the Magic Dragon waltzed in with Tinkerbell on his arm. In years to come, she'd stay in town a few days to hit the produce vendors on Market Street, see a movie or get lunch in a café. She said it made her feel good and feel better yet coming home. We achieved fulfillment as people can in mobility. Things leveled off, and we had love.

Anne Waring is not forgotten. I don't feel responsible for her suicide, as friends can. I added to her disappointment, and I regret our friendship ending. But it seemed only a matter of time under any circumstance. Her depression was clinical. I was not a naturally happy man. We would not have lasted. I think most people marry so the woman can feel secure. Anne never could. Her life ended soon after a failed marriage, and I'm grateful it wasn't to me, proving again how little we know along the way.

I mark history and time as beginning with my first drive out, towing Jim Cohen's *Promise Land Produce* Cadillac. That was also the beginning of the end of nature, just south of town. Development crept south with new dredging for new bridges and roads for more cars, as if the traffic might thin with more lanes to move it. It won't. More cars will ensure more jobs, and so-called growth reached farther south to kill what remained of nature. I bought another two acres for protection.

These days, the scan button on my truck radio stops on Christian talk and Christian music on twelve stations out of fifteen, as if Jesus wants development as much as he wanted St. Louis to win the Super Bowl. It's still good out here, but the blush is fading, and I'm grateful I'll die before it does.

Jim went on ahead in '92 at ninety-seven, which was good for him, his kin averaging early eighties in general, if you don't count them that drowned or died in childbirth. I was eighty-two at the time and would have thought ninety-seven a goodly number of years for me too, my kin showing late eighties on average. You get up near a hundred and know it doesn't happen one day but over time, functions and body parts failing here and there till you just sit there waiting to initial the last chit. Old Jim went good, hardly slowed down from eighty, still dressing himself and eating on his own, and us fishing and throwing the net now and then, till he went on in from his porch one summer morning on the last two hours of flood. He lay himself down in the bed he'd risen from a short while prior and stared at the ceiling.

I was there to see him go, smooth as a shadow fading at sunrise. I didn't want to be obtrusive in that final time with so much family around, but a few encouraged me to lean in close with a farewell from a friend, so I did, whispering in his ear, "Hey, Bubba." I wasn't sad for his death or my loss but trembled into goose bumps, though I couldn't say what from, but it wasn't sadness. Even the tears on my face felt like somebody else's tears on somebody else's face, and when I said, "You the best friend," it felt like somebody else's voice.

He stared up, moving his hand a quarter inch till his fingers touched mine, letting me feel something I'd felt before, something alive and moving into me. Then he died, not fifty paces from where he and his father and his children were born. Those people in town, for whom ancestry and heritage are revered, could only admire such a tight radius to the Cohen homestead. The Cohen radius has stretched many miles in recent decades, to Atlanta, Charlotte, Chicago and other points of perceived opportunity. Now the gentry seeking refuge threaten to displace the homestead and surrounding forest.

I'm not necessarily next, though nobody would say boo if I am. Or be disappointed, given the solitude of a man who outlives his family and friends and is down to polite conversation with his wife. I stay busy, minding the till at the Cohen Bros Salvage & Fixit Garage, or sitting near it among the worn outs, staring at thin air and seeing how it was. I sometimes see a brickbat arcing in flight and can easily view that same scene without it, but I can't know if things would have played the same without that little brick. Things play out how they want to.

I'd rather be planted out here than in town, somewhere between Ledinwah and Bohicket Creeks, unmarked but for the stars and seasons, settling in with the tides and critters. I fancy a shallow hole halfway down a flat, until a storm surge in winter might thin the top layer to reveal whatever nutrients I might provide. I want to help feed a spring brood, to continue the greatest part of my life, my legacy to kith and kin.

They won't do it. It's illegal for one thing to bury someone in the marsh, and it goes against the general order for another. They want us wayward souls back into the fold, to bolster what is held more dearly in town than all the wonder out here. They'll plant me in the Covingdale section, where one spot remains for the sole remainder of the clan, as if my wife and daughter won't count, or maybe they'd only discount my women on account of Aníse getting buried in the Cohen place, and Julya changing her name when she married. Either way, they'll want me under the mud at Magnolia Cemetery, unless they forget, and that notion gives me hope.

Julya got on at the Rockville store; she was so service-oriented and easy with the customers. She often told me of folks from town coming out to size her up, folks who knew me but wouldn't say so, going pink in the face when she introduced herself and offered a handshake and asked who they might be. She married a fellow from Atlanta, after he got lost one day and stopped for guidance. Smitten by the beauty abounding, he stayed on for a while, though Julya swore he'd get none of the you-know-what till he said *I do*; or not much of it anyway. These kids today.

It was Socrates or Plato who wrote about the waters of forgetfulness; I can't remember which. Around here, it's over and out, and them who's left head out to the garden for social ablutions, to recollect and drink. I think forgetfulness in death affects only what was learned in life, like the Dewey Decimal System, or the reason time and circumference are measured on a root of twelve rather than ten, or Latin binomials, or cousins, aunts and in-laws, or generic names of regions or trees, fish, birds or subcultures, like Yankees, flatlanders, grits, spades and the like; you forget the sundry details of civilization. Or your phone number or address. Or the date you were born. Your name.

I think a greater knowing may follow death, when intuition teaches what you learn at last, what the other species sense more easily in life. Aldous Huxley called it *the knowledgeless understanding of everything apprehended through a particular piece of knowledge.* He was likely tripping, seeing God in a grain of sand, or a pencil eraser, or the slight movement of a finger, or the three hundred sixty degrees of every orbit ever occurring in heaven. I wish I'd tried that, just to see.

I think the transition from flesh to spirit is more difficult when the transit begins far from nature, like, say, in town, any town, where local knowledge concerns pavement and commerce, and general information passes for wisdom. Yet even from the urban core, the facts, stats and personal contacts default to a greater knowing at the end. I don't mean you're suddenly smart at death, after a life of vacuous mentality. Take for example the President of the United States of America at this juncture, who best illustrates this point. His biographers record no ideas or positions in his youth. At Yale and Harvard, ideas and positions are presumed but in him were absent. He got by as an heir, avoiding the misspeak that might irk the patriarch in the glory days of youth, liquor, cocaine and leg. Party stalwarts join the refrain: *youthful indiscretion.* I suspect no discretion whatever. I think George II will meet his maker knowing little else but what the cue cards tell him, not a bad man but better served at a lower station. Who could imagine a worse president than that?

I'm old-fashioned, a dyed-in-the-wool Southern Democrat who sees no value in the two-car suburbs with new appliances, who sees no absolution for a mean spirit or material growth.

I have more faith in my cat Ruby, walking regally across the deck, jumping onto a chair and from there to a low overhang off the roof and easing on up to the ridge, where she fluffs, squints at the green-tinted sunbeams and seems to sense the world around her more than her president. That's the knowing available to some of us, before or after death. Maybe things are best perceived from a rooftop, or at least from a reasonable distance.

We put Jim Cohen out with the rest of the Cohens, under a good size magnolia by the pond they called brackish, because it broke off from a curve in the creek about a hundred years ago and stayed half salty in spite of its freshwater spring. I knew the place well and went there often for serene stillness. Nobody else went out there because of the graves, except for Jim, who went out for something else. He showed me the place some years ago, pointing out how the creek had snaked in and back out in tighter curves, till two of the curves pinched to touching, to form the pond and leave it, right on top of the freshwater spring. That made him wonder, and he showed me how the pond had become fresh enough to host dragonfly larvae. He pointed out what was plain to see, iridescent blue green dragonflies dipping their tails to the surface, dropping their eggs. "D'enfant skeeta hawk cain't drank no saltwater now."

He makes me laugh; baby mosquito hawks can't drink saltwater. I cupped a handful and tasted fresh.

He showed me how to scratch an itch for old times, when mystery and adventure waited around every bend. Nothing scared shit out of Jim like lightning, and I shared that fear. Most people head inside at the first flash. The air and humidity in this region pump ions up to discharge right now, on so much current the bolts crack and thunder like warheads. Not that anyone would fire on Wadmalaw. Who'd care? Unless they missed the nuclear submarine base up in North Charleston and hit here by mistake.

Everyone gets caught out sooner or later, driving down the road if nothing else. Jim Cohen got caught often as not in his bateau, with nothing for it but to row for home. That was years ago. Years later he stacked three old tires out by the pond and family gravesites, because he believed the lightning didn't take nearly so quick to freshwater, and if it did, *de sparit ob de fambly* were there to save him, and if they didn't, there wouldn't be so far to carry his body. He got me to help him carry three more tires out there and *stackumup* one gray, blustery afternoon to demonstrate, showing me how to sit on the tires in order to achieve a poor man's grounding. He warned as well not to tip the whole load over, unless I got stuck, and then there wasn't nothing else for it, if a man wanted out.

We wedged into the tire stacks as the clouds got dark and thick and the bolts came crashing, first a mile out but jumping fast to a hundred feet out. The squall soaked us to the bone, lightning cracking for ten or twelve minutes, thunder booming like bombs.

When it passed, we were ready to head home with nobody restless anymore. He didn't press me for thoughts but seemed satisfied. He warned that if I came back without him, don't forget to check *in dem rubbah tah fuh dem rattuh snek wid dem cawton in e mouf,* which he had forgot to do, but *neh min'; dem snek be's sceeyid as us two foo, fuh true, don'chu know.*

I haven't felt restless enough to try that one again but did go back out to the freshwater pond a few times for the stillness. I don't know if they'd allow me in for the long haul, but I wouldn't mind helping Jim feed that tree. I might see how his kin would feel about a plain pine box and me in it. I'd go away in no time, no marker necessary, unless they want to say something about a loving husband and father.

I had a few chats with Julya on the sins of squandering and the prudence of investing for the future, reinvesting the dividends, never touching the principal or losing sight of the greatest wealth of all.

I think Waties Waring was my friend and mentor, that he and I reflected the prevailing influences around us, for better and worse. We arrived together, long way around, adapting to a truth forced upon us, each in our way.

Aníse and her cousin Jim unveiled that truth for me and remain steadfast in quelling my doubts, and so does the beauty abounding.

About the Author

Robert Wintner has authored fifteen novels, three memoirs, four story collections and five reef photo books. *In a Sweet Magnolia Time* came out in 2005 from The Permanent Press, Sag Harbor, NY, and is presented here again in perspective. Robert Wintner is the nom de plume of Snorkel Bob, Hawaii's biggest reef outfitter. He lives on Maui with his wife Anita, Cookie the dog, Rocky, Yoyo, Inez, Buck, Tootsie, and Coco the cats, and Elizabeth the chicken.

www.ingramcontent.com/pod-product-compliance
Lightning Source LLC
Chambersburg PA
CBHW051414170626
46809CB00006B/2152